The Split

Randi Harvey

The Split
Copyright © 2019 Randi Harvey
All rights reserved.

ISBN 978-0-578-62182-1 (print)

Cover art by Derick Snow

First Edition: December 2019
Version 1.2

This book is dedicated to

GEORGE

GJ

and

COLTON

You are where my life began, and my love goes on
forever...

ACKNOWLEDGMENTS

Where to begin?

A huge thank you to my editor John McNabb, who made me feel safe throughout this process and will probably cringe when he sees this excerpt in that I edited it myself. Your sidebar comments made me laugh, and your perceptive, yet kind, critiques gave me the courage to keep on keeping on.

Tami Miller Davis, my bestie from the westie, allowing me to read all of the wonderful works you have created, inspired me to write my own. And when I said I couldn't ever write a book because I can't edit worth a damn, I do believe you said, "You hire someone to do that, silly."

You not only read my novel, but printed it, marked it up with brilliant insight (and comma corrections ☺), and mailed it back to me. Tam, your life is a whirlwind of busy. Yet, you took the time to go above and beyond for my first novel. I cannot fully express my gratitude. I love you, sister from another mister.

To all the people who were on my beta reading team, thank you for hanging in there despite my complete lack of comma usage and overuse of swear words. Your insights and honest opinions gave me the nerve to publish.

Derick Snow, the moment I saw your art I was in awe. Though it took three years, I knew one day I would have you create something beautiful for one of my projects. Your cover art is haunting and beautiful. Sara Weiderholt would be proud.

To my parents, mom/Denise and dad, thank you for investing in our family's cabin in Lincoln, Michigan. It all started there, sitting at the table and listening to the woods sing one July morning in 2018. But more than that, thank you for your support and for making me feel proud about the cock-a-many plans I come up with.

Mom/Kelly, I can't quite put into words how happy I am you have been with me every step of this process. You're my biggest cheerleader. And right, wrong, or indifferent, your endless supply of encouragement has made me believe I can accomplish anything.

GJ and Colton. Sitting at the cabin one summer morning sipping coffee, I watched you play with your toys. When a thought occurred to me, I would literally do anything to keep my boys out of harm's way. And from that instinct, Sara's life began to take shape. You two are my greatest gifts. Mama loves you.

George, my everything. For all the times you reminded me I was going to be late (like literally just now) because I was lost in my story, for every coffee you brought to my office, for all the times you made food for the boys and me, thank you. For every iota of backing you have given me over the past year, thank you. You always encourage me to follow my dreams. But little do you know, I am already living them. <3

CHAPTER ONE

Five fan blades. One, two, three, four, five. Sara closed her eyes. *I'm going to barf.*

Ok. Today, I have to go to the thrift shop and see if any new dining tables have come in. Oh, and I can see if they have any jean shorts. My old ones ripped.

Dan laid down on her body and grunted. She could smell the dollar store body wash on his skin. The sick smell of cheap strawberry made her almost gag. Much better than smelling him though.

His head now blocked her ceiling fan distraction. She moved her gaze to his skin. Just a bunch of cells. He was so close that Sara could see the triangular patterns that made up her husband's largest organ. He would, however, beg to differ. Eight inches he always claimed. *Hardly.*

Maybe that was normal. Dan's most cherished item size, that is. How the hell would she know? Besides him, every other man she had been with was not by choice.

Man parts are weird.

She noticed Dan had an odd mole on his shoulder. It looked pre-cancerous: odd border, the color had changed over time, growing. However, the call to the doctor would never come from her. She smiled. Sara imagined the baby

1

squamous cancer cells playing on his birthmark. They were stacking centrioles and learning to climb mitochondrion.

Sara was very impressed with her ability to remember her high school biology class. Her teacher was an old angry lady who had missed her dreams of becoming a famous lab rat at some fancy Ivy League university. Instead, she was stuck in shitty Michigan at a high school of a few hundred students who were as dumb as their parents when she had taught them twenty years earlier. Her teacher wore round spectacles circa 1900 with a gray beehive hair-do and bell bottoms. Sara always thought she looked like various time capsules had vomited on her. Her name was Mrs. Humper. *Hilarious*, she thought and stifled a laugh.

"Flip over," he whispered.

With pleasure.

This would be the only position her husband could get there. Like a dominating dog. But for Sara, that meant it was almost over. She looked at the hem of the sheet starting to fray. The tag was on the wrong side. How could she have missed that? She'll need to wash the sheets and turn them the correct way, tag to the bottom right.

The carpet was worn. Sara had discovered a new color in the fibers last week during her spousal devotion: light gray. She had always thought it was a beige multi-colored generic carpet. The kind you used to see on the racks at local hardware stores. The cheapest, lowest-end carpet a rental home could buy. But there it was, light gray, shining its shaggy head like a beacon of *You're Middle Class, lady! Congratulations!*

Sara learned to utilize this time for list checking and rechecking, analyzing past conversations, and appreciating the little things. Like carpet fibers. Sara sighed heavily. Then Dan sighed heavily. Sara immediately snapped out of it, pretending her sigh of life mediocrity was sexual desire. She felt him collapse on her with a waft of salty, strawberry scent filling her nostrils. *I have to buy a new body wash.*

Dan kissed her ear and rolled off her. "So," he said,

"what's your plans today?"

He grabbed *her* hanging shower towel and wiped himself off, throwing it on the ground next to the hamper. She reached down to pick up the towel. "Well," she started, "the gym, then grocery shopping."

He had already shut the door of the bathroom before she had finished her sentence. She looked at the towel. *Thank god for birth control,* she mused even though it was harder and harder to find. Those little pills were a gift from God. And her God was definitely a woman.

Sara toweled off her body and turned to the mirror. Her long brown hair was still curled from the day before. Sara tilted her head back and forth, making duck lips. She had forgotten to wash her makeup off, so she had a smoky look to her eyes. She kind of liked it.

She pinched her back fat. No noticeable change. She angled her leg and flexed. *Rectus femoris* was defined more than yesterday. She had drank vodka last night, she noted. Dehydration was great for muscle definition. But god she hated her breasts and stomach. Perfectly formed abs and pecs lay beneath her "mother leather," as she so fondly referred to her post-partum skin. Her friends gawked and swooned at her body. Some even chided her for the dedication she held for her physique.

"You go overboard," her bold friends would say, "you're almost forty. And we have much bigger things to worry about than our looks."

But what no one knew was this was Sara's control. Her one self-possession that no one could take away. She wanted to be perfect. And even though she knew she would never be, her constant drive at trying to be was all she had.

Sara compressed her flattened chest into a sports bra and went to the kitchen.

Amy was sitting at the table on her phone. She was talking to Anthony. Because that's all she ever did. *Young love*.

Amy giggled at whatever dumb poorly-written sentence

Anthony had texted. She looked up at her mom and gave her a smartass look as though Sara was intruding on her private conversation.

Young, dumb, *love.*

Sara stared at her daughter, now that her back was turned. *Smooth*, she thought, watching Amy try to hide the mysteries and depth of their teen love.

It was like looking into a mirror. Amy had her heart-shaped face and olive skin. Her eyes were dark brown and big. Her lips were full, and she had perfectly straight teeth without the help of an orthodontist. Not like they could have afforded or even found one.

Sara smiled. She loved her firstborn so much. "Would you like a piece of quiche, sweetie?" Sara said.

"Are there eggs and cheese in it?" Amy responded without looking up.

"Well – yes," Sara said, "it's quiche."

Amy sighed and threw her phone down, glaring at her mother. "And do eggs and cheese come from an animal?" Amy asked like she was talking to a child.

If only Amy loved me as much as Anthony. Sara gritted her teeth through a forced smile. "Well, yes but I thought-" Sara started.

"And a vegan doesn't eat animal products no matter how nice," Amy put in air quotes for effect. "The packaging says they treat their livestock, right?"

Sara took a deep breath, "A simple 'no' would've been sufficient."

"I don't like dumb questions." Amy grabbed her phone and began texting again. "Nothing animal goes into this body."

Her signature loud thump interrupted them as Marie jumped the last five stairs.

"Except your ape boyfriend," Marie chided.

"Screw you!" Amy yelled.

"I don't like sloppy seconds," Marie said with a wicked grin.

"No one would ever give you firsts, you ugly cow!" Amy shrieked.

Sara rolled her eyes as she took Amy's slice of quiche and set it in front of Marie at the table. "Girls," Sara warned, and was ignored.

"Oh," Marie continued, "I forgot to tell you. I used all of your tree-banging, granola shampoo, so I replaced it with dollar store soap."

Amy gasped and touched her hair. Amy had scrounged up the ingredients to make her vegan shampoo from various shops and neighbors. It was a big source of pride that she made it herself. "You wouldn't," Amy growled.

Marie nodded with a mouthful of quiche, "Pretty sure I heard the whales screaming all the way from the Atlantic."

Sara sat back, watching the tennis match. Marie was Dan's twin. Like Amy, Marie had Sara's heart-shaped face, but everything else was Dan: his hair, eyes, personality. The last part made her cringe. Marie displayed Dan's famous ability to find what makes you hurt and use it as a weapon. Her sandy blonde hair whipped back and forth as she cocked her head, bullets flying from her mouth. Amy didn't stand a chance. Amy was book smart, pretty, popular. Marie was mouthy, rough, and street-wise. The conflicting sister scenario was so basic and cliché it was out of a storyline. *Maybe this is par for the course*, Sara thought, *a tale as old as time.*

"Guess you're part of the animal cruelty problem now too," Marie smiled. "Wanna go hunting with dad and me this weekend?"

"I hope you die!" Amy yelled and ran upstairs.

"Enough!" Sara raised her voice to meet theirs.

The complete lack of respect everyone in the house gave her was so commonplace Sara barely registered it anymore. She would've never spoken to or in front of her father that way.

Sara poured herself a cup of coffee and sat next to Marie. Marie's blue eyes stared into hers for the briefest moment, and then back at her plate. "You shouldn't let anyone talk to you that way," Marie said.

Marie's choice of the word *anyone* did not go unnoticed. "Well, I shouldn't have pressed the quiche issue," Sara said, clicking her wedding band on her cup.

"You asked if she wanted some food," Marie said, flatly.

They sat in silence. The birds were chirping outside. Sara used their calls to center herself when the real world got to be too much. She knew every one of their names and sounds. She could tell if they had babies or flew south for the winter. Her favorite of them all was the Willow Ptarmigan. Sara smiled to herself. They sounded like a tickled frog that had inhaled helium. Every morning she would hear two Willow Ptarmigans call out to her. Even though war raged a few hours south, they reminded her the world could still be funny. And every morning Dan reminded her that the world, in fact, was not.

Dan had gotten out of bed one morning yelling and cursing. He was again angered for being woken by their drunken frog calls. Sara always rolled over to hide her smile. But this morning he lifted the mattress, nearly knocking her off the bed. "Dan, no," she begged him, struggling to untangle herself from the sheets.

He was already out of the door with his shotgun when she pulled herself upright. "Dan wait!" Sara called as he pulled the trigger, releasing hundreds of buckshot into two small birds.

Click, click, click went Sara's ring on the cup. No birds sang for a week after that.

Sara shook her head because today was a good day. The birds' memories were short-lived, and they sang this morning.

"Mom," Marie started gently.

Marie's kind voice was so out of character that Sara's head snapped up to verify that her youngest child was still sitting there. "I am going to join the Gray's when I'm seventeen," Marie said.

Three more months, Sara thought. She looked into Marie's

face and saw long-braided pigtails and trips to the Wisconsin Dells.

"I won't be here to stand up for you," Marie continued, and Sara looked down, "Freddie did. Then I took over. But you are going to have to do it when I leave."

Sara smiled briefly and took a deep breath. She reached for Marie's hand. "I'll be fine."

The familiar thud of Dan's footsteps echoed down the stairs. He was dressed in his police uniform, complete with his Gray's Pin. Sara smiled at him, hoping today was the happy slot of the Weiderholt Roulette Wheel. One could never tell with Dan. Super high days meant the entire family took on massive house projects or went door to door passing out pamphlets about the Gray agenda signing kids up to enlist. Down days? Sara cringed thinking about it. Dan poured himself a cup of coffee and eyed Marie and Sara speculatively.

"Did she pray before breakfast?" Dan asked sternly.

No winners. No winners. Spin again tomorrow.

Marie's shoulders hunched. "Of course," Sara answered, a little too quickly.

Marie looked at her mom and then smiled at her dad. "Good morning, dad," Marie confirmed.

Dan huffed and looked around for something to justify his rage. The kitchen was spotless. The décor had been dusted. Breakfast was prepared. Nothing out of place. He eyed Sara over his coffee mug as he took a long sip.

"How does your day look, sweetheart?" Sara asked, trying to distract.

Sara knew he was supposed to secure a Gray rally today. These were dire times. Ever since the war started, food and goods were rationed, people were joining the army, and attacks were ever-prevalent. But they lived far to the north of any action. Still, hearing of the mass airstrikes and chemical warfare taking place in New York, LA and Boston made everyone on edge. These rallies were to gain more support from the Swiss, who could tip the scales in their favor. "Swiss" were so-coined because they were citizens choosing to remain neutral in the face of the conflict. They gained the nickname from Switzerland's stance in WWII. Sara thought it confusing.

Sara hated what was going on in her country. And while she didn't know if she completely believed the Gray's position on everything, she hoped for the war to end soon so Freddie could come home.

Dan opened the fridge. "Where's the milk?" he asked.

Sara closed her eyes. *Fuck.*

Sara opened them and saw the toes of Amy's shoes hiding on the staircase. Amy knew better than to walk into this oncoming storm. Marie re-hunched and braced for impact.

"Oh, Dan," Sara said looking up at him, "I am so sorry. It was on my list and I overlooked it. I am so sorry."

Dan slammed the fridge door. Sara and Marie jumped. So did the shoes hiding on the stairs. "Milk is rationed, Sara," Dan started slowly, savoring her fear.

He had found an error and a rationale for the bubbling anger that laid in wait. No longer was it his fault he was angry. It was hers. Dan turned slowly and crossed his arms. His eyes sparkled with malice. "Now we won't have milk for another week," Dan cooed.

"I know. I'm so sorry," Sara stuttered.

Dan charged forward and grabbed Sara by her upper arm. Sara gasped. *Always the upper arm,* unhealed bruises screamed from beneath her sleeve.

"I try to make everything so easy for you," he growled, "because time and time again you confirm to me how fucking stupid you are."

"Dan please," Sara whimpered.

"I write something on the list so you don't forget," he continued, "because your life is so hard sitting at home all day with *so* much to remember."

Marie sat positioned behind Dan and was able to wipe her eyes unnoticed.

Sara noticed.

"I am forgetful," Sara said, "and I am so sorry to you and the rest of the family for my mistake. My head has been preoccupied with the upcoming rally."

Dan's grip loosened a bit.

"I wanted to surprise you," Sara thought quickly, "I was planning on going door to door today to get people to show up. Gather more support."

Dan released. Sara felt the blood reenter her fingertips. Dan's eyes shifted to Marie, who had been pretending to eat like an extra on a sitcom. "Your Mother is an idiot," Dan said to her, "but loyal. That's what's important in a woman."

Marie shook her head in silent agreeance. And the hidden toes made their appearance. "Good morning, dad," Amy smiled with all the poise of a method actor.

"Girls," Dan said ignoring her, "I expect you to be at the rally early. Wear your pins and look respectable."

"Yes, sir," the girls said.

He turned, heading towards the garage, "And don't forget our gas rations this week. Empty cans are by the house."

Dan walked out, slamming the back door. Sara exhaled with the girls as if on cue.

"I'm really sorry," Sara said to both or no one.

Marie rolled her eyes; her lips pressed so tight she thought they would bleed. She dumped her half-eaten quiche in the sink and followed in her dad's footsteps.

~

Marie followed her dad out. He most likely saw her but pretended he didn't. Marie hopped on her bike and headed for town. She pedaled in the lowest gear the entire way, even up hills. Tears flowed backward, drying before they could drip from her face. She hated them; all of them. Her sister was the biggest bitch alive. Her father was a monster, and her Mother was a spineless doormat. How could she be genetically related to any of them? *I am the white sheep*, she kept repeating.

Yet as her dad drove past her in his police cruiser, she couldn't help but feel a ping of admiration. She wanted, no, *needed* his approval. Half the reason she planned to join the military was to see the pride in her father's face like he had when Freddie joined. The other half was to put as much real estate between her and her horrible family as possible.

By the time she reached Main Street, her leg muscles screamed in pain. She parked her bike by the town coffee shop called Gather. Colin O'Ryan was sitting at one of his café tables outside waiting for her. He waved when he saw her coming and looked concerned when he really saw her up close. "Rough morning?" he asked gently.

Marie took a deep breath, leaning her head against the brick building Colin's parent's owned. "Sorry dude," Colin said.

Colin knew her life at home was less than healthy. Marie hated it when someone felt pity for her. So she grabbed her backpack and started rummaging through it. She grabbed a binder and tossed it on the table. Colin leaned in and flipped the cover. He gasped. At least twenty plastic pages held dozens of Magic the Gathering cards in perfect condition.

"Where in the hell did you find these?" he said in disbelief.

The production of anything besides basic needs for life and war were eradicated. At first, it was temporary to focus on the necessities. But now there weren't enough people in the country to start manufacturing luxury items, even if the war ended tomorrow.

So many people were dead or missing in such a short time, Marie still couldn't wrap her mind around the numbers.

"I broke into Mrs. Balletti's house," Marie said with a shrug.

Colin's eyes got wide. Marie smiled back. She showed him inside her bag. Freddie's best friend was such a goodie-

goodie. She loved to see his shock at her schemes and colorful words. Colin shook his head of curly strawberry-blonde hair and went back to flipping the binder's pages. Marie had always thought Colin was cute. Anyone with eyes could see that. He was the stereotypical blonde-haired, blue-eyed, straight-out-of-a-Grimm-book prince.

"I found them in her son's old room," she beamed, "Gen Xer's had the coolest shit."

Colin rolled his eyes and thumbed through the pages. "Holy cow, Marie," he looked up at her, "an Assassin's Trophy card!"

Marie smiled. "I thought you'd like that one."

She hated to admit it. But this game had become her whole world. Gone were the days of playing on computers and video games. Gone were the sexting and gossiping on the latest social media app. Not that she was ever old enough to have participated. The internet was a non-functioning, slow, and unkempt technology of the past, and international sites were blocked. With no one left to update it, it became obsolete. Even if they did want to access old 2018 viral videos seen millions of times, the means of getting internet were either damaged or non-repairable. So kids got creative. And the joys of old became commonplace again.

Along with basic teenage terrors, Marie thought as she saw the dumpster fire of Watertown pull up beside them.

Marie covertly slid the binder into her bag.

Brett leaned his head from the driver's side window. "Hey Marie," he said.

Brett was the absolute worst. He had a buzzed haircut and a chipped tooth. He wore camo everything, with a hook in his hat, and a hunk of chew pinched in his cheek. Brett made her physically ill.

Marie ignored him and took attendance of the gang filling the rest of the seats: Scotty, Mitch, and Benji. They couldn't share a brain cell between them. It was then that she saw Anthony slouching in his seat in the back. *Sheep*, she thought angrily.

"You have a real shit choice in company," Brett continued, nodding at Colin.

"Funny," Marie said back, "I was about to tell your minions the same thing."

Brett ground his teeth and turned his attention to Colin.

"Drafting sixteen-year-olds now, White fucker," Brett smirked, "only a matter of time till you and me face off lead to lead in the field."

Colin crossed his arms and looked at the ground. Colin's family hadn't declared a side, which meant the Gray-claimed city of Watertown, South Dakota put the O'Ryans on Team White.

"Don't you have something to set on fire?" Marie distracted. "Or maybe a squirrel to torture?"

Brett looked Marie up and down and licked his lips.

"You need to stop fucking Honkeys," he said, nodding Colin's way, "and let a real man show you a good time."

Anthony sat up. "Dude let's go."

"Tempting," Maire said casually leaning back, revealing her stomach, "but I wouldn't want to piss your hand off."

Marie gave Brett a jerking off motion and then gracefully flipped him off. Brett turned red. Colin tried to hide his smirk, and the gang began braying like donkeys.

"Fuck you!" Brett said, "Your sister's hotter."

Marie felt her rage boiling. Anthony punched Brett in the arm. Marie stood up and charged the car, stopping only a foot from it. She cocked her head and said with a vicious calm, "I want to hate you, Brett, I do."

Marie allowed the dragon that lived inside her to escape a bit. "But I feel sad for you. Years of inbreeding. No education. Large forehead. But do us all a favor? Instead of spraying your testosterone-filled rage about the streets of Watertown, fill the emptiness your father left you with alcohol, like the generations of your worthless family before you."

Colin stopped laughing and looked at Marie with wide

eyes. Brett's friends stopped laughing too.

Brett's father had drank himself to death the summer before. He was a mean, abusive, all-too-familiar son of a bitch. Marie and the town all knew about what had transpired. Brett had found him drowning in his own vomit and tried madly to revive him. The entire town watched the tough, classic bully sob and wail as they put his father in the back of an ambulance to take him to the hospital. She crossed her arms as Brett's mouth fell agape with so much sorrow and anger he couldn't form a sentence. Marie looked from face to face of the boys before her. "Well this has been," she grabbed her bag and dryly looked at her audience, "fun."

She held the last word for effect.

"Come now Colin," she finished, "I'd like some coffee."

The bell rang as the door opened and closed. Colin followed her inside, rubbing his hair and pacing. "That was," he started.

"Necessary," Marie finished.

Colin raised a brow. "I was going to say ruthless."

He followed Marie to the back and began to pull the cards from the binder. Not wanting to have Marie turn on him, Colin set to pull apart the binder. Colin gasped as he combed through the collection. Marie smiled. "Marie," Colin said, "this is just too much."

"I found this too," Marie said pulling a bottle of liquor from her bag.

Colin wrinkled his nose. "It's like nine in the morning."

Marie shrugged and took a swig. It tasted like fire. *Good,* she thought, *pain is good.*

Her pulse was still racing from the encounter outside. How dare they suggest she and Colin were together? Colin was her only friend. Granted he was Freddie's friend first, but Colin was special to her. Marie took another big swig and felt the heat spread through her veins. *Anger and an empty stomach, this should go well.*

She handed the bottle to Colin, who eyed it suspiciously.

"Do not make me drink alone," Marie said, a little too firmly.

Colin sighed, "You're terrifying, you know that?"

And he took a sip. Colin began coughing. Marie watched him, bemused. He was handsome. Why hadn't she ever pursued him before? They made sense. They were of similar age. They loved the same things. Marie's eyes fell on his lips. Before she knew what she was doing, Marie leaned over the pile of nerd bounty and kissed him. Her head swam. Colin froze. He tasted like liquor and toothpaste. She crawled closer and leaned more into him. She felt him relax a little and kiss back. Then softly he took her arms and pulled her away. They sat there looking at one another. "I thought I'd try it," Marie whispered.

"Oh yea," Colin said cautiously, "And?"

Marie looked for the right words.

"It was," she hesitated, "it was like kissing my brother."

Colin gulped and laughed out loud. She fell back into her spot, confused. Marie didn't get the joke. Colin stared at her for a bit and began shuffling the new cards.

"It definitely was not like kissing Freddie to me," Colin smiled.

~

When Marie slammed the door shut, Sara looked up at Amy. Amy was texting again. It was like the thing grew from her arm. Cell towers were still somewhat functional, but the internet was all but gone. If only the two luxuries were switched. "What are your plans today?"

Amy either didn't register the question or chose to ignore it. Amy was probably doing both at the same time. When did Sara become so invisible?

Sara sighed and rubbed her arm, checking over her shoulder even though she knew Dan was gone. "Well," Sara said, walking to the sink and rinsing out her mug, "I'm headed to the gym and then to try to find some milk."

"And go door to door to invoke Gray pride in the hearts of the Swiss?" Amy asked without looking up from her phone.

Sara rested her hands on the sink and took a deep breath. "I am doing the best I can," Sara said, "Can someone please give me a break?"

Amy looked up and crossed her arms. She chewed her lip.

My mini-me, Sara thought.

Amy tucked a dark hair tress behind her right ear. "Dad is stressed," Amy tried, "we all need to be at our best. Once the war is over, everything will be better."

Would it be? Sara was reminded daily of the effects of the war. People disappearing, some fleeing, some joining the ranks, some executed. Everything was rationed. The schools had temporarily shut down. They said it was for safety. But it was mostly because there weren't any teachers left to teach. It was controlled chaos in Watertown, and they were thousands of miles from the fighting.

When had it all gone so badly? At first, it was fighting amongst the government officials. Then it crept over to the die-hard political fanatics. It oozed onto social media. Soon friends were battling friends. And neighbors were fighting neighbors. People who seemed to be on the same side began beating different drums. And then there was the first airstrike.

Sara remembered exactly where she was when it came on the morning news. When they still had morning news. Dan was having an "up" day. She was wearing her old robe she loved, that badly needed washing. She was rubbing at a coffee stain when the announcement came over the TV. Atlanta had been bombed. The house froze. The smell of bacon burning always brought her back to that moment. When they still had bacon.

Even the news reporters were stunned. Amy cried and ran out of the room to call Anthony. Marie sat speechless on the carpet, her mouth opening and closing like a fish without water. Freddie went to Marie and put his arm around her. Dan's up mood went down, and he paced the family room, cursing and throwing things. Sara tasted bile.

It was the pivotal moment for the country. The match that lit the tinderbox. Both main sides blamed the other. The planes that had dropped the bombs were civilian corporate jets that had been fitted with weapons. They were traced back to an executive airport in Chicago. Over 75,000 people died from that day in the bombings. The people in the area blamed Washington DC for not thwarting the attack. The local military bases were mayhem. Such anger from the domestic terrorism led subordinates to overthrow their leaders. And the next airstrike occurred not even twenty-four hours later, under complete secrecy.

The country, which was still weeping for the deaths in Atlanta, learned on the morning news of the military airstrike on the executive airport and the west side of Chicago. A gut-wrenching 25,000 Americans lost their lives by the hands of their own people.

Washington went into complete chaos. The government officials chose sides. The President tried to declare martial law. And in the middle of a press conference asking for calm on both sides, a lone female walked up to the President and shot him in the face.

No one tried to stop her.

President Kukolny's brains sprayed on the secret service officials who made no move as she approached.

Jessica Smith was the official name released. Sara remembered the video that played over and over of this woman walking through the crowd. She wore a dark blue smart-looking suit. She had a staff badge. Her hair was dark brown and curly. Her eyes seemed glazed over and tired. Her mouth sat in a perfectly straight line. No malice on her face. No tears. No words. Like a fembot fatale, following orders.

After the assassination, she was taken away. Ms. Smith went to trial and sat in her same smart suit, looking straight ahead. Her attorneys would whisper to her from time to time. After a while, Jessica Smith would turn and look at them with bewilderment on her face. It was as though she had no idea who they were. Ms. Smith would then go right back to her fembot face until the end of the day.

She was sentenced to death and went to a maximum-security prison. There were rumors she had been kidnapped or freed. But the official report was Ms. Jessica Fembot Smart Suit was executed by lethal injection that following spring.

The Vice President, Vincent Gray, declared himself the new Commander in Chief, whose supporters were then coined the "Grays". The Leader of the House, Michael White, declared that Gray was unfit for the position.

Mr. White and his supporters were convinced Gray had orchestrated the assassination. Michael White, of course, was then the leader of the Whites. Congress split along with the citizens. And overnight, the United States of America was thrown into its second civil war.

The problem of the division was over ideals, not borders. Fighting broke out in all the major cities. Millions of people fled to Mexico, Canada, and other countries offering refuge. Airstrike after airstrike took out major city after major city. And the day the first chemical warfare was unleashed on Nashville, Freddie decided to sign up for duty. *Oh, Freddie,* Sara thought, *my sweet baby boy.*

Sara remembered the look of determination on her middle baby's face that day.

The man who stood in front of her suddenly seemed like a stranger. He was tall like his father, with his a chiseled jaw and blue eyes. But his face and hair were all his mama's. Freddie had her darker waves and a crooked smile. He was still lanky at eighteen, but she could see the muscles building from beneath that bony frame. She had tried for years to fatten him up. Sara opened her mouth to contest and nothing came out but sobs.

"Mom, I have to go," Freddie said soothingly, "it's my duty. We

need to end this, so we can all go back to normal."

Dan had walked into the room and took in the scene. "So you told her?" He said flatly over Sara's loud sobs.

Freddie held and hushed his Mother. She cupped his face, trying to remember every detail. Where had his chubby cheeks gone? When did this beard stubble appear? You grew up and I didn't even notice, Sara thought.

Freddie looked so dashing the day he left for training that she caught herself forgetting to hate every moment of it. Dan slapped him on the back and gave a speech in the middle of Watertown square. "These fine people are sacrificing their lives and time with their families, so that we all may be unified under the true policy and ideals of this great nation." Dan said, "God bless you all, and may your courage inspire others to take arms against the White Rebels."

The crowd cheered. Many of the people from Watertown came out to say goodbye to the nearly two dozen men and women going off to serve. The entire town showed up to send their town heroes off. Even a makeshift band came together to play patriotic music. Smiles were had by all, except for Freddie's best friend Colin. He wore a hoodie, trying to stay unnoticed since the town thought his family was undeclared White supporters. Sara saw him standing in the back of the crowd. His eyes were red and puffy. He kept wiping his nose on his sleeve. Sara looked at Freddie, who was smiling confidently, listening to his dad speak. Freddie's eyes scanned the crowd until they fell on Colin. Freddie's breath caught and he lowered his eyes.

Colin and Freddie were inseparable from as young as Sara could remember. They almost looked like brothers. They acted like brothers. That is, until they reached around thirteen years old. Right away, Sara noticed the change in both boys. Colin and Freddie began to hang out alone in Freddie's room with the TV blaring. Sleepovers became just the two of them instead of their crew. When Sara was home alone with them, she saw them sneak touches and glances. Whenever another friend was around or Dan was home, the boys snapped into macho mode and covered their tracks well.

All of Sara's suspicions were circumstantial until the day she forgot her gym key. She opened the door and ran upstairs to her room. Freddie's door was ajar, and she heard quiet moaning. She opened it to find Freddie and Colin kissing in their underwear. Sara was so stunned that she just stood there, unable to speak. Colin's eyes opened just enough to see her and gasp. Freddie fell off the bed and Colin tripped backward, hitting his head on Freddie's desk. They were both flat on their backs, like dead cockroaches with erections. The loud thuds broke Sara's shock and she turned around and shut the door, apologizing loudly.

Sara sat on the couch turning her key over in her hands. Suddenly, Colin bolted down the stairs and out the front door without a word. Freddie came down a half-hour later fully clothed. Thank god, Sara thought.

He had been crying. Sara searched his face. He was in so much pain and fear. "Come here, sweet pea." Sara said, opening her arms.

Freddie launched himself into her with such force it knocked out some of her breath. He cried and then apologized. Then cried and apologized more. Sara said nothing and smoothed the hair on his head. They sat like that in silence, with the occasional shuttered breaths that happen after a hard cry. She held her son like that for an hour. Then they heard the garage door open. Freddie shot up and looked terrified. Dan was a believer to his core. And anything that went against his ideals was an abomination. Dan would beat Freddie senseless and then go after Colin if he ever found out. And Freddie knew it. Sara took his face into her hands, "You are perfect."

"Now go upstairs and get your face right." Sara said, and Freddie fled to his room.

Freddie stopped halfway and turned around. "I love you, mom."

Sara snapped herself from her memory and looked up at Amy. Would it ever be the same?

"Will it ever be the same?" Amy asked again with less attitude, a pleading look in her eyes.

"I hope so." Sara said.

Amy nodded slightly and went back to texting Anthony. Sara stood up, grabbed her keys, and purse, which held Freddie's last letter. They had received it a few days prior, and Sara made a copy to give to Colin. It was too risky for a Gray to send correspondence to anyone remotely affiliated with Whites, let alone a same-sex lover.

The first time she had gotten a letter from Freddie, she was ecstatic, and while everyone was happy to hear from him, they didn't share her unrelenting joy. Dan thought she was too emotional, and that her excitement deterred from the honor that was serving. Amy was too self-absorbed, and Marie would read the letter and then go to her room, locking her door.

One of those afternoons, when she had been left alone at the dinner table clutching Freddie's written thoughts, it occurred to her. There was one person who would share her joy. Sara jumped in her car and sped to Gather. From that day on, she began meeting up with Colin secretly, and they would comb through Freddie's letters, smiling and laughing. They would pick apart every sentence and gush over his adventures. They'd joke about statues being erected in his honor and then laugh about the word "erected". Theirs was an unlikely friendship, but their mutual love for Freddie kept them going.

Sara nearly skipped up the sidewalk to the coffee shop. The door opened, and the bell rang. Colin turned to greet the customer. "Welcome to…" Colin started, "Sara!"

Sara smiled and waved the letter in the air. His face spread into a similar smile, and Sara went to their spot in the back room. "When did this one come?" Colin asked.

"A few days or so ago," Sara apologized, "sorry it's taken me so long, but I couldn't get away."

Sara handed him the letter. Colin took it, handing Sara her coffee just the way she liked it: two pumps of sugar-free caramel syrup with three fake sugars. Her dear sweet Colin had no idea how much that meant to her. Colin caught her staring at him with so much love. "What?" Colin said.

"You are such a wonderful young man," Sara said.

Colin smiled, and then began to read.

Hello everyone,
I hope you are enjoying the summer weather up there. I am not.

Marching in full gear is miserable when you are sweating through it. We are headed to the east coast. I can't say much more than that. I am hoping once we get through this big stronghold, the war will be coming to a close. We haven't seen a lot of action, though. I am really getting homesick. I know I shouldn't be. I'm lucky. A lot of my friends here don't have homes to go back to. I will be so ready to come back to you all when this is all over. I really miss family and friend.

Colin's eyes got big.

"I don't think the missing S was an accident." Sara giggled and nudged Colin with her shoulder.

Colin blushed and continued.

But what gets me through is knowing what I am doing here will ultimately end this thing. And then I can go home. No more drafts. No more deployments. Schools will be back up and running, and I can go to college. We need a doctor in the family!

Love you ALL so much,
Freddie

Colin sighed and leaned back on the empty shelving. Only a year ago these shelves would've been filled with dry storage and baked goods waiting for sale. The fridge behind him held only a few jugs of milk and a bottle of pop.

Sara smiled as she looked at Colin immersed in the words of his deployed love. She felt so protective of him like he was her second son. Maybe when the war ended, they could come out and live a happy life. They would probably have to move. But they could still be together. Sara admired their love like one observes a zoo animal. She was completely in awe of it. Something she had never seen in real life. Something rare. Something almost extinct. Sara suddenly felt guilty about the way she mocked Amy and Anthony.

Colin tried to hand the letter back to Sara. "No, you keep it." Sara smiled.

Though not seemingly possible, Colin smiled bigger and

held it to his chest. The doorbell chimed. Sara grabbed her purse. "I'll just go out the back." Sara said.

She turned and found herself face to face with Dan.

Dan's eyes grew big and then dark. "What are you doing here?" Dan asked with restraint.

Colin was terrified of Dan too. The poor kid froze, sliding the letter into his back pocket. "You said you were going to the gym." Dan said louder, "What are you doing with a man in a back room?"

Dan seemed to grow a foot taller as Colin shrunk. Sara scrambled for a way to calm him down. "Colin is hardly a man," Sara joked, "but I'm sure he appreciates the compliment."

Dan's hands balled into fists. He already didn't like Colin and his family. He only came to Gather because they were one of the few places left that had real coffee. Dan didn't even pay. He simply said civil servants earned these privileges. Dan approached the counter and glared at them both. "Why are you here?" Dan punched out each word.

"Milk," Sara said matter-of-factly.

"Milk," Dan repeated.

Sara reached into the fridge next to her and pulled out one of the jugs. "I saw Colin in town, and he told me he could spare one." Sara said.

Dan eyed Colin suspiciously as Colin wagged his head in agreeance.

Sara turned to Colin and smiled. "Thank you so much," Sara said winking at him, "you saved me some serious embarrassment at the Weiderholt house."

"Of course, Mrs. W," Colin said shakily.

Sara walked past Dan to the door. "I'll just take this home. Then I'm off to the gym," Sara said to Dan and walked out the door.

It chimed *GOOD ONE* in Sara's mind, congratulating her for quick thinking. *Not today, Dan Weiderholt, not today.*

~

Sara swung by the house to drop off the milk and made her way to the gym. She worked out with a group of women from town. They were considered the town cliché. Always in everyone's business and up on the latest gossip. And always trying to act like the country wasn't in the bloodiest war the world had seen. They kept up their monthly ladies group meetings and played Pokeno the first Tuesday of each month. Each one was either a widow or had a husband fighting. Each one considered themselves Sara's best friend. And Sara loathed each and every one of them.

As Sara entered the gym, the cackling hens were leaving. "Sara!" they almost screamed in unison, giggling and jumping up and down like middle school girls.

"Where were you?" Jackie asked.

"You missed it," Kristen chimed in, "Hadley farted on the treadmill. We all thought we were going to die."

"I did not, Kristen," Hadley yelled, turning red.

"Lovely," Sara giggled, turning into one of them in an instant.

Sara's survival skills were at an expert level. "You need to quit drinking those homemade shakes. They are rotting your insides," Sara whispered to Hadley.

The girls laughed, and Hadley rolled her eyes, grinning sheepishly. "So where were you?" Jackie asked again.

A few of the girls tried to hide their concern. Dan's temper was known throughout the city, and women took note when a hen was acting suspiciously in long sleeves during the summer or wearing sunglasses at night. Sara waved them off, "Oh, I had to drop off some milk at the house. I forgot to grab some, and Colin lent me a jug from the bakery."

"How'd Dan feel about drinking *White* milk?" Hadley stabbed.

The girls nudged her, and Hadley looked down. Sara couldn't help but hold herself where the bruises were already formed.

"So," Jackie changed the subject quickly, "Smoke Show was asking about you."

Sara rolled her eyes and smiled. The allusive Smoke Show Samuel. Watertown's favorite personal trainer. And by "trainer" one would mean the guy who, pro-bono, ran the town gym. He was from the south and had been swept up in the early conflicts. Which was why he had only one leg and one eye. The town knew he had relocated looking to start anew after being injured. And Watertown adopted him with open arms. Regarded him as a hero. It didn't hurt that he was impossibly handsome - even minus some body parts - and was a Gray Supporter. The ladies of the Watertown Gang were enamored with him and most workout sessions involved gawking and creating colorful imagery about his nether regions.

"Because one of the Watertown's hens was missing from the flock, I'm sure," Sara answered Jackie's remark, "see you all tomorrow."

Sara waved goodbye as she entered the gym. The gym was old, but Sam kept the place clean and running. Not many people used the gym besides the clique. But the occasional elderly man came in to use the cardio machines. One was finishing up when she set her stuff down on the weight bench. "Good morning, Mr. Wheeler," Sara greeted the familiar old-timer.

Mr. Wheeler tipped his baseball cap towards her, "Fine day, Mrs. Weiderholt. Samuel said to lock up when I'm done, by the way."

"I'll do it when I leave. Enjoy your day," Sara said stretching her arms.

Good, she thought, *I can take this hot thing off.*

Sara unzipped and escaped her steam room of a hoodie and sighed in relief. She frowned at the hand-shaped bruise on her upper arm. She touched the finger marks gently. *I should've remembered the milk.*

She began with a quick warm-up of jogging then jumping jacks. Sara relished working out alone. The girls loved to talk and lean instead of keeping their heart rates up. It drove Sara crazy. She was going to push it today. She needed to sweat out the adrenalin from the morning. Sara grabbed a pair of mismatched twenty-pound weights and began squatting. She set them down and began to jump squat. Her quads burned. *Good.*

She wanted to feel pain today that didn't include her family. The music in the gym was a mixed CD because the radio was so hit or miss. It had top 40s from the 80s until before the war. She didn't care for the songs much, except one. The electric clicks began, and Sara smiled. She set her weights down. The familiar *ooh* faded in. The bass line kicked, and Sara was full-on dancing on the top of the bench. "*Clock strikes upon the hour and the sun begins to fade; sooner or later the waiter bends, and I'll waste my use away*," Sara sang into her thumb, butchering the lyrics.

Sara threw her hair back and forth and ran in place as the chorus geared up. "*And when the night falls my lonely heart calls*," Sara wailed in an off-key rendition "Whitney" would despise.

The chorus exploded and Sara sang along, letting the day escape from her. She pulled out some old dance routines she remembered from her cheerleading days and even tried a herkie jump.

"Nice," a voice came from the other end of the room, "but the lyric is 'still enough time to figure out how to chase my blues away'."

Sara froze. *Someone kill me please.*

She looked up in the mirror to see Smoke Show Samuel staring at her in the back doorway. His arms were crossed, and he had the biggest smile on his face. His one crystal blue eye crinkled at the corner, looking her up and down. "Oh, come on," SS Samuel continued, "don't let me stop you. It's nice to see you have a fun side."

How are his teeth so perfect?

That was the only thought Sara could muster. Sam finally relented and walked up to her. "I'm sorry," he said, "I should've announced my entrance. But it was too cute watching you."

Sara closed her gaping mouth and uttered a barely-audible, "Yea, right."

Sam smiled again and picked up Sara's weights and replaced them on the rack. "So, what are you doing today?" he asked. "Since the crew isn't here, I thought you might actually get a workout in."

Sara was finally able to form a sentence. "Circuit training with jumping and weights," she blurted a little too loudly.

"Cool," Sam said, "can I jump in with you?"

Sam's sentence cut off, and Sara followed his eyes to the massive bruise. Sara's heart stopped for the second time in three minutes. The whole town knew, and the whole town treated her like a kicked puppy. She quickly grabbed her hoodie and threw it on. Sam met her eyes, and Sara could see him trying to hide anger and pity.

"Yes, please," Sara answered quickly, "let's start with lunges."

Sam ran his hands through his ebony hair and nodded. He grabbed her a set of twenty-pound weights. He took the thirty-fives. He smelled like a body spray commercial.

They worked out in silence for a few reps when Sam smiled. "You know," he said, "you've been working out here for almost a year, and I don't think we have ever said more than "hello" to each other."

His southern accent was edible. Sara looked down and smiled. "I guess it's because I am a mom and a wife and a hen," she said begrudgingly, "not much else to say."

"Why do you hang out with those women?" Sam asked through heavy breathing. "And no offense if they are your ride-or-dies. You just seem to be above their level."

Sara met his eyes in the mirror. "What do you mean?" Sara said, breathing heavy too, hers not from the cardio.

Sam set his weights down and began jumping lunges. The fact that he moved as though he didn't have a second-hand knee-down prosthetic left her in awe.

"Well," he started, "you don't say a bad word about anyone. Even if they deserve it. Those women don't talk about anything besides each other, people in town, or what I'm packing."

Sam smiled at her and looked at her sideways. "You caught that, huh?" Sara said turning red.

"You seldom say anything but when you do, it's kind, a distraction, or intelligent," he continued, "the company you keep just seems beneath you."

Sam's eyes trailed to her covered arm with his inflection on *the company you keep*. Sara stopped jumping and turned to him. "It's a small town with a lot of history," Sara said, furious from embarrassment, "you work with what you have."

Sara grabbed her bag and water bottle. Samuel sat down on the bench with his arms on his knees. His gaze followed her as she walked towards the door. Sara stopped and turned around. "We can't all be war heroes," Sara snapped, "sometimes we're just the people in the crowd."

Sara burst from the door and charged down the sidewalk, hiding her tears from people passing by.

Who was he to judge her? Sara hastily wiped her tears away, screaming at herself to buck up. Suddenly, she felt bad for snapping at Sam. He was right. About all of it. Her shame and ignominy led to fury. Sara never wanted to see that gym again.

CHAPTER TWO

Amy sat looking at her phone. The screen was blank, but her thumbs moved vigorously over the empty text window. She counted the steps her mother took when she arrived home to put the milk away. Amy knew she'd eventually leave to go to the gym. Only a few more moments and she would be alone again. She could feel her mother's eyes on her and heard a click of her tongue in dismay. Always on her phone is what they all thought. No one had caught on that she was only on it in front of them. A perfect excuse to be excused from the chaos.

The daily disfunction in her family drove her mad. Quite literally. She used to count items and sort them. But that drew too much attention. Then Amy began taking small pieces of toilet paper and pushing them under her nails. She knew it was insane. But the pressure and the slow recession of her flesh under her nail meant she controlled something. Unbeknownst to her family, Amy even went through a period of pulling the back of her hair out. Strand by strand, the tiny stabs of pain distracted her, comforted her. That all changed when she met Anthony.

Amy set her phone down and remembered back to the day they met.

She had just started her second year at middle school. Due to lack of funding and teachers, the schools were combined throughout each county. Many families couldn't get their children to the remote schools, so slowly kids stopped going. And with the state's government in disarray, forcing kids into attendance disappeared. But their family was lucky. The county seat was in their town and thus, the schoolhouse.

Amy was sitting at her desk in homeroom. She and her friends were all combing over the latest picture filters when Anthony walked in. He was tall, with dark hair and eyes. His skin was tanned even though it was September in South Dakota. But his eyes were this hazel that made her insides melt. "Who is that?" someone said behind her.

Amy swallowed and closed her mouth, noticing it was open. The new boy noticed the stares and look directly at Amy. Amy's heart pounded. The new boy kept his gaze as he walked towards her. The girls began to giggle when he put his book bag down and slid into a desk beside her. "Hi," he said, "I'm Anthony."

Amy smiled again. That was six years ago and the start of a romance which continued to this day. She still couldn't believe he was a year younger than her. He was so mature, even then. Far taller and more man-like than half of the high school kids. He was an instant heartthrob, and Anthony Gomez chose her.

Amy unlocked her phone and texted him.

Me: Where are you, hun?
My Sweetie: At the beach. U coming?
Me: Duh … lol…be there in 10…love you
My Sweetie: Awesome! Luv u 2

Amy grabbed her purse and rode her bike to Shady Shore.

~

When Amy arrived, the usual suspects were gathered around acting like assholes. But as she walked up, the antics amplified. *Apes*, she thought snarkily, *every one of them*.

Secretly, she loved it. Amy knew she was pretty. She tried to act coy about it, but she was ever-aware that the smallest bat of the eyes or purse of her lips got her anything she wanted. Well, almost anything. Anthony came trotting over and walked her bike to the rack. He kissed her over the handlebars. "Hey sugar," he whispered on her lips.

Amy swooned even after all these years. They were the *it* couple, and everyone wanted to know one thing.

"Get married already!" Benji's latest arm candy yelled.

"Get a room!" Benji hollered.

Amy looked at Anthony and threw her arms around his neck. "Yea," she whispered in his neck hugging him, "when are we getting married?"

Anthony pretended to not hear her, kissing Amy deeply. "Seriously," the girl of the week said, drawing out the word, and the gang laughed.

Amy couldn't remember her name: Christy, Christa, Crystal? Not like it mattered. He'd be onto the next by the end of the week. Watertown was small. But many transplants moved there to get away from the fighting. Kids who were drafted moved out. Families who were displaced moved in. Which meant there was a large cache of new blood for the Watertown thugs to prey on. "I know you heard me," Amy pushed again.

Anthony pulled her away and looked in her eyes, "Amy, stop."

Amy frowned. "Why?" she asked, starting their weekly battle.

"You know why," he said peeling himself from her.

"It doesn't make any sense," she huffed, crossing her arms, "don't you want to be with me?"

"I am with you, Ames," he said for the hundredth time, "But I am eighteen and either of us could be scooped up at any moment. And what then?"

"All the more reason to," Amy said, looking away from him, "plus, I could avoid the draft if I'm pregnant."

Anthony glared at her and walked away.

"Ok," Amy resigned running after him, "I was just kidding."

The group sat on around a picnic table and shot the breeze. Some played cards; Amy watched Benji take Christ -*y-a-in* towards the woods. Amy rolled her eyes. He was harmless really. Amy saw through most of the boys she hung out with. The one thing they all had in common was their fathers. They all had either died or come back hardened from this war or the wars fought before. Benji and Mitch cycled through women to feel loved. Brett was an asshole because his dad treated him as such. Scotty barely spoke, but to be accepted he would do anything anyone asked. Amy frowned. What did that mean for her?

She looked out at the water. Muddy and cold Lake Kampeska where no one swam anymore was a reminder of where she really was. The once beautiful city of Watertown was rundown because there wasn't any money to care for it. And the park always was filled with teenage townies because there wasn't much for kids to do.

Amy sighed, looking at their "beach". It was such a perfect metaphor for the current status of the country. Sad, dirty, rundown, and everyone who lived in it still acted like it was paradise. Because the memory of how wonderful this place was before the war was all they had to hang onto.

Anthony pulled her arm and nodded to the park facilities. "Shall we?" he smiled.

Amy grinned. They snuck away to the heckling of the remaining picnickers to find a quiet place. They walked into the women's bathroom. There was an unwritten rule about the bathrooms in Shady Shores. The men's toilet was where you did your business. And the women's was where you did your real business. The two walked into a literal steam room of sex. Amy could smell the heat.

Anthony looked under the stalls. All were taken. Anthony saw Benji's shoes and pounded on the door. His girl squealed. "Taken!" Benji yelled.

"We all know you only take sixty seconds, Ji," Anthony said, "times up, minute man!"

Female snickering came from within. Amy smiled and leaned on the wall. The sounds of clothes being hastily adorned made Amy laugh out loud. Benji emerged red-faced. Anthony raised an eyebrow. Arm Candy walked out with a saunter. "There's always tomorrow," she cooed to Amy as she followed Benji out.

"That one may stick around," Amy said, watching them go.

Anthony grabbed her hand and pulled her into the stall. Her mouth was on his before he could lock it. They pressed their bodies together and Amy felt him through her pants. She milled on him, egging him on. His hands found her shirt's hem and ventured up to her stomach. Amy let out a gasp when his cold hands touched her boiling skin. Every time he touched her, she felt her body respond. Amy unbuttoned his pants, making sure to rub him in the process. Anthony braced his hands on the stall walls. She pulled him from his jeans and placed him in her mouth. Anthony sighed and gently held her head. It made Amy so happy to please him. She would do anything for this man.

Amy stood up as he sat on the toilet lid. He pulled down her leggings and kissed her stomach. "Please," she begged quietly.

Anthony wagged his finger at her, pressing his finger to her lips. She put his finger in her mouth. Anthony smiled, taking his wet finger and sliding down her stomach. Amy let out a moan as he slipped it inside her. He covered Amy's mouth with his other hand, snickering. Amy rocked on him. Blood rushed in her ears and she felt herself about to go over the edge. She bit down on his finger. Anthony let out a yelp and pulled her down onto him. They sat there without moving for a moment, two bodies as one. She ran her fingers through his crew-cut hair. She could feel her pulse everywhere. "I love you," she whispered.

"I love you," he answered.

They began again in perfect sync. Amy felt him getting close to the edge. It was only then the thought occurred to her. As he began to finish, Anthony started to lift her from him. But Amy wrapped her legs around him tightly, braced and stayed put. "Amy," he gasped as he tried to buck her off. But it was too late, and she felt him release inside. Amy sat back and smiled at him.

Anthony's eyes were wild. "What in the actual fuck, Amy?" he said pushing her off of him.

"What?" Amy said innocently.

"You know damn well what," he said buttoning his pants.

He shoved her out of the way and stormed out of the bathroom. Amy leaned on the stall wall, tears filling her eyes. All the sounds of love stopped abruptly after their commotion. Amy wiped her eyes and put herself back together. When she got back out to the picnic tables, Anthony was already gone.

~

Sara spent the next few days in her daily monotony. She woke and went for a jog. Cooked. Cleaned. Sunday, she went to church. She listened to the news with Dan and agreed with every point the Grays made. "The Whites are sheep," Dan said smugly, "every last one. They expect us to live with their ideals. It all looks good on paper."

Sara nodded vigorously. She never did understand which ideals they intended on making them live with. And Smoke Show Sam thought she was so smart. He's the fool. Sara realized she was grinding her teeth. She didn't understand half of the things that went on in her daily life. And the way Sam had looked at her with such pity. *Ha*, she thought, *you're the one-legged man entering an ass-kicking contest. I should march down there and give him a piece of my mind.*

The memory of Sam's gaze flooded back her, and again she was on fire. That is before he saw Dan's marks. Then it was a feeling of embarrassment. A man like that couldn't possibly be looking at her. She was old and had weird skin. She was a mom and hadn't done anything exceptional with her life. *No*, she thought, *it was in her mind. How dare he confuse me! I need to head down there and clear the air.*

Every one of the last six days Sara had forced herself to not go near the gym. When the girls asked where she had been, Sara feigned being sick. When her daughters asked why she wasn't obsessing over her latest workout plan, Sara said she now fancied running. Lying to them was easy. Getting the SS Samuel out of her thoughts was becoming more and more difficult. The over-analysis of the last day at the gym should've been tedious but it was like watching her favorite movie. It replayed over and over. The girls razzing her for Sam always being there when she was. Mocking the way he ogled her. Always managing to work out next to her. Perhaps it wasn't in her imagination.

"Sara," Dan said, "hello?"

Sara had been drying the same dish for several minutes. Startled, she set the plate down. "What has gotten into you?" Dan said, and was cut off by a rolling blackout.

"Dammit," Dan said, shoving himself back from the table. He stormed outside to see if the neighbors were out as well. Dan insisted on a gas generator, so they would never be in the dark. Sara watched him throw the blue tarp off of five gas cans they had stored behind the garage.

Sara took her chance to get away from his prying eye. She ran upstairs and locked the bedroom door.

Undressed, she stood in front of the mirror. Sara let her mom bun fall down her shoulders. Her dark hair cascaded over her breasts and she ran her fingers through it, smoothing it. Sara turned to catch the light of the fading sun. Slowly she ran her hands down her body, trying to feel it as a man would. Her heart pounded in her chest as she thought of Sam's gaze on her. Sara's hands cupped her breasts and her nipples hardened at the thought of him. Listening for Dan, she licked her lips. Dan didn't allow locked doors in the house. Sara was taking a risk in her mind and in the flesh. Almost without permission, her hands grazed down over her mound. She frowned at the amount of hair. She hadn't worn a swimsuit small enough to even need to trim. Dan wouldn't allow it. Sara hadn't shaved in years. Undeterred, her hands slipped between her legs. She sighed at the fantasy of Sam's touch and felt her hand get wet.

The downstairs door suddenly slammed. "Sara!" Dan yelled.

In twenty seconds, Sara was dressed and walking down the stairs.

"Yes?" she responded.

Dan eyed her suspiciously. Sara wiped her hands on her pants. She could smell her own pheromones. God, she hoped he didn't too.

"You're sick," Dan said, repulsed.

She was indeed flush and her heart was racing. Dan was, fortunately, a germophobic. She couldn't overplay her excuse often but used feigned illness to rid herself of unwanted sexual sessions with Dan.

"Oh, I don't think so," Sara said, "just hot because the fans turned off."

Dan relaxed a little. "So, what are your plans tomorrow?" Dan asked, and without interest he added, "don't forget our gas rations."

"I think I'll go to the gym," Sara said, hiding her glee, "I want to try something new."

~

The girls were all squealing and jumping when Sara's Jeep pulled into the gym parking lot. They reminded her of Shitzus, and it was certain they too peed a little when excited. "I'm so happy you're here," Jackie sang, "together again."

"It's not the same without you," Hadley added, "we get nothing accomplished and end up going to Gather and eating whatever Colin has."

"Don't tell Dan though." Kristen said.

Sara smiled despite herself. Her heart was hammering in her chest. And she felt exposed as her freshly-shaved parts rubbed on the crotch of her yoga pants. She hoped they wouldn't notice that her hair was done and that she had on a bit of makeup. She normally looked like a vagrant when working out.

Sara tried to be blasé as she walked through the gym doors. She subtly looked around, searching for Sam. The only people in the gym were a few older ladies on the elliptical. Sara's heart sank. "Sara," Jackie called, "earth to Sara!"

The other women giggled as they set their towels and waters bottles down, preparing for another long workout of their mouths. "Um, yea," Sara said, "sorry. I guess I'm still a little out of it."

"So, leg day?" Hadley asked.

"Yea, sure whatever," Sara sighed, setting her things down.

All that hype for nothing. Sara had prepared a speech to put Sam in his place. And her disappointment had all to do with not being able to use it. At least, that's what she kept saying over and over in her head. Sam was usually there in the mornings to open and would drop in throughout the day to make sure the place was still standing. She must have missed him. Sara reached down and grabbed a kettlebell. "Squats then sumos," she prompted as the girls settled into gossiping about a townie who had bad teeth.

"They're like yellow chicklets," Kristen giggled, "I mean we still can be hygienic is all I'm saying."

The other women nodded in agreeance. "Gross," Jackie said, "maybe gargle with nail polish remover?"

"And we're squatting and we're squatting," Sara tried again lowering the bell between her legs and standing up, swinging it to shoulder height.

"Yea yea yea," Hadley conceded, grabbing a bell.

Sara laughed. It was nice to be around non-familial humans again, even though they wouldn't have been her first choice in friends. Even relationships are rationed these days. They finished their first circuit, of which Hadley complained the entire duration. "You're squatting five pounds," Sara said, laughing as Sam walked in from the back office.

Sara's eyes locked with his. He was as frozen as she. Sara stood with her weight dangling from her fingertips. When she almost dropped it, she snapped back to reality only to see Sam smile at her. His smile faded and his face became solemn. He nodded towards the restrooms.

"Where are you going?" Danielle asked.

Sara set her weights down. "Too much coffee," she said and headed to the back hallway.

This is it, she thought, *I'm going to tell him where he can go.*

Her heart was hammering in her chest, and she tried to ignore the same in her leggings. She turned the corner, and there he stood. His blue eye gleamed as he stared at her. He waved her into his office, and he shut the door.

His face betrayed so many different emotions, Sara had a hard time keeping up. But the one she didn't expect was longing. He took a deep breath and lowered his head. A lock of ebony hair fell and Sara's knees about buckled. "I'm really glad you came back," he said without looking up.

"Yes, well, LA Fitness isn't building a new facility here, so," she said.

Sam looked up smiling. She visualized herself being scraped off the floor. *I have been through harder times than this*, she thought and took a deep breath, steadying herself.

"What you said was incredibly invasive," Sara began as rehearsed, "and while I know you were trying to help…"

"I'm so sorry, Sara," Sam interrupted.

He took a step towards her. She could smell his freshly-showered skin. "That's ok," she responded automatically.

He took another step closer. "No it isn't," he continued, "I care about you. And when I thought you were in trouble, I didn't think."

Another step. She could smell the gum he was chewing. *My God, I can taste him.*

"I think the world of you, Sara," Sam said, "but when you stopped coming. And I didn't see your face every morning."

Sara tried without victory to keep her mouth from gaping.

"I just," Sam continued, "I just felt like the brightest part of my day went dark."

I can't breathe. I'm having a stroke, yup, stroking out.

Another step.

But then the realization hit her. Sam was going to kiss her. What was she going to do? Let him? Have an affair? Secretly meet SS Sam in the women's bathroom at the only gym in town? *Yes! Yes, this is what I want. It'll all work out. These things always do, right?*

Sara almost laughed out loud. The image of Dan sprang into her mind. This was a bad, bad idea. Per the usual, she saddled her fairy tale and came back to her real life. "Sam," she started carefully, "you're very sweet. But I am going to go back to the gym."

Step back.

The shine of his eyes promptly went out, and it broke her deeper than she could've imagined.

"We're good," Sara finished, touching his arm and turned to leave.

"Are you wearing makeup?" Sam asked.

Sara froze with her hand on the knob. This was a mistake. She had cast a line and that was wrong. She promptly opened the door and went back to the hens.

CHAPTER THREE

Sara returned home after her barely-executed workout. She rested her head on her front door, tears streaming down her face. While at the gym, Sam walked the floor, mysteriously needing to clean every surface. Sara avoided eye contact with him. She avoided everyone. The hens cackled and swooned over Sam. A loud laugh from Hadley startled her enough to lift her eyes from the floor. Across the room, Sam watched her. Their eyes met. Quickly, she looked away. "Did you all see the stack of newspapers that made it to the gas station?" Danielle asked. "It's basically nothing but pictures of what different cities look like. It's just so awful."

"Please tell me Vegas is still standing," Kristen joked, "after all these years of slumming it, I'll need a glittery girls' trip."

The girls all squawked and agreed. Soon, they were all planning outfits and excursions for a city that was most likely flattened. "You should've seen Dallas," Kristen began again, "it looks like the moon there are so many craters. And the skyline looks like a mouth of broken teeth."

The girls all started cackling again, except Jackie. Sara's eyes shifted to her. Jackie began to breathe heavily. Jackie had moved to South Dakota from Texas when they were all in high school. And apparently, Sara was the only one who remembered. "It's really not funny," Sara said quietly.

"Oh lighten up," Hadley said.

"Seriously," Kristen continued, "That was a split town anyhow. At least half of them were Whites."

Jackie slammed her kettlebell to the ground. The girls all got quiet. "Vegas is dust along with all the people in it," Jackie said with an intensity Sara hadn't heard before. "Nellis Air Force Base was just outside of the city. All the military cities were targeted first. You might want to rethink your girls' trip. I hear Dead Wood's nice this time of year."

Jackie grabbed her things and stomped out of the gym. Sara couldn't help but look at Sam. He watched Jackie go and swallowed hard. "Not cool," Danielle said to Kristen.

"Oh, who cares," Kristen said flippantly, "I hear they are only Gray cardholders, so they could stay in Watertown."

Sara gritted her teeth. Those were dangerous accusations.

"And I also heard her husband has a computer he built in the basement that can access the internet."

That got Sara's attention. Jackie did always seem to be in the know. What if she could find out where Freddie was? It wouldn't really keep him any more or less safe, but it would be comforting to know where he was. Selfishly, Sara thought of all the ways she would use instant access to information: finding the name of a long-lost song, checking the weather, self-diagnosing a rash. Sara wasn't ever tech-savvy, but she missed the days of digital ease with a passion. Sara gathered up her things. "I think I'm going to call it a day too," she said, heading towards the door.

She didn't look back to say goodbye.

~

Sara was busy preparing dinner when her daughters began filing in. She had the hardest time cooking for Amy and her specific diet choices. Rations were mostly canned or boxed food, and unless it was marked "vegan," Amy wouldn't eat it. Sara always gave the impression each meal was seamless to prepare, while in actuality, she spent half her day staring at her cabinet, planning how she would feed her family. Tonight they were having Chicken Ala' King. Amy's less the chicken, cream-based soup, and bread. So Amy would be enjoying Bean Ala' Pita. Thankfully Sara had the forethought to snag any spice she could find. Sara even had a little herb garden in their backyard. So whenever a meal tasted bland or musty, Sara dumped herb after herb until it tasted like normalcy. As much as she hated the hens for acting like a war wasn't waging, she spent most of her time making her home peaceful.

Amy came down first. Sara motioned for her to set the table. Sara watched her when she wasn't looking. Amy looked upset. And as badly as she wanted to ask, Sara wanted to avoid her teenage angst even more. So silent she stayed. Marie took the stairs one at a time and plopped into her chair. Sara always thought it was funny that families had assigned dinner seating. Sometimes she wanted to sit elsewhere just to add spice to their rationed life. The garage door began to crunch and the sound of an old cruiser pulling in filled the house. *And that's why I don't*, Sara thought with an eye roll.

Dan hated change. He yearned for his days in the military. And he ran his family as though he still was. "Hi honey," Sara tried, "how was your day?"

Dan grunted and hung his jacket up in the closet. Amy and Marie sat down and waited silently as Dan took his chair. Sara took her place at his side. He opened his hands to them. They completed the circle and bowed their heads. "Thank you for this food and for another day to wage your will. Please give strength to the Gray Main and bless us with a return of our country. In your name, we pray."

"Amen," they all answered.

Dan tucked his napkin on his lap and began to serve

himself. Only then did the rest of them dig in. "What did you all do today?" Sara said trying again.

"I hung out with some friends. Played cards," Marie said into her plate.

Sara smiled and nodded. Slowly, she took a bite of food, watching her family. Amy sniffed her meal and then took a bite, finding it acceptable. Dan was cutting his chicken into equal-sized pieces. He took a bite. "It's good," he mumbled.

Sara smiled and her heart slowed a bit. "Amy, did you have fun at the beach?" Sara asked, "it was a nice day. But I'm sure the water was…"

"It was fine," Amy snapped.

Sara and Marie looked up from their plates. Even Dan paused mid-bite. "Was there an issue at the park?" Dan asked pointedly.

"No," Amy said trying to adjust her attitude, "It was just…fine."

Dan sized her up. "So I heard there was a newspaper at the gas station," Sara said, trying to change the subject, "that showed pictures of major cities across the US."

Dan nodded with a grunt, forgetting Amy's blatant lie. "I have a copy in the cruiser," Dan said shaking his head, "some of our best strongholds…leveled."

"Were any of them near Freddie?" Marie asked.

Sara saw the hurt in her eyes. "No," Dan said, "none of them were in his area. But it's great to see the progress we've made taking the White cities. Definitely more of them taken than ours."

That confused Sara. Watertown wasn't truly Gray. Many families tried to stay neutral or pretended to be Gray because they didn't have the means to go to a friendly city. Dan spoke of the military actions as though he was still enlisted. As though he was directly involved. Dan would say once a military man, always a military man. Sara knew it was an honor to serve. But he seemed to use it as an excuse to order them around like they were new recruits. He'd say his iron fist and type A idiosyncrasies were out of his control because once…always. Dan's refusal to change was because there wasn't a problem. His surroundings were to bend to him and thus, so would they. Marie finished her plate and dumped it in the sink. "Thanks, mom," Marie muttered and ran back to her room.

Amy grabbed her plate and a few empty serving dishes and excused herself from the table. Sara and Dan ate in silence. And she found herself wondering about Sam. She wondered if he ate alone, if he had any friends. Sam most likely had a girlfriend; every woman in town fell all over themselves when he was around. Yes, he must have had a girlfriend. Sara had totally misread their interaction. "Sara," Dan said, his voice annoyed.

Sara looked at him blankly. "Are you listening to me?" Dan said with raised brows. "I asked if you wanted to see the newspaper."

"Oh," Sara said shaking the Sam smoke from her mind, "no, not really. Too sad."

"Seeing our enemies defeated is sad?"

"No," Sara dodged, "I mean seeing our people and their cities demolished. Seeing cities I wish would have found the way before they were destroyed, it's sad. That's what I mean."

Dan nodded and sat back sipping the whiskey Sara had poured. "Plus I get updates from Jackie."

Dan's brows shot up. "Jackie Gunther?"

"Yea," Sara said collecting their plates, "her husband has a working computer. Isn't that amazing?"

"Like the internet?"

"Um," Sara now slowed, realizing her folly, "I'm not sure. I guess so. The old internet that we all try to use."

Dan rubbed his chin. "Old internet wouldn't have updated information on the war," Dan said, "But international internet certainly would. Very interesting."

Sara went to the sink and began scrubbing the dishes in panic. She knew that international internet was frowned upon by the Grays. It was said it gave misinformation, altered news and couldn't be trusted. Moreover, it was known people used it to get out of the States or give information from the inside. Who they were giving information to, Sara had no idea. But she knew it was bad to be associated with international internet. And now she had just outed a woman and her husband.

Later that night, Sara laid in bed staring at the ceiling. It was so dark she resorted to counting the sounds of the fan blades cutting through the air. She chewed her lip until she tasted blood. What had she done? She knew Dan wouldn't hesitate to turn Jackie's family into the Gray Main Authorities. Dan loved to brag about his connections and applaud the brave men and women who turned in traitors. Sara promised herself she would warn Jackie in the morning. And it wasn't too much after that resolve when the sun came up.

~

Sara paced the kitchen, waiting for it to be 7 am. Marie and Amy eyed her but didn't ask why she was so fidgety. At precisely eight, Sara drove to the gym. She couldn't raise suspicion. Sara went about her morning like every morning: made coffee, cooked breakfast, and tidied up. Sara kept her speed under control as she drove down the main street to town. And on the route sat the Gunther's home. She saw the lights before she saw the house. Sara felt bile rise in her throat as she slowly drove past. Gray MP vehicles dotted their lawn. Uniformed men were taking equipment out of the house and in the back of a van sat Jackie's husband, Justin. His head hung and shoulders slumped. Sara looked around for Jackie and her small children but didn't see them. It was the only small mercy Sara felt.

As her Jeep passed the van, Justin looked up. Sara saw him look at her with such grace. He wasn't afraid. He was just waiting. An MP slammed the back door and climbed into the van, driving away.

Sara pulled into the parking lot of the gym. She stepped out and threw up. Pinning her arms to her stomach, she held her sides, trying hard to silence her sobs. *I did this.*

She had slipped and told Dan. Sara couldn't let the hens know what she had done. Standing up slowly, she gathered herself. Taking a sip of water and retying back her hair, she slammed the Jeep door. Which left her face to face with Sam. He stood outside the gym's back door watching her. The look on his face crushed her. It was so incredibly sad and broken. He knew. Sam nodded towards the door. Sara followed, pushing past him into the gym. He stopped her, taking her hand. "Hey," he said quietly.

Sara began sobbing. Sam took her in his arms, smoothing her hair. "It's ok," he kept saying, holding her tight.

God, he felt good. The safety of his arms made her feel guilty for enjoying it. She cried harder. After she had emptied her eyes, she pulled back to look at him. Sam tucked a hair behind her ear, running his thumb over her cheek, wiping away the last tear. It was then she heard the crying from the other room. Sara took the briefest moment to look into his blue lone eye and broke away. She ran into the gym and found Hadley crying on the weight bench. Danielle was rubbing her back and handing her toilet paper to wipe her nose. "She's gone," Hadley cried into her hands.

Sara looked at Kristen who was leaning on the wall with her arms crossed, looking not a bit sympathetic. Hadley looked up at Sara. "They're all gone," Hadley said of the Gunthers.

~

Sara went home. She couldn't stand being around anyone. When she got there, Dan's cruiser was parked next to a car she didn't recognize. She came in through the front door to see a man who likely owned the mystery car. He was in casual clothes but looked expensive. He was handing Dan an envelope, which Dan checked, revealing a wad of Gray cash. Sara glared at the two of them. She could smell the aftershave on the stranger, and his leather shoes were new, a style she hadn't seen before. The man quickly turned around, leering at her. "That's my wife," Dan said tucking the money in his pocket, "don't pay her any mind."

Sara watched the man shake Dan's hand and let himself out as though he had been a guest before. Dan leaned back on the couch, reaching his arms back. "Who..," Sara whispered, "What did you do?"

"My civic duty," Dan said with a grin, "and I'm feeling generous."

He stood and scooped her into his arms, kissing her. Sara knew better than to struggle. Dan was almost giddy as he led her to their bedroom where she knew she would be counting fan blades. Sara completely submitted and gave into him. So numb to what she had done, Sara accidentally let herself feel some pleasure. She hated herself for it. When they had both finished, Sara took a shower. She was too ashamed to cry. Too dazed to feel. Which is why at four in the morning, Sara felt no fear as she slipped from the bed and out her front door.

Sara jogged towards Jackie's house. She pushed her jog into a sprint. She wanted to feel her legs burn. Sara wanted to punish herself for what she had done. As she neared the house, Sara's lungs screamed for her to stop. But she pushed on until she was there. Blinded by her pain, Sara almost ran into Jackie's mini-van parked in the driveway. Jackie was rushing around it, pulling its striping tape from the sides. "Jackie," Sara whispered.

Jackie dropped the tape ball, clutching her heart. "Oh my God, Sara! What are you doing here?"

What *was* she doing there? "I…I," Sara stuttered, "I'm so sorry about Justin."

Jackie rushed around the car, finishing her task and checked on her sleeping boys in the back. "It's not your fault."

Sara's heart dropped. She knew. "I didn't mean to say anything, I swear."

Jackie stopped and stared at her. She took Sara's hands. "None of this is your fault," Jackie said in that voice Jackie had taken the day before, "they were onto us for a while."

They? Us?

"Where did they take Justin?" Sara asked, watching her climb into the driver's seat.

"He's dead, Sara," Jackie's eyes only betrayed the smallest hint of sadness, "they executed him last night."

Sara clutched her chest, still heaving from the run. "But," she gasped, "no trial?"

Jackie took a deep breath, looking in the rearview mirror at her sleeping sons. "We knew the risks," she said, giving Sara an even stare, "and for all we've been able to do it was worth it."

Jackie took a deep breath and stared blankly into the windshield. Jackie was a few years younger than Sara. She had blond hair cut into a bob. She wore glasses and was a bit overweight. She always seemed younger than she truly was to Sara. But in this moment, Jackie was like a warrior with the wisdom of a hundred lifetimes. "You should volunteer," Jackie said turning those wise eyes to her.

Sara shook her head, not understanding. Jackie turned the van on, cringing when its engine echoed down the street. "We could use more like you," Jackie said and rolled up the window.

Sara watched her drive down the street without headlights on.

CHAPTER FOUR

Sara spent the next several days going through the motions. The Gray Authorities executed Justin Gunther. Jackie and her boys had disappeared. The town was on fire with the news. Some thought Jackie was taken into custody. Others believed she and the boys had fled. But all agreed they were treasonous wolves in sheep's clothing and that Justin, at least, got what he deserved. Even Hadley had resorted to pretending she and Jackie hadn't been close friends since high school. All of them made Sara sick. She couldn't even look at Kristen. Sara barely spoke to Dan. And instead of submitting to Dan's daily verbal degradation, Sara shot back. She hit him with an *I disagree* or *I don't think you are right*.

The consequences of these outbursts throbbed under her hoodie as she drove to the gym. Sara found herself angry without an outlet. Old habits like tapping doorknobs and counting everything began once more. And to her horror, Sara had begun hurting herself again too. The angry red marks on her wrist stung. But it felt so good to snap her hair tie on them over and over again. Her hair itched to be pulled.

Walking to the gym, she went straight to the elliptical.

"Well hello to you too," Kristen said with an attitude.

The hens watched her work out for a minute and then decided to ignore her too. Subtle chuckles and hushed tones proved Sara was the shiny new gossip toy. And Sara couldn't have given a single fuck. Justin was dead. Jackie was in danger, and it was all her fault.

Her breath caught, and she choked back a sob. Off-balance, she lost her footing and her knee slammed into the cup holder, tearing a hole, in her favorite yoga pants. They were black with wear spots and a faded DKNY logo written down the side. Not fancy, but they always made her feel good. And with the new hole, her pants said DOKNY with blood showing through. She did feel like an ass. "How goddamn appropriate," Sara hissed through gritted teeth.

Sara stomped over to the hens. Danielle and Hadley watched for Queen Hen Kristen's reaction. Kristen put her hands on her hips and cocked her head. If she flapped her arms, Sara would laugh and then punch her. "Do you guys have a Band-Aid?" Sara asked begrudgingly.

"Oh, now you can talk to us," Kristen snapped back.

Oh, please flap your arms, you snub-nosed bitch.

Danielle giggled, and Hadley looked down at the floor. "I have a lot going on, ok," Sara said, bearing down on her urge to tear Kristen's face to pieces.

"Well, so do we," Kristen said, pointing at the hens. "Our best friend was a traitor."

Sara sighed and turned, heading to the bathrooms. "Our families hung out for goodness sakes. Who knows what her kids told mine!" Kristen yelled to her back, "It's not all about you."

Sara walked into the bathroom and shut the door, locking it. She leaned her head on the cool metal door. She stared at the mosaic pattern on the tiles. *One, two, three, four.*

Tears wet the triangles and squares. She eyed her leg. It was already starting to bruise. *What's another one?*

A gentle knock tapped on the other side of the door. "Sara?"

Sam's deep voice came through muffled. "Are you ok?"
No. Never. Never have I ever been ok.

"I'm fine," Sara said clearing her throat.

Quickly, she turned on the faucet and washed her hands, throwing some water on her face. "I have Band-Aids," Sam said through the door.

Sara swallowed and looked down at her bleeding leg. Unlocking the door, she cracked it open. Sam's face stared back at her. No one had ever looked at her like that in her life. There was so much empathy and kindness. Sam reached through the crack and took her hand, squeezing it. "Come on," he nodded to his office.

Sara followed and sat down in his office chair. He gathered some supplies. Moving the new hole around, Sam assessed the damage. "Don't sue us, kay?"

Sara laughed, despite herself. A nose bubble popped in the process. Sam saw it and fell back on his butt, quietly laughing. *Kill me please.*

Any feelings of anger or sadness were instantly replaced with pure mortification. "Here," he said, handing her a tissue.

"Thanks," Sara turned fuchsia.

Gently, he cleaned the area with an alcohol pad and bandaged the small cut. "It's going to bruise," Sam said, standing up and staring down at her.

"I know," Sara said, looking down.

Sam searched the room with fire in his eyes. Sara was all too familiar with bruising, and Sam knew it. Sara stood flexing her leg. "That feels good," Sara said, trying to be casual, "thank you."

Sara turned to go. "I'm sorry about your friend," Sam whispered.

She looked over her shoulder. His face was coated with thick worry lines that she hadn't ever noticed before. His one eye brimmed with tears. "I'm sorry for everything."

Sara froze. Her heart started pounding. Her hand was on the knob. All she had to do was turn it and walk away from this situation. Sara felt his hand slide into hers, and in one beat, Sam had turned her to him. He slid his hand into her hair and cupped her face. They stared at each other. Sara searching his face. *Walk away. Walk away.*

Gently. Slowly, almost asking, he pressed his body into hers. Sara's eyes closed as his lips gently met with hers.

Her body was on fire as she wrapped her arms around his neck. Sam's mouth parted - she tasted mint. Their tongues danced, and she felt him harden on her thigh. Sara had never wanted someone as badly as she wanted him right then. Hands slid down her body, pulling her closer, and he backed her into the wall. His mouth explored her neck and Sara threw her head back, banging it on the shelf. Her squeal made him chuckle. "Oh it's like that," Sara whispered.

She reached for him inside his gym shorts, which was all the license he needed. He yanked down her leggings and turned her around. The feeling of Sam sliding inside made Sara's vision swirl. *Is this how it is*, she thought, *could this possibly be how it's supposed to feel?*

A man who had just been a friendly acquaintance was now filling her, making her knees weak. Sara gasped and he covered her mouth, softly laughing in her ear. Sam began to move faster. Sara felt herself getting close. Was it possible for a woman to get off this way? The universe answered as they both climaxed together, sagging to the floor.

Sara heard Danielle's loud laughter from the next room. It broke her trance enough to pull away from Sam. He looked in her eyes and held her face. "You are the most beautiful woman I have ever known," he whispered.

Sara smiled. She couldn't help it. Nothing she ever dreamed came true. No positive thinking ever came to fruition. She was always last place, worst-case scenario, the beaten dog. "I have to go," Sara whispered back.

Sam ran his hands through his hair. His chest rising and falling from the exertion. "See ya tomorrow," he said expectantly.

"To work out, yes," she answered slyly.

He laughed out loud at that. "Sure," he said with a grin.

~

Sara apologized to the hens on her way out the door. She claimed her leg was too hurt to continue. The girls didn't need much convincing and all made plans to go to Colin's for coffee.

Sara flew through the familiar roads. And suddenly everything looked new. She noticed depth in the color of the brick houses. She saw the dark edging of the clouds, puffy and whipped. A hawk soared through the sky on a thermal. The high was so effortless. For the hawk and Sara both. She kept yipping like a dog. Bubbles of joy boiled through her, needing to escape. She thought she'd hyperventilate. There should be guilt for feeling this way because of recent events. But Sara couldn't help it.

She pulled into the drive, and her heart hammered to a stop. Dan's car. He was home early from work. "Be cool," she prepped herself.

It was just once, she thought, *not like you had an affair. Not cool, but not a full-blown affair.*

Sara opened the garage door to find Dan sitting at the laptop typing something out. He did this one finger at a time. Everything about him was infuriating. But nothing would dull her mood.

She burst through the door, and Dan looked up from the laptop briefly. Then his eyes flew to her face. *He knows.*

"You look lively," Dan said leaning in his chair, "feeling better, I see."

He's smiling, she noticed.

Smiling Dan had only a few provocations. One was passion. Sara's body heaved at the thought of him. "Nope," Sara lied, heading for their bedroom. "Period started."

"That's fine with me," Dan answered, hollering up the stairs after her.

"And diarrhea," Sara called back.

She heard Dan gag as she shut the door. Sara leaned back on it and hugged herself. She tried to recall every moment. The way he smelled. The way he tasted. She could still feel his hands in her hair.

She locked the door and threw off her leggings. Sara explored herself in ways she had never thought to. She imagined it was his hands inside. Rocking her hips, she quietly moaned for him.

When Sara finished, her hand was soaked with her need for the SS Sam. She laid back on the pillows, watching her chest rise and fall. She could see her pulse in her belly.

There was a sudden click in her mind. She never wanted to stop feeling this way. She was going to have the feeling again. And the plotting began. *Just to see him*, she reassured herself, *nothing more. Not cool. But not an affair.*

She was instantly addicted to that feeling. And Sara would have it again.

~

After Sara had collected herself, she went downstairs and found Marie working in her math book. Schools hadn't been open for almost two years, but Sara felt compelled to ensure the kids were educated. She delighted in reviewing the complex math problems and science workbook with her children. She had always had a knack for school. Sara had always wanted to go to college. But when Amy came into her life, it was all survival mode. And when she married Dan, the subject was not to be broached. "How's it going?" Sara said, kissing the top of her head.

"Eh," Marie answered, "I hate matrixes."

Sara smiled, and Amy came skipping down the stairs, phone in hand. Sara moved to the sink and began cleaning up dishes her family threw there. But it would not get her down today. No amount of cooked-on grease would dampen her mood. "Hi sweetheart," Sara said.

"You're chipper," Amy said without looking up.

"You think?" Sara brushed it off.

Marie sat watching the exchange. "Yea," Marie added, "you're grinning like a loonie toon."

Sara shrugged, "Just a nice day."

"Guess your anal leakage issues have subsided," Marie grumbled.

Sara grabbed the sink sprayer and shot Marie in the head. "What the hell?" Marie shrieked.

Amy looked up and started giggling.

"You think that's funny," Sara said and raised the sprayer.

"Don't you dare get my phone wet," Amy yelled.

"Better detach it from your arm, daughter," Sara teased, following her with the sprayer.

Amy made a run for it, and Marie jumped in her way. Marie looked like a drowned albino rat with half her hair soaked. Amy squealed, and Marie jumped on her. Amy managed to toss her phone on the counter before Sara got her square in the face. Marie was cackling like an old woman, and Amy was screaming, kicking out of her grip.

Finally, Amy broke free. "You guys are f'ing crazy, you know that!" Amy shouted.

Sara and Marie both looked at each other and began laughing hysterically. Amy grabbed her phone and wiped her face on her sleeve. "Ha ha ha," Amy groaned, trying hard to hide a smile.

Dan charged in from outside and saw the mess. "What the hell is all this?" he demanded. "Who was screaming?"

"The sprayer got stuck," Marie answered quickly.

"Yea," Amy added, "Mom got it working, though."

Both girls grabbed a towel and began wiping up the floor. Sara's heart swelled.

Dan rolled his eyes and went back out to the garage, muttering about women. Sara found another towel and got down on her hands and knees with her daughters. They all smiled at each other. They were still her babies.

"I love you," Sara said.

"Love you too," the girls echoed.

~

After Sara cleaned up, she had a chance to collect her thoughts about the day. She had to keep it business as usual. Couldn't set off alarms. She grabbed her grocery list and headed to the market to shop for dinner.

She drove past the gym and craned her neck to get a glimpse of Sam. The place looked empty. Sighing, she continued driving. She was so excited to go to the gym in the morning she was shaking. Pulling into the parking lot, she leaned her head back. She felt drunk. Her hand found its way between her legs and she moaned. *What am I doing? I'm like a horny teenager.*

But that didn't stop her. She began to micro-analyze every moment of what could have only been two minutes of pure ecstasy. She felt herself throb again. Sara closed her eyes and breathed in the remembered scent of him.

Knock. Knock. Knock.

Sara yelped. Kristen yelped. Sara clutched her chest. "Oh my god," Kristen said muffled through the Jeep window, "you scared me to death."

Oh god, Sara thought, *what did she see?*

Sara slowly opened the Jeep door. "Are you ok?" Kristen asked. "Were you sleeping?"

Sara crossed her arms uncomfortably. "Uh, yea" she agreed, "I slept horribly last night."

"Aw," Kristen said linking arms with her, "shopping buddies?"

"Sure," Sara answered begrudgingly.

Apparently, all was forgiven. Sara sighed. *Keep up the façade.*

The women entered the bustling County Fair Food Store. The store was as old as the town. It had that small market feel. The County Fair Food Store had only five aisles that once carried every type of food imaginable. The produce section she took for granted was now a harvest ghost town. She sometimes dreamed about bananas. A staple once so plentiful was now more valuable than money.

Because the summer was coming to a close, locally-grown fruits and vegetables would find their way to the shelves. But they would be scooped up so quickly, most families went without. Canned produced was rationed. *So there's that*, Sara said to herself.

Sara's eyes grazed the empty aisles. She used to stand in those aisles trying to figure out what type of bread she wanted. Now she stood longer in a line to get one loaf. Shopping, as Kristen had so annoyingly called it, was more like waiting. You brought your vouchers and waited in line to collect your food.

Sara lacked in about every area in life, but she could cook. If there was one thing she could give her family, it was a semblance of normalcy at dinner. She'd make yeast taste like parmesan cheese. She could take bread and turn it into a cake-like dessert. Bartering with her neighbors helped her find missing ingredients or spices to make tacos or a like-meatloaf. It was about the only thing Dan praised her for. Never to her personally, of course. He couldn't have her thinking she was of any value. But Sara heard through the grapevine that he often bragged about her skills in the kitchen.

Sara stood with Kristen in line. Out of her reverie, she realized Kristen had been talking the entire time. "So he thinks it's like an STD or something, and I'm all, Jason," Kristen paused for effect, "it's a friggin' ingrown hair."

Kristen started laughing loudly. Some of the people in line gave her a dirty sidelong glance and turned away from them both. "Do you remember all those pimple popping videos online?" Kristen asked.

"No, I don't think so," Sara said crossing her arms and avoiding eye contact.

The war had caused the systematic dismantling of most online sites. Sara remembered the days she could search the answer to any question in an instant. "So guess what I did?" Kristen geared up.

The woman in front of them was rolling her eyes, crossing her arms, screaming non-verbally, *Shut the fuck up, lady.*

"I got in between his legs and popped his nard pimple," Kristen laughed.

At this, Sara heard audible gasps from the peanut gallery. Another twenty minutes passed before it was their turn. Kristen handed the clerk five coupons for bread, milk, cans of beans, and butter. Sara handed him one for eggs and one for cheese. The clerk was in a Gray military uniform. He looked the same age as Freddie. Except, he was missing both legs. When he looked up at Sara, an old man stared through his young eyes. Sara's eyes misted. "Egg, cheese, milk, bread, beans, butter," the young boy's voice creaked.

Sara had been wrong. He was younger than Freddie. The clerk handed them their groceries and they walked back to their cars. "How old do you think that kid is?" Sara asked Kristen.

"I don't know. Maybe sixteen," Kristen guessed.

Sara choked, "Sixteen!"

Kristen shrugged.

"But he's too young to serve," Sara added.

"No," Kristen said, "they changed the draft age to sixteen a few months back. I guess they are starting with the boys."

Sara froze. Her mouth gaped, and her breath caught in her throat. "But this thing is going to be over soon," Kristen tried to reassure her.

Sara didn't answer. She opened her Jeep and collapsed in the seat. She was clutching her bag of groceries to her chest. "Sara, don't worry," Kristen tried to console her, finally reading someone's body language correctly, "they aren't going to draft the girls at first."

Sara turned her Jeep on and sped away without a response.

Sara knew men were being drafted. The age kept getting lower and lower because they kept running out of recruits. The news outlets blamed it on the defection of American citizens to other countries, but the massive death toll was truly to blame. Everyone knew it, but no one spoke of it. Still, Sara didn't think girls would be on the draft list ever. Even with all casualties, she didn't even consider it a possibility.

Sara burst into the house. She slid to the floor and sobbed. How could one day swing so wildly?

How long Sara wept, she wasn't sure. But a thought crept into her mind. Dan knew. The girls knew. But no one had told her. On cue, she heard the garage door open. Dan walked in, giving her a dirty look as she sat on the floor, eyes red with tears. "Some serious mood swings this month," he said, reaching in the freezer for some ice.

Sara sat fuming. She wrung her hands, gauging her move. Dan rolled his eyes and poured a glass of whiskey.

She stood and smoothed the front of her shirt down. Class. She chose class. "Are you aware the draft is now opened for sixteen-year-olds," Sara started, "and that it will be opening for females when the boys run low?"

Dan sighed and leaned on the counter. He knew. "Sara," Dan said like he was talking to a child, "you are a hysteric. The smallest thing sets you off. So.."

Dan shrugged.

So you didn't tell me, you fucker.

Noting her fury, Dan rolled his eyes. "Yes, this is unexpected. But this war will be over soon, so it won't affect this family."

"You said that about Freddie," Sara said coldly.

Sara remembered vividly when the draft was reenacted. She cried and cried. The fear of her baby boy being drafted wasn't palatable, and the taste made her sick. In every war ever fought, draft meant death. And a lot of it. So when Freddie volunteered to serve, she felt betrayed. She stood in the town square in the cold every Friday morning to check the draft roll call for her child's birthday on the community bulletin board. And each time the page was void of Virgos born on September 4th, she cried. But all her praying was for nothing.

"This whole war is a disaster," Sara began to lose her class, "it's not ever going to end, and it's taking my babies away one by one."

Dan took a step towards her. She had over-stepped her bounds. "I am hearing that you don't seem sure of our cause," Dan said softly.

Sara choked back tears. The door slammed, and Amy walked into the kitchen. She looked up from her phone long enough to see the tension. "What's going on?" Amy said, alarmed.

"Your Mother was just declaring her lack of support for the Gray cause," Dan stated.

Amy's eyes shifted to her Mother. "You found out," Amy whispered.

Sara threw the groceries off her arm onto the counter and stormed up the stairs. Once safely in her bedroom, she crawled into bed, clothes and all. She covered her head with the blankets to blot out the sun. Her soul was exhausted. She wanted the sadness and fear to leave her, and she only knew of one way to do it.

~

Sara's eyes were wide and staring at the ceiling when her alarm went off at 6:30 am. She had barely slept. Her arms shot out, shutting it off before the third blast.

She smiled amongst her guilt. Her sleeplessness should've been caused by the impending doom of her country and the possible drafting of her daughters. But thoughts of Sam swirled in the blackness of her bedroom. The night was a tennis match of tears, then thoughts of Sam. She tried to keep her anxiety and passion quiet. Dan was a light sleeper, and the thought of him on her made Sara ill.

So she contended with dreaming of what would happen and how it would happen. What would she wear? How would she get him alone?

She launched herself from the bed and quickly showered. Sara was giddy and bouncing around like one of her annoying Shitzu friends. She suddenly saw all the 'to-do' about releasing glee. Sara just hadn't had much practice in experiencing it. Sara threw on her now-favorite yoga pants. She set the coffee pot for Dan and headed out to the gym.

The streets were just beginning to emerge from the darkness of the night. The sunrise was beautiful. Sunset in morning: sailors take warning. Sunset at night: sailors delight. That was something her father always said. She hoped this wasn't foreboding for how her day would go. She began to think about Amy and Marie in a Gray's uniform, and her heart raced. *No, keep your eye on the prize.*

Sara parked a little too aggressively in front of the gym. Her Jeep was up on the curb as she stepped out. She didn't care. She ran towards the door and saw the lights were on. The door opened with a familiar squeak and Sam looked up from a machine he was repairing. He had his shirt off, and he was sweating. Belts and machine parts laid all around him.

"Sara," he whispered and stood.

Sara smiled, her chest unable to get enough air. She took a step towards him, and Mr. Wheeler walked out of the bathroom hallway. Sara's face fell. "Oh, good morning Mrs. Weiderholt," the elderly killjoy said, "you're early."

"Good morning," Sara mumbled and walked to the weight bench.

Sam smiled and turned back to the machine. "I'm so sorry, Sammy. I can't figure out what I did to the thing," Mr. Wheeler confessed.

"You didn't do anything wrong," Sam assured, looking past him at Sara, "these things happen."

Mr. Wheeler began mounting a new machine. Sara imagined him being flung off the end. She didn't even feel guilty about it. Sara grumbled to herself as she grabbed two twenty-pound weights and began sloppy deadlifts. Sam watched her with amusement. She looked at the clock. It was 6:45. The ankle-biter crew would be there any minute.

"Mr. Wheeler," Sam interrupted her thoughts, "I really should make sure these machines are sound before I have you on them."

Sara turned and hid her smile.

"Why don't you come back this afternoon?"

Mr. Wheeler sighed and agreed. Sam shuffled him out of the gym.

The look in his eyes when he turned to Sara made her mouth water. They both ran to the office. He swung the door shut, locking it and grabbed her waist. They came for each other so quickly he bit her lip. Sara yelped. "Oh, my god are you ok?" he laughed.

She answered by tangling her hands in his hair. Suddenly, everything was gone. The stress. The draft. The war. Her past. She was alive.

A small moan escaped his lips as she took hold of him through his pants. *My god, not all men are created equal.*

Sam put his hand down the front of her faded DOKNY pants and rocked his hand against her body. Sara was going to burst. He had touched her for only a moment, and she wanted to explode like a prepubescent boy.

Sara lowered the front of his pants and returned the favor. He wrapped an arm around her waist to hold them both up. They found a rhythm, and after what couldn't have been longer than three perfect minutes, they both gave way.

Locked together, they found their place on the floor. He pulled her into his arms and kissed her head. They laid there in silence for a while.

"I've wanted you since the moment I saw you," he whispered.

Sara looked up at him and smiled.

"Why?"

"For everything I said before and more. Beautiful, smart,

kind, and while the other women gawk at me like a piece of meat or a broken toy," he paused and took her in again, "you've never looked at me like that."

"Wouldn't that mean I wasn't interested?" Sara replied.

Sam laughed. "Yea," he said, "but then you wore perfume."

Sara leaned in and kissed him again. "I want more of this," Sara whispered into his lips.

"Oh thank god," he whispered back, locking his hands into her hair.

He laid her down on the floor and began sliding down her waist, kissing her stomach as he went. The front door squeaked open. And the sound of hens filled the gym. Sam shot up and Sara gasped. *No, no, no, NO*, Sara screamed in her head.

"I'll distract them," he smoothed her hair and smiled, "head to the bathroom."

Sara got up and kissed him again and nodded. With a quick slap of her ass, he rose and went to the flock. Sara quickly slipped out of the office and into the women's restroom. She hugged herself and jumped around. Looking at her reflection, she looked flush and happy.

"Sara," called Hadley, "where are you?"

Sara flushed the toilet and washed her hands. "Coming," Sara laughed at her pun.

~

Sara slammed her bedroom door behind her. She leaned against it and began to laugh. At first, it bubbled out of her quietly, but soon she was in hysterics on the ground, rolling from side to side. She could still taste him. And she wanted more.

Sara rolled to her side and saw a sock under her bed. Dan's sock. She took a deep breath. She had to get herself under control. No one could see the change. The magnificent, life-altering change in her being. Sam had lit a fire inside her she never knew existed, and she felt she could light the world. But if Dan ever knew, he would kill her. She knew in her heart, he wouldn't let her live with such transgression. Sara also knew she was addicted. One hit and she was hooked.

Sara reached under the bed and grabbed the sock. She rolled to her back. Fan blades. *One, two, three, four, five. You. Will. Keep. Your. Composure.*

She sat up, tossed the sock in the hamper, and headed to the shower.

Marie and Amy came home at around five o'clock. The door slammed, making Sara jump. *Showtime.*

Marie plopped down at the dining table, and Amy hopped on the counter. Doing this without the use of her hands always impressed Sara. Sara smiled looking at her. Amy suddenly looked up at her mom and gave her a funny look, "Are you making monkey bread?"

Upon hearing "monkey bread," Marie's head shot up, sniffing. "Oh my God, you are," Marie exclaimed, "and Chicken Ala' King!"

Marie jumped up and practically shoved Sara out of the way, reaching for toasted sliced bread. Rationing didn't allow for fancy items like rolls, brown sugar, heavy cream and the like, but Sara was going to make this meal like it was still 2019.

Sara swatted Marie's hand away from the goods. "Not until your Father gets home," she laughed.

Amy sat studying the situation. Sara tried to avoid her gaze but she could practically hear her gears turning. "Are you wearing makeup?" Amy pried.

Dan barged into the kitchen. Sara was actually glad. *Mark this day in history.*

Dan took a deep breath. "Did you make my favorite?" Dan too eyed her suspiciously.

Sara inhaled. Time for an Oscar-worthy performance. "Listen, I wanted to apologize," she began, "I haven't been very supportive or really there, if you will, these past few months."

Dan grabbed the bread forbidden to Marie and sat down, tossing it in his mouth. Marie scowled. Amy's eyes narrowed.

"I'm really proud of what this family and our cause stands for," she continued, "I've just been so worried about our family. But I promise I will show my patriotism and support more openly."

Dan crossed his arms, clearly pleased. Marie, catching on, looked at Amy.

"Because it's not about me."

It's all about him, she thought.

Amy returned Marie's gaze and they both looked at their mom.

"Well," Dan said slapping his legs and standing up, "that's the smartest thing I can remember you ever saying."

Sara smiled. *Hook, line, and sinker.*

Dan came in for a groping hug. He inhaled her freshly-lotioned body and squeezed her butt. "Mmm," he whispered in her ear, "I'd like to more of this spirit later."

Sara's heart dropped but not her smile.

"I'm going to change," he said slapping her rear as he walked away.

Two ass slaps, one day. Sara wiped her hands on her apron, turning to her girls. They both leaned on the counter, arms crossed.

Too much, Sara cursed herself.

"So," Amy began, "are you leaving for Michigan, or can we expect to all be murdered in the morning?"

Marie gasped and elbowed Amy.

"Well," Amy retorted, "She's acting like it's the last supper."

"Seriously you two," Sara said, "I'm sick of the fighting. I'm trying to smooth things over."

They both returned her stare, not budging. Sara dug in. "Listen," Sara whispered, "I don't want to get hurt, ok?"

Amy and Marie visibly deflated. Sara felt guilt swim over

her. "If I don't behave, you know what happens," Sara dug in further. "You don't want that for us, right?"

Straight to hell. Sara was going straight to hell. The girls both murmured and shook their heads. "Ok," she said, "then please be on my side. Now grab some plates and set the table."

Happy to have the conversation ended, Sara's daughters began their task. Sara excused herself to the family room and covered her face with her hands. Her first casualty. Manipulating her daughters so she could have an affair. She finally said it to herself: the word affair. She smiled. How evil can she be? *Very*, she thought, *I will do anything to be with him.*

~

Marie had her thumb in her mouth. She was a chronic thumb-sucker as a child but graduated to nail-biting, as it was disgusting but more socially acceptable. Something was off with her mother and it was driving her mad. Her mom was never happy. She would smile and have better days than others, but the happiness she displayed today was very strange.

"Marie. Marie!"

Colin's voice broke through her trance. Marie looked at him. "You ok there champ?" Colin laughed at her, "it's your turn."

Marie pulled her wet thumb from her mouth. She laid down her card. "Hedron Scrabbler," she said tossing the robotic-looking spider down in front of him.

Colin pursed his lips and hummed to himself, peering at his cards. He looked like a girl trying to take a selfie. Marie wanted to punch him. She threw her cards down, "I'm going home."

"Why?" Colin said clearly offended. "What's up with you today?"

Marie stomped in a circle, crossing her arms and fought

back tears. She eyed Colin and he stared her right back down.

"Fine," she said throwing her hands in the air, "let's start with my dad is an abusive prick, and we live in constant fear. I literally detest my sister. As in, I legitimately think she is the dumbest bitch on earth. My mother is a pushover and allows us to be subjected to him. I can never make anyone happy with anything I do. We are at war. I miss good cereal. I miss school. I miss watching dirty videos online."

That made Colin raise a brow.

"And every day I wake up wondering if today is the day Freddie dies." she finished.

Colin deflated before her eyes. *Great*, Marie thought crossing her arms, *messed up again*.

"We all miss him, Mar," Colin said quietly staring at the ground, "we all just have to be positive that one day we can all sit around watching porn."

Their eyes met, and they burst out laughing. "You're disgusting," Marie said picking up her backpack. "And an ass."

Colin stood smirking and wrapped her in an awkward hug. "You're not alone." He said. "We're all scared, but at least we have Magic the Gathering."

Marie smiled into his collar as they stood to embrace. Marie let her tears fall. She was so tired of being in fight-or-flight. Colin smelled good, and she buried her head into his hoodie. "Alexa," he said.

Marie leaned back and gave him a look. "Who the hell is she?"

"Ya know, Alexa, what's the weather today? Alexa, who won the game last night? Alexa, I miss Alexa."

Marie laughed out loud and punched him in the arm. "I'll see you tomorrow, nerd." Marie said, escaping.

She appreciated Colin more than anyone else in her life, but she needed to be alone. And maybe a sandwich. Which these days meant homemade pita bread and whatever you could find to cram in the middle. One day seeing their bare cupboards, she got creative and made a pickled-beets-and-cornflakes-wrap with mustard. It was as awful as it sounded. But her father made her finish the entire thing. "Our brave men and women are on the front line eating weeks-old dried meats and rice cakes."

Marie refrained from rolling her eyes at the memory. Even away from his presence, she feared him. Taking a deep breath, she laughed to herself walking out the door.

So, Colin missed internet hubs. At one point everyone had an Alexa, or Google, or Quartana. What the populace didn't know was everything said was recorded and kept in some cloud. And at the beginning of the war, some techie realized they could do audio searches through the saved files to find pockets of the enemy. Marie couldn't remember which side did it first, but it wasn't too long before everyone was using Alexa as a glorified paperweight. Even if people still used her, there wasn't much those hubs would know anymore. They had to go back to the old ways of guessing.

Walking out of Gather, the sun blinded her. Covering her eyes, she squinted, trying to find her bike, and then she saw a familiar Jeep parked in the back lot across the street. Marie hopped on her bike and pedaled towards her family truck. No one was inside, and no other cars were in the parking lot. *Odd.*

Marie walked to the back door of the gym. She'd make her mom take her home and fix her some food. Not for nothing, her Mother could make anything taste good. The back door clicked shut behind her as she walked down the hallway towards the gym. Hushed voices and giggling came from the room to her right. Suddenly, the door opened and the gym manager, Sam, walk out embracing a woman. They were kissing and he was grabbing her ass. She was about to turn around in full blush when she saw the familiar worn leggings. Marie couldn't help gaping at her mother grinding on another man. The thought never even occurred to look away. So when Sam looked up from kissing down her mother's neck, he froze. Her heart was pounding out of her chest. *How could she? How dare she?*

Her dad was not a great man, but this? Marie turned and ran. Busting through the door, she hopped on her bike and sped home. She barely registered her mother's voice calling, "Marie!"

~

Amy wrung her hands as she stood waiting for the door to open. She hadn't heard from Anthony in two days. At first, she tried to give him space. She knew what she had done was incredibly stupid, but this couldn't possibly break them up. He couldn't end things over her wanting to be with him forever.

The door creaked open, and Anthony's mom greeted her with a wide smile. "Hi Amy," she said and called over her shoulder, "Anth, Amy is here."

"Hi, Ms. Hadley."

Anthony's Mother looked straight out of a 2000's girl band video. She had her hair in the most obnoxious pigtails, a baby T-shirt that said "angel baby", and pink velour jogging pants. It was hard to tell these days if people dressed in dated fashion because of the war or choice. The faintest whiff of cotton candy lotion invaded Amy's nostrils. *Choice*, Amy thought, breathing through her mouth.

Anthony's mom turned back to Amy and leaned on the door frame. "How are you all holding up?" she probed.

Amy crossed her arms and faked a smile. Who? Freddie, her and Anthony, her parents, the war? So many horrific options all quieted with one response, "As well as can be expected. Thank you."

Anthony appeared behind his mother, and he looked at her with such distance that Amy's eyes teared. Ms. Hadley looked from one teenager to the other and raised a brow, but clearly had no intention of leaving. At this, Anthony sighed and began walking down the sidewalk. Amy was left jogging after him. Out of the corner of her eye, she saw Ms.

Hadley standing in the window, trying to be out of view. She saw her mood ring glinting in the sun. *Everyone in this town is so nosy*, Amy raged.

"Wait," Amy said trying to catch up.

Anthony walked faster. "Anthony," she whimpered, "please."

Anthony turned so quickly and charged towards her that Amy tripped into him. He grabbed her too roughly as she fell. He took her arms and growled inches from her face, "What the fuck were you thinking?!"

Amy swallowed and blinked back tears. She knew this dialogue. "I am so sorry. I won't ever do it again, I swear."

Anthony, realizing her fear and his grip, released and began pacing. "You could be pregnant right now, Amy," he said with his hand on his head.

"I'm not."

Anthony turned around and stared at her. Amy saw his resolve soften and Amy went to him, wrapping her arms around him. "I'm not pregnant," Amy repeated, "I started last night."

Anthony's hands slid up her body and embraced her tightly. "You sure?" he choked out, holding back his tears.

"Yes," she said, crying. Or at least she would be sure when her monthly visitor showed up in two weeks on schedule. Or so Amy prayed. "And I will never do that to us again."

Anthony nodded and crushed Amy in a bear hug. All was resolved. Amy smiled into Anthony's Stussy shirt, his soap smell replacing his mother's cotton candy odor.

~

"Shit," Sam said into Sara's neck.

Sara's heart was so happy. She had managed to sneak away for an additional workout session without causing notice. They were only able to steal a few moments together, but in that time Sara had pleasured Sam in his office. The sounds of town seniors huffed and puffed in the next room. Sara smiled at the thought of appreciating the once-annoying sound of the gym filled with elders' emphysema, which helped drown out their quiet sighs.

They should've looked before they opened the door. "We've got company."

Sara turned to see Marie standing in the hallway, her mouth gaping open. Then she took off running the way she came. *No!*

Sara ran after her. "Marie!"

But she was already turning down the street on her bike. Sam ran out after Sara. Slamming back into him, she ran back inside for her purse. "Sara, wait."

Her hands were shaking. *No, no, no.*

"We can explain this to her," Sam started, "maybe it's time people knew."

Sara stared at him, her eyes wild. "Do you know what we've done?"

Shoving past him again, she ran for her truck. Sara threw it into gear so quickly she almost t-boned Mrs. Blaskow. Slamming on her brakes, she mouthed "sorry" to her near-victim and waited impatiently for her old Buick to clear the intersection. Sara sped home. She had to get to Marie before she saw Dan. So focused on her task, Sara didn't see the police car parked across the street from the gym.

Sara pulled into her driveway. Dan's car wasn't there. She thanked whatever God still listened to her and ran inside.

"Marie," Sara yelled seeing her bike laying on the lawn.

Sara threw her keys on the counter and began running around the house. "Marie!"

Sara searched the bedrooms and ran into the living room and right into her daughter sitting on the couch cross-armed and red-eyed. Sara knelt beside her and tried to take her hand, which was quickly snatched away. "Marie," Sara began.

Fuck, she thought, *what the hell do I say?*

Marie faced away from her and was stoic except for her quivering lip.

"I can explain."

At this, Marie snapped her head around. "Explain what," Marie said with such intensity that Sara sat back on her heels, "that you have lost your mind since Freddie left? Or why you let the world treat you like a doormat? Or is it the skanky affair you are having with the one-legged gym pirate?"

"Please don't call him that."

Marie's eyes bulged. Sara knotted her hands. Freckles: one, two, three, four. Marie raged, "Do you have any idea what is going to happen to you if dad finds out?"

Sara looked up at her pleading. If Dan did find out, she was a dead woman walking. She didn't know how, but he would end her. "Please."

Sara took her hands roughly. "Jesus," said Marie standing up, leaving her Mother on her knees begging, "I'm not going to say anything."

Sara put her head in her hands and wept. "But he will find out," Marie growled, "And when he does, you better run."

Sara wiped her eyes and looked up at her daughter. "Thank you."

Marie rolled her eyes and went to her room.

~

It should have, but being caught didn't soften Sara's resolve to see Sam. Over the next few weeks, she did whatever she could to get out of the house to see him. Sara should've been in the best shape of her life as much as she worked out. But no one in the family seemed to notice. Marie, however, barely made eye contact with Sara.

Sara kept up the charade. The house was spotless. Dinners were always made and milk was never forgotten. Sara met with Sam every morning, and every morning they had an almost spousal routine. He had her coffee waiting, and she would bring him a snack. They made love and then would hold each other until someone entered the gym. Sara would sometimes park down the street and walk to her Jeep to then drive it to the parking lot. No one seemed to notice a thing, except for Sara's new chipper attitude. This worked for Sara. She was happy. Until one morning Sam was holding her, per usual, and he started massaging her shoulders. Sara sighed in appreciation. "I love you," Sam whispered.

Sara looked up at him and smiled. "I know," she said, "and I love you."

Sam lowered his lips to hers and held her face. He searched her eyes with such intensity that one eye could search. "Let's run away together."

Sara laughed.

"I'm serious, Sar," he said, "I want us to be together."

Sara sighed and stood up, putting on her clothes, knowing they hadn't much time left.

"I thought you said loved me," he said, running his hands through his perfect hair.

Sara furrowed her brows at him. "You're not serious," Sara said. "Where would we go? We have no money, hell, money doesn't even really exist anymore."

"You and I could figure it out." Sam rose, taking her hands. "I need to be with you."

"I can't leave my children," Sara said flatly.

"They aren't kids anymore, babe," Sam continued.

Sara stared at him and shook her head.

"Then divorce Dan."

Sara tore her hands away from him. She felt her blood pressure rise. "Do you have any idea what he would do to me if I tried to divorce him?"

Sam turned from her and began to breathe heavily. He slammed his hands against his shelves and Sara jumped. "I know what he has done to you," Sam whispered, "and I want to kill him for it."

Sara went to him and wrapped her arms around his waist. "This is going to have to do for now," Sara said into his shirt.

He turned and lifted her chin. "Promise me we'll start to make an exit plan soon," Sam whispered, hearing the front door open, "I want forever with you. I want to be our own little family."

The hens began to cackle from the doorway and Sara headed for the office door. "I'll step out and act like I'm just coming in, okay babe," Sam smiled, "I love you."

Sara smiled, following him out and mouthed it back as she slid into the bathroom. Sara stared at her reflection. Could she leave Dan? Restraining orders were not only impossible to get but also completely unenforced, especially since the assailant was the one who would have to do the enforcing.

Sara smiled again to herself. Having a family with Sam? She imagined him coming home and her holding their little boy. He'd look just like daddy but have both eyes and legs. Sara giggled at her sick joke. She leaned on the wall. *Oh, man*, she thought, *a baby.*

And then it hit her like a freight train. Babies. What date was it? Sara frantically pulled out her phone to check the calendar. The fifteenth. It couldn't be. When was her last period? Sara racked her brain trying to remember when she had started it last. It must have been her and Dan's last fight. She had run out of her pills the week prior and forgotten to ask around for more. How could she have forgotten? She paced the bathroom, her heart pounding from her chest. When *was* her last period? It had to have been around the 11th of the month before. A week late. She gasped, "Oh god no."

Sara exploded from the bathroom, almost knocking Kristen over. "Excuse you," she said loudly.

Sara raced towards the front door. "Where are you going, crazy train?"

Sara left the hens gawking at her quick departure. So fast

she had departed that she completely missed Dan's cruiser sitting half-hidden behind the building.

~

Amy walked down the empty aisles of the old market. Most people came here and stood in line for food. But there were a few goods stacked here and there for purchase. Amy had to be discreet. She made sure to come at a slow time, and the place was nearly empty. She walked past a gift card tree that was collecting dust. Amy glanced at the old store names they would never be used at like 18 For Life, Bullseye, The Goods.

Ridiculous names, she thought to herself.

But she couldn't deny the fond imagery of being very young and walking through most of them. "Hi, Amy."

Amy jumped and saw a woman from church walk around the corner.

"Hi, Mrs. Grove."

"How have you been? We really miss seeing Freddie around town," she said, squeezing Amy's shoulder.

"We're getting by."

Amy was mentally shouting for her to leave.

"Well stop by sometime," Mrs. Grove continued, "we miss having you over."

Amy nodded and looked away. Mrs. Grove sighed and smiled. Mrs. Grove's husband and daughter, Ashley, had both died fighting in the war. Amy used to play with Ashley when they were young. Mrs. Grove now lived alone, and the medications she needed to keep her in this dimension were almost impossible to get. Amy watched Mrs. Grove invite a few more invisible people to her house as she walked down the aisles. Mrs. Grove was a nosy woman who annoyed everyone she encountered, but Amy couldn't help but feel bad for her. Amy swallowed and turned on her heel and walked to the back of the store. She exhaled when she got to the feminine products. Her eyes landed on her prize: the pregnancy test. "Test is accurate up to 3 days past your missed period," Amy whispered, reading the box.

Amy was one week late. She swallowed and slid the test into her purse. "Can I help you find something?"

Amy yelped. One of the workers was standing behind her. "Oh I am so sorry," she said gently, "didn't mean to scare you."

Amy grabbed a box of tampons. "Do you have more of these?" she improvised.

"Just the one box," the worker said sadly, "these are a luxury these days, ya know?"

Amy nodded and put them back. "I'll see if my mom still wants them."

"See if I want what?" Amy's mother's familiar voice echoed from the row over.

Amy felt herself dissolve. *What was she doing there?*

Her mother never shopped on Wednesdays. Her mom came around the corner with the oddest look on her face. Amy knew she had been caught. "So do you want these?" Amy held up the box, keeping up the façade.

Sara cocked her head and looked at the clerk who stood there smiling. "Not especially," Sara answered slowly.

The three of them stood there in silence for a minute. "I'll just let you two discuss the tampons," said the clerk, excusing herself and giving them an awkward look.

~

Sara watched the clerk go and turned back to Amy, "You know we can't afford these."

"I just thought," blood rose in Amy's cheeks, "I just…never mind."

Amy shoved past Sara and ran for the door. Why was she here? She never came into this store. Sara's blood pressure finally returned to normal. Tampons! Of all things to want. Why not just ask for a new car or a vacation to a theme park? All three were about as equally unattainable.

Sara sighed, looking over her shoulder one last time as she grabbed the pregnancy test. At least Amy's little fit got her out of the store. Now Sara only had to dodge the prying eyes of the townies. One failed move and the whole town would be talking about her possible new addition. And she could only pray they would all think it was Dan's. Like Frogger in her favorite childhood video game, it was time to jump to the register, avoiding people. "Sara," a familiar voice echoed.

"Oh hello, Mrs. Grove," Sara responded through her teeth, putting the test slightly behind her, "how nice to see you."

"I just saw Amy," she pried, "everything alright."

You nosy nothing better to-do miserable...

"Oh she's fine," Sara cooed, "just being a teenager."

"I do miss seeing your Freddie around town," the women dug, "how are you all doing in these delicate circumstances?"

Sara resisted the urge to strangle the old woman, even though everyone knew she was crazy. "We hold onto the fact that his work is of noble purpose," she replied, giving her nothing.

"But you must feel just awful," Mrs. Grove continued.

"Is that Danielle?" Sara interrupted trying to escape to the check-out.

If she were in a real Frogger game, she'd be dead by now and run out of lives. "I heard her husband has been hitting the...," Sara whispered making a drinking motion.

Mrs. Groves's eyes got large looking at Danielle, taking in her next victim. Danielle stood in line waiting for her rations. "I wish she had more support from her family," Sara said, throwing the hen under the bus.

Mrs. Grove clicked her tongue and hurried away to stand ever so conveniently in the ration line. She didn't even say goodbye to Sara. A wicked grin splayed across Sara's face as she made her way to the counter. A young clerk stood up abruptly. People didn't buy much these days, and the market workers showed a merciful sense of normalcy. "Will this be all?" the boy's voice cracked.

He was so young he didn't understand the gravity of Sara's purchase. *Thank god for small miracles,* Sara thought, relieved.

Sara paid the boy and shoved the stick into her purse. She left the Jeep parked at the market and walked down the street to the gym. Sara went in through the back door. She suddenly felt sweeping arms pull her into a bear hug. Sara let out a squeal. "You smell so good," Sam whispered into her hair.

"Put me down, Sam," Sara said flatly, "how'd you know it was me anyhow? Hug random gym lunks often?"

Sam closed the door and leaned back on the wall, crossing his arms. His crooked smile made her insides melt. "Who else would be coming in my back door?" Sam smiled.

Sara began to pace the hallway. Sam began to see her worry. "What is it?" Sam stood up. "Did that mother fucker touch you again?"

"No," Sara snapped.

How was she going to tell him? Sara could set the clock better than the Mayan Calendar with her cycles and here she was late. Very late. Sam grabbed her hand and she turned to look at him. She loved him so deeply, her heart ached. She also knew what he would ask of her once he found out what might be growing inside her. "If you don't tell me," he said, "I'm going to have a heart attack."

"I'm late," Sara admitted.

"For?"

"You cannot be that dense," Sara said pushing him in the chest.

Sam's look of confusion went to surprise then pure joy. "Oh Sar, are you sure?"

Sara dug in her purse angrily and yanked out the test. "Not entirely."

~

Drip. Drip. Drip.

Sara drummed her finger on her thigh in beat to the leaky faucet Dan still hadn't fixed. This was the longest three minutes of her life. She leaned her head back on the cabinet in her bathroom. She had run upstairs after seeing Dan's cruiser gone. She didn't care if the girls were in the house. Sam begged her to take the test with him, but she needed to do this alone.

The stick sat in front of her, looming like an ammonia-smelling magic eight ball. Are you carrying Sam's baby? Ask again later. *Precisely sixty seconds later*, Sara thought, checking her watch for the hundredth time.

Sara began to imagine what she would do. She pictured a blue-eyed boy with his daddy's big smile. She fast-forwarded to a toddler being thrown in the air, giggling uncontrollably. She smiled thinking of Sam coming home to her after work and having dinner ready for him. Her older children would visit, now grown. They would dote on their baby brother. And Dan would be gone. *Dan*, she thought, *he'll never let me go.*

Sara looked at her wrist. The thought had gotten her past the sixty-second mark.

~

Amy's lips were so chewed she began to taste blood. She didn't have the nerve to take the test out of her purse. But when she heard her mom's car coming down the drive she tore the test from the packaging, peed like a racehorse, and ran to her room with the stick in hand.

She set it on her dresser and sat on the bed in front of it. She rubbed her stomach, praying. *Please be in there.*

Her eyes shifted to a picture of her and Anthony. They were playing volleyball at the beach that day. They were both tanned and happy. It was less than two years ago. Things had changed so much in just that time. The war still seemed so far away. Freddie hadn't left yet. People were optimistic it would be over soon, and Amy had the rest of her life ahead of her. She wanted to go to college and be a nurse's assistant. She'd move to a bigger town, find a cute apartment in the middle of it. Amy wanted new friends, a new job, a new life with Anthony.

She glanced at the clock. Three minutes were up. She stood quickly.

~

She grabbed the stick. Two pink lines.

~

She grabbed the stick. One pink line.

~

Anthony sat on the couch watching old DVDs, drinking a cup of tea. It wasn't iced because the freezer didn't work, and it wasn't hot because their microwave didn't work. It wasn't even tea. It was a mixture of dried mint leaves his mother had tried to grow in the garden. But his mom drank it because it made her feel full. He was halfway through some lame horror flick when he realized he hadn't been watching any of it. Amy was driving him insane. He loved her, he did. But the constant barrage of questions about their future was getting so old. Weeping from the bathroom interrupted his thoughts. He set down his cup of weed juice, grabbed a fresh cup of water, and headed for the hall closet. There weren't any clean towels. Anthony sighed and grabbed his shower towel from his bedroom door. "Mom," he said, gently knocking on the bathroom door.

"Go away," she said still crying.

"Come on mom. Open up. I've got a glass of water and a fresh towel."

Silence. Then a click signaled she had unlocked the handle. Their dance had begun. Anthony stepped inside. There were the usual suspects. Her crochet hook laid on the counter covered in his mother's drool. Splatters of vomit lined the inside of the bowl and the plate of food she had been eating was sitting on the sink. "Too much lunch?" Anthony asked gently handing her the towel and cup of water.

His mother simply nodded. Her eyes were red and puffy, and her hair looked like a rat's nest. Anthony went beneath the sink and grabbed the toilet brush and some of their homemade vinegar cleaner. It had been so long since they could afford the good stuff. He tried not to look too hard at his broken mother. She used to be so beautiful and so full of life. Then his father died and she did along with him. Anthony thought she'd bounce back, but it had been nearly four years, and she was getting worse. "Thank you, baby," his mom said gently sipping the water.

Anthony nodded, putting the cleaning supplies back. "This isn't what it looks like," she lied again, "the food was bad. That's why I had to get rid of it."

Anthony crouched down and smoothed her hair. "I know mom," he lied again.

She smiled at him, and Anthony saw the row of once-white teeth now eroded, yellowing and rotted. No dad. No dentist. No money. No future. "Come on," he said, helping her up, "let's watch the rest of *Texas Chainsaw Massacre*."

He watched her stagger to the family room and collapse on the couch. He could never leave. He knew he was stuck with her forever. It made him sad, but he didn't resent his mom. Collecting her plate, he took it to the kitchen to wash. *No future*, he thought silently, looking out the sink window.

~

Amy tore into the instructions and held the paper to the test. "One line," Amy mumbled, "not pregnant."

Her eyes unfocused. She eased slowly back to the bed. Tears streamed down her face. A baby was her ticket out of this house. Her ticket to be safe from the draft for two years. It was Amy's only plan to escape the events she had no control over. Now she was stuck in this hell hole with the threat of her number being pulled at any moment.

Amy's tears turned to sobs. She grabbed a pillow to muffle her cries. She never really wanted a baby. The thought made her so nervous her palms would start to sweat. But what was more nerve-wracking was the thought of going to war or worse spending another year in this house.

Amy heard someone flush a toilet. *Shit.*

Amy stuffed the test into her backpack and ran down the stairs. She'd throw the test in the bushes somewhere between there and Anthony's house.

~

Sara's mouth went dry. It wasn't possible. She had taken enough of these tests throughout her life to know what two lines meant. She was pregnant with Sam's baby. Sara's lunch began to crawl up her esophagus. She was a dead woman. If, not now, when Dan finds out, she would be a dead woman. Sara covered her mouth, and her brain began working furiously. She could run. But what about the kids? She could try to find someone to give her an abortion. But doctors were almost impossible to come by, let alone one who would do that. Most had fled the country out of fear of being jailed or worse.

Sara stood and lifted her shirt. Not even the hint of a bump. She could hide it. But for how long? Sara pulled her hands through her hair again and again. *I could hide the pregnancy*, she thought, *it's almost winter. I could hide the bump and give the baby away.*

No, someone would notice in this town. One of the hens for sure. She could pretend it was Dan's. *No, that'd be impossible*, she thought.

She hadn't slept with Dan in weeks. Unless. Sara dropped to her knees and reached the toilet just in time.

Sara was just finishing brushing the acid from her teeth when she heard the familiar sounds of squeaking brakes. The door opened and shut. A duffle bag was thrown by the door. The water turned on as Dan washed his hands. Then the fridge opened and the sound of whiskey being poured into a glass. It was a symphony of sounds that alerted her to showtime every afternoon. And now was her ultimate opus.

"Sara!" Dan yelled from downstairs.

"Up here," Sara said as calmly as she could.

Dan's prodding footsteps led up the stairs and down the hall to their room. The door swung open, and Sara laid on the bed posed and naked for him. Dan's brows raised. "Hi," Sara said meekly.

"Hello," said Dan closing the door, "what's all this?"

Sara crawled to the edge of the bed and pulled him to her. Sara felt his just-washed, clammy hands trail down her back. She swallowed, "I haven't been a good wife lately."

Dan huffed and took his hands off of her. Sara quickly grabbed them and put them back around her. "Listen," she continued, "I am out of my mind worried about Freddie, ok?"

Dan sighed and looked back into her eyes. There was skepticism but an underlying hunger. She reached up, placing a hand on his cheek, "Make love to me, Dan."

"Are you still contagious?" Dan questioned.

"It was something I ate, really," she insisted, "I would never put you in danger."

Her acting was perfection because Dan seemed to believe her enough to put his mouth on hers. *I'd serve you food with live Ebola if I had it*, she thought, trying to distract herself.

Behind her eyes, she saw Sam's smile and heard his laugh, which kept her from pulling away with disgust when his hands lowered and cupped her ass. His finger found its way to her warmth. She gasped with surprise which he took as passion. *Good*, she thought.

Dan laid her down and began kissing her greedily as he disrobed. "I've wanted you so bad, Sar," Dan whispered into her neck.

Sara kept her mind on what was at stake. Dan's hardened length found its way into her. She felt him lean on her body as he thrust faster. His mouth kept trying to find hers, and she would turn away, crying out in false delight. He stopped suddenly and grabbed her chin. "You know I love you, right," Dan said breathlessly.

"Of course I do," Sara responded quickly.

His mouth found hers again, roughly exploring every inch with his tongue. His pace quickened. Sara felt him squeeze her breast. He released inside of her with a gasp. He tried to pull away, and Sara grabbed his hips keeping them connected. Sara needed him to remember this moment.

Dan looked into her eyes. Sara smiled. To her astonishment, Dan began to cry. Sara's eyes widened. "I'm sorry," Dan said sniffing, burying his head in her shoulder, "I know I'm not perfect. I know I have messed up with us. I'm just so happy you're mine."

Sara gaped at the ceiling as her husband sobbed in her hair. She rubbed his back and thought about the small child growing inside her.

~

Sara avoided the gym, the hens, and the outside world for a few days. She needed to be alone. So when Sara finally appeared in Sam's office, Sam almost leaped from the chair and put her in a tight hug. "Where have you been?" he whispered into her hair.

"I slept with Dan," Sara said quickly.

He pulled away from her and looked into her eyes. Sara braced for impact. She avoided him because Sara knew she wouldn't lie, and she was terrified of the fallout. Sam took a deep breath and gave a weak smile. "Ok."

"Ok?"

"You did what you had to do," Sam said, tucking a strand of hair behind her ear.

"Didn't you hear me?" Sara said pulling away, throwing her hands in the air, "I cheated on you."

Sam rubbed his jaw and sat down in his chair again, "I'd hardly call that cheating. I know what you did was to protect yourself. Our baby."

Sara turned to him aghast. "How are you not mad?" Sara whispered.

It baffled her how leveled headed he was. Every hurdle he welcomed head-on: their love, this baby, she being married to a psychopath. Sam smiled and pulled her into his lap. His kind eyes made her insides weak. Sam cupped her face and kissed her deeply. "I love you," he whispered into her lips, "and there is nothing you can do that will change that. Dan is dangerous, and we don't have a plan yet. That baby is going to keep on growing. So you made sure to keep yourself safe."

Sara's eyes filled with tears.

"I cannot imagine how hard that was for you," said Sam, "and I want you to know that we will figure out a way to keep you safe and be together."

Sara just shook her head. Never in her life had a man made her feel worth anything or taken away her pain, given support. Sara leaned her head into his, "Thank you."

Sam held her face and kissed her deeply. Tears wet both of their faces and Sara wasn't sure whose were whose.

~

Life went on. Routines were kept. Sara walked down the street towards her house. The sun was shining, and the clouds were big, white, and puffy. Her body was humming. A loud bus zoomed past her. It was painted black with big letters on the side: Gray Recruits. The bus filled with newly-drafted soldiers would've made her take pause and silently pray for the men, women, and now children who were being whisked away to their certain deaths. Selfishly, Sara knew nothing could spoil her mood today. She had left her daily meet-up with Sam in the woods near the lake.

After finding out about the baby, they both decided it was too risky to see each other at the gym. Sam had surprised her the week before with a walk through the woods to an old hunting shed. He had cleaned it out and added some furniture. Sara had brought flowers and they spent an hour or so there every few days playing house. It was the happiest Sara had ever been. She would be in tears every time they said goodbye. Sara sighed, thinking about the love they made that day. He filled her with such heat, she blushed thinking of him climaxing on top of her. His dark hair would fall in his eyes as he looked up whispering, "I love you."

It was like a dream. The thought shattered when she heard a scream. Sara's head snapped towards the sounds. She saw three men in front of Colin's store. Colin's mother was screaming as they kicked a small form on the ground. She saw Colin trying to rip the men from the man lying there. "Fucking dirty Whites!" one man yelled as he kicked.

"You're all traitors!" another yelled.

"You're going to kill him!" Colin's mom screamed.

Colin managed to grab the shirt collar of one of the large men she now saw was one of the townies, Brett. Brett turned and threw Colin with barely an effort. "Hey!" Sara yelled, running across the street, "knock it off! All of you!"

The men briefly backed away. "This doesn't concern you Mrs. Weiderholt."

"The hell it doesn't!" Sara said with the sternest voice she could.

Colin's dad lay limp on the ground, bleeding from a head wound. "These pieces of shit are White spies," one townie said. His name she couldn't recall.

"Spies," Sara lamented, "in Watertown? You need to quit reading the crap they pass around at the park, you guys."

"How can you back them up after what's happened in Louisville?" Brett said, wiping his brow.

Sara paused. She hadn't heard anything about Kentucky. "What do you mean?" Sara asked, distracting them by putting herself between them and Colin's dad.

Colin and his mother had run to her husband's side, and they were wiping the blood away with her shirt. By now, the commotion had brought out several people to the street, including Sam, who had just gotten back to the gym himself. Sara and Sam locked eyes, and Sam disappeared into the gym.

"The Whites invaded Louisville. They executed any solider they could catch and gave an option for civilians to join the Whites or be a dead Gray. That's why we need to get rid of every single White in this town!" Brett yelled to her and the onlookers.

"So Watertown doesn't become Louisville!" one of his friends yelled.

Sam came running across the street. He knelt alongside the O'Ryans, assessing the damage. "I highly doubt the White army is targeting small towns in South Dakota. And even if they are, it doesn't permit you to assault private citizens," Sara said.

Brett eyed Sara with rage and took a step towards her. Sara felt the heat of Sam stand up behind her. "It's time to go, boys," Sam said with an intensity Sara hadn't ever heard.

She felt her face flush. Brett spat a wad of chewing tobacco towards the O'Ryans on the pavement. "You're lucky you're the sheriff's wife," he said over his shoulder as he and his friends walked away.

To Sara's disgust, some of the townfolk clapped and hollered in support of their savagery. Sara turned to Sam, looking into his eyes.

"What's going on here?" Dan's voice cut through the moment.

Sara jumped back too quickly and looked down at her

hands. Her heart hammered in her chest. "Those guys beat up Mr. O'Ryan," Sara answered.

Dan looked from Sam to Sara slowly. His gaze fell on the O'Ryans. Colin's dad was finally sitting up, holding his hand to his head wound. Dan sucked a piece of food from his teeth, "I'd suggest you register for a side to avoid these types of altercations in the future."

Colin's eyes glared at the sheriff with a level of intense hate that made Sara look away. Sam interrupted the next altercation by leaning down to pick up Mr. O'Ryan. "I'll make sure they get home alright."

Sara watched them walk back into the store and the townsfolk go back to their business now that the drama had ended. "Such the martyr, that one," Dan said from behind Sara, sliding a firm hand onto her shoulder, "people like that best be careful. Martyrs are martyrs because they always end up dead."

Sara wrapped her arms around herself, tears blurring her eyes.

~

After the fourth day of the coffee shop being closed and no sign of the O'Ryans, the town had all realized they had skipped town. Marie said nothing when her peers fantasized about what had become of them. "I'll bet they were spies and went back to the White Army to tell them what they found out about us," said Chase.

"Like what," said his sister McKenna, "like you still wet the bed?"

"Fuck you, McKenna."

The kids all laughed. Marie picked at the dried wood on the picnic table. "I bet Brett and his friends killed him," Todd said with a smirk of satisfaction, "but they had it coming. We can't have the enemy living right beside us."

"I heard Colin was gay," an older boy named Luke said.

"No, he wasn't."

"Yup, I heard he was banging some dude one town over."

The kids all erupted into gasps of disgust and laughter.

"There's no way. All the time Marie spent with him in his basement," Todd spat.

Marie's arm shot out so quickly, it even took her by surprise. The crack of his larynx on her forearm was audible. He dropped in a heap on the ground gaping his mouth like a fish. She was on him in moments. The sounds of the kids screaming faded, and everything became very slow. Calculated. Her fists lost feeling after the second punch. Marie's arms went in a rhythm that echoed the wet sound of blood with every jab. Every moment of every bit of fear, sadness, and rage went into the nose of this poor boy. And she loved it. Marie felt fucking happy. And that emotion made her stop in mid-punch. She crawled off of him and stared at what she had done. The voices of the kids all came rushing back, filling her ears and overwhelming her senses.

"What the fuck, Marie?"

"How could you?"

"What is the matter with you?"

"White lover!"

Todd moaned on the ground as the kids all hovered over him. Marie stumbled as she stood, unable to take her eyes off of the destruction of Todd's face. She ran. Marie ran so fast to her bike and was racing down the street before her feet had even touched the pedals. The kids behind her stood speechless as she fled.

Marie ran up her stairs into her room. Both her parents were in the kitchen but said nothing as she sped past them. Amy was in the hallway and was almost knocked over by her.

Marie shut her door and locked it. Her dad was going to find out what she did to Todd. Marie looked down at her mangled hands. They were cut and already starting to swell. She tried to flex them and stifled a sob. A soft knock. "Mar," Amy said quietly, "you ok?"

"Go away," Marie sobbed.

Amy's soft footsteps sounded her retreat, and Marie almost begged her back. She felt so sad and so alone. No one had heard from Freddie in weeks. The White Army was pushing further north. And more and more of her neighbors were being called up for duty.

Marie couldn't even begin to think of her Mother and that pirate. Last and selfishly worst, Colin was gone. She was certain the family fled because all of their belongings were gone. Marie had gone to Gather every day and looked in the windows. She would sit outside for an hour pretending to read a comic book, praying they would come back. During one of those long sits, she noticed it. Sticking out from the back of the welcome mat was a Magic card: Colin's Timetwister card. It was super rare and before the war would've been worth a few thousand USA dollars. But more than that, it was priceless to Colin. Marie picked up the card and flipped it over. A small heart with a smiley face was written in pen on the back. Marie blinked away tears.

Marie pulled the card from her wallet and looked in her mirror. She looked like a stranger to herself. Her big, puffy blue eyes were bloodshot, and her hands looked like they were cartoons. Suddenly, a rattling of the doorknob led to its opening. Amy set the screwdriver on the dresser and quickly closed the door behind her, locking it again.

Marie sat down on the bed and looked away.

Amy had a grocery bag which she pulled two bags of ice, towels, a bottle of water and bandages. Marie looked up at her confused. "It's kind of spreading like wildfire," Amy admitted quietly, "I thought you could use a hand."

Marie rolled her eyes.

"What?" Amy asked confused.

Her complete lack of common sense made Marie laugh out loud. Amy smiled despite herself, still not getting it, and went to cleaning off Marie's hands. Marie gasped as the water hit her bruised skin. Amy took her time and worked silently. Marie could feel her heartbeat slowing in her hands through the simple gesture of someone loving her.

"There," Amy said placing the ice bags on Marie's bandaged hands.

"You going to be ok?" Amy asked gently.

"I'm just…"

Marie couldn't find the words, "I'm just so.."

Amy leaned in and hugged her sister. Marie cried into her beautiful brunette hair. "Yeah," Amy said, "me too."

~

Sara set out early that morning for her new running regiment. She hated running. Despised it. But now that Sara was running towards her storybook life, she was like the wind. A few weeks had passed since she found out about their baby. Sara should've been terrified. She should've been spending every waking minute formulating a perfect plan. Aside from hiding White dollars and Gray currency in a baggie in the back of the toilet, she had barely even tried.

Sara unlocked the shed door and walked into their little sanctuary. They had made a little bed in the corner, and Sam had brought two chairs and a little table for the other corner. Sara sat down on the bed and pulled her backpack off. She had brought a sign from her house to add to the décor. Sara knew it was stupid, and this wouldn't last. But she was going to ride this happiness train until the wheels fell off.

Sara had just stepped away from the wall where she'd hung a light blue sign that read *Home Sweet Home* when Sam stepped in. Sara turned and smiled. "Good morning," Sara said.

Sam dropped the bags in his arms and replaced them with Sara. He squeezed her and leaned back to look into her eyes. "You're beautiful, you know that," Sam grinned.

Sara rolled her eyes and looked over his shoulder at the goodies he brought. "What's on the menu today?" she asked hungrily.

Sam began unpacking some bread and jam in old mason

jars. "Made this myself," Sam winked.

Sara set the items on the table and began to dig in. It was so nice having someone take care of her. The simple gesture made her want to cry. "How are you feeling?" Sam said, taking her hand.

Sara shrugged. "Fine, I guess."

There was one family practice in town but not an OB-GYN for hundreds of miles. Prenatal care, along with any other care outside of a simple sinus infection, was all but gone in Watertown. Even finding vaccines was a process. Thankfully, her kids didn't need to be on the now-yearlong waiting list. But this new child would be living in a whole different world. Instinctively, Sara placed a hand on her belly. They grew silent as they looked into each other's eyes. Sam got up and knelt beside her, placing his head in her lap. Sara stroked his soft dark hair. "We are going to figure this out Sar," Sam swore.

Sara looked at her newly-hung sign. What were they going to do?

~

Life went on. To keep up the façade, Sara went to the gym twice a week with the hens. The difference was Sara now jogged from her home; cardio was her new favorite pastime. Or so she needed everyone to think. Sam was lucky she loved him more than running. Sara slowed to a walk as she approached the hens at the front door of the gym. They were all clucking away, but something was off. There were no sounds of catty laughter or gossip. The mood was truly panicked. "What is it?" Sara asked, out of breath.

The women parted, and the front door of the gym was broken in. Sara's eyes bulged. She ran into the gym. "Wait," someone called, "the robbers could still be in there."

The gym was relatively unscathed. But the light was on in the office. Sara sprinted to the back and threw the ajar door open further. Her hand covered her mouth so she wouldn't scream. The office was torn apart. The struggle that occurred was epic. Nothing remained on the desks or shelves. And blood was all over one wall and the floor. Sara could see pieces of black hair on the ground. "Oh my sweet God," Danielle whispered over her shoulder.

"We need to call the police," Hadley said pulling out her phone.

Sara ran out of the office and opened the back door. Sam's car was still parked in the lot. Sara put her hands on her head. *No, No, No.*

Sara ran back into the office. Hadley was already on the phone with the police. Sara slowly sank to the ground. The women were all in a frenzy, pointing out clues and guessing what could've happened. Kristen was on the phone with someone from town. Hadley was covering her other ear trying to hear the police officer on the line. "Guys," she tried to shush them, "Guys shut up!"

Everyone stopped talking. Hadley answered with several *uh huh's* and *yes sirs* and she hung up the phone. The women all leaned in. Hadley swallowed, "He was taken into custody. For draft dodging."

The women all gasped and turned slowly to Sara sitting on the floor. It was at that moment Sara realized they all knew. Maybe not all of it, but they knew enough of what was going on between her and Sam. *And if they all knew.*

Sara shot to her feet. Knocking Danielle completely over, she bolted to the door. Her legs burned and her arms pumped. Sara sprinted from downtown to her home. Dan couldn't know. *He couldn't know!*

Her lungs felt like they were on fire. Her body screamed for her to slow down. But she didn't stop until she got home. She ran through the front door. Her heart was pounding as she looked around for Dan.

Run.

That's all her brain could formulate. She darted to her room, grabbed a duffle bag, and threw in clothes and shoes. She bolted to the bathroom, grabbing a few items, and took the lid off the toilet to grab her stashed money. *The girls are at the park. I'll grab them, and he can cool down.*

Sara took the stairs in two strides and landed with a thud and stopped dead. Dan sat at the kitchen table. Sara lost her bladder. "Dan," she choked.

She could hear him grinding his teeth. Dan tilted his head back and forth, tasting his rage. He took a deep breath and looked at her, his blue eyes like ice.

"Dan," she changed gears, "what's the matter?"

He studied her. Sara could've sworn he almost smiled. She took a step back. Sara realized he had been waiting for something like this to happen. An excuse was all he needed. "Dan," she tried again, "talk to me."

Dan reached under the table and threw the *Home Sweet Home* sign on the table. Sara's insides turned out. "Going somewhere?" he asked, looking at her bag.

Sara turned and ran for the door. But he was so fast. He was on her before she could touch the knob. Sara screamed for help and Dan put his hand around her mouth. She couldn't breathe. He threw her on the ground and straddled her. "Wait," she begged, "it's not what you think. He just runs the gym."

"Not anymore," Dan sneered.

She was going to die. She began to buck and claw at his eyes when he put his hands around her throat. *No*, she thought, *please no.*

Not Sammy. Not her sweet Sam. Her vision began to blur.

Ding, Dong.

There was the slightest release of her neck and she got a breath. But the hands tightened again. Now she saw stars.

Ding, Doing. Pound, pound, pound.

"Fuck," Dan growled.

She felt him release and roll off of her. She gasped for air, holding her neck. She rolled to her side as Dan opened the door. Her eyes were so watered she couldn't see who it was. Male voices conversed as blood flow returned to Sara's brain. Suddenly, she felt a tight grip on her arm. "Get up," Dan whispered, "I'll deal with you later."

He propped her up next to him in the doorway. Sara wiped her swollen eyes. Two officers stood on her porch holding a letter. They looked at Sara alarmed and exchanged glances. "Mr. and Mrs. Weiderholt," the older one began slowly, "it is with our deepest regret we have come to inform you your son Frederick…"

His voice melted. And Sara passed out.

~

The next few days evaporated like smoke for Sara. In the whirlwind of it all, Dan had put the affair on the back burner. Sara hadn't even asked where Sam was. Sara laid in bed all day counting the fan blades. Amy and Marie tried to get her to eat. The hens visited but tired of her quickly and went back to their lives. Dan slept on the couch. She only rose to use the bathroom. When her period started, she didn't even cry. On the seventh day, she looked into the mirror. She looked like a zombie. Her skin was ashen. Her hair was a mess, eyes red. "Mom," a small voice called.

Sara skipped washing her hands and oozed back into the room. Marie smiled gently. "You're up."

Sara hung her head and sat on the bed. Marie walked to her and sniffed. "Maybe a shower today?" she suggested lightly.

When Sara didn't respond, she handed her a letter. Sara looked at it. It was from Freddie. For the briefest moment, Sara thought he may be alive. There was a mistake.

Seeing her reaction, Marie quickly said, "He mailed it the day he died."

Sara reached out and took it. Sara pressed it into her chest and gasped for air. "Momma," Marie whispered and sat with her mom.

No one had called her that in years. "Let's get you a shower and brush your teeth," Marie said, smoothing her mom's hair, "then we can read it together."

With the promise of Freddie's last words, Sara went to the shower. Marie turned it on and set a towel on the toilet. With a small smile, Marie shut the door. The sound of the shower hurt Sara's ears. Slowly, she peeled her old clothes from her body. Her neck was still bruised but had turned a yellow-green color. No one had said a word about the injury. The water ran down Sara's emaciated body and cleansed her spirit. It felt better than she had expected. She turned the water off and dressed.

~

Sara hadn't moved from the chair she had been placed in. Apparently, she was unnerving family and friends by looming in doorways or hiding in bathrooms. There were 133 flowers on the front panel of her skirt, 576 ceiling panels, and a perfectly symmetrical spider web in the bottom of the pulpit. She named the little lady spinning it Michelle. Michelle was so busy with her work, she hadn't noticed the funeral occurring just behind her. Michelle wasn't married. She was a widow, for her husband's half-eaten body was wound up in the corner of her perfect home. *What a fabulous life*, Sara thought, y*our kids hatch, and they are off to live a happy life of web crocheting. And when your husband makes you angry, you fucking eat him.*

Dan probably tasted like stale beer and old feet. No, she wouldn't ever eat Dan. That's where she and Michelle differed. But she'd sure like to wind his drunk ass in rope and let him starve to death in the basement of her perfect crocheted house.

Sara refused to call it a funeral. She refused to look into the casket. She begged Dan to keep it closed, but he wouldn't have it. "We must allow the family to gaze upon what a true hero looks like," he preached. "The fact he was returned to us at all is a miracle."

Dan wasn't wrong. Most people who died in this war

were never returned to the families. Because they A: didn't have the means to do so or B: there wasn't much left.

Dan stood during this tirade at dinner the week before. Like a sweaty preacher at an unairconditioned Sunday service, he paced his lectern. The power was out again, so the fans weren't running. He hadn't had his night-whiskey. That made him sweat even more because the afternoon-whiskey had left his bloodstream. There was a small window between the fury of sobriety and the fury of drunken stupor where Dan was jovial and, at times, reasonable. So, Sara had taken her chance to beg Dan to reconsider keeping the casket closed.

Her husband made eye contact with each family member, asking for someone to challenge him. And when his eyes had fallen on Sara, she knew she had chosen incorrectly. Fury of sobriety was still in full swing.

"We must allow our family and friends to see what true animals the White Main can be," he said patiently like he was talking to a child, "because what Fredrick Francis Weiderholt died for will be an important part of the overall victory for the Gray's and a return of the true United States of America."

The silent downtrodden stares into their plates seemed to be enough of an agreement for Dan. He took a deep breath and ran his hand down his sweaty face. He then pointed his moist finger in Sara's face. "You better keep your mouth shut during that funeral," he growled, "because if I hear you utter one word of your negative bitchy bullshit…"

Sara raised her eyes to meet his which narrowed on her immediately. "You'll discipline me in front of everyone," Sara whispered.

The hand swung so quickly Sara didn't even see it. The next thing she knew, she was on the floor. Amy dropped her spoon. Marie slumped further into the chair, trying to be absorbed by the floral cushion.

A baby crying a few rows over snapped Sara out of her

flashback. She glanced at the new mother. Must have been a high school friend of Freddie's. She cooed and bounced the baby with perfect instinct. Sara felt her eye twitch, and her gaze moved to the father. His back was to Sara, and his face was buried in his phone listening to a news bulletin on the radio. *Update: 1,277 more confirmed dead in the battle of FLGA. While sources point most of these causalities from White Main forces, loss of life occurred on both sides. Due to this mass casualty, White Main has now opened the draft to married females 18 to 35. Draft numbers are expected...*

The mother's eyes met Sara's, and she grabbed her husband's phone. She cleared her throat angrily and meekly smiled at Sara. A small burst of signal from the dying radio they all still tried to access. How fortunate. The universe had quite a sense of humor. Sara sighed.

Where was she? Oh yes, the saga of Michelle. She noticed a white moth had trapped itself in her web. Its wings fluttered and strained, but it was of no use. Once Michelle had you, you were had. Michelle leisurely began spinning the moth's tomb. "Make it quick, Michelle," Sara whispered, "don't be a showboat."

"What the hell is that supposed to mean?" Dan grabbed her arm.

"Get up," he growled pulling her to her feet.

Dan dragged Sara to the side of the casket. "They are about to play taps," he growled, "pay your respects."

That'll bruise, Sara thought as his hand released her upper arm, so cunningly placed as to not show.

She had grown accustomed to wearing long sleeves, even in the dog days of summer. So she had pulled out her favorite sweater for the occasion and was sweating like a whore in church. *Quite literally*, she thought, briefly thinking of Sam.

Everyone had filed out and was waiting in the hallways where the military bugle player stood at attention. This was to be a private moment, but Sara could see everyone in the hall craning their necks to see the family's reaction. It's like a train wreck. They want to see the pain in others. Not because they like to see others in pain. Because it meant that at that moment the pain is not happening to them. *Well*, Sara thought, *I won't give them the satisfaction because I am not looking in that fucking box.*

Sara made eye contact with Hadley and Kristen who had made zero effort to hide their nosey gawking. They quickly looked away once caught. Dan grabbed her again and shoved her up to the shell that was once Freddie, "Pay. Your. Respects."

Sara accidentally looked down. He looked nothing like Freddie. This man was an imposter. He was swollen. His lips weren't right. His head appeared to almost be sitting on his shoulders. It was worse than the wax figures at museums. This was clearly a mannequin. It wasn't her baby. She was about to announce to everyone there had been a mistake. Then she saw it. On his left hand was a scar from his 10th birthday party where he fell off his new trampoline and had gotten stitches. And then the ear lobes. The ear lobes had the half-healed large holes from the huge gauged earrings he'd gotten at fourteen without their permission. She reached into the casket. "Mom, stop," Amy sobbed.

Sara moved his collar from his shirt, revealing the fatal wound from the battle sewn to the best of the mortician's ability. There sat his birthmark.

Sara was instantly back in the hospital. She could smell the blood and her legs were numb. Dan hadn't made the delivery for reasons she couldn't remember. Sara was tired and a bit confused from the meds they had given her. Suddenly, a nurse handed her a tiny bundle of blankets. Peering out was a tiny face.

She moved the blankets away from his face, and she saw his ducky-shaped spot. She kissed it and the tiny baby cooed. She was in love.

Her vision swirled.

~

The lights flickered again. Sara sat on the couch in her house. Dan had rehung the *Home Sweet Home* sign on the wall. It had been one month since she'd hung it in Sam's shed. The clock ticked. Her eyes were raw. The lights went on, then browned and went out. She stood robotically. It was getting cold outside. Sara walked to the garage to turn on the generator. *The groceries. They'll go bad*, Sara mumbled in her head.

There was mail on her doorstep. Pick up the mail. Look through the mail. It was like living a program. She flipped through the paper which held a church flyer, Gray propaganda hand-written by a neighbor. Sara dropped it on the ground. And then she saw a white envelope addressed to Marie. Sara opened the letter knowing what was inside. Her hands began to shake.

Marie Ann Weiderholt, you are hereby ordered for induction into the Armed Forces of the Gray Main United States Army and are to report...

Sara shoved the letter into her back pocket. *No.*

Sara walked to the generator. "I have to get the generator on," she said to no one.

Sara's eyes bugged, and the ground moved beneath her feet. She walked to the back of the garage and pulled back the tarp revealing their five gas cans. She picked one up. *This can't be happening. Not again.*

Right foot. Left foot. Right foot. How could they take another one of her babies? *How?*

"I have to get the generator going," she repeated, lugging the heavy can to the old Honda machine, "I have to…"

She swallowed gently, her throat still aching from the bruises of Dan's chokehold. Sara paused, leaning a hand on the cool brick of her garage. She screamed. The force with which she did echoed and birds took flight from the oak tree in the back yard. Somewhere close a dog began barking.

Sara listened to the soundwaves bounce until they fell silent. Her throat hurt in a new way, a better way. Her head cleared. She stared at the can in her hands. She turned and looked at the full cans behind the garage. In a blink, she was in full force.

Sara began pouring the cans into the tank of the Jeep. Then she raced upstairs to grab a bag. Sara stuffed clothing into it and ran to the girl's room. Pulling out Amy's backpack, she rummaged through her drawers, pulling out underwear and socks. Sara moved with purpose she had never felt, with determination she had never known. Sara repeated her fury of movement with Marie's backpack. Again, she grabbed her toilet money.

After grabbing a grocery bag filled with food, Sara threw everything in the back of the Jeep. She didn't even look at the house in the rearview mirror as she headed for the park.

~

Amy leaned her head on Anthony's shoulder. His arm gripped her tighter as they looked out at the lake. She watched kids playing and mothers chasing their toddlers. Men and women exchanged pleasantries and gossiped. Most likely about the Weiderholts. They were now on the list. The list of families that people gave sad smiles to. The ones where horrible casseroles appeared on their doorstep in the hands of women trying to get a glimpse of what their family had thus far avoided. The too-loudly spoken, *I'm sorry* or *thoughts and prayers*. It made Amy sick.

"I am truly sorry for your loss, Amy."

As if on cue, a friend of her father's walked past them sitting on the picnic table. "Terrible loss," a rough smoker's voice said, "such a wonderful young man."

Amy was so numb, she didn't even look at him. "Thank you, sir," Anthony answered for her.

Thankfully, the man didn't venture further into a conversation about Freddie's sacrifice, his heroics, or how this war would be over soon. "Come on," Anthony whispered.

He took her by the hand, and they walked to the shore. "I think this is the one, Anth," Amy whimpered, "this is the straw that's going to break my mom."

Anthony looked at her side longed, "You really think so?"

"My dad did something to her again," Amy began cautiously.

It was very dangerous to speak of what the whole town knew. She and her siblings avoided most beatings by fleeing when he was in a mood. It suddenly occurred to her that her mother never did. It was as though she waited for his rage. Maybe it was to direct it away from them. Amy wiped her eyes. "I just keep thinking, who's next, ya know?"

The sand crunched beneath their feet as they rounded the corner towards the parking lot. "Maybe if we got married," Amy said.

Anthony let go of her hand and turned, "Don't start."

"I'm just saying," Amy began to get frantic, "maybe we could get a pass from joining or being drafted if we're newly married or if I'm..."

"Stop it! You know that's not how it works, Amy," he said sternly, "and that would leave you pregnant and me off to god knows where. It is not going to happen until this is all over."

"Amy!"

The argument was interrupted by her mother parked fifty feet from them. Sara was waving Amy over. Amy's attention was drawn to the backpacks thrown in the back and Marie sitting solemnly in the front. She clenched her fists and growled. "I told you," Amy snapped, "she's broken again, and now we are off to my Aunt's."

That was her mom's safe place. Throughout the years, when it got really bad between her parents, they were packed up and drove to Aunt Emily's. She wasn't really her mom's sister. It was a distant cousin, and she lived in a boring suburb outside of Detroit.

Anthony sighed and put his hands in his pockets, looking away from her. Sara yelled again for Amy to get in the Jeep. "I am getting off this carousel with or without you," Amy said stomping towards her mom, "when I get back from Detroit, I want commitment. Concrete commitment."

Marie was staring blankly out the windshield. Amy looked from her to her mother, who was noisily climbing back into the driver's seat and adjusting her mirrors. Amy cursed to herself and climbed into the back. "Off to Aunt Emily's we go," Amy said flatly and watched the park get smaller as they drove away.

Anthony stood in the parking lot, watching them drive away. He raised his hand slightly in goodbye. But Amy's tears blurred before she saw his gesture.

~

Marie watched the light poles zip by in perfect rhythm. When she was little, she'd pretend there was a giant who would jump from pole to pole chasing her as they sped down the highway. Those were the days when they still went on vacation to the Wisconsin Dells or Mount Rushmore. Marie always complained about how boring those trips were. And now she'd give anything for her life to be that simple. Marie barely registered her Mother yelling for Amy to get in the Jeep. Her mom had found her outside of Gather. She was there waiting for Colin again. Marie carried the Timetwister card with her everywhere she went now. She knew Colin wasn't coming back, but she still rode her bike there every day since the soldiers knocked on the door to give their condolences. Her mother was catatonic. Her father was acting like a maniac, telling anyone who would listen about the heroism of his son. All Marie had wanted was for her and Colin to grieve together.

Dead. Freddie was dead.

The White Main had killed her brother and taken her already-fractured family and decimated it. Marie always had a dragon that lived inside her. She had known it from a young age. If left unchecked, it would tear through anything in its path. She flexed her hands that were still healing. Todd found this out the hard way. Once when she was around eight years old, a boy at the park took her hat. He wasn't trying to play keep away. In fact, he immediately handed it back to Marie when he saw her face. In hindsight, he probably was trying to flirt with her. Her parents got a phone call home about what she had done. If it weren't for her father being who he was, she'd have been expelled. The stone she threw at his face broke his nose, and it remained crooked until she last saw him boarding a bus for Recruit Training. Marie didn't even remember his name.

Her pulse beat in her fingertips and ears. She wanted to release the dragon on the people who took away her brother. "I'm joining when we get back," Marie said suddenly.

Her mother became very still. Amy snorted from the backseat. Marie settled into her seat. She leaned her chair back and closed her eyes. *I want the front line*, she thought, *I want to be where I can make them hurt the most.*

~

There was a hole burning in the pocket where Sara had stuffed Marie's draft letter. Hands gripped tightly at ten and two. Her knuckles were white. Amy was trying without success to get a signal. Giving up, she threw her phone in her bag. "Great," she huffed.

"Guess you'll have to talk to us," Sara joked.

Amy huffed louder and reached into the front seat, turning the knobs on the radio. The snowy static was ominous. There weren't many stations left transmitting anything, let alone music. Sounds of voices came through and Amy paused. "Two hundred dead after another battle in…"

Marie pressed the first button her finger could find.

"…*around the Christmas tree have a happy Holiday*."

Christmas music began to flow from the speakers. Amy and Marie groaned, and Sara smiled. She loved Christmas music, and to her surprise, the girls didn't move to turn off her CD. "Everyone dancing merrily in the new old fashion way," Sara began singing a bit off-key.

"You may get," Marie started to mumble, "a sentimental feeling when you hear."

Sara slapped the steering wheel to the beat, "voices singing let's be jolly!"

"Come on Amy!" Sara hollered over the music as Marie turned it up.

"Deck the halls with balls of jolly," Amy groaned from the back.

Sara laughed. "Not even close," Marie chided as she hid a smile, looking out the window.

The sun was beginning to set, and they were almost to Minneapolis. Sara knew she could use either currency there if she stuck to marked Gray businesses. An old VW van passed them in the opposite direction. Sara's mind drifted to memories of dozens of cars on these interstates. Memories of the problems everyone complained of before, like traffic or seasonal allergies. Sara would give anything to sit in traffic en route to a pharmacy where the aisles were lined with every medication known to man.

"Santa Baby" had popped up next, and both girls sang along, lost in their thoughts. The white lines whipping by in a rhythm let her mind relax, and for the first time in weeks, she thought about Sam. She couldn't bring herself to consider what Dan could have done to him. Sara had tried to call his cellphone a few times, but it went straight to voicemail. A few days after they found out about Freddie, Marie had come into her room. Sara only knew because she felt the bed sag where she sat. Marie and Amy had taken turns bringing her food and trying to coax her from the bed.

But on this particular visit, Marie brought news.

She had heard from the townies that Sam had been rounded up by a bounty hunter. Someone had tipped him off that Sam was a defector. Sara had no idea. Sam hadn't mentioned it. To the best of anyone's knowledge, he was a war hero who narrowly escaped with his life in some battle. But in these times no one could be sure who anyone was anymore. It was so easy to slip away and disappear. Sara knew immediately what that meant for Sam. Death or the front line. Either way, death.

She tapped her fingers on the wheel to the beat of *Mama Got Ran Over By A Reindeer*. "Disappear," Sara whispered to herself.

The thought was interrupted by dings from both Amy and Sara's cellphones. Amy shot up and grabbed her phone. "About time," Amy said, settling in for a recapping of the day's events with her friends and no doubt Anthony.

Sara glanced down and saw several notifications from Dan. Sara quickly turned the phone over, but not before Marie saw it. Marie sighed and rolled her eyes, crossing her arms. Sara pretended not to notice and looked for a turn off for gas. They turned off the interstate down what used to be a busy road in the middle of Minneapolis. Now barely any cars drove the streets. The Jeep still had most of a half tank left, but Sara took no chances. You could be stranded so easily on abandoned roads with no services for hundreds of miles. Sara went through a mental checklist of what food items she brought. Enough for the trip down to Emily's house if there were no detours, checkpoints, or other unmentionable roadblocks she had heard happening to lone cars on the interstate. Rumors circulated about road pirates and bounty hunters taking anything or anyone for a profit. Sara thought it was to keep people from fleeing but wasn't about to take the chance.

A big strobe light beckoned her from the exit. A newer well-kept gas station appeared a few miles down from the exit and had its lights on. A large American Flag in the muted color gray waved from the top of a large flag pole. "Anyone have to go to the bathroom?" Sara asked, opening the door.

Marie jumped out and walked towards the building without answering. Amy ignored her completely, her face lit up by the cellphone screen. Sara sighed and followed Marie into the building. The door rang a bell as they stepped inside. The gas station was surprisingly well-stocked. There were bottles of water, some bags of snacks, candy, and even a working fountain pop machine. A pleasant-looking older man was at the register. He was a cheerful grandpa sort with a thinning head of silver hair and droopy brown eyes. "Good evening, Miss," he said with a smile made of false teeth.

"Hi there," Sara answered, "that big strobe is a good idea. Led me right to ya."

"That was the owner's idea," said the man, "helps a lot of people find us."

"What type of money do you take here?" Sara asked.

"The only money that's gonna matter by the end of the year," he said with an edge.

Sara pulled out her Gray money, "Oh, of course, I just meant do you take rations and old money too."

The man smiled. "My apologies," he said, watching Marie admire the fountain pop machine, "people can be quite difficult when they try to pay with their useless White backs."

"Thirty on pump two please," Sara said handing him the Gray cash, "has there been any news? About the war ending, I mean. You mentioned it being over this year."

A radio softly spoke from the back counter. It was fuzzy, and Sara could only make out that it was a talk show. "From the stations, I get out here," he said with a reassuring smile, "the Gray's numbers far exceed the White's, and we are pushing them out of all the major cities."

Marie edged closer to the conversation, trying to seem oblivious.

"That's really good news," Sara said, looking over at the Jeep.

They needed to get on the road. "And the other radio stations?"

The man looked at her like she had two heads. "You know," Sara tried again, "the White-leaning ones? Are they hinting at what their counterattacks might be or where?"

The man began laughing. "I don't listen to that crap, sweetie," he wiped his eyes, "it's all propaganda."

"Of course," Sara smiled, hiding her disdain, "oh honey, put that back. We have snacks in the car."

Marie put the sucker back on the shelf. "No no," the man said, "go ahead and take it. It's probably expired anyhow. Not that sugar does."

Marie smiled and thanked him. "She reminds me of my daughter when she was younger."

Sara smiled at him as she ushered Marie towards the door. "How old is she now?" Sara asked over her shoulder.

"She would've been thirty-five this year," he answered solemnly, "but she fought hard, and her death will be remembered as a victory when we win. You wait and see."

Sara plastered a smile to her face that didn't reach her eyes. "Thirty on two," he repeated turning on their pump.

Sara nodded politely and walked back to the Jeep. "That was nice of him."

Marie glared at her mother and totted off to the Jeep. Marie had climbed in the front and slammed the door before Sara made it to the pump. Sara sighed and wrung her hands. The sun had fully set, and the blackness of night made the city eerie. She knew there were thousands left in this city, but without much access to power, it was mostly dark. She tried to imagine what it once looked like only ten years prior while she filled the tank. Tall buildings lit like Christmas trees lined the night sky. You didn't need a compass. You could navigate by where you were in relation to the IDS Tower. Now that GPS was non-existent and/or unreliable, good old fashion maps had made a comeback.

Good thing her father showed her how to use any kind of map that existed: topography maps, aviation, and nautical charts. She knew what the symbols and lines meant. They spoke to her like someone telling a story. Not that she needed a map to get to her cousin Emily's. She had made that unharmonious trip more times than she could count. And they all were for one reason: Dan. Though she tried not to let onto Emily about how bad the relationship was, she always seemed to know. "You should leave," Emily had said more times than she could count, "you're stronger than this, Sar."

Sara could've written the speech out verbatim. And each time she felt energized by it. And each time Dan would apologize, and she would go back. Sara could feel in real-time her brain and body going from a place of *I'm going to leave*, to *I'm scared*, to *it's too hard*. And each episode she'd lie to herself about how this time was different, and this time he'd change. She was so scared that the lie felt so easy to believe. And here she was again, pumping gas in Minneapolis and repeating history. Her phone buzzed again in her pocket. The white glow of her screen lit her eyes. *I know. Call me back now!*

Sara shoved her phone in her pocket and hooked the hose back on the pump. Dan knows what exactly. *There is a lot to know right now*, Sara chewed over in her mind as she got into the car.

She took Marie's summons, so he couldn't know that. Sam was in some boot camp or worse. Colin's family was gone. She had disposed of the pregnancy test. So what did he know?

"Ready?" Sara said in a voice that was way too chipper.

Marie ignored her. Amy barely gave a noise in response. "Yay," Sara said sarcastically, "girls' trip."

The Jeep pulled out from the station. "*Do you hear what I hear?*" the radio sprang to life.

"God no," Marie said hitting the buttons again.

A news station filled the Jeep. "…in the Minneapolis

area. Take cover."

"So what are we going to listen to then, Marie?" Amy shot from the back seat, "news?"

Sara craned her neck to listen to the report. "Oh piss off Amy," Marie jabbed back, "I'd rather listen to raccoon porn than your oo'ing and giggling over Anthony's dick pics."

"Girls," Sara said, "quiet."

Sara was pulling onto the highway, and the signal got fuzzy. Sara pulled to the side of the road to see if she could get the signal to hold. "Jealous much?" Amy teased, "Did Colin not send many your way before he ran off?"

"Fuck you, Amy."

"Girls!"

"Colin and Marie sitting in a tree NOT f.u.c.i.n.g."

"There's a K in *fucking*, dumbass."

The sirens stunned them all into silence. "Mom?" Amy sat up in the back seat.

"*Reports of White airstrikes have been substantiated. Repeat. If you are in the Minneapolis area, please take cover.*"

"Shit," Sara mumbled, throwing the car into drive.

They sped down the highway through the center of the city. *Shit, shit.*

The sirens were haunting background noise over the news reporter Sara had all but tuned out. They were on the west side of the city, and 494 took them south past the middle of it. They still had at least twenty miles to pass the city. Sara punched the pedal to the floor. The old Jeep engine roared down the expressway. The speedometer raced up the half-moon towards a hundred. Marie quickly fastened her seat belt, and the second click told Sara Amy had done the same. "Look around," Sara ordered, "do you see anything? Lights in the sky, planes? Anything?"

Though Sara had tried her hardest to avoid any news on the attacks in the south, Dan insisted on picking them apart at the dinner table. "They should've done this." Or, "The flank was completely open, and we could've had them."

Though she never absorbed much, one point jumped

from her memory. "Whites completely level Gray cities, regardless of who is in them." Dan would seethe. "And if Grays followed suit, this war would be over!"

Sara knew this attack would be bad if it happened. She wasn't about to stick around to find out. The sirens echoed one another in sequence. Sara saw a sign for 94. "Eight miles, girls," Sara said, "we're almost out of town."

Amy and Marie were frantically looking out the windows for anything in the sky. Just when they thought it might be a false alarm, they all heard it. A once often-heard roar in the sky meant a plane was overhead. "Look," Amy pointed out the passenger side window.

Sara leaned over to Marie's seat. "Momma!" Amy yelled.

The glow of five jets in the sky in a V formation was coming in fast from the south. Amy screamed. "They're shooting stuff towards us!"

Sara leaned down just long enough to see balls of light explode from beneath the planes. Sara turned the headlights off. The bombs and the planes seemed to be racing towards the highway they were speeding down. "Come on, come on," Sara said, drowned out by the roar of engines.

The bombs rained down overhead. Sara was in awe. They looked like 4th of July fireworks. It reminded her of summers on Lake Superior in her hometown of Paradise, Michigan. It was her favorite time of year, besides Christmas of course. Everyone would gather on the beach covered in bug spray and drinking their favorite pop. Adults would have booze in theirs of course. Everyone would be talking and laughing until the fireworks started. Then they were all in stunned silence of their light. Sara couldn't help but think they were just as beautiful.

Marie and Amy screamed. The bombs hit the ground not a mile from their Jeep. The Jeep shook from the explosions, then shook from the jets cruising over their heads. The girls watched, and Sara heard the melee of bombs hitting the city over and over. Sara heard the planes get far away and then return. "Where are they?" Sara yelled, "They're coming back! Where are they?"

"Where we just were!" Marie cried.

Sara looked up in time to see the bombs fall over the west side of town. Sara sucked in a breath. There was a huge fireball reaching up to the sky where the gas station strobe has once been. She knew the gas man had finally been reunited with his daughter.

Sara's phone buzzed again. Tears blurred her vision as she looked at the screen.

DAN: BC she didn't report, she is now a war criminal…it's bad enough you disgraced yourself. but now you have done it to our daughter. Get your ass home!

Sara watched the jets flash across the sky the way they came. "What are they doing this far north?" Amy whimpered.

"Where are the fucking Grays?" Marie yelled over her.

Amy sniffed and leaned up towards her mom and sister, "Is anywhere safe?"

The sweat from Sara's hands was dripping down the steering wheel. She wiped them quickly off on her pants. Sara was sweating so bad, it looked like she peed her pants. And on second thought, she believed she very well may have. They crossed the Mississippi River and headed into the darkness towards Michigan.

~

The silence in the Jeep was thick. The only sounds came from Amy sniffing in the back seat. Sara tasted blood. One of her many stress habits had left her with half a chewed lip. She looked over to see Marie doing the same thing. *If they have gotten this far north, are they in Detroit? I should call Emily.* Sara's thoughts raced.

Her phone buzzed. She glanced down and saw Dan's name and didn't read it. *I know this story*, she thought.

Anger. Threat. Apology. Promises. Her return. Sara looked at the girls. They may have been almost adults, but they looked so small. The fires from Minneapolis were in her mirror too. Signs for Chippewa Falls glowed in her headlights. Highway twenty-nine was the way to northern Michigan. God, she missed her home. Even though she only spent her childhood there, it was where her heart stayed. Aside from moments with her children, it was the only time she had been happy. As hard as she tried, memories of her father faded with time. The most bizarre parts of him, though, stayed crisp and clear in all her senses. She could imagine his hands like a photograph. They were big and strong with a little dark hair on the knuckles. He could turn screws with his nails. Smiling, Sara thought of how he'd always give her morning juice in a teeny Dixie cup, even when she was a teenager. "I'm not a baby, dad," she would tease him.

"Just trying not to be wasteful," he'd say sheepishly.

In hindsight, maybe he gave her kids cups because it made him feel like she was still his little girl in some way. Those days in her home brought her so much joy. *Home*, Sara thought.

Sara's heart quickened. "Home," she whispered.

And as the rolling clouds of smoke billowed into the air, the old black Jeep turned off Interstate 94 and headed north on highway twenty-nine.

Preparing a speech in her head, Sara waited for the girls to notice the turn-off. But the horror of the events had left them all in their heads. Thankfully after only a few minutes, her daughters had fallen asleep. They inherited that trait from her. Most people, in times of stress, can't sleep. But Sara would fall asleep due to over-thinking. Her body would be so exhausted from worry and stress she would almost fall asleep driving. Oddly, she was so clear at the moment. Sara thought of the people who were no longer on this earth. She shook her head sadly. They were here, and now they are not. *It's all so fragile*, she thought to herself, looking at Amy sleeping in the back.

"What am I going to do?" Sara repeated to herself.

She had been racking her brain on how to handle her situation. The decision had been made that she wasn't going to Emily's. Sara didn't even call her to begin with. It would be the same go-around. Now she was headed to her childhood town of Paradise, Michigan. But what then? Dan wouldn't look there first, that was for sure. But eventually, he would figure out where she went. *Maybe we could try to go to Canada.*

The fantasy of fleeing to Canada was something every citizen of the broken country fantasized about at one point or another. Some spoke of it openly. But these days most people kept the dream to themselves out of fear of being accused as a traitor or draft dodger. Canada was still allowing refugees seeking asylum, but rumors were they were semi-closing the borders due to conflict between the Whites, the Grays, and Canada's government. Canada vowed to not interfere, and opening their borders would be cause for another war, Dan had assured her at dinner one night. "Those syrup-drinking hippies need to stay out of it," Dan said after drinking deeply from his whiskey.

That evening he was in a particularly good mood. So everyone hung on his every word and nodded vigorously when a substantial point was made. Sara remembered the look on Marie's face of complete admiration. Sara tried not to be resentful. She really did. But anger boiled inside of her for always being last on everyone's mind in the family, for being discounted. She took a deep breath. She was going to get the girls to Canada if it was the last thing she did.

Sara began making a mental total of the cash she had on hand. She had heard paying for a border crossing was expensive. Maybe someone in town would be able to help her. The border crossings would be dangerous. News reports of raids and armed military officers at the points of entry, or in this case exit, were heavily patrolled. Sara thought of the thousands of days she had spent on the Superior shore. Canada was nearly a swim's distance away. *How ironic*, she thought, *we could almost canoe there.*

Her brain light bulb going off made her eyes hurt it was so obvious. Doyle. Her father's best friend lived in Paradise his whole life with no interest in ever leaving. His family had lived there since beaver trappers settled in the 1700s. And he had a boat, a big fishing boat. He would help. Wouldn't he? She hadn't seen him since her father's funeral. It was no secret he wasn't thrilled with Sara and her choice to leave town to live with Emily and her parents. But he was her dad's best friend. He had been family. A renewed sense of security washed over Sara. There was a plan.

Sara was looking for another gas station turn-off. It was past midnight, and the Jeep's tank was hovering between half and a quarter tank. The thought of going into another big city made her stomach turn. She decided to stop well before Green Bay. More signs appeared showing facilities available. The first sign showed several hotels at the exit. All the hotel names had been spray-painted

Her heart pounded as she turned off the exit when she saw a sign of gas stations available. Two were left without crossed-out marks. "Right or left?" Sara said to no one.

~

Amy began to stir when she felt the car slow and turn, "Are we there?"

"No honey. Getting gas."

Amy shot upright. "Don't worry. I turned off well before the city," Sara reassured her.

The phone buzzed, waking Marie from her sleep. The signal was reaching them again from Green Bay, and Sara blacked out her screen quickly. "Will you just answer him?" Marie groaned rolling over. "Let him know we are making a quick stop to see Aunt Emily, and then we'll be home before Labor Day."

Sara ignored her tone, changing the subject. "This is such a nice time of year by the lakes. I used to vacation all around the coasts when I was little."

Marie sat up and rubbed her eyes. A large green sign with miles to go appeared in the darkness. "Green Bay," Marie said cocking her head, "why are we going to Green Bay?"

"We're not," Sara wasn't exactly lying, "different route. Safer, I think."

"Pretty sure nowhere is safe anymore. Especially in any of the big cities," Marie poked at her eyes, then wiping the eye snot on the seat.

"Can you stop being so negative?" Sara chided.

"I'm not really interested in your maternal guidance or optimism at the moment."

"Mouth, young lady!"

How dare she? Marie thought.

How dare she try to act like a governing body of anything after what she had subjected them to? Kidnapping her from her home to go on a pointless road trip and then almost getting bombed. *Mother of the year right here.*

The phone buzzed again as her father called for the hundredth time. Marie snatched it from the console. "Give it to me," her Mother asked pulling into the well-lit station, "Marie please."

"Let it go, Marie," Amy said from the back.

Amy shook her head and sighed, grabbing her mother's purse. "Thirty bucks?"

Sara nodded and Amy went in to pay the clerk.

Marie looked down at the glowing screen. Dozens of missed calls from her father, Aunt Emily, and her mother's friends. Then she saw the text notification and clicked it.

DAN: BC she didn't report, she is now a war criminal...it's bad enough you disgraced yourself. but now you have done it to our daughter. Get your ass home!

Marie's hands began to shake. "Who," Marie said quietly, "whose number got called?"

Sara knotted her hands. They were sore from so many years of it. She noticed how the veins bulged from the backs of them. Dehydration and age had made them almost alien to her. Her young daughter's voice seemed like a stranger.

"I'm not letting you go," Sara whispered.

"Don't you dare," Marie charged her, "Don't you dare tell me what to do! You broke the law. You made me break the law. You *lied* to me. I don't want to be here with you!"

Marie got out of the Jeep and slammed the door. "I want to fight for my country, for my brother. I want to finish what Freddie started."

Sara got out and grabbed Marie's arm, "Wait, please."

Amy trotted back out from the store. "They took old money if you can believe it," she said, stopping upon seeing the two, "What happened?"

Marie threw the phone at her mom. Sara's road-mapped hands barely protected her face from the blow. "Your mother knew my numbers were called and has been on the run with us so I don't report!" Marie yelled at Amy.

Amy's eyes widened.

"You have never stood for anything. Dad was right all along. I hate you!"

Marie stomped off in the direction of an old mini-mall across from the station. Sara exhaled and ran her fingers through her hair and leaned down to assess the phone damage.

Amy began filling up the Jeep, watching her mom pick up the shattered pieces of the cellphone. "We're not going to Detroit, are we?" Amy asked hooking the gas nozzle.

Sara shook her head, "I need your phone."

~

Marie began to walk faster and faster in time with her ragged breaths. The tears running from her eyes made it almost impossible to see. "Marie, wait," her mother called, "it's not safe."

She would never let anyone, especially her feeble mother, see her in a moment of weakness. She was a Weiderholt. The sun was below the landscape, and the shadows lengthened on the ground. Marie thought of her brother, and she began to pump her arms into a run. She crossed the street, turned right and ran down some old forgotten road. She was running and sobbing so hard she didn't notice that the stores she happened upon were raided. She didn't notice her reflection in the shattered windows of the pharmacy. Her nose didn't pick up on the metallic tinge in the air. Marie's lungs were about to explode when she slumped down the side of a brick building in the center of a mini-mall in the forgotten town. Burying her head in her arms, she muffled her scream. *Enough*, she thought, *pull it together. I'll just call dad on Amy's phone, wait here for him to pick me up, and explain I was taken against my will. What happens to mom is her problem.*

Marie wiped her face with her dirty hands and took a deep breath. She choked on her spit, gasping for air. A gasp echoed from behind her. Marie froze. She slowly turned around. On the ground behind her were the darkened silhouettes of six bodies. The one closest to her twitched and gurgled again. Marie's hand went to her mouth, and her eyes bulged. The girl wasn't much older than Marie. Her face had been beaten, and her blonde hair was matted to her face. Her eyes looked at Marie, pleading, unable to speak. Marie rolled to her knees and removed the girl's purse, which was tightly wound on her neck. "What happened?" Marie whispered. "Where are you hurt?"

The girl reached for Marie's hand, covering it in thickening blood. Marie looked at the ground and saw it shining. There was a pool where she had been sitting. By the time Marie glanced back at the girl's face, she was gone. Marie rocked back against the wall in disbelief and heard muffled voices. A scream echoed through the parking lot. Marie peered around the wall, dropping the hand of the dead girl. Three men and a woman dressed in uniforms were dragging a woman down the street. "Shut the fuck up!" one man shouted.

The moon reflected through the street like a spotlight. It was only then Marie saw a dozen more dead lying in the parking lot. Marie's eyes went to the Gray Main flags on the coats and sighed in relief. *The good guys.* She put the girl's purse around her neck. *They can alert the families of what happened here, and they can direct me to the nearest reporting post. Damn Whites.*

She began to approach the group and saw one of the men crack a woman in the head with the butt of his gun. Marie gasped and hid behind a car. The man grabbed the woman's white floral skirt and threw it over her head. The woman screamed begging him to stop. "I'm on your side," she pleaded, "I am a registered Gray!"

The man yanked his pants down and threw his pelvis into her backside. She screamed, begging for him to stop. The larger man rolled his eyes and began checking pockets of the dead with the female soldier. The other man, who was wearing boots too big for him, laughed and rubbed his crotch.

"We need to clear this place, asshole," the woman said, riffling through a woman's coat pockets, "finish already."

"I'm next," the big-booted man shot back.

The bag the female soldier was holding was thrown to the ground. She walked over to the rape scene, raised her gun, and shot the woman in the floral skirt in the head. "No, you're not."

"You fucking bitch!" big boots yelled.

"What the fuck, Heather?" the rapist screamed, rolling off of the body. "You could've fucking shot my dick off!"

The woman raised her gun to the rapist. "If we are late getting back to post and/or don't have enough goods, we will get rations again or fucking worse. So put your micro-cock back in your pants and help me find valuables or so help me."

The two men looked at each other. "Fine," the rapist grumbled, buttoning his pants.

Big Boots grabbed his sack off the ground and followed the woman soldier. Marie released the breath she'd been holding and stood back up slowly. Just as she turned to run back to her mom, she smacked into a light pole. She yelped, immediately covering her mouth.

Big Boots stopped and turned around. "Did you hear that?"

The soldiers all stopped what they were doing and turned towards the sound. "There! On the sidewalk," Heather pointed, "Hey, you! Stop!"

Marie turned and bolted. Her body moved like it was on octane. The adrenaline coursed through her veins, pumping her arms and legs. Marie could barely see the ground. She prayed she wouldn't trip again.

"Stop now!"

Shots fired and whizzed past her, hitting the street close to her feet. Marie turned down the corner where she had left her mom and sister and began screaming. "Turn on the truck! Get in the truck!"

Sara and Amy looked up and saw Marie sprinting towards them. "What the hell?" Amy said squinting.

Sara's eyes widened at the sight of her disheveled daughter. "Is that blood?" Amy whispered.

"Get in the car," Sara ordered, "*Now!*"

The engine roared to life as the soldiers turned the corner. Amy climbed into the back and threw the door open. She screamed at Marie. "Get in!"

Marie threw her body forward. She could hear the crunching of Big Boots getting closer. Her lungs were about to burst. Her muscles screamed to stop. Fifty feet until she was at the Jeep. She saw her mom start moving the car in anticipation to flee. "Run Marie!"

She could hear the sound of the man grunting and breathing hard to catch up. *Five feet.*

Marie leaped.

~

Dan threw his phone on the table. Emily was either lying or hadn't heard from Sara yet. *Where did that woman go?*

Normally, Emily gave him an earful when they had a bad episode. She would curse him out, vowing to break his neck if he ever touched Sara again. Like she could. The fat sow was as nimble as she was skilled at hand-to-hand combat. Dan spun the glass slowly on the table. No. Sara didn't go to Detroit.

Dan flexed his fists, wanting to hit something. He was hard on Sara, he knew. But he only wanted to make her the best she could be. Look at the woman he had made her into. She was a fine cook and an excellent mother. Dan provided a home and a car. Everything she was and had was attributed to him and his kindness all those years ago. And this is how he was repaid: an affair and the kidnapping of his children. Dan sat back in his chair and looked at the clock; it was just after nine at night. His thoughts went to the one-legged traitor and their encounter. Dan wanted so badly to kill him. To make him scream first and then shoot him in the head. He would've liked Sara to watch. For her to know the extent of what he would do for his wife. Sara was his, and that man had made Sara turn on him and her children. Dan knew that if Sam showed up missing the town would start to ask questions. It was too messy. So after a thorough beating in the gym office, he knew Sara would eventually happen upon, he called the bounties on him. They were there in an hour and took the barely-breathing adulterous bastard to his front-line grave. The look of pure hatred on the man's face made Dan smile. *She's mine. She will always be mine*, Dan recited.

Dan called in a few favors to make sure Sam ended up right where he belonged. Within one month, that piece of shit would be in the thick of the battles somewhere to the south. Between IUD's and chemical warfare, he'd be missing a few more parts if he ever made it out alive. Dan smiled to himself.

The house was quiet and clean. With only him in it, the place felt a bit empty, not that he minded. Freddie was the only child they had planned. Once he had his son, that's all he needed. But one month Sara forgot to take her pills and Marie was a product of that mistake. Dan was always apologizing or cleaning up after Sara. He should be happy about her absence. But Sara had his children, one of whom didn't show for her summons and was now the talk of the town. This, of course, reflected badly on Dan. At the department, people would quiet down their hushed gossip as he walked into the room. Dan told everyone she went on a sabbatical because of her state of mind due to Freddie's death. "My wife is unwell," Dan would insist with a stern tone, "you all know how unwell she can be."

Dan assured them that once Sara was in cellphone range, he would inform her of the summons and Marie would be on the first bus to proudly serve her country. People would nod their heads with a smile that didn't reach their eyes.

Ding dong.

Dan set down his empty glass and answered the door. Anthony stood on the porch with shoulders stooped. "Good evening Mr. Gomez," Dan said with a friendly smile, "come in. Come in. Can I get you something to drink?"

Anthony tried to stand up a little straighter to hide his fear. Everyone in this town feared Dan in one way or another. They knew of his deep ties to the Gray Higher officials. Some of it was true because of his time served years ago in Afghanistan; other rumors weren't. But he wasn't about to correct them. "I, err, no thank you, sir."

Dan motioned for him to sit at the table. Anthony sat and began to knot his folded hands in his lap. Dan smiled again to the boy as he poured another heavy drab of whiskey. Dan raised his glass while Anthony his brows, "Sure I can't offer you some?"

"No thank you, sir," he said much too quickly, "I don't drink, sir."

"Probably for the best, son."

Dan took a long sip of his drink and slowly made his way to the chair next to Anthony. His dark hair was freshly cut high and tight, and he wore a nice button-down shirt. This boy wanted to make a good impression. *What is he so afraid of me knowing?*

"I am sure you are aware Amy isn't in town," Dan began gauging.

"Yes sir," Anthony answered meeting his gaze. "Well, I assumed so, sir. Mrs. Weiderholt picked her up from the park yesterday afternoon."

Good. He was spilling already. Dan nodded thoughtfully. "Son, I am very worried about my wife," Dan said. "She hasn't been herself since Fredrick's passing, and I fear she may not be making decisions with all her faculties."

Anthony swallowed. "Moreover," Dan continued, "I am more concerned for my daughters."

The boy sat up at this and leaned in. "Why? Is Amy ok?" *Got em.*

"Well, see that's the thing," Dan said sadly shaking his head, "My wife isn't answering her phone. I believe she is on her way to her family's house in Michigan."

Anthony nodded, "Yes she goes there when there is trouble in the house, right?"

Anthony's face paled and if he could have covered his mouth, he would have. Dan's ear's burned. He knew the town folk assumed, on some level, there was unrest in their home. But to have a child call him out on it was unconscionable. *Steady yourself, Dan.*

Dan wiped a hand over his sweaty face pushing his bangs from his bloodshot eyes. His blond hair was too long and needed a trim. Sara needed to get back soon. "Yes," he kept his voice even, "we do sometimes have issues. Like all families."

"Of course," burst Anthony, "I didn't mean."

Dan raised a hand, "No offense taken. I'm not perfect. But Mrs. Weiderholt is unwell, and I worry about her hurting herself and by proxy, the girls."

A beat. Dan watched it sink in. "Do you know where they are, Anthony?"

Anthony shook his head and looked down. "Amy calls me whenever she gets a signal."

"So where are they now?"

"Last I heard from her, they were headed towards Minneapolis."

Dan leaned back in his chair and scratched his chin. That was on the way to her bitch cousin's house. Maybe Emily was lying after all. Dan sat up and leaned forward, putting a hand on Anthony's shoulder. "Thank you, son."

Dan could see the edges of tears he was fighting to hold back. "You are aware of the people I know within the Gray government?"

"Yes sir," Anthony said.

"I want the love of my daughter's life to keep his own," Dan said with a fatherly tone, "you helping me get my family back ensures that."

Anthony looked confused. Dan fought back the urge to punch him in the face. Dan sighed, "I'll make sure you are in a paper-pushing position, son, if you are ever drafted. I have that power, you know."

The boy's eyes got bigger. "So if you hear from my little girl again," Dan said, "you need to let me know immediately."

"Yes, sir."

Dan watched the teenager walk down the street to his house. Anthony wasn't his first choice for Amy, but he was easily controlled and that didn't always come cheap. The screen door slammed behind him as he went back inside. Without Sara there to cook, he was left on his own to figure out dinner. He pulled out the bottle of whiskey and dumped in another large pour. *I'll make some cereal*, he thought, taking another deep swig, knowing full well that Jack D would be his only dinner guest tonight.

~

"Is everyone ok?" Sara asked, peering through the

rearview mirror.

She could see four soldiers' silhouettes against the lighting of the gas station. Beams glowed in the back seat like tiny spotlights seeping through the bullet holes. Sara's eyes fell on the face of her youngest daughter curled into the side of the seat. Her eyes moved to the road, staring blankly ahead. Amy's soothing words blurred into the sounds of the engine. Sara looked back at Marie, seeing the eyes of a person who was no longer a child. They were the eyes of a soul who had experienced something so traumatic they would never be the same. Sara knew this look from her reflection when she was a child. There was nothing she could say, so she didn't.

"Marie," Amy started again more urgently, "god, Marie, please. What happened?"

Amy grabbed a pack of butt wipes from the backseat pocket and tried wiping the drying blood from Marie's hands. Marie's head wagged back and forth, and she gasped for air. "You're safe. You're safe," Amy hushed, gently wiping her cheeks where blood-smeared like war paint, "you're safe now. They are far away. Mom is taking us somewhere safe."

Amy handed Marie a bottle of water. Marie took it. She didn't drink from it, only holding it and squeezing the plastic lightly. It made a quiet crunching sound that made Sara's ears want to bleed. "They were all dead," Marie said between gasps.

"Who was dead?" Sara asked gently.

"I don't know who they were, mom," Marie said desperately, "but there were Gray soldiers there. And I thought they were there to help."

"Well weren't they?" Amy said confused.

Marie shook her head and took a long sip of water. "They were most definitely not."

Sara chewed her lip as Marie delved into the story of the mini-mall parking lot. Amy covered her mouth and gasped. Sara's eyes lined with tears. "That doesn't make any sense,"

Amy sat back in the seat after Marie finished, "I thought we were the good guys."

Sara knew the war wasn't that cut and dry, but Dan had led her to believe the Whites were truly evil. However, Sara always knew it wasn't as simple as "that religious group is all bad" or "that group of people is out to get you". It was hard not to fall into the over-used rhetoric or memes she would see online and on TV. Though she was devoutly a registered Gray, the mere fact Dan supported everything they stood for was enough for Sara to reflect on her position.

"Those were not the good guys," Marie said with a growl.

Sara saw Amy's hand slide into Marie's. And for once, Marie didn't let go.

The white lines ticked by again in a rhythmic pattern. Any other time it would have lulled Sara to sleep at this late hour. But she was wide awake. Where would she go once they got to Paradise, Michigan?

About an hour passed, and the girls had fallen asleep. Sara began to see signs for Green Bay. They would avoid big cities like the plague now. Sara began looking for another turn-off for gas as the Jeep's clock flipped to two in the morning. There wasn't much open at this time, she knew, but with a half tank of gas, she'd have to start trying.

~

Amy's eyes burned. But it was the sound of her phone pinging to life that brought her out of sleep. Amy fumbled for her phone with relief. Signal.

ANTHONY: *Where are u? r u ok?*

They must have just passed Green Bay. Amy rubbed her eyes and wrote back.

ME: *Somewhere in Wisconsin. I've been better.*

ANTHONY: *u need to get back here Ames. Ur dad is looking for u.*

Amy sighed and looked up at her mom and sister in the front seats. She knew her dad would send Marie off to fight. And after everything they'd seen, maybe it was better to lie low for a while until this mess passed.

ME: *Listen. Things are really weird right now with my family. I know we'll be back sooner than later. But my dad knows we're fine. And please don't tell him we talked, ok? My parents just need a little space.*

ME: *There was a bunch of jets that bombed Minneapolis. We were right there when it happened. I was so scared.*

No answer. Amy swallowed. They wouldn't be gone forever, surely. This was temporary until things, all things, settled down.

ME: *And then Marie found some soldiers who shot at us. We're ok tho. And they were Grays, babe. Listen, I don't think going back the way we came is safe now.*

Silence.

ME: *U and me r still ok, right? I know we left on shitty terms. But you still love me, right?*

Another long pause left Amy checking and rechecking her signal.

ANTHONY: *Of course. But please keep me updated on your whereabouts.*

Amy raised an eyebrow. *That was formal.*

ME: *Um ok Well I love you*

ANTHONY: *I love you too.*

Amy sat up and crossed her arms. The sun was beginning to hint at its appearance over the horizon. She wanted to go back to be with Anthony more than anything. But these past few hours had changed her. Amy knew going back at this moment meant certain demise for her sister and truthfully, her mother as well.

Amy chewed her lip as her mother veered off an exit to a gas station whose lights were on. Her mom looked back at her, noticing she was awake. "Keep an eye out."

Amy nodded and watched her mom walk into the store. Amy sat up and looked around for any people. There was only one old Buick parked on the side which was most likely belonged to a store worker. Hopping into the driver's seat, Amy began flipping through pictures on her phone. She paused at one of her and Anthony kissing. They made a heart shape with their hands. She was smiling slightly from something Anthony said that made her laugh. Amy's heart ached for him. Maybe once Marie and her mom were settled, she could go back. They could start again. Clean slate.

~

Anthony took the phone from the table and slid it into his pocket. Dan watched him thoughtfully digesting what the texts had said. The boy had done as he asked, so that pleased him. As soon as he heard from Amy, he had come to the house to tell him. But something still didn't sit right with the brief text conversation. After word spread of the Minneapolis attacks spread a few hours prior, he knew the girls had to have been somewhere close. *Looks as though they got a front-row seat.*

Dan smiled and ran a hand through his blonde hair. Serves them right. Perhaps Sara will realize she is in over her head and come back. He had tried Emily again, and she didn't answer. "If you hear from her again, I need to know immediately."

"Yes, sir," Anthony said raising his eyes.

"The girls are in obvious danger and we need to get them home."

The boy nodded.

"You can leave now."

The boy turned so quickly on his heel he almost smacked into the fridge. Dan smirked as Anthony hobbled his way out the front door and shut it gently. Dan sighed and rose to refill his glass. Opening the fridge, he realized there wasn't any food. "Fuck," he said, slamming it.

He was distracted at work and he hadn't eaten a proper meal in two days. Dan felt the rage building inside him. When that woman got back, he'd teach her a lesson. He'd need to practice restraint because he could so easily go too far like he had the day they found out Freddie was dead. It felt so good to show her how powerless she was.

Walking to the radio, he turned it on and snow sounds loudly poured from the speakers. Dan began to turn the dial to find something reporting on the attacks. Suddenly a song came through. The lyric was so distant yet so familiar he grasped the countertop for support.

Trip to Garden Grove…smelled like Blue dog inside the van…

He slid down the sides of the cabinets and grabbed his head. Dan's memories flashed back to a time when he was small.

"Sublime" was playing on the radio and acrid, meth smoke hung in the air. His parents were arguing in the next room, and he heard something break. Danny picked up his stuffed bunny and walked to the kitchen, stepping over trash and things on the ground. His mother was lying on the ground with blood on her face. She seemed to be asleep. Dan's father was washing his hands in the sink cursing. Danny knew better than to hang around and so he turned to leave. "Daniel."

The deep slurry voice stopped him in his tracks. "You

got something to say, boy?"

Danny shook his head slowly as his big blue eyes filled with tears. A large hand reached out and grabbed his arm.

The radio suddenly cut out and began hissing with the sound of snow again. Dan shook his head. He fought back emotion and slammed his hand on the counter. Again and again, he hit the cheap Formica until he heard a crack. In his whiskey stupor, he couldn't tell if it was his hand or the counter. He curled into a ball on the floor and cried until he fell asleep.

~

"Marie, wake up."

Hands roughly shook her from a deep sleep. The dreams were of fire, but Marie couldn't place if she was frightened or not. Her mother's hands grabbed her again. "Marie!"

"What?" Marie said sitting up rubbing her eyes.

Amy was leaning into the front seats with a wild stare in her eyes. Bright lights blinded her and ahead a large sign said "checkpoint."

"Amy, get your licenses. Marie, tell them you don't have yours."

Amy fumbled for her purse, pulling out her ID and Gray Card. There were three cars in front of them. One of which had a barking dog walking its perimeter. "What are they looking for?" Marie asked.

"Defectors," her mother whispered.

Marie's heart dropped. "What am I going to do?"

"Just let me talk. Let me figure out something to say."

Marie's heart was beating out of her chest. This was it. They were going to discover who she was and that her number had been called. At best, she could say her Mother didn't know, and then she would be packed off to the nearest camp for training and then fighting. At worst, they could be executed. The soldiers looked young and not too different from the ones back at the mini-mall. Marie tried not to pee her pants as a tap came at her window.

Her Mother rolled the window down. "Good morning," her mother said sweetly.

"IDs please," the soldier said, shining a light into the Jeep looking around, "traveling somewhere?"

"Visiting family in Michigan," she spoke again with a smile.

"Where?" the soldier said, taking Amy's cards and reading them.

"Sault Ste. Marie," she answered.

He pulled out a machine and swiped the picture ID. A green light glowed on the top and he handed the cards back to Amy. He reached past Marie to grab her mother's cards. His uniform was worn and too big for him. Marie took a chance to look up at the sentry as he swiped her mother's ID. He couldn't have been older than seventeen. He had crooked teeth and bad acne. His crew cut appeared to be blonde. And then his brown eyes turned to her. "Where's yours?"

"She doesn't have an ID sir," her Mother apologized, "we seem to have misplaced it."

Eye snot was in the corner of one of his eyes, and white gunk strung from the corners of his mouth. A seventeen-year-old with bad hygiene was about to send her to her death. The boy began to look harder into the cab of the Jeep. "Everyone's got to carry ID," he said quickly, "step out of the car."

"Now hold on a second," her mom started as the solider tried to open the Jeep door, which was locked.

"Open the car door, ma'am'."

"She just hasn't been able to find it."

"Please, we were just trying to get to our family's house," Amy interjected as the situation escalated.

"Open the door!"

The soldier's shouting got the attention of another, and he began to approach the Jeep. Marie's panic was rising, and she felt a tug at her throat. The strap from the dead girl's purse was cutting into her neck. "Wait," Marie said over the arguing.

She began digging in the purse for the dead girl's wallet. Marie pulled it out, "I have it!"

Everyone stopped yelling. "I found it," Marie said with an extra dose of teenage attitude, "jeez."

The soldier frowned and grabbed the two ID cards Marie had dug out of the wallet. He shined the light on them. "What's your name?"

Marie heard the silence as her Mother and Amy stopped breathing. "Charlette."

"Charlette, what?"

"Charlette Ann Miller."

Her mother and sister were made of stone. The soldier looked at the ID and then to Marie. She knew she didn't look exactly like the girl in the picture. Same hair and eyes, by the grace of some god, but the picture was old. Like it had been poor Charlette's original driver's ed picture at fifteen. "Birthday?"

"May 30th," without missing a beat.

The soldier sniffed and wiped his nose on his hand and swiped the ID. The light illuminated green. Marie's chest relaxed.

"Zodiac sign?"

Marie looked up to see the solider grinning at her. She could almost hear his mind say, *gotcha*.

"Gemini of course," Marie leered at him, "the most bipolar and difficult signs to get along with."

Rolling his eyes, he handed the IDs back to her without a second glance. "Welcome to Peshtigo, Wisconsin. You're free to go."

Her mother rolled the windows up and, with all the restraint within her, creeped slowly and cautiously out of the checkpoint. They sat in silence until the lights of the near-disaster were out of sight. "What in the hell, Marie?" Amy shrieked, "where did you get that and how did you.."

"That was the most brilliant thing I have ever seen,

Marie," her mother interjected.

"And then when you acted like such a brat," Amy laughed sitting back, "oh my god, it was perfect."

"Whose IDs are those?" her mom asked.

"There was a girl in the parking lot where the soldiers chased me," Marie began, "I took it when she died because I thought maybe the soldiers would help find her family."

Amy blew a big breath she'd been holding out and sat back in her chair. "I looked through it after we escaped the gas station," Marie said quietly, "I wanted to know her name. And she has the same birthday as…"

"Dad," Amy and her mom answered together.

"He is definitely a Gemini," her mother said, shaking her head.

"He is definitely an asshole," Marie echoed.

The truck fell silent. Her mother began to chew her lip. Marie looked at her hands in her lap and thought of all the times she avoided the situation between her parents. How many times had she ignored the bruises or the fear that was palatable in their sad home? She spun a ring on her finger that she never took off. It was a silver band with a small V bent on the top. She had found it at a thrift store when they were looking for clothes. The shop clerk smiled at Marie as she admired it on her hand. Marie asked how much, and the clerk told her to keep it. It was such a simple gesture but it had touched her so much. That small act of kindness had been such a source of light that day.

Marie showed very little kindness to anyone. It was incredibly intentional. Many people's pain manifested into over-eating or low self-esteem. Marie's was a white blinding rage. What scared her most of all was how much she liked to release it. But sitting here with her mother and sister after witnessing the brutal truth of their situation from the bombing and mall slaughter, Marie felt a clear calm. "You can never go back," Marie said quietly.

Amy looked up from her lifeless phone. "What do you mean?"

"Mom can never go back," Marie said, "he'll kill you."

Her mother's shoulders visibly slumped. "I will never leave you," her mom whispered.

Marie nodded. "I know that. That's why I don't want to go back either."

Her mother's eyes still fixed on the road, filling with tears.

"Now hold on," Amy interrupted, "I have a whole life in Watertown. You can't just expect me to walk away from it. I know things are crazy right now, and we are laying low for a bit. But when this all settles, I'm going back to Anthony."

Marie turned back to her sister. "That's your choice. But I will never step foot in that town again. And neither will our mother."

Amy sat back, rolling her eyes. Marie wanted to knock them out of her head. Marie may not do things right very often, but this time she would. She would protect her mother and sister if they let her. They would escape. Now all they needed was a plan. Marie stared out the window as the truck fell into silence. Everyone seemed to ponder where they fit into the future. Old billboards whizzed past them with advertisements for businesses long gone. Marie saw decaying houses and abandoned cars littering the highway. They were rotting. And staying in Watertown meant her family would too.

~

The sun was beginning to rise and light up the horizon. Sara smiled. Michigan was an absolute beauty in the summer. They had passed the *Welcome to Michigan* sign four hours ago. And when they did, a rush of joy and excitement filled Sara. Home. She was finally home. The waters of Lake Michigan sparkled in the new sunlight. Not many people knew of the wonder of the North. But most northerners liked it that way. There were places for tourists to leave their trash and have their fun with the locals. And they were named Mackinaw Island and Traverse City. Places up here in the U.P. were untouched and wild. That was how Sara wanted it to stay. She had passed several small base camp turn-offs on their way here. She tried to even her breathing. The two different militaries were everywhere looking for defectors and arresting people who tried to help them. *Arrest at best*, Sara thought grimly.

Sara should have been exhausted, but she found herself wide awake. She decided they would go into Paradise and act like they were visiting her old stomping grounds. Sara would take the time to look for familiar faces. If she couldn't find Doyle, perhaps someone could help with how to get out of the US. Sara pulled up to the Berry Patch Restaurant off the highway. She took a deep breath. For the first time in decades, she was home.

They were all starving. Panic and fear kept hunger at bay. But now that they were at their destination, their stomachs were audible. "This place is cute," Amy said, raising her phone for a signal.

Their phones had been essentially paperweights for the last several hours. Phone towers were an odd commodity up here, even before the war. Marie had ignored her sister for the remainder of the trip. It was hard to see her girls upset with each other. Sara was going to make it better, and food would be a great way to start. Bells chimed as they walked into the store. It looked much as it had almost twenty years ago, except for the shelves being a bit barer. But to her surprise, it was still quite well-stocked with crafts and local goods. A man walked out from the back. He was older than Sara with a belly and a smile. "Good morning, three for breakfast?"

"That would be great," Sara said, "what form of payment do you take?"

The man waved his big hand, "We take what you have."

He grabbed menus and directed them to a booth. There were a few locals she didn't recognize sitting at a table on the other side of the restaurant. Only a thousand people lived in Paradise. Sara once knew everyone and everyone knew her, but she had been gone for a long time. The place even smelled like Sara remembered. Wooden tables lined the dining area with pictures of the town's history adorning the wood-paneled walls. "Do you work for the Woods?" Sara asked, remembering the family who owned the place.

"Nope," he said, "bought it from them several years ago. I fixed up the back, and I lived there with my daughter. Are you friends of theirs?"

Sara noticed the table of locals turn around and smile, looking at the new Berry Patch Owner. "Well I grew up here, and I just knew them because," Sara said, "Paradise, ya know?"

"Welcome back, Miss?"

The girls looked at their mom with caution in their eyes. "Rayl," Sara gave her maiden name, "Sara Rayl and this is my daughter, Amy, and niece, Charlette."

Amy and Marie smiled but said nothing. "Amare Wilson," the man said, nodded his balding head, "My daughter, Ife, will be out to take your order."

Sara watched the man walk away. Her daughters all exhaled. "So I'm your niece, huh?" Marie said with a grin.

Sara shrugged, "I improvised."

The hinges of the kitchen door squeaked, and a beautiful girl walked out of the kitchen. *Coffee*, Sara's heart beamed when she saw the pot in her hand.

All three of them turned their mugs over immediately. "Good morning," Ife said, "anything besides coffee?"

Her braids clinked when she leaned over to fill their coffee cups. Sara noticed Marie staring. Ife made eye contact with Marie and smiled too. Marie's face reddened and looked down. "Three glasses of water and I think we are ready to order," Sara said without asking the girls.

She felt her stomach digesting itself. Ife took their order and walked away. Marie lifted her eyes again to watch her go. Minutes later a bell dinged, and Ife came out with mounds of steaming eggs, potatoes, and toast. Sara thought she might cry. "Are you all passing through? On holiday?"

Sara shook her head with a mouthful of mashed potatoes. "Just seeing a few friends in town."

Ife looked a bit taken-back. "What friends?" she said a little too loudly.

They all looked up from their meals. Ife smoothed her apron down nonchalantly. "Maybe I know them. This town has seen a lot of change though."

Sara mulled that over. The town looked exactly the same, but when searching the faces of the people roaming the streets when they walked in, she didn't know a single face. Sara listed off several family names of people she thought may help them. One by one, Ife said they either moved, had gone to war, or she didn't know them. *Odd*, Sara thought, taking another bite of egg.

Trying a few more names, Sara said, "Let's see what about the Kubats or VanderWeels? Doyle Bedford?"

The mention of Doyle's name made Ife's eyes widen. "Yea," she said with a tone that suggested he wasn't her favorite person in the world, "he's around here still."

Sara nodded. Luckily, the one person she had somewhat of a plan for was still a resident. Still so strange that everyone she knew seemed to be gone. But that was the United States today. A massive ghost town. Sara sighed and took another long sip of coffee.

"You like Magic the Gathering?," Ife said to Marie.

Marie choked on her water. "Um, yea. How'd you know that?"

"Your shirt," Ife smiled, "I used to play all the time."

Marie nodded, looking down at her black dragon shirt that read "Got Magic?" Shyly, she went back to her eggs. "I'll go get some more joe," Ife said, walking into the kitchen.

"Who's Doyle Bedford?" Amy asked.

"Old family friend," Sara said, watching the table of men in the corner staring and speaking in low tones, "with a boat."

The girls looked at each other. Jamming her knuckles in her eyes, Sara began to see double. She needed sleep. After leaving the Berry Patch, they went to find a room. As much as she wanted to find Doyle immediately, she knew they all needed to reset. "Vagabond Motel," Amy read the sign as they pulled up to the local hotel, "sounds swanky."

Marie hissed at her sister. Their refusal to speak to one another wasn't remedied by hash browns. Sara shook her head and grabbed their bags. "It's nice," Sara promised, "I know the owners. Or did know the owners."

Once in their room, Sara dug around her bag for her toothbrush. The people working there were very friendly and accepted the money Sara had without question. But they were, like everyone she had met so far, strangers. When she asked what had happened to the Hewit family, they brushed off the question, handed them keys, and went back to straightening up the office. Each daughter had taken a bed. Amy was fiddling with her phone. She had obviously gotten a signal because she began texting furiously. Sara went and sat on the bed. It groaned with the sounds of old springs. The maroon floral bedspread was soft but ancient. "Amy," Sara began, "I need to talk to you about Anthony."

Amy's eyes didn't look up, "Yea?"

Sara placed a hand on Amy's leg. "Amy you cannot tell him where we are."

Marie muted the TV and listened. "He's worried mom," Amy said with an attitude.

Sara sighed, "Tell him we are ok. Tell him we are still en route to Detroit. Tell him anything else but where we are."

Amy dropped the phone in her lap. "I am not staying here. And you still haven't explained why we need a boat."

"We need to get Marie to Canada."

Marie sat up. "What," Amy yelled, "are you insane?"

"It's the only place she'll be safe."

"And what then, mom?" Amy continued with tears welling in her eyes, "You just expect me to walk away from everything because you and dad fight and *she* got drafted?"

"It's not safe in this country right now," Sara began.

"Well I'm not going," Amy said crossing her arms, "I'm going to catch a bus and go back to South Dakota. Anthony and I are planning our life together, and he can keep me safe. You two can do whatever you want, but I am going home."

"Always thinking of others," Marie chided.

"Oh get bent, Marie," Amy yelled back, "You act like you are all of a sudden so on-board with running away with mom. This was probably your plan all along. Because you hate SD. You have no friends except Colin, who is gay! And everyone knows you threw yourself at him, and he didn't want you either. You want everyone to be as miserable as you are!"

Marie threw the remote at Amy, hitting her square in the forehead. Amy let out an ear-piercing squeal, covering her face. Eyeing Marie, Sara grabbed Amy's hands, trying to see if it drew blood. And by the time she looked back, Marie was gone.

~

Boiling blood was making Marie's face sweat. Amy was the biggest narcissist on the planet, and she hoped the remote cracked her head wide open. How dare she? It was true Marie hated Watertown, but the situation they were in was hell. She would never have wanted this outcome.

Would she have?

Marie shook her head. *No*, she thought, *Amy was selfish. I am doing what's right for my Mother.*

Thoughts of Colin seeped into her mind as she walked down the street. In hindsight, she had never really liked him in that way. She blushed thinking about the kiss. Marie hoped he and his family were alright. "Still hungry?"

A voice interrupted the sounds of her head and her feet crunching gravel. Marie looked up and saw Ife taking a trash bag to the dumpster. The Berry Patch sign was just overhead. This *was* a small town. Ife saw Marie's fury and raised a brow. "Everything ok?"

"Yes. No," Marie put her hands in her pockets, "I don't know."

Ife put her hands on her hips, studying Marie. "Want some rhubarb pie?" Ife motioned to the Berry Patch, "I made it myself."

Marie swallowed down the rage and looked up at Ife. Her dark skin was flawless, and her large brown eyes sparkled. She couldn't have been much older than her, but Ife seemed so much bigger. She gave off an air of maturity that made Marie feel like a sulking child. Marie's heart began to beat fast. Ife smiled bigger, "Come on. It's on the house."

Marie sat in a booth, and to her surprise, Ife sat across from her, handing her the small plate of bright red pie and a cup of coffee. Marie took a bite. It was the best thing she had ever tasted. Rhubarb wasn't anything they rationed in Watertown. She didn't know what it even was. "Good right?" Ife said. "Dessert makes everything better. So you want to talk about it?"

"My sister's a bitch."

Ife laughed out loud. It was the happiest thing Marie had ever heard. "Yes, they most definitely can be," she replied, "but remember she's still your blood. What's your name?"

Marie paused, "Charlette."

Saying her sister was the absolute worst out loud did make it seem childish. Every sibling fights and her reaction was a bit over the top. Ife sipped her coffee, looking at Marie over the rim. "So," she began again, "just passing through? Will you be staying long?"

Marie shook her head. "We will be heading out tomorrow. We are just saying hello to some old friends of my mother's"

Ife nodded her head. "Like that Doyle guy?"

Marie paused her chewing. "I think so. My mom just wanted to say hi."

Ife placed her hand over Marie's. And to her surprise, Marie didn't pull away. Marie grabbed back. Ife's eyes were lit with concern. "You need to be careful around that man. He's an odd duck."

Marie looked down at their hands. "I'll be sure to tell my mom that. But it sounds like she's known him for a long time."

Marie pulled her hand from the grasp. "People change," Ife said with a sad smile.

Marie wiped her mouth with a napkin and took a quick sip of her coffee. She needed to get out of here. Ife seemed really sweet, but this whole town seemed off. "I'm going to head back," Marie said over her shoulder, "thanks for the pie."

Marie was almost in a jog by the time she got back to the Vagabond Motel. She burst into the room and found her sister lying with an ice pack on her head. Her mom gave her a dirty look. "Sorry," Marie said tightly.

Amy scoffed and rolled to her side, ignoring her. Her mom rose. "Come on. We can't wait until morning." She said. "I need to find Doyle and I'm not leaving you two alone. Or I will be saving you from each other and not the draft."

Marie rolled her eyes and followed her mom out of the room. They got in the Jeep and turned back out on Hwy 123. "Where are we going?" Marie asked.

"There's only one place Doyle would be and there are only three of them in town."

~

Sure enough, they found Doyle at the second bar they tried. Marie turned her nose up at the smoke that filled the small dive bar. The smell of it almost covered up stale liquor refermenting in the bar mats. Fruit flies flitted about, and Sara swatted them away from her eyes. The Bar, as it was so aptly named, had been a staple watering hole for the fringes of Paradise. Layers of dust covered the heads of mounted deer on the walls that had been shot decades before. The wood paneling was home to hundreds of fishing trinkets collected over the almost hundred years it had stood. To Sara's surprise, she knew the bartender. She was the mother of one of the guys she had gone to high school with. When they locked eyes, Sara knew immediately she had been recognized. But revealing herself to Doyle would've alerted the entire coast anyhow, so Sara just smiled. "Hi, Ms. Sue. How ya been?"

"My god is that little Sara Rayl?"

From the corner of her eye, she saw Doyle stiffen. "You betcha," she answered, eyes flitting to Doyle.

"And this must be your daughter," Ms. Sue inferred.

"Niece," Marie interjected, "I'm Charlette."

Sara hid the startled look in her eyes. So this was going to be a thing. Marie was always a step ahead. "So how is Andy?" Sara changed the subject.

Ms. Sue paused and then began vigorously wiping down the empty bar top. "Died," she said, "Somewhere in Georgia."

Marie looked at her feet, and Sara shook her head. "My deepest apologies."

Sara took in Ms. Sue. The experts can say what they will about the effects of nicotine, but Ms. Sue looked like she hadn't aged a day. A few more lines and her hair had gray roots, but Sara found herself thankful for a familiar face. "Well belly up," she said with a heavy northern accent, "Can I get you something?"

Marie fought and failed to keep the disgusted look off of her face. Sara internally sighed. "No thank you," Sara said, "we were looking for someone."

Sara nodded her head to the end of the bar. Ms. Sue looked at Doyle and nodded sadly. "Well let me know if you change your mind."

Sara took a deep breath and walked to the end of the bar. "Uncle Doyle," she said cautiously, "is that you?"

Sara felt Marie take a step into her like she did when she was a child. She couldn't blame her. Doyle looked like a crusty, half-dead pirate. His clothes were dirty, and his shoes had holes in them. He had lost most of what hair he had left from twenty years ago, and it was all white. When he turned to face them, he was missing most of his side teeth, and the ones in the front were yellowed and crooked. Doyle was a sight for sure. He leaned back in his bar chair and crossed his arms. The familiar pouch of tobacco in his lower lip was prominent. "Well well," he started with a thin raspy voice, "you've made it back home."

Sara tried to breathe through her mouth. His breath would knock over a horse. "Just passing through actually."

Doyle worked on the chew like a cow with cud. Sara had never much cared for Doyle. But when you live in a small town, friends were at a premium, and her father was friends with everyone. But he always gave Sara the creeps. "Can we sit and talk?"

Doyle shrugged and waved to Ms. Sue. "An order of fries and another round."

Sara watched Marie check the booth quickly for smears of unmentionables on the seating. Marie eased across as Doyle plopped down across from them. "This is my niece, Charlette."

"Nice to meet you. Where is your husband?"

Sara placed a reassuring hand on her daughter's leg that was uncontrollably bouncing under the table. "That's why I am here. We are having difficulties. And I am looking for a change."

Doyle raised an eyebrow. Just then Ms. Sue laid down a beer and a shot of whiskey for Doyle with a basket of fries. They shined with grease and smelled of year-old oil. Doyle grabbed the ketchup and drowned the once-potatoes in a sea of red. "What's that got to do with me, eh?"

Sara took a breath and tried to ignore the way he ate. "Do you still have Medea?"

Doyle stopped chewing. "Do you know how much

trouble I could get into taking you across the border in my boat? If that's what you're asking."

"I know it," Sara's heart began to beat fast, "but we are out of options. We are looking for a new life. Please. You are the only person I can turn to. You were my dad's closest friend once. I am begging you."

Doyle's eyes darted between the two. "Is it just you two I will be committing treason for?"

Sara's body sagged. *Oh, thank God.*

"Yes, actually."

Sara noticed Marie suddenly finding the ring on her finger incredibly interesting. "My daughter. My oldest. She wants to go back to South Dakota."

Doyle finished his fries and threw back the whiskey. "You just up and left."

Sara looked down and wrung her hands. "I did, yes. It was too difficult to stay."

He nodded. "Yes, you were in quite a predicament if my memory serves."

Marie looked at her mom, confused. Sara swallowed. Doyle waved again at Ms. Sue for another round and sat back, resting his hands on his potbelly. "Meet me at my dock at midnight tonight," he instructed, "the trip will take about a half an hour without lights. This is Gray territory, and they patrol these waters from time to time. I'm sure you saw the checkpoints on the way up."

They both nodded. "We don't have any money," Sara blurted out.

"I figured you didn't," he said flatly, "it's a short trip. Consider it a favor to your dad."

CHAPTER FIVE

I'm on a boat.

Sara exhaled for the first time since forever. Her eyes fell on Doyle searching the storage under the cabin seats. "I have blankets in here somewhere," he mumbled looking up at the girls, "wouldn't want you to catch a cold."

Marie looked blankly out the window, her hands folded neatly in her lap. Tendrils of blond hair were matted to her forehead. Remembering the girl she had been just a few days before was nearly impossible... that girl was gone forever. All the years Sara had cursed the heavens for her strong-willed daughter. Now she thanked them on bended knee for their forethought. Sara prayed Marie's strength would carry her through this trauma. Everyone had a cache of strength, patience, and empathy. Marie was so much like her when Sara was young, it was staggering. Sara blamed her forfeiture of dignity to her strength cache being used up.

When had it happened? she thought. *When did I go from being the girl who had such glorious plans to the shell? The doormat?*

Through immense begging on her part, she had talked Amy into coming on the short voyage. Her heart was utterly broken at the thought of not seeing Amy for a long time. She couldn't bring herself to believe it would be forever.

Sara wanted every last second to try and talk her out of going back to Watertown. Amy and Marie hadn't even looked at each other. There was a huge welt on Amy's forehead as the reminder of why. Her thoughts were interrupted by Doyle draping a dark blue wool blanket around her shoulders. "I apologize for the smell," Doyle shrugged, "I haven't used them in a long……"

The musty scent of the blanket had reached her nostrils. She knew it was too late. The scent reached her chemoreceptors, which activated electrical impulses sent to her brain, triggering perception and then memory.

At some point, she had lost consciousness because you can't come to if you haven't gone out. However, she kept her eyes firmly shut. For if she couldn't see what was happening, then it couldn't be real. The most painful part at this point was a rock lodged in her back. The man was so much bigger than her, and his body weight and thrusting made it dig further into her skin. She almost asked him to give her a second to remove it.

I wonder what's for dinner? Sara thought, opening one eye.

Her head was lying to the side and directly in her vision was a perfect birch stick. The stick was perfectly straight, and the edges were beautifully broken. A dog would love that stick, Sara thought, I want a dog.

Sara realized her disconnect. She was being raped and all she could think about was if her dad would have left her dinner out and a pet. Sara was starving.

Her memory flashed further back in time.

Her pulse quickened. "I said what are you doing here?" a man asked flatly.

Sara wrung her hands, looking at the ground. She had mud on her new LA Gear sneakers. Her dad was going to be mad. He had saved up for those shoes and gave them to Sara for her birthday. "Hey girl," the man asked again.

"I was building a fort," she finally looked up at him.

Sara wiped her nose on her arm, leaving a snail trail down it, gluing the hair to her arm. She was trying to look tough.

The man had greasy brown hair, long in the back. His bottom lip was puffed out with chew, and his teeth were the color of rotting leaves. His D.A.R.E shirt had the collar cut off and his jeans were too big for him. "I need to take you home," he said with a flat tone.

He looked like a man she had seen in town before, but she couldn't tell. He probably wanted to help.

"Alright," Sara whispered.

He took her hand roughly and her breath caught, her hair stood on end, adrenaline pumped through her veins, and it all screamed to run. But she didn't run. Sara followed blindly further into the woods.

The man crushed her body beneath him trying to kiss her. When he tore her My Little Pony underwear, she thought, Why didn't I run?

When the searing pain of her situation made her fall limp, she calmly thought, I'm going to die.

Sara's thoughts jumped forward like being thrown through a wormhole. She kept tying and untying her shoes. It may have been hours, minutes, days but she began to hear yelling in the woods. From her hiding spot beneath an ancient maple tree, Sara saw light beams waving hello. Through her tears, the foggy lights looked like the strobes that signaled the JC's haunted house every October. She kept thinking it was only July. How could it be time for Halloween? Then she heard her daddy. "Sara!"

Then a chorus of voices. "Sara!"

It was a cacophony of safety trying to find her. They sounded like Sunday service when churchgoers tried to be in unison during the Apostles Creed. Sara swore she even heard Pastor Michell in the accompaniment. She had just started catechism classes and had gotten a star on her chart for memorizing the first section. I believe in God the Father almighty, she silently recited, maker of heaven and earth and in all things visible and invisible.

What if I'm invisible? she thought.

Sara opened her mouth to scream and nothing came out. She cleared her throat and wiped the dried chew from her lips and cheeks and tried again. "Here," eked out in barely more than a whisper.

Her face smelled like mint. But the chew tasted like a campfire. The voices seemed to be going in the wrong direction. NO, she thought.

Sara tried to get to her knees and her legs and hips screamed in

pain. She slipped on the blood and pee that had puddled beneath her.
"Daddy," she finally spoke, climbing towards the safety lights.

"Daddy. Daddy!" Her voice got louder. "Daddy!"

"Over here!" Her dad's best friend, Doyle, yelled and shined his
flashlight in her eyes.

Sara saw a tunnel of light. "Mama," she whispered.

She felt salvation when familiar arms scooped her up. Kind hands
passed her back and forth as she was carried and covered with a musty
wool blanket. Blankets smell badly in heaven. She looked down at her
dirty LA Gear. Honor thy Father and Mother. She hadn't. This is
hell, she thought and then passed out.

Sara's head snapped up and was thrust back into the now. Her hair was wet; her breath staggered. She swallowed and almost gagged from the taste of imagined chew in her mouth. "You ok?" Doyle asked.

"Yes, I'm fine, thank you."

Sara laid her head back on the cabin wall. She could hear the steady waves lapping on the hull of the boat. Paradise laid in the distance of the setting sun.

Sara knew she'd never see her childhood home again. She couldn't figure out how she felt about that. Somewhere ahead was an island just inside the Canadian border. No one lived there. Absolutely no one. It didn't even have a name. As a child, her Father dared her to make the twenty-mile swim. "I could do it, daddy," Sara said defiantly.

"Oh I don't doubt that Snickerdoodle," he said with a smile, "but
this is lake sturgeon mating season. Although, I don't think the big
ones are in these parts."

Sara audibly swallowed. "You know the ones," he rambled,
scratching his chin, "the seven-footer Uncle Bob caught when we were
kids. About sixty pounds I believe it was."

Sara's eyes got larger. "My word," he exclaimed, "don't ya know
that fish was about ten pounds bigger den you!"

The water suddenly seemed much too cold to Sara. And just past
where she had focused on jumping in seemed much too deep blue.

Sara smiled to herself, remembering. Daddy had a way of getting people to see the error in their ways without telling them straight. It was a gift.

Her smile faded when Sara remembered back to the night her father had left her alone for too long. He always got her a sitter if he was going out with his friends or had some errands to run. So that night when he said he'd be right back but left her alone was odd.

Lap, lap, lap, the waves licked the side of the hull. It melted with the memory of the sound the hose made after her daddy showered beside her window that night. When her daddy finally had gotten home, she had looked at her glowing clock. Mickey pointed to the three and the twelve with his white-gloved hands. When she was sure he wasn't beneath her window, she crawled to her knees and peered out. Even a month later her hips ached if she ever was in one position for too long. She quietly grunted into a position to look out her window. Her father was lighting a fire in the middle of summer. Not entirely odd in that northern Michigan could get chilly even in July. But today it had been one of the hottest days of the year. The worst drought of the 80s they'd said.

They. Sara was always perplexed on the perpetual truth from "they, them, who". Who on earth were these endlessly intelligent people? Where did they get their knowledge? Could they share it with her? Could they tell her why her daddy was standing by a large bonfire naked throwing his clothes into it? He burned the handle of his shovel too. But where was the spade?

An hour later, he had dosed the fire and come inside. Sara pretended to sleep when he checked on her. She could smell the campfire. Her heart began to pound. The hose began to drip again. *Lap, lap, lap,* went the waves and hose in her reality and mind. The next morning her daddy was up before her and in the kitchen making his famous pancakes. The ones in the shape of an S with chocolate chips. "Good morning, Snickerdoodle," he said with the biggest smile.

Something she hadn't seen him do in weeks. "Morning, daddy," she said sleepily, rubbing the sleep from her eyes.

He laid the biggest S she'd ever seen in front of her, complete with brown-sugared bacon, eggs cut into squares, and toast with jelly. "Eat up, baby," her daddy chirped as he started washing pans.

Sara, still a bit confused, started to eat. Something was different. A cloud was lifted. She'd always had a knack of sensing what others felt. Maybe that was it. Her daddy had finally forgiven her for getting lost in the woods.

"Hey Sar," her father pulled her from dismantling her S which now was two small c's, "we gotta talk about last night, ok?"

"M'kay," she agreed with a mouthful of S.

"People might come to the house asking about last night. Like where I was or if I ever left," he said, still washing dishes, glancing over his shoulder, "it's very important to say that I was here the whole night."

Sara was young. But a night with the minty D.A.R.E graduate had changed her. She didn't exactly know what had happened, but Sara felt all the rage of the past four weeks boil to pinpoint focus. *I will protect my dad.*

"Actually," she mumbled through sugared bacon, "we were up watching movies because I had a bad dream. Until about 3:30 I think it was. Then you insisted I go to bed."

Her dad held her gaze. He finally blinked and shook his head. "That's my girl."

Sara launched from the table, and her dad caught her in mid-air. Sara sobbed. Her daddy sobbed. "What's my job?" he cried.

"To keep me safe," Sara answered as she always did when poised that question.

"I failed you, Sara," he choked, "I'm so so sorry, baby."

"It was my fault," Sara cried harder, "I should've never been out so far."

"Listen," he brought her to his eye line, "we're a team. And we

are never going to let anyone hurt us again. Never ever."

"*Never ever."*

Lap, lap, lap.

"Mom," Amy whispered through Sara's memories, "we're stopping."

Sara sat up. The engine stopped. They were slowing down. The lights of Paradise were barely visible, but she still couldn't see the Goulais Bay shore. "Doyle?" Sara called.

Maybe the engine quit, she thought, walking to the helm.

Sara glanced at Marie, who was still looking out the cabin window. Sara smoothed her sweaty hair back and looked for their captain. "Doyle!" she called again.

Sara heard creaking floorboards from the front of the boat. Doyle appeared like mist. He looked comically accurate with his captain hat, slickers, and pipe sticking out of his missing tooth space. "Sara, it's time to discuss payment," he said flatly.

I know that tone.

"We don't have much money, Doyle," Sara said calmly, "I told you that. We're trying to get safe. You said you'd help us."

Doyle raised his hands, silencing her.

"I know you don't have money," Doyle said pulling out his pipe and licking tobacco from his tooth hole.

He couldn't help but look over at Marie and adjusted his pants. *No.*

"Are you kidding me?" Amy shrieked.

Upon that, Marie turned sharply, eyes wide. Doyle pulled out a gun. "You don't get nothing for free."

"Mom, do something!" Amy yelled.

"Uncle Doyle, you can't be serious," Sara tried reasoning, "what are you doing? You're like family to me."

"Lots has changed kiddo," Doyle said plainly, "and I ain't your Uncle."

Doyle moved with more agility than a man his age should and fixed the weapon at Amy's head. "Mom," Amy whimpered, "do something please."

Marie sat transfixed, watched the drama unfold. "I'm not gonna ask you again," Doyle said to Marie.

"There is no way we're going to let you do anything to her, you creep!" Amy yelled, her voice echoing off the boat walls.

"Amy," Sara ordered to silence her, shifting her eyes to her youngest daughter, "Charlette, do what he says."

"Are you insane?" Amy yelled again.

"It'll be alright -- Charlette," Sara said with a pause, "just go with him."

Marie stood up, eyes wide, and Doyle pointed the gun at her. "Down," he motioned to the cabin below.

Sara stood. Amy sat dumbfounded. "There's nowhere for you to go, eh," Doyle spoke calmly, almost father-like, "once this is over, I'll dump your treasonous asses in redskin territory and us Grays'll be better for it."

~

Marie was standing in the stairwell leading down to Doyle's "payment". What was she going to do? She looked at the old man as he kept his attention on her mom and sister. He still had the gun pointed at her head. He stunk. Soon, so would she. The mouth of the cabin felt like it was swallowing her as she took one more step down, gun pressed into her ribs. "Now," he cooed, smiling at her licking his cracked lips.

The movement behind Doyle happened so fast. Marie barely realized what had happened when Doyle slumped forward. Marie felt warm splatters on her face and Amy screamed from above. *Oh, God*, Marie thought, *I'm shot*.

But there was no sound. Doyle groaned and threw himself towards her mother and sister. Only in the light did she see the dent in the side of his head and her mother on the deck wielding an oar.

Marie wiped the blood from her face and launched

herself over the dented Doyle. Her eyes burned from the tears Marie hadn't notice she'd shed. "Where are the keys?" Her mother spoke with such authority Marie and Amy both gaped at her wide-eyed.

Marie noticed the gun that had been knocked from Doyle's hand and rushed to pick it up. Without looking at her, Sara took the gun from Marie's shaking hand and handed Marie the oar. The fear gave way to rage, and Marie wound up like her softball days.

Doyle spat blood and a tooth from his mouth. "You are a dumb, fucking cunt you know that," Doyle growled.

"Doyle," Sara roared and cocked the gun like she'd done it a million times, "the keys!"

Doyle started to laugh. "You know we all thought that husband of yours was such a fool marrying you and you're inbred," he began, "I already called em'. I know one of your bitchlets ain't givin' their real names because you're defectors."

Sara's face fell. "Called who?" Amy half asked her mother.

"You fucking asshole!" Sara yelled. "You were my dad's best friend!"

"And you killed him!" Doyle roared, wiping blood from his mouth.

Marie and Amy looked again at their mother. "I didn't make him have a heart attack, Doyle!" she screamed.

"No," he said, "but when your daughter is the town mattress cousin banger…"

"Doyle," she asked again, "the keys."

He pulled them from his pocket. Sara nodded at Amy. Amy moved to take them, and Doyle threw them into the lake. The women collectively gasped as the water plopped. "There's a real big bounty for deserters," he smiled, "but I would've turned you in for free."

The echo of the gunshot made Marie's head spin. She thought she had broken an eardrum. Dented Doyle was now Dead Doyle with a hole in the front of his head. Amy covered her mouth and screamed. Marie looked at her mother. Like a character out of an action movie, she stood holding the gun. The breeze took her hair up, and she looked like a wild woman. With deft hands, Sara cocked the hammer back and counted the rounds, looked in the barrel, and then snapped the barrel back into place. She put the gun in her back waistline.

"Girls," she said calmly, not taking her eyes off Dead Doyle, "I need your help and we don't have much time."

~

Blind white rage. Sara felt it so piercingly that when she pulled the trigger it was in slow motion. It wasn't passion or revenge. But purely to end the existence of someone trying to hurt her children.

Amy, Marie, and Sara grabbed the man's legs and arms dragging him to the side of the boat. "Wait," Sara said and checked his pockets. She found no keys, but a lighter and a few spare bullets. "Ready?" Sara asked.

The girls replied by grabbing his limbs and lifting. The splash of Doyle hitting the water stiffened Sara's resolve. *One down.*

Sara saw Marie staring at her. Marie was frozen, tear-stained vertical stripes on her cheeks. Sara grabbed Amy's and Marie's hands. "Girls," Sara said steadily, "we don't have a lot of time. If Doyle was telling the truth, soldiers or worse will be here soon. There are bases set up along Michigan's border looking for people like us."

Amy started, "Mom, we could tell them it was an accident. That we didn't realize Marie had been called up. Dad would vouch for us. We could go home."

Marie pulled her hand from her mother's and pointed her finger in Amy's face. "You just want to go home to your fucking boyfriend! What is wrong with you!"

Amy bit back at her words, her hand automatically going to the bump on her forehead.

Sara squeezed Amy's hand. "Punishment for failure to show is front line or death," Sara said, "there is a no-tolerance policy because of all the draft jumping. If they catch us, we could be executed on the spot."

Amy's eyes filled with tears. Sara grabbed her hand tighter. "Amy if we stay, we die," Sara said.

Amy wiped her eyes and nodded. "Amy, I want you to go down below and look for a kettle or pot," Sara said, "and any food you can find."

Amy ran down below. Sara turned to Marie, who stood at attention ready to take orders. "I need you to find matches and any type of fuel."

Marie nodded and turned to start when Sara grabbed her hand, which was slick with sweat. "I'm sorry," Sara said.

"Mom," Marie said, squeezing it, "so am I."

Sara nodded. Taking the briefest moment to watch them, she held her breath as they rummaged through the boat. *I will keep them safe.*

Sara pulled every life jacket from under the seats and began to strap them together. She found a water-tight bag. It was old, but she hoped it still was sound. Sara went over to the helm and switched on the navigation. Marie walked up to her mom with matches, a lighter, and lighter fluid. "I thought he threw the keys out," Marie asked.

"He did," Sara responded, "But boat navigation systems run off the battery. No engine required."

Sara flipped the power switch on and the board came to life. She pored over the screens. "Ok," Sara said, using her finger to follow the lines of the coast and their location, "Damn."

Amy came up from below toting a bag of supplies. "What is it?" Amy asked.

"We are two miles from shore," Sara answered.

"From Canada," Marie said with hope.

"No," Sara said, "from the Michigan shore."

Marie looked out where the shoreline showed the flicker of lights to the north. "So how long will it take to paddle there?" Marie asked.

Sara grabbed the garbage bag out of the can and turned it inside out, dumping out the garbage. She started to fill it with the supplies the girls had found around the cabin. "We're swimming," Sara said without looking up.

"You're crazy!" Amy shrieked, backing up into the railing.

"I'm not swimming that mom. It's freezing. We could drown," Marie agreed.

"This time of the year the water is about sixty-five degrees. Cold, yes. Deadly, no," Sara began as she started to take off her clothes and put them in the dry bag along with the guns, a blanket, matches, and lighter. "It will take about an hour for us to push this raft I made to shore."

Naked, Sara grabbed a life jacket and put it on. Marie and Amy stood frozen. Sara walked to them and grabbed their hands. "I need you to trust me," she started, "we don't have time to argue. The MPs could be here any minute."

"Where will we go when we get to shore?" Amy started to weep.

Sara squeezed their hands and pulled them into a hug. "I have a plan," Sara answered, "I am not going to let us die. You have to trust me. Now hurry!"

Marie had already started to disrobe, and Amy then followed suit. They stuffed their clothes in the dry bag and put on their life vest. Sara lowered the makeshift raft into the water, holding onto a strap. Marie went to the edge and looked at her mom. Sara nodded. Lowering herself into the water, Marie let out a yelp. "Is it cold?" Amy asked wearily from the boat.

"It's like Destin, Florida," Marie answered from the water, "just no salt, no sun, and the enriching fun of almost certain death."

"Marie," Sara warned.

"Come on," Marie said, smiling at her sister, "give me your hand."

Marie helped Amy up onto the raft. Sara lowered the bag

of food and the dry bag down to them. She took one last look at the boat, ransacked and covered in Doyle's blood. She then turned to the faint lights of Paradise in the distance. Sara slid into the water to join her daughters.

~

Amy was freezing. They had been kicking for what seemed like ages. It could have been forty-five minutes or sixty seconds but the cold had seeped so deeply into her bones she was starting to lose basic understandings of time and space. The lights of the city seemed to be getting farther away. Her legs were beginning to ache. She stopped kicking and the sudden lack of body heat from the exercise made her insides frigid. Amy started to kick again. She rested her head on the raft. *I wonder what Anthony is doing.*

She imagined his warm body holding her and watching a movie in her basement. It was in that basement they waited for her parents to fall asleep.

Anthony and Amy locked the basement door and lit candles. Anthony laid her down on the bed they made of couch cushions and soft blankets. He was always so sure of everything he did. So when Amy saw apprehension in his eyes, it took her back. "Are you sure you want to do this?" Amy asked.

"Of course," he admitted, "I'm just. What if… What if you don't like it?"

Amy placed her hand on his cheek. "There is no one I want to experience this with but you."

Anthony smiled, back to his confident self. He slid his hand down her stomach to her brand-new neon pink lace panties she had worn for this special occasion. Moving them aside, he slid in a finger. Amy rocked with his hand. She moaned. He covered her mouth, shushing her laughing. "You'll wake them up," he smiled.

Amy kissed his hand and rolled out from under him. Amy took her clothes off as Anthony watched. Amy knelt and helped him out of his. They held hands, kneeling face to face in the candlelight, Toto singing quietly about Africa in the background. "Ready?" Anthony asked.

Amy nodded. Anthony laid her on her back. She suddenly remembered it hurts the first time and mildly panicked. But before she could react, Anthony slid himself inside. "Oh!" Amy said, startled.

Anthony stopped. "Are you ok?" he said, concerned.

Amy smiled, "Yea. Don't stop."

They fumbled through their first encounter, smiling and learning each other's bodies until Anthony came. Anthony collapsed on her. Amy smiled, running her hand up and down his freshly-shaved head. He felt like a teddy bear.

"You didn't get there," he said, disappointed.

"It's ok," Amy smiled, "we can try again tomorrow."

Anthony smiled and kissed her forehead. They then sat up and realized their folly. "Oh. My. God," Anthony stuttered.

The blanket they had laid on was covered in blood. They sat in scared silence for a beat. Rushing quickly, Anthony grabbed a towel from the bathroom. Amy began to wipe her legs down and started to laugh. Anthony hushed her as he rolled the blanket up and stuffed it into his bookbag. "What are you going to do with it?" Amy asked, not able to control her laughter.

"I'm going to burn it in our fire pit," Anthony hushed her again.

"That's my mom's favorite throw," Amy whispered.

Anthony smiled, his perfect white teeth gleaming. Amy melted every time she looked at him. His tanned skin. His dark hair and big brown eyes with sweeping eyelashes. She'd love him forever.

"Not anymore," he grinned.

Marie broke her reverie. "The lights are getting far away mom," Marie said, trying to hide her panic.

"There's a current, hun," Sara said, "it's pulling us south at about a centimeter per second."

"Oh, God," Amy said, "it'll pull us to sea."

Marie kicked Amy, "The sea is like thousands of miles away dummy."

"This is nothing. In the winter, the current increases twenty-fold," Sara said.

"How do you know all this stuff?" Marie asked huffing with exertion.

"I grew up here," Sara answered.

They kicked in silence, only the sounds of their breath filling the air. "I'm really cold, mom," Marie said finally, "and tired."

Sara started to rub her shoulder with one free arm. "Let's tell stories," Sara said quickly, "how about the day you were born?"

Amy smiled. She loved that one. Mostly, because it embarrassed the hell out of Marie. But to her surprise, Marie said, "Yea, tell that one."

Amy heard Marie's teeth start to chatter and her heart sank. "Yea, mom tell that one," Amy said loudly and started to rub Marie's other shoulder.

"I wanted your birthday to be June 26th so that way you'd be six twenty-six because your sister is seven twenty-seven," Sara started. "You must have heard because you made your debut at 12:46 am."

"And I didn't cry right away, right?" Marie added.

"Nope," Sara continued, "the midwife was worried, though she tried not to let on. They started by rubbing you harder, then I saw her gently pinch your butt, which got you going, and you started to quietly cry."

Amy smiled to herself. She had heard this story so many times that she could have recited it as though it had happened to her personally. *That pinch must have unplugged your little booty*, her thoughts began the story again.

"That pinch must have unplugged your little booty," Sara said, "because you started to poop on me. The midwife rushed to grab some towels to try to wipe us off. But you just didn't stop. And this isn't like a grown man's poop. This is the newborn black tar stuff that doesn't smell but stains and sticks to everything."

Marie laughed. *Good*, Amy thought, *stay awake sister*.

"That poor woman went through every towel in the birth center. You were so past your due date, you had two weeks of newborn poop diapers explode on me in fifteen minutes."

"Sorry, mom," Marie laughed.

"You still hold the record at that birth center for the largest baby born there," Sara concluded, "nine pounds three ounces."

"I still can't believe you delivered us all without drugs," Amy added.

"Well after your Buddha baby sister," Sara said, "I knew my body was done making babies."

"Or," Marie said, "after me, why try to improve on perfection?"

Amy and Sara laughed.

Amy leaned to look up. It was so dark, the sky lit up like a Christmas tree. It was then Amy saw the arcing green waves in the sky. It was so beautiful it almost distracted from the tightening of her muscles and aching joints. They had to be getting close. They had been swimming for what seemed like hours. Amy could just make out the tops of trees.

We have got to be getting closer.

Amy suddenly felt a warm rush on her torso. "Oh, yes," Amy said, "warm pocket."

Sara looked at her daughter, "That's impossible. It's over eighty feet deep."

Marie burst out laughing. Then Sara started laughing. "What?" Amy yelled not understanding.

"Never have I ever been Marie's toilet," Sara said sarcastically, gasping between laughs.

Amy sat puzzled until it came to her. "You're disgusting, Marie," Amy said punching her with her free arm.

"But you're warm," Marie laughed.

Amy was warmer she admitted to herself, begrudgingly. "Scuba divers often pee in their wet suits when getting into cold water," Marie said, with a smirk.

"Fine. That's how we're going to play this," Amy said emptying her bladder.

Marie moaned in pleasure. "What is wrong with you, freak?" Amy yelled.

They all laughed and enjoyed their newly-found warmth. "This is a weird day," Marie said.

"I love you girls," Sara said.

"Love you," both girls said together.

Their statement was cut short by the sound of an engine. "Mom," Marie panicked, "is it them?"

They all stopped kicking and looked at the boat which was about a half-mile away. The boat threw its emergency lights on when it approached Medea. An announcement came from the deck, "This is the United States Grays. Please come to the deck with your hands up."

"Kick girls," Sara whispered, "if they search the area, they will find us."

The women began to kick madly beneath the water, trying to not make any sound. Amy looked back at the boat and could make out people boarding. They shined their flashlights about, and she could imagine them discovering the gruesome scene. She imagined them trying to deduce what had happened. Was the blood from the dodgers or Judas Doyle?

Amy's foot grazed something and she stifled a scream. "Shhh," Sara said, "sound travels faster on water."

"My foot just touched something," Amy whispered.

They kept kicking. "Oh," her mom exclaimed, "mine just did too. I think we're almost here."

The ground began to rise to their feet and before the MPs had even left Medea. Amy sunk to her knees when they got on the shore. She flipped over and laid on her back, looking at the sky. Sara knelt beside her. "I know you're tired," Sara said sitting her up, "but we aren't safe yet."

Amy saw Marie opening the dry bag. She dried off quickly and threw the towel to her mom. Her mother started drying her body off and Marie put her clothes back on, quietly moaning. "Oh, dry clothes feel so good," she said in bliss.

"Amy," her mom begged, "you have to get up."

Amy looked out at the Medea and didn't see the MP boat. Her eyes searched the waterline and saw the boat doing passes back and forth with a searchlight. The world was completely silent. This was weird because she could see her mother moving her lips when she got close and the boat must have had an engine. Her heart was beating out of her chest, and she wanted to lay down and go to sleep. Hands tried to pull her up from the sand. *Thump thump thump*, her heart echoed in her ears.

Amy tried to stand and her legs gave out. Familiar hands took off her life jacket. Tears ran down her face, and Amy's teeth chattered. Suddenly, she felt a warm towel drying her off. Marie threw the towel on the raft and sat Amy down on the towel. Amy couldn't take her eyes off the boat passing closer and closer to shore. She was frozen. Panic and hypothermia had rendered her useless. They were all going to die.

Amy felt her leg lift and watched Marie and her mom slide her underwear up her legs. "You have to help us, Amy," Marie said so kindly Amy couldn't believe it had come from her sister.

Amy tried her legs again and stepped on a sharp rock. The pain was like smelling salts to her system. "I'm ok. I'm ok," she repeated, grabbing her shorts and pulling them up.

Marie and her mother's face showed relief, and they went to grab the other items. Amy finished putting on her clothes, "What do we do now?"

Sara grabbed the bag of food and threw the dry bag at Marie. "Grab the raft and connect it to our life vests," she ordered, "we need to drag it into the woods with us."

They stepped off the shore into the woods off the southern coast of Lake Superior. Only after climbing the hill to a safe distance did Amy dare look back. The MP boat lights were sweeping the shore where they had been sitting. The women picked up their pace deeper into the woods and towards their mother's unknown plan.

CHAPTER SIX

It was a moonlit, warm night for northern Michigan. But the cold swim had chilled them all to the bone. They had walked for what had seemed forever, taking turns dragging the life vest raft and carrying the bags. They also took turns tripping on anything and everything on the ground. "How much farther?" Amy whined.

"When we get to Shelldrake River," Sara answered.

They had passed several cabins on the shore crossing over a road. Most of the cabins had been burned. Marie suggested they take shelter in one until morning. Sara knew that was too risky. Dan had told her about the vacation homes on the shore being run through by Grays looking for deserters and people trying to hide. Several small battles had been waged by innocent people not wanting to be part of the fight or looking to flee. The people who had the idea to flee in the beginning were now long gone. The people who had the idea too late were also long gone. Luckily, It had been years since the border battles, and they were all one with the earth in one way or the other.

Sara was getting delirious with exhaustion and hunger. By Sara's estimate, they had traveled about an hour; therefore they were about two miles from the shore. They had to be getting close. The conversation between her daughters got her attention. They seemed to be chatting pleasantly enough. *Small miracle.*

They needed water. "I'm so thirsty," Amy echoed Sara's thoughts.

"I'm *so* thirsty," Marie mocked, "we're all thirsty Amy, god."

"Shut up, Marie," Amy snapped, "you have more fat to store fluids than I do."

"Don't blame me, tiny tits," Marie shot back.

There went that.

"Girls," Sara chided, "the last thing we need is..."

Sara paused. "Water," Sara whispered.

"The first thing we need is water, mother," Amy said.

"No, listen," Sara hushed, "I hear water."

They all fell silent and heard a faint trickle like a leaking faucet.

"We made it!" Marie shrieked and took off running toward the sound.

Sara and Amy followed suit. Within one minute, they were all on their hands and knees at the side of the Shelldrake River, drinking in big gulps. "I think I just swallowed a pebble," Amy coughed, laughing.

"This is the best water I've ever had," Marie moaned.

"OK, girls," Sara stood up and walked to a large maple tree, "we'll set up camp here and get our bearings in the morning."

Amy sighed as she slumped to the ground on the raft. "We need to make a fire and warm up," Sara continued, "then well grab some food."

Sara went into the woods to gather some sticks and twigs to start a fire. She bit her lip. The current had pushed them. But how far? Sara shook her head. No use worrying about it now. They would know in the morning.

When Sara got back, she was pleased to see the girls had started unloading and making food. Sara moved away pine needles and leaves from the ground to create a dirt patch and began stacking up the wood for the fire. She deftly placed the kindling under the tented sticks and logs, then placed dried pine needles and grass inside. One match lit the fire, and the women all gathered round, warming their hands. Marie passed the can of beans to her Mother. "Thank god for pull tabs," she chuckled, "am I right, mom?"

Sara smiled and dumped some of the beans in her mouth. She chewed thoughtfully. This was nice.

Was she insane? *Nice?*

But something about having her girls with her in the middle of the woods. Woods she knew intimately. Woods she could draw a map of from memory. The danger was, at least for now, a safe distance away until daylight. They were hydrated, warm, and fed. She wanted to stop time. Shifting her eyes to Amy, she noticed her pouting. "What's wrong?"

"It has pork in it," Amy said, crossing her arms stubbornly.

"Oh for fuck sake, Amy," Marie crowed.

Holding a finger to Marie to shut it, Sara said, "This one time would be ok, Amy."

Amy shook her head and grabbed the crackers and began crunching. Sara sighed and passed the can back to Marie. Marie was staring at her. She looked so much like Dan with her hair slicked back, it was like looking at an old picture of him. "What?" Sara asked with a laugh.

"How do you know all this stuff, mom?" Marie asked.

"I dunno. Girl Scouts. Your grandpa," Sara waved it off.

"No way," Marie kept at her, "you knew the names of the townies out here. The currents, the water depth, and temperature. Doyle knew your dad. I thought you grew up downstate."

Sara moved her gaze to Amy who was looking blankly into the fire. "No more secrets, mom," Marie said, "we need to know what is going on. What's the plan?"

Setting the can down, Sara rubbed her face roughly. She took a deep breath. "I was raised here. I moved downstate when I was seventeen. My dad has a cabin up here. Well, it's actually mine. It was left to me after he died."

"So, we're going to your dad's old cabin," Marie gathered. "How far are we?"

Sara looked over at Amy chewing her lip. *She knows something is off.*

"I won't know until morning," Sara answered, "and it was my dad who taught me how to live off the land."

Marie sat thoughtfully and grabbed a handful of saltines from the box at Amy's feet.

"Mom," Amy said after being silent for a while, "what did Doyle mean when he called me an inbred?"

Marie's eyes darted back and forth between her sister and Sara. At this, Sara locked her eyes on the ground. She had hoped so deeply that Doyle's jab at her and her first child went unnoticed.

"Mom?" Amy asked again.

"Amy," Sara started, "I don't want to do this now. We need to keep our wits..."

"Is dad my real dad?" Amy interrupted.

Sara's chest ached. She knew this day would come. But she couldn't have imagined it would be here. Hundreds of miles away from their home in the middle of the woods fleeing execution in the worst war ever fought.

"Mom," Amy said quietly.

"No."

Amy got up and marched into the woods. Marie stopped eating and set the crackers down. "This has been a real shitty vacation, mom," Marie joked.

Humor. Aside from rage, Marie's favorite coping mechanism. Sara was stoically staring into the fire. A tear ran down her cheek just like the night she had met Dan. "Mom," Marie said gently, "are you ok?"

Every year her Father's family got together for a barbeque reunion of sorts. They'd rent a picnic area and camp at a state park in Timberlost. She was sixteen and had just gotten her first bikini. It was a pair of yellow boy shorts and triangles for the top. Sara had her hair in two pigtail buns on top of her head. She was sporting her strawberry Lipsmackers and greased up with Sweet Pea lotion.

Her trip to Sault Ste. Marie the week before was like a dream come true. She had saved for months to get some super trendy clothes from 5-7-9 and accessories to knock boys dead and make all the girls jealous. 6R Clairol Red had turned her brown hair into a vibrant color. Semi-permeant of course, because her dad wouldn't allow anything that didn't wash out. This trip was her trial round for her new look. She and her dad showed up that Friday and Sara was the object of everyone's ooh's and ahh's. Mission accomplished.

Sara laid out on the dock the next day soaking up the coveted northern Michigan sun. She heard footsteps and was suddenly cast in shadow. She sat up covering her eyes and saw her dad's cousin's kid, Rodney. "Hey asshat," Sara groaned, "you're in my light."

"Like you're gonna get a tan anyhow," Rodney joked, "you're like a fucking vampire."

"Then how am I out in the sun?" Sara said.

"Yea well," Rodney racked his brain for a comeback.

"Tell you what," Sara mocked, "when you think of something, let me know."

Rodney rolled his eyes, "Dinner's ready. Your dad wanted me to come and get ya."

Sara stretched, adjusted her bikini top, and grabbed her towel. She trotted to catch up with her cousin. "So what're the plans for tonight?" Sara asked.

Sara caught Rodney looking at her chest. Gross, Sara thought, boys are all the same. Pathetic.

"Well when the adults start getting drunk around the campfire," he stated, "we'll all be getting drunk in the middle of the woods."

"Sweet," Sara smiled.

Her cousins were a hoot. And while most of them lived relatively close to one another, they didn't get to let loose and hang out like this but once a year. Sara changed out of her swimsuit and put on her jean skirt and baby doll tee. It was blue and said "Angel Baby" on the front. She tossed her hair in a messy bun and sprayed herself down with bug spray. The adults were already drinking around the fire.

Her dad and Doyle were arguing about topics they agreed upon.

"Hipple needs to be out there every game," her dad continued, "If they do that, this is the Lion's year."

"They're just not going to win, Eddie, with Danielson in every game," Doyle shot back, "and we haven't seen a team like this since we were kids."

"But we need a QB that'll," her dad noticed Sara standing there, "hey snugs, what's up?"

Her dad tugged her shirt down to cover her belly. Batting his hand away, she gave him a dirty look. "Kid's bonfire," Sara answered, "out by the old marina."

"Ok," her dad said, "be back by ten. We are going floating early tomorrow."

Sara waved in agreeance as she trotted off to the marina. Floating was a Michigan pastime in which you sit in a half-deflated inner tube and sail down a slow-moving river and try not to drown. Small towns are quite resourceful when it comes to entertainment. When she got to the festivities, they were already off to a loud start. Someone had a boom box playing Barenaked Ladies. Some locals, not that there were many, had come out too. Being from a small town meant anytime tourists, or Fudgies as they were so aptly named, came up for the summer, hook-ups were abundant. Sara saw a cute brown-haired boy on the other side of the fire looking at her. Sara smiled back. Suddenly, someone put a cold bottle on her bare back. Sara squealed.

Rodney laughed as he handed her a bottle of Zima. "You asshole," Sara laughed and took the bottle, "quite a showing this year. All the locals came out."

Taking a long swig, Sara saw a few familiar faces from the years before. She waved at a girl she hung out with last year but couldn't remember her name.

"Hey sweetie," another girl said, drunkenly hanging off of an older guy's arm, "jello shot?"

Sara took one and threw it back. The lime favoring was barely tasted over the cheap plastic bottle vodka.

"Oh my God," the girl shrieked as N'Sync came on the radio, "I fucking love this song."

The girl grabbed Sara's hand and led her to the boom box and started dancing. Sara laughed and joined in. Halfway through her

Zima and not even to the chorus of Bye Bye Bye, Sara started to feel drunk. Rodney handed her another Zima. "Come on lightweight," he urged her, "keep up."

Sara could barely stay on her feet when her favorite song came on – The Sign by Ace of Base. The crowd groaned as she began swaying to the ballad.

Sara took her hair down and raised her arms to the stars. She felt invincible. She felt sexy. Sara felt hands slide up on her hips. She looked over her shoulder and saw a brown-haired boy dancing with her. She smiled and kept moving. Other people started dancing too. Those unlucky souls who hadn't paired off sat and watched. Sara noticed her cousin watching her. Rodney was swaying too. Although his lack of rhythm came from far too many Natty Lites.

The next song started and before she could even recognize what it was someone pulled her hair and screamed. The ground came up to her face as Sara was being dragged by an unknown assailant. People started yelling and there was commotion all around her. "Let her go, Shawna," the brown-haired boy yelled, trying to untangle the ninja bitch from Sara's hair.

Sara began to swing wildly at the body in front of her screaming, "You fucking slut! That's my boyfriend."

The blind punches and the commotion of people trying to free her hair ended as quickly as it started. And as suddenly as she had been in a scuffle, Sara was now on her ass looking up at the brown-haired boy and the ninja bitch fighting with each other. "Shawna" kept trying to hit him and her friends were trying to tear her away, issuing such reassurances as, "He's not worth it," and "Fuck him, Shawna, let's go."

Shawna took one last look at Sara and said, "You better watch your ass, bitch."

She took off running towards the parking lot, "I'm gonna key the fuck out of your truck, Tommy."

"Shawna, no!" brown-haired Tommy yelled, chasing after her.

He turned briefly to Sara, "I'll be right back. I'm so sorry."

Sara watched "Tommy" chase after her assailant. She then noticed everyone staring at her. Some of the locals were laughing. Others looked at her with pity. She hated that. She hated it when people viewed her as weak and unable. "Yea, well," Sara yelled, "fuck you too. Shawna."

Sara walked over to an unguarded plastic bottle of vodka and took a swig. "Let's get fucked up," Sara said to Rodney.

He smiled, "Don't have to ask me twice."

Sara used her recklessness as a shield for the utter humiliation she felt. She drank, cussed, danced, and picked fights with anyone in her sightline.

When another cousin named Emily tried to pick her up off the ground for the tenth time, Sara spewed, "Get off of me cow!"

Emily's eyes filled will tears as some nearby kids started to snicker. Rodney slurred, "Why don't you go find some water for her and I'll find a place for her to lay down."

Rodney hoisted Sara up and they walked to an outbuilding at the end of the marina. He wiggled the latch and slid the door open, revealing canoes, oars, and life jackets. The movement of him jiggling the door open made her nauseated. The world was spinning. The world was winking in and out.

Rodney propped her up on the wall and pulled a bunch of jackets down and laid her on them.

Sara collapsed on the jackets and smelled the plastic mixed with light mildew. She must have passed out because one cannot wake if one has not slept. She felt tugging on her legs. I'm going to throw up, she thought and she blacked out again.

The loud screeching of metal on metal brought Sara a bit more into consciousness. She still felt her head being jammed again and again on a wall. "Oh my god, Rodney!" Emily screamed.

Sara's head came to a stop, and her cheek felt like the Indian burns her friends would give her on the playground. Sara was able to turn her head at precisely the wrong moment. Just in time to see an audience of teenagers, Tommy included, with looks of mockery and horror. They saw me puke, she thought but didn't remember doing it.

"Get off of her!" Emily screamed again.

The sound made Sara's head want to split in two. She was about to tell Emily to shut the fuck up when she felt a weight lift off her and felt a warm sensation down her leg. She looked up to see an embarrassed Rodney put his penis back in his pants. Just before he *zipped them, he gave her a mournful look and ran out of the shed.*

A familiar shriek came from the teens, "Holy shit, Tommy," Shawna crowed, "your new girlfriend just fucked her cousin."

Shawna and a few of her friends began to laugh. Emily rushed to Sara's side, pulling her panties up and her skirt down. Emily pulled Sara to stand and started walking away from the crowd.

"She'd rather fuck her cousin than you," Shawna laughed at Tommy, "way to pick em, loser."

Sara's eyes met Tommy's as she walked away. He gave her a dirty look and walked in the opposite direction. "It's ok," Emily said, "let's get you back to the campground."

Sara took a deep breath and looked at Marie after finishing her story. She was terrified to see Marie's reaction to this reality. This long-held secret of shame. The fire licked upwards at the sky; it glowed Marie's features a beautiful orange. She looked like a sculpture. A sad, heartbroken piece of art.

"So, the next morning I woke up," Sara finished, "and the entire campground knew. Felt like half of the state knew. Rodney and his family had already left, and I never talked to him again. And about fifteen years ago, I heard he was killed in a car wreck. So, there was that."

Sara wrung her hands. "My father barely spoke to me that day when we drove home," Sara continued with a sob, "He was disgusted with me. I knew that it was my fault."

"Oh mom," Marie said, staring blankly at the fire.

"My dad kept saying he wasn't feeling well," Sara said, "we were unloading our equipment, and he fell. I thought he had just tripped or something. But he…it was a massive heart attack."

Marie's hand went to her mouth, and she looked out at the forest, choking back a sob.

"The doctors told me he was dead before he hit the ground," Sara began chewing her lip.

Sara took a deep breath and rubbed her arms. "So, I went to live with your Aunt Emily and her parents in

Milford, downstate. They moved there when we were in the 5th grade, but she and I always stayed close. They were the only people who would take me in. And within two weeks, I met your dad."

"Did dad know?" Marie asked.

Sara nodded.

She recalled when she had figured out the ongoing food poisoning wasn't rotten Big Boy's burgers. Sara sat on the floor of her Aunt's master bathroom and looked at the stick for at least an hour. She was about four months along. And she and Dan were deep in a teenage love affair less than a month strong. It was fast and hard. Dan made her feel safe and cherished. So, when she broke the news to him that she was pregnant and by whom, his reaction shocked her stupid. Dan had thrown her against the wall of his basement bedroom. He called her every name he could think of and then slapped her.

Sara sat on the floor, crying and ashamed with a fat lip, as Dan stormed up the stairs and slammed the door. About a half-hour later, Dan came down the stairs and kneeled in front of her. "I'm so sorry, baby," Dan began, scooping her up in his arms, "and I can't stand the thought of another man's baby in my girl."

Dan lightly ran his fingers across Sara's busted lip. "I love you," he said, "who knows?"

"No one," Sara lied.

"Let's get married," Dan asked, "We'll tell everyone it's mine."

Sara's back ached from where she hit the wall. And her eyes were swollen from crying, and she tasted blood. But through watering eyes, she saw her knight in shining armor. The one who was going to make everything better, and for the first time she felt safe. So at seventeen, she became a mother and a bride.

"I realize now," Sara said finishing her story, "that was the first time I had willingly handed over my dignity."

Sara felt bile climb up her throat. Marie stood suddenly

and sat next to her. Wrapping her arms around her mom, they sat there for a long while. Then Marie got up and walked into the woods.

~

Marie was furious. How could anyone let those things happen to them? Not so much the rape, but the abuse from another person. She felt so conflicted. She loved her dad, idolized him. But why on earth did she feel that way? Marie had personally witnessed his behavior towards her mother. And while she hated it when it was happening, she just as easily slipped back into day-to-day life after they had made up. Pretending to ignore the long sleeves her mother wore or the abundance of eye makeup she would apply now made her feel so ashamed. And after all the things her father had done to her mother, the smallest glimpse of his love towards Marie made her melt.

She hadn't walked very far when she saw Amy sitting at the base of a large tree. "If you came to give me any shit, so help me…" Amy said between sniffs.

Marie slid down the trunk to sit next to her sister and wrapped her arms around her. Amy, startled by the rare affection, froze. Slowly, Amy's arms slid up to hug Marie back. Marie couldn't recall the last time she had hugged Amy.

Amy was the beauty with all the friends, who had higher aspirations to help the world. She didn't get amazing grades but she didn't need them. The most popular guy in town was her boyfriend. Amy was fit and vegan and everything Marie pretended to hate. As a child, Marie wanted to be just like her. Until one day, a teacher who'd had her older siblings in the years before said, "Freddie is the smart one, and Amy is beauty. So, what does that make you?"

Marie was so embarrassed. All the kids were looking at her, waiting for a reply. It was in that moment she wanted to be nothing like either of them. Marie realized she could never be brilliant like Freddie, and she certainly wasn't beautiful. So, she'd be tough. She'd be strong.

"This is awful," Marie whispered.

Amy began to cry harder. "How could she do this, Marie," Amy said, "what are we doing out here with a mother like that? We need to go home."

Marie sat back and wiped Amy's cheeks. "You're wrong," Marie said.

Marie leaned back on the tree and retold her mother's story. She kept in every detail, so Amy wouldn't be in the dark anymore. Amy didn't interrupt or ask questions; she just listened.

After Marie finished, she reached over and grabbed Amy's cold sweaty hand. It was shaking uncontrollably. "Come on," Marie said, pulling Amy to stand, "let's go back."

Amy wiped her nose and then her hands on her pants. "Ok."

~

Amy emerged from the woods to see her mom in the firelight. Weeping hard yet silently, she hadn't noticed them walk up. Amy felt her heart drop. Her mother had learned to do this. No one cried so void of sound. "Mom," Amy said quietly.

Sara looked up startled and wiped her eyes quickly. Amy was shocked at how quickly she could snap into a mode of perfect normalcy. Again, learned. Sara stood, and Amy walked to her and wrapped her in a hug. Marie sat next to the fire and wrapped her arms around herself. "I'm so sorry," Sara chocked back a sob, burying her head into Amy's shoulder.

Amy backed up and grabbed her mom by the shoulders, looking deep in her eyes. Looking back at her, like a mirror, her mother looked so afraid. They looked so similar and were so close in age, they could be sisters. "No," Amy said with such solidarity even Marie looked up, "You are done being sorry. None of this is your fault."

Sara stared at her daughter. "I'm really tired," said Amy, suddenly feeling the weight of the day.

It felt like ages ago that they had boarded creepy Doyle's rape vessel. Marie sighed and brushed her pants off and walked to the mound of life jackets. Amy followed her and looked back at her mom, "Aren't you coming?"

"Someone has to stay awake just in case," Sara answered, "I'll take first shift."

"Ok," Amy yawned, too tired to argue.

Amy curled up behind Marie and snuggled her. Marie wrapped her arms around Amy's.

.

CHAPTER SEVEN

The moon was high in the sky, lighting up the forest like a stage. Everything felt silver and mystical. Sara had no reason to feel at peace and safe. Yet there she sat, happy, content, and feeling free for the first time since her encounter with Rodney. *So ironic and bizarre.*

She looked over at the heap of life preservers and daughters. She smiled. They still slept like they did when they were kids. Amy was on her back with her arms curled up like a T-Rex. She looked as though she was faking it and would spring to life if you got too close. Now her sweet baby Marie was on her side with a jacket in between her legs. As a child, she would use her stuffed dinosaur, Little Foot. She took that thing everywhere, Sara reflected. It was so stained no matter how many times she washed the thing. It looked like it had leprosy. Marie would talk to it when she thought no one was watching. One time, she heard Marie talking to Little Foot, and Sara stood outside the door to listen. "Look what you did," Marie yelled at Little Foot, "you spilled your food!"

Sara's heart began to throb painfully in her chest. "You are so stupid!" Marie yelled and threw the dinosaur across the room.

Sara entered and scooped Marie up in her arms and cried. "I'm sorry, mommy," Marie said petting her hair, "I won't play that game again."

Sara blinked hard at the memory. Why had it taken so long? Why did she allow herself to be treated that way? Why did she subject her children to it? She knew why. Fear. Fear of being alone. Fear of making it on her own. Fear of what Dan would do to her.

But sitting there she was a new person. Sara felt it in her veins. She looked back at who she was only a few days ago, and it was as though she was reflecting on a story she had read or gossip of someone in town. Certainly, not her. Not she who had fled with her daughters to escape Dan and the draft. Not the woman who took a life to save their own. Not the woman who was going to get them to her cabin and then regroup. Regroup to figure a way out. A place for a new life.

Sara sat up taller and took a swig of water. She munched happily on a cracker, too excited to sleep.

~

Sara watched the girls stir as the sun was hinting at its arrival. The air was crisp even though it was late summer. Amy and Marie groaned from the uncomfortable bed. Amy stretched and slapped Marie in the face. "Ow," Marie yelped, "move over."

"You move over," Amy sat up looking around.

Her hair was sticking up with twigs in it. Sara giggled. Amy looked around, not remembering where she was. Then she locked eyes with Sara. Sara saw the light of understanding blink on. Marie groaned and grabbed the towel they used as a blanket and rolled over.

"Good morning," Sara said quietly.

Amy yawned, got up, and sat next to her mom. Amy laid her head on Sara's shoulder, taking a big breath.

The birds were singing to them. Maybe they remembered her from the stories their grandbirdies had passed down.

There once was a human named Sara,
Whose singing sure would've scared ya.
But she'd feed us each day.
Kept predators away.

Damn, Sara couldn't think of another word that rhymed with Sara.

Sara felt drops hitting her shoulder. Amy was weeping. "Baby," Sara said, turning Amy to face her, "what is it? I mean I know it's everything, but what can I do?"

Amy was now sobbing uncontrollably. The sound made Marie sit up. She rubbed her eyes and saw her sister. Marie looked down with a sadness Sara didn't think possible.

"It is everything," Amy agreed, "I'm not dad's. We killed a guy last night. I'm wet and tired, and I smell really bad."

Marie stood up and sat on the other side of Amy. "I want to go home," Amy continued, "but I know that doesn't exist anymore. I just want things back to normal. But then I guess your normal was horrible which makes me feel even worse. I miss Anthony and…and…I started my period."

They all sat for a moment in silence. Then they all burst into laughter. They laughed until they cried, then Marie choked on her snot, and then they laughed again. Sara untangled herself from her daughters and grabbed the towel. With a knife she took from the boat, she cut a piece off. She handed it to Amy, "I give you the origin of the phrase: the rag."

Marie grinned, and Amy made a face. She took the rag and went to find a distant tree. "When you get back," Sara said to Amy, "I'm going to tell you both the plan."

Sara watched Amy walk away and then started to pick up their supplies. Marie followed suit. "Should we leave the life vests here?" Marie asked.

"I think so," Sara said, "if they come looking for us, this isn't going to give them a good indication of which way we went."

"Which way are we going?" Amy asked as she walked back to camp.

Sara divvied up the crackers between them, making sure the girls got two more than she. The girls munched away while she laid out the next day.

"I grew up in a cabin with my dad a few miles from here," Sara started, "We follow this river until we come to a bend. I'm not sure how far the bend is, but I know it's going to take half the day to walk to it. Then we use the sun as a compass about one mile northwest to the cabin."

"When's the last time you were there, mom?" Marie said through chewed cracker dust.

"I was sixteen, but I would map search it from time to time," Sara answered.

"Are you sure it's still there?" Amy asked.

Sara took a deep breath, "No. But I am the one on the deed. My dad left it to me. And I feel like if anything had happened to it, I would've been notified."

The girls looked at each other.

"Ok," Sara said, "plan B is if the cabin isn't there, we'll know by tonight. We have enough food to get us through until tomorrow morning. Then we can walk into town and figure out something else. But we have to be careful that no one recognizes us. I don't see how they would because I don't seem to know anyone there anymore. Well except Doyle."

They all got very quiet. "We met those people at the diner," Amy said suddenly.

"I'm sure the whole town knows something is up," Sara continued, "so let's just hope we don't need plan B."

Marie nodded saying, "Over the river and through the woods…"

Amy took her mom's hand. "To grandpa's house we go," she said, and they began to walk north towards the unknown.

CHAPTER EIGHT

It was such a drastic difference from the night when they were swimming in freezing waters to now sweating, traversing the river's edge towards Pa's cabin. The girls had taken to calling the grandfather they never met "Pa" during their hike. Grandpa was a mouthful between gasps of exhausted breath, so Pa it was. Sara kept a watchful eye on their location and the sounds of anything mechanical to notify them of danger. But from time to time, she would peek a glance at her daughters walking side by side and chatting. Marie's blonde hair was sticking up and dirty. Poor Amy's waves were turning into dreadlocks and she had so much foliage in it a gardener would be impressed. Sara prayed the cabin would still be standing. The girls asked some questions about their Pa and what the cabin was like. Sara answered honestly. "He was the best man I've ever known," Sara said. "He looked just like me but taller. He would've been to the moon over you kids."

Now they were all silent, listening to the river waters and wildlife. Sara knew them all by heart. The warbler and wren would call, the tapping of a woodpecker busy with his daily chores. Light shined through the pines and made the forest magical. The smell of sap and rich dirt was the tale of her childhood, and the story made her heart swell. It was then she saw it. The hard western break in the river that made a loop and flowed back. The distance between the river's edges was barely thirty feet. How many times had she played in this river loop? How many forts had she built in the large oak tree at the top of the hill she now stood in front of? The old oak was bigger but as familiar as her own hands. A smile broke on Sara's face. Amy and Marie flanked her. "Are we here?" Marie asked.

Sara nodded. She looked northwest to where her childhood home sat only a mile from this bank. Smoke rose from the treetops. Her heart sank. "What is it?" Amy said noticing her change.

"We are going to walk up the back way," Sara began, "there are huge blueberry bushes about fifty feet from the house. You'll hide there while I check the place out, ok?"

Amy let out a big breath, and Marie nodded. Her girls needed rest and safety. And god help whoever was in her home. Sara drew the gun and began up the hill.

~

No one spoke as they approached the stone cabin. It was just as Sara remembered. The front porch was held up by large stone pillars. The Adirondack chairs her dad built were sitting on the porch. Albeit a little worn, they were still in one piece. Off to the wooded edge of the property, two deer hung from a tree waiting to be butchered. And to her surprise, her childhood vegetable garden was tended to and had large tomatoes growing on large vines. The wooden sides had been repaired and peeking from the edges were squash blossoms and heads of young cabbage. Sara's eyes went skyward to the large stone chimney on the side of the house. It released puffs of smoke like an enormous pipe.

Sara motioned for the girls to follow her to the large bushes. They all crouched down, and Sara handed Marie the gun. "You pull back the hammer like this," Sara showed them, "line your sight, exhale, and then pull the trigger."

Marie nodded; her face was surprisingly calm. Amy, however, was shaking like they were back in the lake. "If anything happens to me," Sara said, "wait until you are sure it's safe and then run into town. Call Aunt Emily."

The girls nodded solemnly. Sara got up, and Marie grabbed her arm, "Please come back."

Sara smiled. "I will sweetheart. It's just in case."

I hope.

With that, Sara walked along the bushes and backtracked to come at the cabin from the side. She slid from tree to tree, bush to bush, to get under the window of the kitchen. Sara pulled out Doyle's pocket knife. It wasn't much, but at least she'd have something to protect herself.

Sara took a deep breath, pushing her hair out of her eyes, and raised herself up on her toes. She came face to face with a young man washing dishes in her sink. He screamed. Sara screamed, and she took off running the way she came. Sara heard the door rock open. She looked back long enough to see the man holding her father's shotgun. "Hey! Wait!"

When she turned back around, she slammed into a tree trunk. Her brain rattled in her head. She saw black stars. When her eyes focused, she saw the man only twenty feet from her taking her in. He began to raise the gun. "Don't you fucking move!" Marie's voice boomed from behind him.

The man jumped and dropped the gun. Sara rolled on her stomach, trying to get up on her knees. She saw Marie stalking towards the man with the gun drawn. Amy was behind her with a large stick raised like a club. Sara gathered her wits and ran to get her dad's gun and pointed it at the man. His dark curly hair looped around his ears. "Get on the ground," Sara ordered.

"Please don't shoot," he begged, muffled by the dirt he was now face-down in.

"Who are you," Sara asked, "and why are you in my house?"

"I didn't know it was your house," he said pleading, "I needed a place to stay, and I found the cabin about six months ago."

Amy peeked out from behind Marie, and Sara saw the man look up. They locked eyes, and Amy quickly looked away. "Listen," he started again, "I didn't mean to scare you. Please... I didn't think anyone lived here."

Sara couldn't exactly blame him. No one had lived there for twenty years. And she had to admit, the house looked very well-kept. "Get up," Sara motioned with her gun, "sit down. What's your name?"

The man sat down on the dirt and rubbed his face with his hands. "Brian."

Sara saw tears brimming in his dark blue eyes. He didn't look like a murderer. His big eyes were framed with dark thick lashes. He was tall, almost a foot taller than Sara. But he was very thin. "You can't stay here," Sara said flatly.

The man nodded his head vigorously. "You can get your things," Sara said, "and by your things, I mean not my things. And then you have to go. I don't want to catch you here again."

The sound of tires crunching up the distant road made all of their heads snap to attention. The man shot to his feet. "MP's," Brian whispered.

"Mom, we have to hide," Marie said urgently.

Sara slung the gun over her shoulder and grabbed her girl's hands. She dragged them to the side of the house and threw open the Bilco doors leading to the dirt subbasement. "Go," Sara ordered.

The man looked bewildered at their reaction as he watched them descend. Sara gave him a look of pure malice. She caught sight of two trucks pulling into the drive as she shut the doors. It was pitch black in the basement, except for a small window made between a few stones. Sara heard doors shutting and males voices exchanging pleasantries. Sara's heart was audible. They were screwed. Nowhere to go. Nowhere to run. She heard Brian speak first. "What do

I owe the pleasure gentlemen?"

Sara knew she shouldn't but hoisted herself up and looked out of the stone hole. "We are looking for some deserters who were possibly involved in a murder," the older one who was clearly in charge stated.

Brian put his hands in his pockets and shrugged. "That's intense."

Sara heard the sound of footsteps approaching the house. Sara slowly cocked the shotgun and aimed it at the Bilco doors. "Hold on," Brian said.

Amy let out a quiet squeak. Marie rushed to her and put her in a tight hug. The front door of the cabin opened and shut. The pounding of his footsteps rang over their heads. A drip of sweat ran down Amy's forehead into her eyes. She quickly wiped it away and took a knee lining up the sights. The front door banged again. "You guys want some deer jerky?" Brian said.

Sara swallowed and looked back out the hole. The MP's all took a bag of meat Brian brought out from the cabin. She saw Brian scratching his head. "Any idea what they looked like?" Then he laughed, "not like I see people out here ever."

Sara's mouth fell open. *He's covering for us.*

"We saw your chimney smoke, and we thought it might have been a campfire," another said, "but we are looking for three females. A mother and two teenage girls."

Brian shrugged. "I haven't seen anyone," he said, "and you think these girls murdered someone?"

The MP shook his head and threw his hands in the air. "We're not too sure," the older man said, "but let's say our informant is missing, eh?"

"But you said the girls are too."

He nodded. "We found life vests tied together a mile from shore. So we're doing a sweep of the area."

Brian whistled. "That's crazy."

Sara pulled her face away from the hole, realizing she had clawed her nails almost off on the dirt wall. "Well, let us know if you see anyone," the man said.

Sounds of their footsteps going back to their trucks reached Sara's ears.

"These deserters have nothing to lose. So keep your wits and a gun about you."

The MP motioned to the deer with clean shots through their hearts. "But looks like you know how to use one. Good on ya."

Sara felt the bile rise in her throat. She was going to be sick. Marie and Amy exhaled together. And as the sound of trucks driving away reached them, the sound of boots walked to the double doors. Brian threw them open and looked down below. "All's clear."

Sara and the girls climbed out of their hiding place. "Why'd you do that?" Amy asked him.

He paused, looking at Amy a moment too long and then looked at Sara. "You seem like good people," Brian smiled with a mouthful of bright white, straight teeth, "plus anyone who can build a perfect Adirondack chair is alright in my books."

~

Brian sat in her father's old chair. Being back in the old cabin was so odd yet comforting. It was all cleaned up and looked like she'd never left. Brian had done well with what he had stumbled upon. So what's your story?" Sara asked.

Marie stood in the kitchen with the handgun in her waistband. Sara had taken to putting her dad's gun back in its place above the fireplace. Brian ran a hand through his dark curls. "I'm Canadian."

The women all looked at each other. "I was down here going to college, and I got stuck," he said flatly, "I lost my passport and getting a new one through the non-existent Canadian embassy was impossible. So I have been making my way north."

"And then what?" Amy startled everyone by speaking

her first words.

Brian stared transfixed at her, breaking the stare quickly but not before Sara noticed. "I'm walking to Canada."

Marie burst out laughing. Brian turned around with big eyes. "What? I am."

"Every port of entry is teeming with MP's," Sara said sadly, not wanting to foil his plan, "and it's a far swim."

"Where's your sandals, Jesus?"

Brian turned towards Marie. "Hilarious," he said with a look, "I do plan to walk on water. Frozen water. The ice will be safe to walk across in January or February."

"Are you nuts?" Marie said loudly.

"Is that possible, mom?" Amy said to Sara.

Sara racked her brain. The lake did freeze solid at the straits in many places. But the weather and winds during that time of year were deadly, and it was at least a twenty-mile walk to the island. Sara took a deep breath. "Well, it's not *impossible*."

"I missed the freeze earlier this year," he began again, looking at Amy, "so I found this place and started selling deer meat for other goods and growing or foraging for food."

"It's not deer season," Sara said staring off, chewing on his idea for escape.

"People aren't policing that right now, ma'am," Brian said, stepping towards Sara, "by the way, what's your name? I already gathered they are Amy and Marie. But I doubt you'd want me to call you mom."

Marie rolled her eyes and Amy smiled, turning towards the fire, warming her hands. "Sara," she answered, "you can call me Sara."

"Well Sara," he said, raising his arms, "I would be most obliged if I could stay here with you all. I have nowhere to go."

"Oh hell no, mom," Marie said putting a hand on the gun.

Sara walked into the kitchen and gently took the gun

from her youngest. Amy turned and looked up at Brian. "I think he should stay," she said, looking at her mom and sister.

"What?" Marie yelled.

"We could've been in his position in Minneapolis if something had happened to our truck, or what if those soldiers had caught up to us in that small town?" Sara said.

Sara looked at Brian. His pleading eyes were wrought with gratitude as he took in Amy. Nothing about this tall, lanky man gave her any feelings of doubt or fear. And it would be nice to have someone who could hunt and help around the cabin. Keeping up a place like that took a lot of work, and her girls had never even hoed a row. Sara took a deep breath and walked to Brian, "You can stay."

Amy smiled at her mom, but Sara had barely time to turn before Marie slammed the front door.

~

Sleeping arrangements were settled. Without provocation, Brian announced he would take the couch. The girls would share the spare bed. Sara took her father's, which Brian had been using. And though Marie was giving all of them the silent treatment, daily routines began. Brian turned out to be an absolute godsend. He cooked, cleaned, and showed them the vegetables and fruits he had canned. He told them Paradise was too far for him to walk, and transporting items on his bike was near-impossible, so he only made the trip when necessary. Not to mention bounty hunters arrested first and asked questions last. So many Americans claimed Canadian citizenship that it was a red flag for the bounties. But with so few soldiers, patrolling the borders was an insurmountable task. "They only come around if there is a tip," Brian told them over dinner one night, "so I lay low. Only go into town for gas for the generator or if I am out of toothpaste."

Sara took another bite of the venison stew Brian had

made. It was delicious. She took note that he made a separate batch with only root vegetables for Amy. Amy merely smiled at him when he explained it was vegan. Sara had been watching them closely. Brian was clearly enamored with Amy. Asked her questions, made sure she was warm: it was a bit charming. However, she couldn't get a read on Amy. She had stopped talking about Anthony and going back to Watertown. But she knew the topic wasn't squashed. Amy worshiped Anthony. Everyone in town knew she wanted to get married. Everyone in town often asked when they would be married. So the holdup was Anthony. And everyone knew it. Sara had been witness to several hushed phone conversations between them where Amy would beg him to be more present or talk about the future. So there was only one possibility: he wasn't ready.

Sadly, the small acts of kindness from a stranger towards she and her daughters made Sara take pause. She had been handled badly for so many years she'd forgotten what it felt like to be treated like a normal human being. Brian took their plates and went to the sink to wash them. The sound of running water hid the tire coming up the drive. When Brian shut the water off, the sound of footsteps crunched up the drive. Marie launched from her chair. "Someone's here."

Everyone went into action. Marie grabbed the handgun. Sara took the rifle. Sara saw Brian angle his body in front of Amy's. Sara peered out the window and saw someone walking up the porch steps. "Brian," a female voice called.

Brian's shoulders relaxed. "Friend," he said aloud.

Brian went to the door and greeted the visitor. The woman filed out behind him, and Marie found herself face to face with her waitress. "Charlette?" Ife said, puzzled.

"Charlette?" Brian said confused, looking back at Marie, "you mean Marie."

Marie's mouth had fallen open, unable to speak. "Wait you know Marie?" Brian asked Ife.

"I know Charlette," Ife said with a puzzled look, hands

on her hips.

Brian looked incredibly confused. "We met at the diner last week," Sara explained.

Ife cocked her head, taking in the rag-tag team. "Looks like you survived Doyle," Ife smiled, "heard he didn't do so well on the receiving end."

Brian turned to Sara, "The guy you killed was Doyle?"

This was getting messy quickly. Sara looked at Marie, who was staring at Ife with such intensity. She could almost see Marie's heart beating out of her chest. Everyone fell silent. "You aren't going to hear anything about it from me," Ife said with a shrug," Doyle was a dangerous, crazy person."

Brian nodded. Sara let out a nervous laugh, admitting nothing.

"Come on *Charlette*," Ife teased Marie, "help me get the stuff out of the truck."

Marie stood there for a minute frozen. Sara cleared her throat, and she finally came back to earth. "Uh, yeah sure."

Marie followed Ife and pulled out a gas can and a box of supplies. "For the extra can goods from last week," Ife said, pushing past Sara and Amy.

"Nice," Brian said riffling through the box of hygiene items.

Ife stopped in front of Marie and gave her a once-over. "Charlette didn't suit you. *Marie*."

With that, Ife winked, walked into the cabin, and helped herself to some stew.

~

Ife wiped her mouth and thanked Brian for the dinner. "How do we know we can trust you?" Amy asked.

Marie was silent. She couldn't believe Ife was here. She hadn't stopped thinking about her since their first meeting. She lied to herself saying it was because Ife was kind to her that day. But Marie was entranced by her. Her chocolate skin and clinking braids. Her deep brown eyes pierced through her. Marie knew she wasn't much older, but she seemed wise beyond lifetimes.

"Listen," Ife assured her, "Doyle was a black mark on this town. You did a lot of people a favor."

Her mother leaned forward, wringing her hands. "We were protecting ourselves," Sara began.

Ife held up a hand. "The less I know, the better. Right now Paradise is pretty low-key. But when you are in town, keep your head on a swivel. Try to keep to yourself."

They all nodded. Ife stood and patted Brian on the shoulder. "Thanks again for the food advance."

Brian smiled patting her hand. "I knew you were good for it."

Marie's heart sank. She was leaving. She hadn't even said a word except for a barely-heard grunt of assent. The truth was, for all her wit, she couldn't think of a single thing to say. Ife turned and looked directly at Marie. "You all are always welcome at the diner. We'd love to see more of you."

Marie's heart quickened.

~

Amy was sitting on her bed with her phone plugged in. She would only charge it when no one was around. They couldn't find out she was still talking to Anthony. She knew she couldn't go back right then, but the thought of not talking to him destroyed her. What was even more confusing was Brian. She noticed everything he did for her since they'd gotten to the cabin. When Ife came and they all panicked, he had stood in front of her to protect her. For an instant, Brian reached his hand back into hers, guiding her to the back wall. Amy shook her head. The phone screen came to life and lit her face. Somehow a few emails seemed to get through if she walked up the hill from whence they came.

Her phone had dinged when she was out looking for

morels and leeks. When Brian found out she was vegan, he took her out to his favorite spots to find roots and shrooms. Amy prayed Brian hadn't heard it. Quickly, she had turned the phone off, saving the message for later. "So," Brian asked carefully, "do you have any family up here anymore? Or are they all…somewhere else?"

"My dad..," Amy began, her voice trailing.

What would she say? What could she say without giving too much away? "My dad is in South Dakota."

Brian paused to look up at her, his hands covered in black dirt. "He hurt us a lot."

Brian's eyes widened. He stood and dusted his hands off. He gently placed a hand on her shoulder. "I am sorry you had to go through that."

Amy nodded, turning away before he'd see the tears in her eyes. "What about friends," he continued, "Friends that are girls? Boyfriends?"

Amy froze and then continued scanning the ground for nettles. "Um, yea," she said, "I have a boyfriend named Anthony."

"Cool," Brian answered too quickly.

Amy was biting her lip, remembering their time alone in the woods. Picking up her phone, she waited for it to boot up. She wanted to talk to Anthony so badly her chest hurt. The inbox opened, and Amy quickly clicked the email.

Amy,

I hope you are alright. I haven't heard from you in a week. People are getting upset around here. They think your mom kidnapped you guys. Everyone knows about Marie being drafted too. I miss you. When are you coming home? Maybe I can come and get you?

Where are you? I will figure out a way to drive and bring you home. PLEASE write me back.

I love you, Anth

Amy swallowed. *He wants to come and get me.*

Amy set her phone down and laid on the bed. She could

go home. She could be back with Anthony. But what would that mean for her mom and sister? She'd never see them again. But if she stayed, she'd never see the love of her life. Anthony or them. Which would it be?

~

Marie had been waiting for an excuse to go to town. She even had helped Brian, the brainless beanpole, bag his deer jerky. She was so tired of being penned up there with the three of them, Marie thought she'd go mad. And she had a hankering for rhubarb pie completely unrelated to Ife. Repeating that mantra over and over did nothing to calm her nerves about seeing Ife again. But there was just something about being around her. So when they were getting low on gas and loaded on jerky, Marie informed her mother she would be accompanying Brian to town. At first, her mother objected.

"We are going to have to go down there sooner or later," Marie said flatly, "I should go with our knight in shining armor."

Marie spat the last words out. Brian rolled his eyes as he packed the back of the Jeep. Her mother pursed her lips, nodding slightly and walked back in the cabin. The ride took about twenty minutes of winding roads to the open-paved bliss of Highway 123. She saw the sign for the Berry Patch, and her chest tightened. Brian pulled to the back. Amare opened the back door and propped it open with some wooden crates. "Wow," he said, "you made quick work of this batch."

Brian began unloading the bags into a basket Amare was holding. "Well, I had some help this time," nodding to Marie.

Marie blushed and helped unload the last few bags. "That's really nice of you, Ms. Marie," Amare said with a smile, "you are going to help feed a lot of people."

Marie smiled politely and wondered who exactly she was

feeding. Everyone around this town seemed like they were well fed. She blew it off and asked, "Who's serving today?"

Amare smiled again. "The only person who is ever on the clock," he said, "Ife is just inside."

Marie blushed again and said over her shoulder, "Can you pick me up in a bit?"

Brian raised his eyebrows. "So I guess I am a chauffeur service now."

Amare laughed. "It's better than when we made our parents take us to the mall."

"What's a mall?" Brian asked with a smirk.

Their conversation faded behind Marie as she stepped through the doors. Her heart began to beat. She casually looked around for Ife, trying to look cool. The sound of the kitchen doors snapped Marie's head up and met Ife's eyes. "Charlette," Ife said using her alias.

Marie smiled. She actually smiled. "Hey, Ife."

"More rhubarb?"

"You betcha," Marie walked to the booth in the back.

A second later Marie was sitting face to face with her new friend, sipping coffee and eating dessert. Ife was the funniest person she had ever met. They talked about music, Magic the Gathering, and Dungeons and Dragons. They talked about the war and life before it. Ife told her about her mother who had passed away. Marie told her about her dad. Ife listened to Marie's stories of abuse and shook her head with empathy, not pity, in her eyes. Ife was, as Marie had suspected, nineteen. "How old are you?" Ife asked.

Marie opened her mouth to say sixteen. But it occurred to her she had a birthday a few weeks ago. "Oh my God," she whispered, "I'm seventeen."

Ife raised a brow. "You forgot your own birthday?"

"I had a few distractions," Marie said snidely.

Ife's smile faded, and she took her hand. "I'm sorry I didn't mean…."

"No, you're fine," Marie looked down at their joined hands.

Marie gently squeezed. "Do you have a boyfriend?" Marie blurted out.

Ife let go of her hand and sat back, eyes wide. Then she burst out laughing. "Most definitely not."

Marie blushed and took a sip of her coffee. Ife sat and stared at her. Marie's normal instinct would be to look away, but they stayed locked like that for a long time. "Come on," Ife grabbed her hand, "no one should have an unrecognized day of birth."

Marie laughed as she was pulled to her feet. Ife took her through the kitchen to the stock room. Ife was digging around in a pile of baking items. Marie looked around the space. It was lined with canned goods and bottled water. There were knapsacks and rolled blankets. It looked more like a doomsday prep building than a restaurant dry storage. "Found it," Ife said, grabbing something from a box.

Ife crammed a candle into a piece of bread and pulled out a lighter. As she lit the candle and turned off the lights, she softly sang *Happy Birthday* to her. Marie tried hard to fight them, but tears brimmed in her eyes. Ife finished the song and they looked at each other. "Make a wish," she smiled.

Marie blew the candle out, and the room went dark. Suddenly, Ife was pressed against her, holding her in her arms. She brushed away Marie's tears. Then Marie felt their lips meet. Light exploded from behind her eyes. Ife's hands went into her hair, and Marie grabbed her face. Marie lost herself in the moment. They explored each other's lips and Ife's hands roamed her body. Ife's braids jingled in the darkness, and Marie could hear her breath catch. "My dad's coming," Ife said quietly, pulling away.

They both giggled as the door swung open and they pressed themselves against the back wall. Amare sniffed the air. "Ife," he yelled behind him, "do you smell smoke?"

Marie snickered, and Ife pressed her hand to her mouth. "Ife," he called again from behind him.

He walked back out, shutting the door to find his

daughter. Marie felt Ife move away, and the light clicked on. Marie stood slightly embarrassed. "Don't worry," Ife smiled, "he's as deaf as a doorknob. He didn't hear us."

Marie wrung her hands and looked up at Ife sheepishly. "I haven't ever," she began.

"I guessed as much," Ife said taking her hand, "didn't you like it?"

Marie smiled slyly from under her thick blond lashes. "A little too much."

Ife rushed to kiss her again. With the lights on, it made the moment all the more real. "We should probably get back out there," Ife said with a fake pout.

Marie nodded and walked towards the door. Ife grabbed her hand before she walked out. "Come back more often?"

Marie nodded again, squeezing her hand. A pot of coffee, half a pie, and two hours later, a tired Brian came walking through the Berry Patch door. "Remind me to tell your mother what a tremendous help you are in town."

Marie peered over the booth. "What happened to you?"

Brian slumped down next to Ife. "You stink, B," she said wrinkling her nose.

"That's because for the past two hours I have been chopping wood for gas to take back to the cabin," he said, stealing Marie's water and chugging it down.

Marie smiled at Ife, and they touched knees beneath the table. "Come on kid," he said standing and grabbing a piece of pie from her plate, "your mom is probably flipping out."

Brian crammed the pie into his mouth, getting red filling on his face. "You're disgusting," Marie said with a smile.

Brian shrugged and held the door open, "Milady?"

Ife waved goodbye, and Marie walked into the sunlight anew.

~

Sara looked up relieved when Marie and Brian walked through the door. Mentally going over the words of disappointment she had rehearsed while awaiting their return, she stood to scold them. But the look of radiating joy from Marie's face stopped her. Marie was glowing. Sara glanced at Brian, wondering if he was the source of that joy, ready to rip his throat out. But his eyes went to Amy and the empty seat at the table next to her. *Oh, that boy has it bad,* Sara thought sadly, *and not for Marie. Thank the heavens.*

It was obvious Marie was happy for another reason, and she wasn't about to upset that rollercoaster. "Any word from town on the conflicts?" Sara asked them.

They had been so cut off these past few weeks Sara hadn't gotten any news about the world outside of their little cabin. They shook their heads. "MPs come in for random sweeps," Brian said, "and as far as specific details of the fighting…none. There's still a war, and that's all anyone has to say about it."

Sara chewed on that thought for a bit. No one had any idea about the war details. Odd. "Did you see if that woman down at the party store had any bottled water?"

Her name was Denise, she believed. Another local not from her childhood memories, but she seemed to be nice the one time they met several weeks ago. Denise worked as a cashier at the liquor store. Sara smiled at the term "party store." One of the many words Michiganders used that no one else did. They sold all sorts of medicines, drinks, liquor, and some toiletries. If the Berry Patch didn't have it, the Paradise Party Store certainly did.

"No," Brian answered, "I mean yes I got the water, but Denise wasn't there. Like she doesn't work there anymore."

Sara's brows furrowed. Another local she didn't know left. Where on earth did they go? It's not like they could vacation down in Florida. Disney World wasn't throwing the gates open these days. Again, odd. "Mom," Amy said digging around the junk drawer, "look what I found!"

Her dad's old deck of cards. "Want to play some Euchre?" Amy asked.

"I'm in," Marie said, practically floating to the table.

Amy pulled out the euchre half of the deck, nines through aces, frayed from use. She shuffled and dealt out four hands of five cards.

"What's Euchre?"

Everyone turned to Brian in horror. "What's Euchre?" Amy laughed.

"Only the best card game ever played," Marie said through a smile.

Marie smiling, Sara thought, *I'll need to check her forehead.*

"It's like hearts," Amy said smiling at him, "there are trump cards and called suit. It's really easy."

"Sounds really hard," Brian frowned.

"I'm on mom's team," Marie called, plopping in the seat across from Sara.

After two games of Euchre, Amy and Brian were conquered. Though it was a slaughter, they all laughed and enjoyed each other's company for the first time since they had met. Sara had to admit she liked Brian. He was becoming a natural part of the house. But their merry band of misfits needed answers and information. Sara sighed as she got up from the chair and knelt by the radio for the tenth time that day. Through trial and error, Sara found the window sill got the best signal. Though "best" only meant the occasional human voice covered in static. But sometimes, they got lucky. Sara turned the dial. It sounded like a rainstorm. Brian had taken his Euchre defeat on the chin and sat whittling a branch. He pretended not to notice Sara continuously searching for radio life. Marie washed dishes from dinner, and Amy sat at the table putting the cards in their box. Their idle chit chat slowed until only the crackling rush of empty radio air filled the cabin. "Come on," Sara said switching it to AM, "there's got to be someone out there."

Sara got up and sat near the window, angling the antennae. Brian shifted his eyes to her new position with resignation. The radio continued to *shhhhhh* the cabin into silence. Marie shook her head and went back to scrubbing.

"attack on the…shhhhhh," the radio came to life.

The girls shot to attention. Brian stopped whittling.

Sara turned the dial back and a surprisingly clear voice came to them.

"This attack was in response to the White's massacre in Chesterfield OH according to the Gray's representatives. Today's attack left an estimated 25,000 Sioux Falls metro residents dead. The high death tolls are blamed on the inability to track drone bombings and the swiftness with which these attacks can be carried out remotely. Even if alerted, many residents of these communities had nowhere to hide. Our thoughts and prayers go out to the families of the deceased. In other news, Mexico has refused any further American refugees as their numbers who have sought asylum crest over 10 million. Mexican President…"

Amy covered her mouth. Marie got up and paced, looking like she was about to punch a wall. "Sioux Falls," Sara gasped, "I can't believe it's that far north."

Amy wiped tears from her eyes, and Sara got up to put an arm around her. "Why?" Brian croaked.

The three of them had forgotten he was even there. "Why what?" Marie hissed, looking for something to take her rage out on.

"Why are you shocked?" he answered.

"All of the attacks have been in larger cities, and almost all of the smaller ones are in the south or at least toward the east coast," Sara began.

"It's systematic, Sara," he said, "they are picking us off one by one."

Amy sniffed, "Who? The Whites?"

Brian threw his branch. The women all jumped. "None of you are listening!" he boomed.

Marie moved to the kitchen towards the knife block.

"There are no sides," he continued, "no Whites, Grays, reds, blues, north, south. None of it! We are slaughtering ourselves at the suggestion and manipulation of an external group who couldn't beat us from the outside. They are letting us do it from within."

"Oh great," Marie said eying a large knife, "we have a conspiracy theorist with a weapon. Can we *please* kick this looney toon out now?"

Brian ran his hands through his hair roughly. It made his hair stand on end. When he stood he looked as crazy as he was acting. His bright eyes glowed. "It's not a conspiracy. It's happened. It's past tense, Marie."

Sara looked at the whittling knife he held. Noticing her gaze, he grunted and tossed it on the table. "For god sakes, I'm not dangerous," he said, "I'm mad."

"You could say that again," Marie mumbled.

Sara took the knife, folded it, and put it in her pocket. "Mad at who? The Russians?"

"Russia, UK, Brazil, Iran," Brian threw his hands in the air, "they are in every country. They are a group of people with the same goal: keep us sick, in debt, poor, and unthinking."

"So, you are saying there is a group of people that want to take down the US because we go against, what? Their religion? Their master plan?" Sara said, smoothing Amy's soft hair.

"That's stupid," Marie said, "there are plenty of other countries that are westernized. Why not go after them too?"

Brian gave her a look like she was a talking monkey. "Why," Brian started to raise his voice again, "Why?!"

"Brian please," Amy finally chimed in, "we are just trying to understand."

Brian took a deep breath. "Anyone part of United Nations was protected by the United States," he began more calmly, " and the Core… That's what we called them."

Marie rolled her eyes and Brian glared at her, "The Core made smaller attacks on some of the other UN nations, but it was just to annoy. They could never fully infiltrate any of the smaller countries without the US intervening. The Core could never come to full power without the US crushing them."

Losing interest in the knife block, Marie leaned in and

crossed her arms. "Ok," Marie conceded, "let's say you're right. Americans have been arguing about different ideals for years. It was bound to boil over and it did. How did the Core do that?"

Brian rolled his eyes back when she air-quoted *The Core*. "This technique is as old as time," Brian huffed, "the Romans used the Germanic Tribes to fault the civil unrest. The Nazis blamed the Jews for Germany's financial ruin. Lincoln threw the US into our First Civil War because he wanted to trade with France, and they wouldn't until we abolished slavery! And they probably caused those to happen too."

Marie's skepticism was waning. She took a seat at the table and motioned him to continue. "They found and tested ideals that separated us the most and created propaganda, memes and fake news stories and fed it to us online. And we snorted it like addicts."

"You mean like when the Russians," Amy tried to understand, "I mean the Core messed with the elections?"

Brian laughed. It was so loud Sara jumped. "Oh, that was just the beginning," he continued, giddy, "it was just to test the waters. When they saw how successful that was, they continued with fake extremist marches. They invited people through social media to these marches whose online activity showed them to be on the fringe of our society. Then created counter-protester events and invited the other extreme to create tension."

"The riots in DC," Sara remembered.

"Exactly," Brian said, "they hoisted people into office that were so extreme on both sides your everyday Joe felt like his country was being overrun by a rogue government, each side taking issue with the other. This motivated people who would've never gotten involved with any movement taking up arms."

Brian was full-on pacing now. Amy watched him with tears in her eyes. She began to remember the memes she had shared on her page. Political rhetoric that seemed so pointless now. Were they manufactured? Was she part of the chess game?

"The climate in this country was so flammable, all it needed was the smallest spark," he said.

Breathless, Amy whispered, "The assassination."

Brian nodded. Sara gasped. Marie looked at the ceiling, visibly grinding her teeth.

"Both sides denied their involvement, but the social media stories began pumping. Some of them so outlandish it's hard to believe we bought them. But we believed the side we belonged to and blamed the other," Brian shook his head, "we were all so hurt and in shock. The country didn't think. It acted. And the war began."

The cabin fell silent, and the radio picked up where Brian left off.

"...tell the exact death toll for either side. But after the Sioux Falls incident today, the numbers stand approximately at Whites just north of 57.3 million and Grays slightly lower at 51 million...."

Amy sat motionless, large tears rolling down her cheeks.

"Approximately, 150 million have fled the country seeking asylum from an estimated 24 countries. Canada and Mexico boasting the highest refugees at 75 million and 10 million respectively..."

"Shut it off," Marie said.

Sara clicked the radio silent. The cabin didn't move. The air felt thick and musty. Brian collapsed into the chair and put his face in his hands. Marie moved to the sink and began to put the dishes away. Outside the birds sang. The world moved on.

~

"How," Sara broke the silence.

Brian looked up at her. "It's complicated," he answered.

"Try me," she said, "how? How did they know where to bomb? How did they know who was with who? How..."

"Algorithms," Brian interrupted.

Amy sat there looking confused. Brian rubbed his face.

"Algorithms the Core developed gave data on which cities held which side. They sold the information back to us, highlighting exactly which place to attack based on which memes and stories we read, commented on, or shared."

"But no city held just Whites or Grays. There was bound to be people killed from both sides regardless of who did the bombing," Sara concluded.

Brian looked at Sara. He held her gaze, trying hard to form a response.

His family flashed before his eyes.

Begging his sister to leave with him. The underground websites he followed predicted the attack in Indianapolis. He remembered her smile with her crooked tooth in the front she hated. That smile was burned into his mind while she laughed at him, telling him he was crazy. He read too much. He believed anything he read. He was so mad at her, he left in his car. He drove around for a few hours north. When he hit the Michigan border, his guilt set in, and he tried calling his dad. It went to voicemail. He got out of his car at the rest stop. He tried his step-mom; straight to voice mail. Afraid to hold down nine, his sister's speed dial, his finger shook hovering above. A car came flying up the entrance ramp of the stop. It hit the curb and parked half on the sidewalk. A woman and two children burst from the doors. The husband yelled out the window, "You have three minutes. Run!"

Brian trotted over to the car. The guy looked like hell. His face looked badly burned all over, red and peeling like a bad sunburn. "Are you guys alright?" Brian asked.

The guy stared at him like a horn was growing from his head. "Huh?" the guy answered.

"What happened?" Brian asked, not wanting to know the answer.

The mom and kids came running back to the car. They all had burns on their faces. The kids were now wet like they'd showered off. "It's gone," the man said, breaking Brian's stare, "Indy is all gone. They're coming. Run!"

Brian snapped from his memory. The women all stared at him waiting.

"They don't care," Brian whispered.

Marie turned around, "They sold us data on the

propaganda we read that they created to divide us in the first place."

"Yes."

"What about weapons?" Sara asked.

"Most of the ones on the ground were from our military when the formal US government dissolved. That was split among the Whites and Grays," he said, wringing his hands, "the air assault weapons have come from various countries looking to help end the war or fuel it. Hard to say."

Marie came around the corner and leaned on the wall.

"Who the fuck are you?" Marie said slowly.

Brian noticed another knife appear that Marie was trying to keep hidden behind her back. "Marie, leave him alone," Amy said.

"No seriously," Marie continued, "you're here squatting at our cabin and suddenly have a "Ph.D. in Bullshittery". Knowing everything that led the country to war. Maybe you're a Core operative."

Brian laughed. "You're kidding," he said.

"Why should we trust you?" Marie said, "Far as I can see, you're a burglar who broke into my mom's home, helped yourself to everything in it, and is permanently sleeping under our roof. We don't even know who you are."

"He already told us, Marie," Amy challenged her, "he's on his way to Canada."

Brian stood. "If you want me to go, I'll go," he said, "just give me until the winter. I've almost made enough money to finish my trip and when the lake freezes, I'm gone."

Brian looked at Sara. He could tell she had chosen not to speak, evaluating the situation. Her daughters didn't see what he did. Sara was an intelligent observer, and whatever brought them to this place wasn't pretty. It was also obvious she knew Brian wasn't telling them everything. "You're not leaving, Brian," Sara said.

"Mom!" Marie shouted.

"He has been very helpful to us these past weeks," Sara added, "if it wasn't for his hunting, we'd have blown through most of our food by now."

Marie tossed the knife in the sink. "Well when they find our gutted bodies, I'll be sure to use your entrails to spell, *I told you so*," she growled and slammed the door as she fled the cabin.

That girl has some serious issues, Brian observed.

Sara turned back to Brian. "Tell me more about your plans to cross the lake."

Brian watched Marie go and sighed. "I'm sorry," he said, "I didn't mean to upset her."

"It's just a lot for *all* of us," Sara began, "I can't imagine being stuck inside another country going through this. But, look, we don't have a plan. I was hoping we could ride out this war here, but it doesn't seem there is an end in sight. Crossing to Canada where it is safer might be a better option than waiting here."

Brian nodded. "I am waiting until early February. The ice is at its thickest then. I was hoping to find a snowmobile and ride it half the way."

"Only half," Amy asked, now interested in the conversation.

"The ice isn't as thick in the center of the straits," he said, "I know the ice will hold nearest the shore, but I don't want to fall through in the center. So just in case, I'm hiking the rest of the way. I plan on taking enough food to cross and set up camp on the other side. I have no idea how far the next existing town is since the war started. So I am planning for at least three days on my own."

Sara took a deep breath. "That's a long time to spend in the elements on the 46th parallel," Sara said, chewing her lip. "It would be safer to do as a group and we are running out of options if this war doesn't end."

Brian watched Amy out of the corner of his eye. As she processed what her mother was saying, he heard her grinding her teeth. Sara stood, crossing her arms. "We're going with you."

~

"Wait, what?!"

The shout echoed through the cabin. "You can't expect me to go to Canada," Amy said, trying to get her composure.

Her mother furrowed her brow. "I expected after all we've been through you, wouldn't want to go back to South Dakota."

Amy didn't know what she wanted. But she didn't like being told she would never go back to Watertown. She missed Anthony. She missed her friends. She hated always being afraid. "Well," she began, "I don't want to go."

"So what is your grand plan then, Amy?" her mother said with such authority it made her take pause.

Amy didn't have a plan. She planned to marry Anthony and have a baby. That plan was her ticket for safety for at least a little while. She hadn't thought past that. Thoughts about the war never much entered her mind even after Freddie went to it. Her father always assured her they would be victorious and it would end soon. Amy didn't want to think. A simple life where everything was laid out for her was what she wanted. It was cowardly, she knew. And she knew it meant handing her life over for someone else to run, but she didn't care. Safety was all Amy wanted. And now, the realization of that safety net fraying back home made her insides turn. "I'm going for a walk."

Amy stormed out the front of the cabin and began walking towards the stream. She heard the door open and shut behind her. "Go away," she mumbled walking faster.

"I just thought you might want some bug spray," Brian answered gently, holding up a green can.

Amy turned around and grabbed it. Brian again for the save. These past few weeks he had confused and annoyed her to no end. He was always so thoughtful and caring. Everything she wished Anthony would be was standing in front of her wrapped in a gangly curly-haired package. It was infuriating. Amy sprayed her arms, which already had two bite marks beginning to swell. The mosquitos up here were relentless. She struggled to try to get her back and felt the can lift from her hands. "Here," Brian said and sprayed her back, "Want some company?"

Amy turned and looked into his eyes. There was no anger or pity, just genuine concern. His eyes were the most fantastic shade of blue-green. She felt her heart flutter. "Fine," she said quickly, turning back towards the trail.

Stop it, she yelled to herself.

There was nothing more to this than being lonely and scared. Brian was only into her because she was the first female his age that he'd seen in ages. And Amy only felt the smallest iota of longing because she was isolated. *Yes*, she thought, *that explains it all.*

In silence, Brian took up pace beside her as the sun began its late-day summer descent. The colors this time of year made dusk and dawn awe-inspiring. The sound of owls and night animals rising from slumber awoke from around them. Amy snuck a peek at Brian as they neared the river. His dark curls framed his face. They bounced when he stepped. It was slightly attractive, she admitted to herself. As they stepped to the river, Amy sat on a large rock at the edge. Brian took a seat on a fallen tree nearby. "You ok?" Brian finally broke the silence.

Amy sighed and itched the bites on her arms. "I don't know."

"Why can't you all go home to South Dakota?"

Amy paused. Should she tell him? "A lot of reasons," she began, "mostly because my dad is a crazy person."

"Aren't they all," Brian smiled, trying to lighten the mood.

"Not like him," Amy said picking at some moss.

Amy went on to explain that her Father and his issues in part. Enough for him to get the gist without giving too much detail. "And if he finds us," she finished, "he'll send Marie to boot camp."

Brian's head snapped up. "So she did dodge."

Shit, shit shit, Amy scolded herself itching her arms again, the *cat's out of the bag*.

Marie was going to kill her. Her eyes looked up at him pleading. "God Amy, I would never tell anyone."

Amy exhaled, relieved. She had no reason, but she believed him. Brian watched her nails attack her skin again. "You're going to bleed and get them infected," he said standing, looking around the forest floor.

Amy ignored him, itching the other side. "Will you stop," he said, sitting beside her.

Gently, Brian took her arm in his hands. They were warm and she could feel the calluses. Examining the bites, he was so close to her. She could smell the fire smoke in his hair. Amy felt her heart beat faster. *Stop it*, she yelled at herself.

He picked a nearby green-topped plant with a white bulb. "What is that?" she asked trying not to sound breathless.

Brian mashed it between his fingers. "Onion makes the bites stop itching," he said, looking up into her eyes.

Amy's face twisted. "I'm going to smell like an armpit," she protested as he gently rubbed the paste onto her bites.

The itching had already subsided. Brian laughed and began on the other arm. "No one's going to want to be within thirty feet of me," Amy laughed despite herself.

Wrinkling her nose again, she looked up to thank him. His deep blue eyes were locked on her. She felt his thumbs trace small circles on her skin. "I don't think that's entirely true," he whispered.

Amy's heart quickened again, and her lips parted. He began to lean in, sliding his hands up her arms. She felt her pulse in every part of her body. It screamed to be touched. And then she felt the name slide from her lips. "Anthony."

Brian froze and slowly leaned back, his hands returning to his lap. "Anthony," he repeated.

"I want to go back to Watertown for Anthony."

Brian's face betrayed the briefest of pain which he hid instantly. *Such a good actor.*

"Of course," Brian said, extending a hand to help her up, "I'm sure he's worried sick. Are you ready to go back? I'm getting eaten alive."

Amy nodded.

They walked back to the cabin in silence.

~

Marie was livid with her sister. Everyone back home knew Anthony was on a completely different level with their relationship than Amy. And the fact Amy would risk her life to be with him anyhow made Marie see red. *Selfish, self-absorbed, naïve.*

After a walk around the cabin, Marie cooled off. Brian wasn't the worst person she'd ever met, and he didn't tell anyone she had spent the entire day with Ife. And the dork could cook. Marie found herself walking through the front door to apologize to the skinny brillo pad. But she found only her mother inside. Sitting at the table, Sara was poring over maps and making notes on the side. She looked up as Marie came in. "Mom," Marie said, her voice shaking.

In an instant, her mom had scooped Marie in her arms. Marie quietly wept. "What's my job?" her mom asked.

"Huh?"

"To keep you safe," Sara whispered, "and I will do that forever."

Marie knew her mother meant it. Her hair felt wet when she pulled away, and Sara was wiping her eyes. "We will be safe again," she said, grabbing Marie's arms, "if it kills me."

Marie knew the gravity of that statement. Suddenly, the door swung open, and a red-eyed Amy and stone-faced Brian walked through the door. Amy walked straight to the bedroom, shutting herself in. Brian looked at Marie and her mom and shrugged. He sat by the fire and picked up some deer leather he had been sewing. She's j*ust like my mom*, Marie realized, watching Amy retreat.

Amy wanted a savior. Men flocked to Amy, and women cooed over her looks and lady-like qualities. So coddled. So used to being served. *The dumb beaver couldn't take care of herself if she wanted to*, Marie thought, shaking her head.

Marie looked at the clock. It was almost ten at night. Her mother had made her way to her room, kissing Marie on the forehead. Marie laid back on the lounger with her hands behind her head, staring at the ceiling. She pictured Ife's perfect face. She had never been so taken by someone. Marie felt excited and scared at the same time. Their kiss and what played out before and after was on auto-loop. And each time her heart would beat faster. It was driving her mad. Brian made his way to the couch. Marie frowned. The guy was such a chatterbox, and Marie had no desire to interrupt her thoughts at the moment. So when he climbed under a quilt and rolled over without a word, Marie raised a brow. She thanked the god above for the small miracle. Soon the sounds of Brian's familiar snores came from beneath the quilt. The ticking of the clock and the sounds of the night made her feel alone. She didn't want to be alone anymore. *I want to be with you right now*, she thought to Ife through some hoped connection.

Marie laid there listening to the sounds of three sleeping people. *Why can't I be*, Marie thought with a jolt.

Her heart leaped as she sat up with the crazy idea. Quietly she got out of the chair and put on a hoodie. She knew the front door was loud. Gently she turned the knob. It creaked and she froze. No one stirred. After ten minutes of opening an inch and waiting, she was outside. She stared at the two-foot gap to close it. Cursing her sister for having the smaller waistline, Marie proceeded to close an inch and wait for another ten minutes. Finally, the door clicked closed. She giddily put on her shoes. She peered inside, seeing Brian asleep with his arm draped over his eyes. His mouth hung open like a cave. Marie rolled her eyes and made her way to the carport where Brian kept his bike.

Walking the bike for the first half-mile, Marie let out a quiet squeal as she hopped on and headed for town. The fireflies lit the sides of the road, almost guiding her to town.

Suddenly, she heard the roars of an engine. Quickly, she rode her bike off the road. The bike wobbled and she almost fell off as it ground to a stop. Marie pulled the bike into the nearby tree line and ducked down.

It was then she noticed a car parked with its lights off sitting up ahead. It was half-hidden on the other side of the road. A capped pick-up truck with racing stripes driving way too fast sped past her. It hit the brakes and slid to a halt next to the waiting car. The doors of both vehicles flung open, and a man opened the back of the truck bed. Two adults and four small children were ushered from one vehicle to the waiting car. The eldest child and man got in the trunk. The two drivers shook hands as the rest of the family poured into the seats. As the car sped away, the truck driver lifted the cab off the back and hauled it into the woods. Suddenly, the sound of a helicopter filled Marie's ear. The man frantically peeled the stripes from the side of the truck and with a grunt got back in his vehicle and took off in the opposite direction. Minutes later, the helicopter circled the area and then went east. When the deafening propeller sounds dissipated, Marie realized she had been holding her breath. Releasing it, she steadied herself.

Who were they? She could only guess why they were being moved in the middle of the night. She waited in the brush for several minutes before walking her bike to the road. In the distance, she could see the one blinking light of downtown Paradise.

No other cars passed for the rest of the trip. And not one house window was lit. As she neared the Berry Patch, she saw the bedroom window where Ife slept. It was dark too.

Quietly setting the kickstand, Marie stood in front of the window. *What the hell do I do now?* she thought to herself angrily.

She hadn't exactly thought this part through. Escaping her house and making the several-mile trek here, sure. But not this. About to turn back home, she saw a long branch on the side of the café. Grabbing it, she hoisted the large branch back and forth trying to tap Ife's window. The bottom of the branch was the width of her arms and extremely heavy. She heaved it up, swaying back and forth. *Shit shit shit*, Marie cursed herself as the branch slipped out of her hands, making gravel fly.

Embarrassed, with scraped hands, she walked back to the bike to leave. "Marie," a voice whispered from behind her.

Marie froze. Ife stood in the doorway with her arms crossed and a faint smile of amusement. "What are you doing here?"

"I, uh," Marie stammered, "saw a truck moving people. And there was a helicopter."

Ife had the strangest look on her face. "Probably just some kids messing around. And there are a lot of helicopters around here," she said flippantly.

For the briefest moment, Marie wanted to explain further. But Ife standing there barely wearing anything had her blood singing. Without thinking Marie rushed to her, wrapping her arms around her neck and kissing her deeply. She felt Ife smile into her kiss. Ife pulled away. "Miss me already?"

Marie smiled nodding. "Come on, crazy," Ife smiled, taking her hand, "keep it down though. My dad just got to bed."

They giggled and crept up the stairs to Ife's room. When Marie stepped inside, she took in the little loft bedroom. Ife was a bit messy, to Marie's surprise. Her clothes were all over the floor, and she had books stacked everywhere. A cup of tea sat next to her bed next to a picture of who Marie assumed was a ten-year-old Ife, her dad and mom. Ife collected the teacup and a half-eaten piece of pie and smiled sheepishly. A large Magic the Gathering poster hung on the back wall of her tiny room. It was so different from the type-A perfectly clean house her father demanded and her mother provided. Sensing her gaze, Ife began picking up things off the floor, tossing them into a basket in the corner. "Sorry about the mess," reading her thoughts, "I wasn't exactly expecting company."

Marie's face fell. "I can go if you want…"

Ife eyed her. "Do you want to go? You can of course if you don't feel comfortable."

Ife sauntered to her, taking her hand. Marie's blood roared in her head. "It's just," Marie began, "I'm…I've never…"

Ife smiled and took a step closer. "Good thing I have."

Marie felt herself being guided to the bed. Ife laid her down and took her in. "I suppose I could give you a proper birthday gift."

Marie let out a nervous squeak, her voice cracking. Laughing, Ife crawled on top of her, straddling her legs. She kissed her deeply. Slowly she worked her way down Marie's belly, kissing her outside her shorts. Marie's legs felt like Jello. Ife slid her shorts down her thighs, trailing them with kisses and threw them to the floor. "Are you sure you want to do this?"

"Yes, please," Marie begged.

Ife slid a finger into the side of her panties and pulled them down. Marie always thought she'd be self-conscious the first time she did anything with anyone. After she kissed Colin, Marie thought she'd died of embarrassment. But with Ife, it felt right. She felt safe. She felt eager. Ife ran her fingers over the top of her, and Marie shivered. And with one gentle movement, Ife placed one inside of her. Marie rolled her hips with her steady rhythm. "You are so beautiful," Ife whispered.

Marie could only smile for fear of waking the entire town if she spoke. Ife quickened her pace and Marie kept in time with her experienced hands. Marie closed her eyes and felt her hips melt. Then she felt Ife's mouth on her. Marie squeaked again. Ife covered her mouth, trying not to laugh. "Do you want me to stop?"

"Don't you dare," Marie smiled slyly.

Ife went back down, taking Marie in her mouth. Marie rocked with her hands, covering her mouth to shield her moans. She felt herself at the edge of a cliff about to fall. And then like lightning, the earth fell out from beneath her as climax gave way. Her breath was ragged, and she saw stars as she looked down at Ife. Ife was silently giggling and kissed the inside of her thighs. Marie felt wet everywhere. "That was," Marie began crawling to Ife, "that was.."

"Just the beginning," Ife finished, taking her face in her hands and kissing her again.

Marie spent the next four hours exploring Ife the way Ife had shown her. They laid naked talking and then kissing, followed by taking turns making the other melt. Marie couldn't stop. She wanted to feel this way forever. She wanted, *no*, needed more. But the edge of the sky began to lighten as she rested in Ife's arms. "You should probably get home before my dad gets up," she said, kissing the top of her head, "or before any of your family does too."

Marie lazily leaned up on her elbows. "I don't want to go."

Ife touched her nose with hers. "It's just for now. Come back tomorrow. Or today, whatever time it is."

Marie giggled as she pulled her clothes back on. Her body felt alive. Ife walked her downstairs just as they heard a toilet flush. "He gets up early to prep for breakfast," Ife said.

Marie nodded, sad to say goodbye. "Will you stop acting like I'm never going to see you again?" Ife said, giving her one last kiss goodbye.

Marie smiled over her shoulder as she got on her bike. She waved as she set off for home.

~

Sara sat on the porch sipping a cup of coffee. She felt her blood pressure rising as every minute ticked by. She recalled the night's events again in her mind in case she missed something. At just after midnight, she had gotten out of bed to get some water. She stopped to check on the girls like she had every night since they were babies. And Marie was gone. Sara calling Marie's name woke the house, and Brian and Amy rose to meet her with sleepy eyes. "What happened?" Amy asked.

"Your sister is gone!" Sara yelled.

They all went around the house, checking for signs of Marie. Amy noticed her shoes were missing from the front porch. Brian called from the carport saying his bike was gone. No one had heard the front door open Sara was furious. They all knew Marie had made a friend in town. *But to leave without telling anyone!*

And while everyone was pretty sure she left on her own accord, every second that ticked by sent Sara more and more off the edge of sheer panic. The three of them had all been up for hours. Brian suggested he'd go into town when the shops opened to ask if anyone had seen her. Amy said she'd head down the trails around the house in case she got lost or hurt. Sara was shaking too badly to do much of anything but panic when the sound of gravel crunching came up the drive. And just before six in the morning, a disheveled Marie came riding up the road. Sara stood, slamming her coffee down on the bench. "Where in the hell have you been?"

Marie froze, hearing the violence coming from her mother. Amy and Brian came filing out onto the porch. Marie took a breath, smoothing her hair down placing the bike back in the carport. "We have been up since midnight thinking you were hurt or captured or dead!"

Marie put her hands in her pockets and looked at the ground. "You cannot just do what you want here," Sara continued grilling her, "everywhere is dangerous for you, don't you get that?"

Amy and Brian looked at each other and went back

inside, Brian holding the door for her. "Do you know what a dodger goes for these days?" Sara whispered so Brian didn't hear.

"No," Marie answered quietly.

"Neither do I!" Sara screamed unable to control her rage. "But I know it's enough to make my family friend not think twice about turning us in."

"I'm sorry, mom."

Sara wiped her hands over her face, feeling them wet. She'd been so angry she hadn't realized she was crying. "Sorry," Sara threw her hands in the air, "Sorry?"

They stood in silence. Sara rubbed her arms and looked at her daughter. "Where were you?"

Marie looked up, and she almost glowed. "With a friend, I swear."

Sara nodded, wiping her nose on her sleeve. "I thought," Sara began looking away, "I can't even tell you what I thought."

Marie ran and wrapped her arms around her mother. Sara was so startled, it took a second for her to return the hug. Sara smoothed her hair and rocked her back and forth. "Please don't do that again. We need to know where you are."

"I promise," Marie said into her mother's nightshirt.

Sara took a deep breath and turned them towards the cabin. Quickly, Amy and Brian turned, pretending they hadn't been spying from the window. When Sara and Marie entered, they began discussing the next day's event.

Sara yawned. "I'm going to bed. And if any of you aren't here when I wake up, I'll sell you to bounty hunters myself."

~

Marie was shaking from the lecture. It hadn't occurred to her that they'd be awake or so scared. Marie washed her hands and grabbed a glass of water. Amy and Brian eyed her suspiciously. "I'm guessing you aren't going to fill us in on your new friend," Amy asked with attitude.

Marie said nothing.

"Fine," Amy clipped, "I'm going to bed. Keeping our mother from complete hysteria and/or off-roading in the truck at night to find you was exhausting."

Brian watched Amy go into the room and close the door. Marie turned and met his deep blue stare. He smiled, leaning on the counter and crossed his arms. "Fun night?"

Glancing behind her making sure they were both gone, Marie smiled. "Maybe."

Brian shook his head, going to his makeshift bed on the couch. "So next time you want to see Ife, just tell me. I'll come up with some reason to go to town."

Marie's mouth fell a little. *How did he...*

"But your mom is right. Taking off like that is stupid and dangerous. Now, go to bed," he laughed, pulling the blanket over his head.

Marie pursed her lips and rolled her eyes. Her hand grasped the knob when a voice from the couch said, "And your shirt is on backward."

~

Amy sat looking at the stream. Tadpoles were swarming each other in a little pocket of water. Some already had legs. The weeks had begun to race by with no end in sight of the war. In fact, from the bits of townie information and occasional news found on the radio, it was getting worse. Amy got down close to the water's edge and dipped her hand in. The water was so cold. The future frogs swam in circles on her palm. Loudly, a crow called overhead. Amy shielded her eyes to look up through the trees. The black crow was circling the clearing. The sun glinting off its wings creating a phoenix-like glow. "Now see here *Ribbets*," Amy announced to the nursery, "I will stay here for a bit. But I can only offer my protection for so long."

The crow protested from above. Every day was a

monotony of the same thing: wake, do chores, tend to the garden, can, sell what they could in town, eat and sleep. The only thing that seemed to change was the constant influx of new people and the outflux of old. The only positive of this weird place was most of them left behind everything. So the local thrift shop had endless supplies of clothes and trinkets. Her whole family had gotten new clothes and warm jackets since the weather was already turning. Before she knew it, it would be winter and she would have to say goodbye to her mother and sister. Her heart dropped as she realized Brian was on that list too. He never pushed her boundaries, but everyone knew how Brian felt. And Amy adored him, but her future waited for her in South Dakota. Amy couldn't go back to the days of self-harm. Just the thought of being without Anthony had her fingers itching towards her hair, yearning to pull out a strand or two.

Amy gently waved her hand in the water, letting them swim through her fingers. Her fingers were throbbing from the chill. Bored. She was painfully bored. "For my purpose today is great. My purpose today is difficult. My purpose," she paused and climbed to the top of the creek-side boulder, "is to collect firewood and find a place to pee!"

She grabbed a nearby branch like a staff and pounded it on the ground. "Amy," she bellowed, "Queen of the Frog Teenagers!"

Her gusto gave way to the moss beneath her feet. Her rear end slammed on the ground. But her staff aided in her not breaking her ankle; her jeans were smeared in green sludge. Grunting, she slowly sat up, checking for damage beyond pride. She thought, *at least no one was there to…*

A stifled chuckle came from behind a tree. Rolling her eyes, Amy got to her feet. "Real funny, Marie," she called, swinging the staff-now-turned-bat, "Come here and laugh. I dare you!"

But when Brian emerged from hiding with his crooked smile and hands in the air, Amy dropped the branch-staff-bat and groaned. "Queen Frog Lady," he spoke innocently,

"I come here in peace."

Amy grabbed a handful of creek muck and launched it at him. "Hey," he jumped back, "don't kill the messenger."

Amy groaned again and slumped down the creek-side trying to hide her burning cheeks. Brian came up behind carefully. Bowing and gesturing grandly to the spot next to her, "May I, your highness?"

"Oh sit down and shut it," Amy snapped, grinning slightly.

They sat there in silence for a bit. The sun was leaking through the trees, giving everything a filter. Amy's subjects flitted and swam about, oblivious to the war raging just over the water's edge. Amy rested her chin on her knees and glanced at Brian. He was chewing his thumb with such ferocity she thought it would bleed. But sitting this close she noticed the faintest wrinkles on the outsides of his eyes: smiling lines. Amy's heart sank. They were from times when they all had things to smile about. Amy looked him over thoughtfully. Brian wasn't a looker per se, but in the dusk, he glowed. The edges of his face were shadowed and cut. His jaw was strong, and his eyes were the most unique, not quite green or blue. She looked down at his chest and muscled arms. Suddenly, Amy couldn't remember why she ever thought him unattractive. Brian glanced up, catching her gaze. "What?" he said.

"You're biting your thumb," Amy replied.

"Oh," he said rubbing his mouth, "yea, I do that."

He stood. Amy looked up at him and saw the longing in his eyes as he looked at her. Boys didn't have to say it, but girls knew what that look meant. She could tell from their first meeting he felt something for her. Brian's subtle glances in her direction when he thought she was not looking. The extra effort to be standing by her or touching her arm whenever possible. He held the door for her, made sure she had had enough to eat at meals, ensured they were meat-free and carried anything that was in her arms. And without even realizing it, she suddenly felt compelled to be in them.

Brian stood, reaching out his hand to her. Amy slid her hand into his, feeling his rough hands, and he pulled her to meet his face. The creek bubbled. The poles held their breath (primarily because they didn't breathe). The crow hoped someone would make a move because he wanted to eat some baby frogs.

They sat there for much longer than any friends should, studying one another.

Amy's phone beeped. So lost in the moment, Amy didn't even register it was hers. "Is that phone working?" Brian's eyes widened.

Amy quickly yanked her phone out, silencing the email from Anthony. "Um, yes," Amy admitted, "it sometimes gets a signal."

"Is the GPS on?" Brian asked alarmed.

"I don't know," she stammered, "I don't think so. By the way, why were you out here? Were you following me?"

Brian paused, looking vacant, almost through her. He drew a breath and began to walk back towards the cabin. "Your mother wants you home for dinner and asked me to find you."

Amy went red with anger and embarrassment. She glanced down, seeing another email from Anthony.

It's getting bad Amz. You have to get your mom to turn herself in. Ur sister could be in a lot of trouble. Where r u?

Amy crammed the phone into her pocket and began walking back to the cabin, trying to figure out exactly what to say. Her mother made her swear not to tell anyone. *Maybe just a half-truth.*

She wrote him back. *I'm in Michigan. But don't tell anyone. We'll be back soon.*

Send.

Suddenly, her head exploded with pain. She saw black stars and dropped to the ground like a sack of potatoes. She looked up at the branch she hadn't seen, her face buried in her phone. Some of her hair was hanging from it. Amy reached up and touched her forehead. Her fingers came back bloody. She launched to her feet and screamed, her fury giving way.

Brian came flying through the trees upon hearing her yell. "What happened?"

"Everything in this fucking forest is trying to kill us," she yelled, kicking the tree, which sent searing waves of pain into her big toe.

Amy slumped to the ground and began sobbing. Her tears mixed with her blood, leaving a puddle of pink desperation in her palms. Brian straddled her fetal-positioned body and held her. This made her sob louder. She leaned into him, so grateful to be held. Amy hadn't hugged her mother or sister since they got to the cabin. Everyone was so absorbed in their daily survival. It had only been weeks, but it felt like a lifetime ago. Brian used his sleeve to dab the blood on her forehead and smoothed her hair.

Amy took a deep breath and looked into his kind face. "I can't give you what you want," she mumbled, her mouth slick with tears.

Brian stopped and held her gaze. "You may, one day," he said, grinning like a loon, "and I've got at least two more months to convince you."

Amy laughed then choked. She wiped her nose on her sleeve and he helped her to stand. A rumble of an engine came from the direction of the cabin. Amy and Brian froze. They looked at each other and broke out into a sprint towards her mother and sister.

As they got closer, they heard voices. Brian grabbed Amy's hand, "This way."

Brian brought her to the thick berry bushes and began to belly crawl beneath it. The thorns tore and scratched his skin, but he didn't seem to notice. He looked back, "Come on!"

Amy got on her hands and knees and followed him into the bush.

~

Sara was stirring the pot of roots when she heard an engine roar up the road. Sara launched herself to the window and peered out. A military vehicle came to a stop at her front door. *He found us,* she thought frantically.

Sara ran to the bedroom where Marie was napping. "Get up," Sara whispered.

"Huh," Marie groaned rolling over.

"They found us, Marie. Get up!"

Marie shot up and spun in circles trying to get her bearings as to what to grab or throw on. Sara threw shoes at her and grabbed her backpack. *BANG, BANG, BANG.* "Military Police," a loud voice called, "open the door."

Marie and Sara stared at each other, not moving. "We see you're in there," he continued, "now open up."

Sara nodded to the back door. Marie started towards it but saw another solider standing in the back through the window. Marie shook her head no to her Mother. Sara looked around trying to figure out a game plan. *BANG, BANG, BANG.*

Sara stood up and mouthed hide. Marie nodded.

BANG, BANG, BANG. "I'm coming," Sara yelled, "one minute."

Sara opened the door to find the MP standing there with three counterparts. Sara didn't recognize them. They weren't the men who had come all those weeks ago after they killed Doyle. "Hello ma'am," he said, "I'm sorry to bother you."

"No, not at all," she said carefully, "how can I help you?"

"You come out here often?" the officer asked.

Sara looked at the solider on the right who was palming his weapon. "Uh," she began, "not often enough. This is my family's cabin. We come here to escape."

She regretted her choice of words immediately. The soldier cocked an eyebrow, "This is your family's cabin."

Sara held up a finger and walked to the mantle. She came back with two picture frames. "See," she held up the portraits of her fishing with her dad as a kid and the two of them when she was in high school.

The MP took the pictures, looking at them. "You're here alone?" he asked, looking past her shoulder.

"No," she gambled, "my daughter is here too. Honey, can you come here please?"

Marie came out from the bedroom, looking uninterested in the commotion, holding a book. "Yea," she said flatly with such acting precision Sara almost chided her for being rude.

"We have visitors," Sara said.

Marie crossed her arms and leaned on the door. "Sup," she greeted.

"Hello," the MP replied eyeing her, "we are looking for a person who has gone AWOL."

Sara swallowed. A loud hissing came from the stove, making both Sara and Marie jump. "Jesus," Sara gasped, "Sweetie, can you stir that?"

Marie nodded, turning her back to the MP. Allowing her act to falter, she gave her Mother pleading eyes.

"So, you said someone has gone AWOL?" Sara asked.

"Yes," he replied, "we're looking for a man named Joseph Piret. Twenty-five years old; about six foot two, brown hair, blue eyes."

It took all of Sara's effort to not exhale in obvious relief. "Joseph Piret," she repeated, "I don't know anyone around here with that name."

"He could be using an alias," the soldier continued, "have you seen anyone fitting his description?"

Like a ton of bricks, it hit her.

Brian.

What a fool she had been! She was so caught up in her own story she'd barely questioned his. "Is that a yes?" the

MP asked, noting her change in demeanor.

"Oh, no," Sara said, "I was just taken aback that there could be a fugitive running around here. It's a really small town."

Marie kept stirring the pot with such vigor Sara hoped the soldiers hadn't noticed. Some water splashed out, making a hissing sound hitting the stovetop. Everyone just stood there for a moment. "Do you have a way of reaching you if I should come across this man?" Sara asked, trying to wrap up the encounter.

The MP paused, judging her, and then reached into his pocket. Sara studied the man's face if he could even be called a man. He barely crested his twenties. His shadow was visible on his cheeks and she could see the patches where it hadn't even grown in. The MP still had acne and the gaunt look of a Great Dane puppy with oversized paws and scrawny limbs. His motley crew consisted of two men and one woman barely older than he. Sara felt immense sorrow for them. The drafting pool must be down very low. All of the true adults were gone or had fled, leaving children to fill their uniforms. "Here," the MP said, interrupting her thoughts.

He handed her a piece of paper with a number scratched on it. *Tyler Baskins 555-4229.* "Looks like you don't have a landline," he continued, "one of the stores in town has a working phone I'm sure. Call me from there if you see him."

"Of course," Sara replied.

Tyler Baskin the child soldier whistled, and two additional soldiers came from around the back of the cabin. As the adrenaline began to exit her veins, she had a chance to truly look at the squadron. They were indeed children. They had to be her daughters' ages. They looked tired and hid their fear by white-knuckling their guns held tightly to their chests.

The numbers began to rattle off in Sara's head. There were over 300 million people living in the old country. Over half of them now dead. And half of the other half had fled.

All the recent years of building the wall and securing the borders had left most Americans unable to flee. So incredibly ironic that Mexico and Canada now had to prevent the influx of millions of Americans trying to escape the worst civil war in world history.

~

Brian and Amy held hands under the berry bush, watching the soldiers leave. Brian had to pry his hand from hers, noting one of her rings had embedded itself in his knuckle. One of the soldiers had come so close to them they could see the stitching on his pant hem. Brian rubbed his face and rolled onto his back, genuinely checking to see if a puddle had been left where he laid. "Oh my god," Amy gasped, "They didn't take Marie. I thought for sure they were coming for Marie."

Amy began to lose the control she had been holding. Brian grabbed her hand again and squeezed. "Come on," he said.

They crawled back out from the bushes and jogged to the front of the cabin. Brian threw open the front door. "Marie. Sara. Are you okay?" he beckoned.

Brian was met with the wrong end of a shotgun pointed right at his head. Amy gasped, "Mom!"

"Sara, what are you doing?" Brian asked putting his hands in the air.

Sara circled Brian, backing him and Amy into the house, shutting the door. Marie sat at the table looking at Brian with no sympathy. "Mother, what the hell are you doing?" Amy shouted.

"Sara," Brian said in a slow calm voice, "what happened?"

"Who the hell are you?" Sara demanded.

Amy looked at her mother agape and then to Marie, who sat back crossing her arms. Brian's eyes narrowed and he tilted his head. "Brian Miller," he answered, "from London,

Ontario."

Sara cocked the gun. "Try again."

Brian looked at Amy. "Is this what the MPs were here about?" he said slowly.

"Talk."

Brian ran his hands through his hair. He took a deep breath and dropped onto the couch. "Ok," he started, "Ok. My name isn't Brian."

"What?" Amy gasped.

"Sure isn't," Marie chided, "Joey."

Brian rested his elbows on his knees and dropped his head, took a deep breath and looked up at Sara. "They were here for me," he said, now realizing.

"No shit Sherlock!" Marie blared.

"How dare you bring danger to this house. You knew we were hiding," Sara said, "You acted like you were here to help us. But you weren't. You were here to hide too, weren't you!"

Amy finally spoke, "You're AWOL too."

Brian stood up, to which Sara responded by stepping forward with the gun again. Brian sat and began to explain. "I'm from downstate. Yes, my name is Joe Piret. After the Indy bombing, my number was called and I ran. I drove until I couldn't find a working gas station and then I walked down dirt roads until I found the furthest place from civilization."

Amy sat next to Marie and took her hand. For the first time in weeks, Marie didn't take it back.

"I found your cabin, and it was relatively stocked. I had a bunch of cash and used that for food until it ran out. A few weeks ago, I called my grandparents who live in rural Indiana to let them know I was ok."

Brian sighed and pushed his fists into his eyes. When he lowered them, his eyes were wet. "They must have told them where I was."

The gun began to feel heavy in Sara's arms. He may well have been pushing thirty, but Mr. Piret was nothing more than a scared barely-adult just like Marie. "You should've told us," Sara said.

Brian nodded his head in agreeance and put his head in his hands. "I'm so sorry I put you in danger."

His shoulder began to shake. Amy looked at her mother holding a gun and Marie who just stared blankly out the window. Aghast, Amy stood and went to him. "Listen. Yes, you should've told us. But no one," Amy said looking at her family, "could blame you for what you did. Going to that war is suicide. If people didn't know that before, they sure as hell know it now."

Brian discreetly wiped his eyes. Amy looked at her mom with her hands on her hips. Sara sighed and lowered the gun. "No more secrets," Sara said.

"Yes, ma'am," he replied.

"So, Joe is it?" Sara asked.

"No, mam'," Brian said, "Joe is gone. I like Brian. That was my dad's name."

"Was?" Marie asked.

Brian stood and chewed his thumb. He walked to the front door. "They're all dead," he said and walked out of the cabin.

Amy watched him go. She then turned to her mother. "You could've handled that a bit more maturely," she said hotly, "we are not the only people trying to stay alive."

Amy stormed out the door after Brian.

"Brian wait!" Amy called.

Brian stopped walking but didn't face her. She grabbed his hand, "So new Brian. How much of what we know is really you?"

Brian lowered his head. "Everything," he whispered.

Amy walked with him in silence. The birds were chirping and the sounds of small animals scurrying about surrounded them. "Favorite color, food, and TV show?"

He looked at her, tears still steaking his dirty face. "Green, Thai, and *South Park*," he answered, "you?"

"Purple, pasta, *Friends*."

They walked further down the trail. "Any family or friends left, dream vacation, favorite holiday?"

Brian didn't answer at first. Amy waited, raising her eyes to a clearing in the trees. Dusk had allowed a few of the brightest stars to shine through. "Starting at the former," he began, "Thanksgiving, Scotland, and.."

He swallowed. "No. They are all gone from my life in one way or the other."

Amy took his hand and squeezed. "Ok, in order," she started, "Yes. I have a Father. Who I told you about. He's the one trying to find us. For the longest time, I kind of wanted him to. I know he's not a good guy. He treats my mother like, well horribly. And I am so tired of being scared and running. I wanted to go back to my normal, regardless of how dysfunctional it was."

"I miss my boyfriend," Amy continued looking sidelong at Brian in case that wounded him, "I miss my bed. I just want everything to go back to the way it was before the war."

Brian stopped and turned to her. Amy ran her fingers through her hair, "Um. And Mexico, I guess and the 4th of July. Long answer to the short question."

Amy turned red. She talked too much. Anthony always told her that. She lifted to face to him. Brian looked haunted. His eyes were red. He was disheveled, covered in scratches, and berry bush sprigs stuck out from his thick curls. He searched her face. "If I was him, I would've scaled mountains and swam oceans to be with you."

Amy frowned and thought of that day at the park. He didn't want to come. He didn't want to be with her, at least not in the long term. "If I were him, I would've kept you safe no matter the cost."

Amy's pulse thundered in her ears. The reality of what Anthony may never be hit her like a train. Amy wanted to cry. Brian smiled, lifting her chin. He had the cutest lopsided smile. She felt herself leaning into him and took his other hand. "So?" he asked.

"So, what?" she said with tears in her eyes.

Brian smiled, "Next year, Cancun?"

Amy lost her nerve and closed the gap between them. She pressed her lips so fiercely to his she felt his teeth. Brian held her face with his hands and greedily kissed her back. The stress of the past few months began to ease. She had fought this for so long and she hated herself for how good it felt. She pulled away gasping. His deep eyes met hers. God, she loved his eyes deep pools of green-blue. Looking into them now, she knew she had a big problem. A very big problem.

~

The next several weeks passed in a blur of routine. They would get up, tend to the house, make meals, hunt, play Euchre, and then go to bed. And every day Sara would cross off the day on her handmade calendar. She'd flipped to February, counting the weeks until they could leave. It was only then her family could be at peace. Marie and Amy had been getting along lately, which also brought her peace of mind.

And Sara had noticed the sexual tension between Amy and Brian, too. The stolen glances, chances to brush up against one another or go into the forest to forage. Maybe Brian was the push Amy needed to be convinced Canada was where she should be. But even with the promising lead of love to keep her family together, the puppy-dog eyes and deep sighs from the two of them had Sara rolling her eyes behind closed doors. Sara knew it was driving Marie crazy too. Because when she mentioned she was going hunting, Marie shot off the couch and out the front door before Sara could grab her gear. They weren't off the porch when Amy began giggling and Brian's deep voice was whispering sweet nothings. Marie actually gagged. Sara smiled. "You about sick of them too?"

"Yeeeesssss," Marie hissed.

Sara laughed, adjusting her father's shotgun. Brian did most of the hunting but the late distraction of newly-requited love left their cooler nearly empty. Sara felt the weight of her weapon. Her everyday struggles were such that she didn't think of Paradise often. If she was honest with herself, it was far too painful to remember those days: good and bad. But being back home was a reminder of what she was capable of. All the things her daddy taught her had come back so naturally. Was it nice to have a man there to help shoulder some of the responsibility? Sure. But knowing she could do it on her own if she had to was more liberating than she could have imagined. And since the appearance of the MPs, the four of them had laid low, so her skillset had been invaluable.

However, Ife had come several times to barter and stayed for dinner. Years of being manipulated into silence made Sara an excellent observer. And as blasé as they tried to be, she knew something was happening between Ife and Marie. Sara could also tell her girls were reaching their limits of being cooped up in her childhood home, but she relished it. If it weren't for the fear of being caught, Sara would've stayed there. They walked in silence to Sara's favorite bird spot. It was odd hunting with someone. She always went alone. But Marie, accustomed to teenage scowling silence, was a perfect hunting companion. Not too long after they had sat down and settled, the unmistakable sound of turkeys rose from the brush. Without a sound, Sara aimed her gun towards it. Marie held her breath, looking between the brush and her mother like a tennis match. Moments later a gaggle of turkeys waddled into sight. Sara took a deep breath and got one foot under her. She fired once and cocked the gun. The surviving turkeys took to the air. Standing swiftly, she fired again, dropping another from the sky. Marie whistled. "Wow."

Sara turned and smiled at her. "That's the easy part," she said, "removing the feathers and the gutting is a gorefest."

Marie laughed as they walked to the birds. Sara and

Marie stood looking down at the dead birds. "It's sad, though right?" Marie said.

Sara nodded. She never liked to kill anything. But growing up, it was how they ate. Suddenly, a memory of her father struck her.

"You know," Sara said, "Native cultures thank every animal that gives their life so they may eat. They even throw a small piece of meat into the fire as an offering of thanks. Because the animal gave their life, they were able to survive."

Marie nodded, sniffing. "I like that."

"Who taught you to shoot like that?" Marie asked, touching the bird's wing.

"My dad," she said smiling.

Marie looked up at her. "You're like this whole other person I don't even know."

Sara smiled sadly. "I haven't been able to show you," she said quietly, "and that's my fault. Here watch this."

Sara took her hunting knife out and pointed at a large nearby tree. She raised the knife and threw it, hitting the center of the trunk. "Holy shit!" Marie said standing.

"And this here is yarrow," she said pointing to a dead weed, "it can stop excessive bleeding. And there, that's sumac."

Sara pointed at a large stalk with a dried berry-looking bloom on the top. "It can be used to treat eye problems. And the blackberry bushes you see everywhere. Well, those berries can be eaten when you have an upset stomach."

Marie kind of stared at her mom for a moment. Sara blushed. "Who are you?"

Sara laughed, picking up the birds. They slowly walked back to the cabin, enjoying the crisp fall weather. Sara could hardly believe they had been there for almost three months. Their old life seemed like ages ago.

"Where is your mom?"

Marie's question took her off guard. Sara's breath shook as she inhaled deeply. She felt the pulse in her neck quicken.

Her mother was someone she had spent decades pretending not to care about. Sara had pushed her to the farthest places of her mind. Once as a small child, she asked her dad where her mommy went. The look of pain on his face was enough that she never asked again. But people talked. And it wasn't long after Sara had heard through the townies that her mother had taken off to some big city downstate.

"Poor Eddie," they'd say in hushed tones, "left to raise that baby girl all alone."

Sara would lower her head in shame. Clearly, there was something wrong with Sara that her own mother didn't want her. Even as an adult who knew better, the feelings of being unwanted still whispered to her in times of weakness.

"I don't know," Sara finally said, "I heard she was near Detroit, but now…your guess is as good as mine."

Marie was silent for a bit longer, then said. "You got dealt a real shit hand of cards."

Sara stopped and looked at her.

"Like, not for nothing, but you didn't have a mom," Marie continued, "your cousin raped you, your dad died, you married my father."

Sara's swallowed, her eyes burning.

"Freddie died. Sam's probably dead. We're on the run," Marie said, bluntly, "I think we need to burn some serious sage."

Marie looked back at her mother, gauging her reaction. "No," Marie said, taking her hand, "no more tears. Look at what you have done to protect us. To keep me safe. You are a warrior who can hunt for food and make eye drops from weeds. We are going to have a great life in Canada."

Sara pulled her daughter into a hug. "I love you, baby girl."

They stayed like that for a beat.

"I think I need something bigger than burning sage," Sara said, holding her daughter tight.

"We could always sacrifice your firstborn," Marie said, muffled into Sara's chest.

Sara whacked the back of her head playfully and the dead bird's head flopped on Marie's shoulder. Marie screamed. Sara laughed.

~

Amy and Brian stood watching the two walk into the forest. Their fingers reached for each other. When they were sure Marie and her mother weren't coming back, they threw the curtains closed. Brian picked her up and spun her around. He brought his lips to hers. Holding his face, she kissed him deeply. They found every excuse to sneak away to get wood, water, a breath of fresh air. They'd kiss and he'd run his hands along her body. There was only so much they could do in the wet, freezing woods. At the moment, Anthony was far from her thoughts. And each time, she'd tell herself it was the last time she'd let Brian kiss her. But Amy needed human touch. And finally having it made her insides melt. She knew he needed it too. He took a breath between her lips and slowed down their pace, almost savoring her touch. Brian held her face with one hand and smoothed her hair with his other. He touched her as if he had rehearsed it in his head a million times. They both knew being alone in this cabin was going to lead one place. "Wait," Brian said, letting her go.

He went into the closet and pulled out the leather piece he had been working on. "Here," he said, handing it to her.

Amy took the leather and held it up. It was a fur-lined hooded coat. "Oh my god, you made this for me?"

Brian smiled proudly. Amy slid it on, and it fit perfectly. "How'd you get the size right?" she said, admiring herself in the bathroom mirror. "It's perfect."

Brian came up from behind, wrapping his arms around her. "I used your hoodie as a guide. You really like it?"

"I'm about to show you how much."

Amy took his hand and led him to the bedroom. He slipped the coat and her clothes from her body and stood back, taking her in. "Perfect," he whispered.

Amy smiled, sliding her panties off, taking her time bending over. Brian choked. Amy laughed. She unhooked her bra and threw it at him. He caught it with one hand. "Wait," she said and picked up the coat, putting it on with a wicked grin, "I need to break in the leather."

Brian scooped her up and dumped her on the bed with a growl. It was all so new. Being with someone who was so captivated by her. Anthony loved her. She knew that. But she had always been the instigator. The one who approached him for every intimacy, from the first kiss to sex. She pushed the image of Anthony's tan face and dark crew cut hair from her mind and leaned back on the bed. Brian took off his shirt. He wasn't built, but he was fit. Brian had gained some weight in the months they had all lived together, and the dark circles under his eyes had brightened. Naked, he climbed into bed with her. Kissing her deeply, he traced circles around her breast with his fingertips. Amy's body responded. She felt her blood heat. Amy leaned back to see him. They'd never been naked together. "Are you sure?" he said.

Amy nodded, taking him in her hand. "Are you?" she asked with another wicked grin.

Brian moaned, leaning his head back into the pillow. "I'll take that as a yes," she purred.

Amy could get used to being in control. There was no worry about saying the wrong thing to push this man away. Brian wanted her unconditionally, and it felt good. Brian sat up, taking her hand off him. She smiled seeing her handy work. He was more than ready. Kissing down her stomach, Brian reached her. Amy arched her back, pushing into his mouth. They rocked in a rhythm, almost sending her over the edge when Brian looked up. "Oh no," he grinned, "not yet."

Playfully, he slid a finger deep inside her. She was begging for him to move his hand faster. He smiled and clicked his tongue at her. "I want to make you want me,"

Brian whispered into her parted lips.

Sliding his body up against her legs, she felt his hardened length finds its way up her thigh. She edged her body towards it, trying desperately to have him inside. Brian leaned on his elbows, and their noses touched. "I want to make you happy," Brian kissed one cheek, "I want to make you smile."

He kissed her other cheek. "But right now," he said into her mouth, "I want to make you scream."

Brian climbed between her legs, and Amy accepted the full length of him. The power of his thrust about sent Amy over the edge. And scream she did. They had both wanted this for so long it was an incredible release. Placing a thumb on her mound, Brian rocked her hips back and forth. It was so different. Amy hadn't ever been with another man. She felt roguish. She felt alive. Suddenly, stars filled her vision behind her eyelids as he made her fall into ecstasy. Amy felt her pulse in every part of her body as a loud gasp escaped her lips. Brian quickly covered her mouth with his and his climax rocked her body. He laid on top of her, their breath matching. She ran her fingers down his back. He shivered at her touch. "I love you," he whispered into her hair.

Amy stopped moving her hands.

"Shit," he said sitting up quickly, "disregard that."

He quickly got her a towel and wiped it down her thighs. "I'm sorry," he said, "I was in the moment. I didn't mean it. I mean I did. Or maybe I could."

Amy watched him fumbling, and her heart sank. She was playing with him as Anthony did her. Here was a man who truly loved her and she led him on because she wanted to feel wanted. *I am an awful person*, she thought, getting up and putting on her clothes.

"Don't worry about it," she said, avoiding eye contact, "slip of the tongue."

"In more ways than one," he poorly joked, trying to lighten the mood, "Am I right? Eh?"

Amy faked a smile and grabbed her phone. Brian pulled

his clothes on quickly, following her out of the room. "You can't be serious," he said desperately.

"What do you mean?" Amy feigned naivety.

Brian ran his hands through his hair, pacing. It stood up on end. He looked wild. "You cannot be serious! Running off to call, email him or whatever it is you do in the woods that you think you are hiding so well."

Amy looked out the kitchen window, crossing her arms. It was true. Amy did venture to the woods alone as often as she could. She and Anthony emailed back and forth. The emails became less and less frequent. There wasn't much to say anymore. They always went along the line of "I'm in Michigan. I don't know where."

Lie.

"I'll be back in February. Have you thought about our future?"

Anthony's silence.

"I don't know what you're talking about." Amy said, flippantly.

"Bullshit," Brian said, his voice wavering, "Stop it! What is this between us? One minute you act like we are together, and the next you are buried in your phone searching the woods for your lost signal."

Amy turned with tears in her eyes. "I told you I couldn't give you what you want. You know I have a boyfriend who I am going back to as soon as you guys attempt your hike from hell!"

"I wonder what your boyfriend would think of what we just did—" Brian hadn't finished his sentence when Amy's hand connected with his face.

Brian and Amy stood staring at each other. "Fine," Brian said, the light going out in his eyes.

Amy's heart was bursting from her chest with rage. But when she saw the pain on his face, it crushed her. She reached for him, "I'm sorry."

"Don't," he said pushing past her, "don't ever again."

~

Marie watched a disheveled Brian throw the front door open and walk to the truck. She and her mom looked at one another. "That can't be good," her mom said.

The Jeep roared to life and began backing out almost running them over. "Hey, asshat!" Marie shouted.

Brian rolled the window down, tears streaking his face. Marie raised a brow. "Sorry," he mumbled, "I'm headed to town."

"I'm going with you," Marie said, already rounding the Jeep.

Her mother sighed, shouldering the birds again. "Do you think that's wise?"

Marie climbed in and leaned over Brian. He barely noticed, staring blankly out the windshield. "We haven't heard from anyone in town about soldiers since the last raid," Marie said, half-lying.

It was true. Ife hadn't told her about any MPs in the area. But she hadn't exactly asked. They were too busy sneaking off to the woods. And then their mouths were a bit busy tending to other missions. Her mother pursed her lips, which meant she was about to cave. "Fine."

Boom, Marie thought smugly.

Brian turned the car around and began down the drive. As they drove away, the sound of her mom's voice barely registered in her ears. "Be home before sundown."

Marie smiled. *Not a chance.*

Marie was so excited to get off the cabin property she was almost bouncing in her seat. She had completely forgotten Brian was even there until he said, "What is Anthony like?"

Marie turned. "You need to stop letting her lead you on."

Brian shook his head and wiped his eyes. "She's not coming, is she?"

Marie sighed and crossed her arms. "Brian, she told us

all from the beginning she would stay with us until we left. Then she was taking the Jeep back. My mom isn't happy with it, and if I'm being honest, neither am I."

Brian gripped the steering wheel. "It's so dangerous," he whispered.

Marie shrugged. "What are we supposed to do? Drag her to Canada?"

"I just thought," he said, "after a while, she'd change her mind."

Marie wanted to snap at him again. But she would be leaving Ife in two months herself. The truth of it she had avoided for weeks. Allowing herself to only focus on the next time she would see Ife. Without even asking, Brian pulled into the Berry Patch lot. Brian threw the truck into park and looked out the window. Marie suddenly felt sorry for the dope. His wild curls, big blue eyes, and lanky body made him seem like a puppy with too-big feet. And her sister had kicked the poor dog. Marie shook her head and put her hand on his. "Brian," she said, "if Amy can't see what a great guy you are, then she's dumber than I thought possible. Which is saying a lot because I've known for years she's a certified dipshit."

When he turned to her with big tears welling in his eyes, Marie wanted to punch him. *Oh my god, stop crying. Always with the crying.*

She pushed down the irritation. Marie sighed, knowing she was missing precious seconds with Ife. "Anthony is self-centered and a follower," Marie answered, "Amy has wanted to marry him forever. And the dumbass wants nothing to do with it. Honestly, if he could, he'd have moved on. But our town is so small, and there's nowhere else to go."

"That's awful," Brian said quietly, "she deserves better."

Marie had had enough of the free therapy session and hopped out of the truck, grabbing Charlette's purse. She had to buy something to keep up this ruse of important town business. "OK," she said, closing the door and leaning in the window, "good talk."

Brian just stared forward, his lip quivering. *Good lord*, she screamed in her head.

If she hadn't admitted it before, this clinched it. *Thank god I'm into women.*

"Hey," she said over her shoulder, "Go grab a beer and I'll see ya in a few hours."

"But your mom said–" Brian began.

He was aggressively ignored as Marie skipped to the back door of the Berry Patch.

"Hello," Marie sang from the back door.

Ife's dad's head peered around the corner. "Hi Marie," he said.

Marie waved, "Hi Mr. Wilson."

He disappeared and reappeared with a glass of pop-no-ice just how she liked it. "You're the best," Marie smiled.

"So I've been told," he smiled back, then calling to the front, "Ife, your buddy's here."

The sound of her laughter filled the restaurant. Marie swooned. Ife came through the swinging doors. Her braids were tied in a top knot, and she was wearing a Slipknot tee shirt. *Hilarious.*

Her jeans held every curve of her legs. Marie took her in without hiding it. "Hey babe," Ife said, taking her in her arms, "this is a surprise."

Marie kissed her gently. "The boss doesn't let us out of her sight."

Ife smiled sadly. "She's not wrong," Ife said, "MPs are still crawling around this place like rats."

Shit.

Ife took off her apron. "I want to show you something."

"Your dad doesn't need help in the café?" Marie asked.

"Dad," Ife hollered over her shoulder, "I'll be back in an hour."

Marie heard the muffled acceptance from Mr. Wilson in the kitchen as they walked out the back door. They walked south down Highway 123. It was getting really cold.

Northern Michigan was known for its severe weather shifts, and today was no exception. Spring in the morning. Summer by noon and fall by dinner. Thankfully, there wasn't any wind today. So their heavy winter coats and boots kept them warm. They held hands and took turns asking each other questions. "Where did you grow up?" Marie asked.

"Detroit," she answered, "but it wasn't safe there anymore. So we came here. Tried to start a new life. To help people."

Marie bit back the question about her mother. Because she didn't want to invite more questions about her dad. "Does your mom know about us?" Ife asked suddenly.

"Um," Marie shook her head, "I don't think so. Neither does my sister. But Brian does. The dumb oaf is in love with Amy. I think they're a perfect match on IQs alone."

Ife smiled slightly. A car came up the road, and they dropped their hands. The war had brought a lot of old ideologies back, and they didn't want to risk bringing any unnecessary attention. "Where is your mom?" Marie asked, regretting the questions as it left her mouth.

"She passed away from cancer when I was ten," Ife said.

"I'm sorry," Marie whispered.

"Don't be," Ife said, taking a deep breath, "I was lucky to have a mom like her. Even if it was for such a short time."

"You know," Marie said carefully, "you could come with us. To Canada."

Ife took her hand again but didn't answer. "We wouldn't have to hide who we are there." Marie continued. "We could start a life. Go to college. Open a new café, call it The Perry Batch, Eh. We'd have to serve poutine and beavertail, but…"

Ife stopped and looked into her eyes. "I can't."

Marie swallowed. "You could."

Ife shook her head. "I have too much to do here."

Marie let go of her hand and kept walking. "Marie please," Ife trotted up to catch her, "you know how I feel about you. But I can't leave my dad, and we can't leave Paradise. Not yet."

Marie studied the beach to avoid looking at her. Ife took her by the shoulders. "Please listen to me," Ife said.

"What am I to you then?" Marie said, fighting tears "Am I just another Fudgie? Another tourist you fuck and dump?"

"Woah, woah," Ife said taking her hands in her face, "come on now. You know me better than that. Marie, I have never met anyone like you. You are strong and smart. Funny. Beautiful. I love you, okay? But I was worried getting close would make everything harder."

Marie choked back a sob. "You love me?"

No one had ever loved her. Not like this. She tried to imagine dating boys at home. The miserable kiss with Colin made her think she wasn't capable of feeling that way. Like she was a broken toy missing the vital brain cells to process affection. But here stood a woman who took her breath away from the moment she laid eyes on her. And by some miracle, Ife felt the same way. Ife smiled and leaned in, kissing her gently. "Come on," she whispered, "we're here."

They walked down a drive to a long-overgrown parking lot. Marie gasped. It was a carnie fair. An old rusted broken-down fair, complete with a Ferris wheel. The large ride sat rotting. The soft light from the setting sun made the colors explode. It was incredibly sad and beautiful at the same time. "What is this place?" she whispered, afraid to awaken the heavy energy it held.

"It was an old carnie operation," Ife said, jumping into the ticket booth.

The booth had red and white stripes and leaned like Pisa. "How many tickets, my dear?" Ife voiced, twisting an invisible mustache.

"Sixty-nine," Marie answered.

"Boo," Ife hopped out, teasing her lame joke.

Marie laughed and spun around, taking it all in. "Does any of it still work?"

"Oh god no," Ife answered, "I wouldn't dare get on one,

even if it did."

Marie walked further into the ruins. Absentmindedly, Marie took Ife's hand. She didn't feel danger, but walking through the past was overwhelming. They walked past a carnie game with water guns. The mildewed and faded stuffed toys still hung from the ceiling. They kept walking in silence. It was like a living museum. Marie vaguely remembered going to something similar when she was very young. The lights and loud music were too much for her. And her sister and brother teased her when she refused to get on the Tilt-A-Whirl.

"The fair rolled in about three years before my dad and me," Ife said, hopping into a bumper car, "the entire company walked away from it. After one of the big bombings, that is."

"Where'd they go?"

"Who knows. If they were smart, Canada. If they had a death wish, the front line."

Marie sat next to Ife in the bumper car. Ife put an arm around her. Marie was very still. The sounds of the fair all those years ago took over her ears. The lights of the rides going round and round. The smell of burned popcorn and sugar. A man on stilts leaned over to her, putting his clown face next to hers. *Are you having fun?* the clown said to her from the memory.

Marie felt like she was suffocating. Then her brother's hand slid into hers and the image of him filled her mind. Freddie took her hand that day and told the clown to hit the skids. Marie was so thankful. And his voice echoed, *I'll always keep you safe.*

"My brother died a few months ago," Marie said breathlessly.

Ife turned and looked at her. "Why didn't you tell me?"

"I didn't want to," Marie said, stuffing down her emotion, "I don't want to remember him. I don't want to think about my dad. I don't want to think about saying goodbye to Amy. Though part of me is ecstatic."

"Marie.."

Marie got louder. "I don't want to think about the people who died in the war. I don't want to think about what we did to Doyle."

"Marie…"

"I don't want to think about being caught or going hungry. And I don't want to think about leaving you."

Ife took a deep breath. A small breeze lifted a tent flap. But Marie was certain her chilled bones weren't from it.

"I don't know your brother, Mar," Ife said, "and I know he wasn't given nearly enough time. But how lucky he was to have had a sister like you."

Warms tears slid down Marie's face. She missed him so much. His laugh The way he would pretend to be annoyed when she'd spy on him and Colin playing cards. He taught her to play Magic the Gathering, and then he made her part of his tribe. He protected their mother. He managed their dad. Freddie was wise and funny and the light of any gathering. Freddie felt so deeply for everything he held dear. But that was his mistake. Joining the army led to his demise. He loved Marie despite her faults. He loved her mother, sister, and father despite theirs. She was the one lucky to have him. And she should try to live her life in the way Freddie should have been able to live his. "I should head home," Marie said.

Ife nodded, and they started back towards Highway 123. Ten minutes into their walk back they saw the trucks and lights. Ife and Marie looked at one another and started to run. The MP trucks were parked in front of the Berry Patch. And Ife's father was sitting on the front step in handcuffs. "Dad!" Ife yelled running to him.

An MP stepped between them. He was, surprisingly, much older than many of the MPs they'd seen since fleeing South Dakota. Marie looked around at the operation. There were older, clearly more seasoned men and women in well-made uniforms. About fifteen in all, these were most definitely not the child scouts who had come to the cabin all those weeks before. The leader had salt and pepper hair cut military-short with a structured jaw. His badge said Harrison. And his squinty brown eyes narrowed at Ife. "What's going on?" Ife demanded, stepping into his face, "get those cuffs off of my dad now!"

"You better stand down," the MP said, palming his sidearm, "your father's under investigation. If we don't find anything, he's free to go."

Marie sighed in relief. Mr. Wilson was the kindest and sweet person she'd ever met. There was no way he was tied up with anything criminal. Then she saw Ife's face. It had gone ashen, and she took off running into the store. Marie quickly followed, dodging the MP when he tried to grab her arm.

"Ma'am," a different officer yelled, "get back here. Both of you! This place is being searched."

They sprinted up the stairs and found soldiers tearing her room apart. Posters had been torn from the walls, the bed was overturned and the picture of Ife's family was shattered under the boot of a soldier. "Get out," Ife yelled, "we haven't done anything wrong!"

Marie tried to pick some things off the floor when a strong arm pulled her to stand. Marie faced another large soldier gripping her wrists, twisting. He was so close to her face, she could smell his rancid breath and his unshaven face leering at her. Marie spat on him. "Oh, you're going to regret that, girl," he growled.

"Papers," Harrison ordered, entering the room, "both of your papers, now!"

Ife's eyes went wide, looking at Marie. Marie's heart leaped. *I'm dead.*

"I'm waiting," Harrison said, picking dirt from under his nails.

Ife went to her desk drawer and pulled out her Gray papers and draft number, pulling her ID from her purse. Harrison scanned them and searched her face. Sucking at his teeth, he threw them on the floor. He held a hand out to

Marie. Shit Breath still had her by her wrists. Which was good because her hands were shaking. "Let her go, Anderson," he said, annoyed.

Shit Breath roughly released her, and she stood, unable to think. Marie's hands went to her pockets, not sure what else to do, and her fingers gazed Charlette's purse. She quickly reached in for Charlette's papers. *Charlette for the save again.*

Marie didn't look much like Charlette, she knew, but the ID was scratched and bent. She held her breath. Harrison snatched the items and looked carefully at them. He got to the ID and looked at Marie. He held the ID out further from his face, squinting at the picture. Marie felt the vein in her neck pulse. Ife glared at Harrison with pure malice. Harrison sniffed and threw the papers to the ground. "Let's go," he said, flippantly motioning to Anderson.

Marie yelped in pain as Shit Breath grabbed her and dragged her down the stairs. Ife was being pulled by the other officer, swearing and flailing behind them. Harrison led the foursome outside. The MP's threw the girls out into the parking lot. Mr. Wilson hung his head. "Dad," Ife whimpered when two soldiers dragged him to stand.

One of Harrison's grunts whispered something in his ear, and the officer smiled. "Mr. Wilson," he said, his voice thick with arrogance, "it seems you have been hiding quite the operation here."

Marie looked at Ife, but Ife only stared straight ahead, willing Harrison to catch fire. Ife's face was wild with blind hatred. The commotion from the café led to three soldiers carrying tubs out to the parking lot. Harrison dug around in a few, clearly looking for something specific. "Here we are," he pulled out a handful of documents and ID cards, "a lot of paperwork for a man who makes shitty omelets."

"They're not mine," Mr. Wilson said flatly.

The look in Mr. Wilson's eyes said everything. Mr. Wilson wasn't getting out of whatever mess this was, and he knew it. "Whose are they?" Harrison said, approaching him, bending down to his eye level.

"I couldn't tell you," Mr. Wilson said, meeting his gaze.

Harrison nodded with a smug purse of his lips and paced like a cat. "Do you know what the penalty is for harboring, aiding, or assisting fugitives, Mr. Wilson?"

Ife began crying quietly. Marie felt her wet tears slide down her face as a familiar black Jeep came around the corner, parking a few yards away. Brian got out of the truck with his hand on his head in panic.

"Death," he said, then pointing at Ife, "They must be hers."

Marie tried to stand up but was quickly shoved down by MP Shit Breath who proceeded to kick her in the ribs. Marie saw stars and felt her lunch rise. "No," Mr. Wilson said quickly, "She's a just kid. She doesn't know anything about any of this."

"Is that an admission?"

Ife crawled on her knees to Harrison begging. "Please, sir. He's wouldn't do anything like that. Please let us go."

No one spoke. The wind stopped blowing. Even the cicadas held their breath. Harrison growled and drew his weapon, pointing it at Ife's head. The girls screamed. Marie's captor kicked her again. "Shut the fuck up."

"Well," Harrison said, "is that an admission? Are you helping fugitives? Is she? I'm confused."

By this time, some of the locals had come out of their cars or stopped to watch. Marie saw some were crying. Others covered their mouths in horror. The Wilsons were the cornerstone of Paradise. They were always there to lend a hand, a dollar, or a piece of pie. The entire street was silent. So much so that everyone heard Mr. Wilson whisper, "Yes."

Marie watched from a prone position as Harrison walked up to Mr. Wilson and shot him point-blank in the head. The ground spun. People shouted and cried out. But Ife's blood-curdling screams filled the street. Chaos erupted. Ife ran to her dad, trying to pick the pieces of his head up. Blood covered the sidewalk and door of the Berry Patch.

"Load up the supplies and paperwork," Harrison ordered.

Harrison turned towards the onlookers who were now crying and holding one another. "This is what happens when you interfere with Gray operations. There are no exceptions," he yelled to the crowd, "Traitors die."

Shit Breath gave Marie another kick aimed at her face and spat in her hair. Luckily, she braced for it, her fists taking most of the impact on his boot. Marie gasped for air, watching the MPs load into their trucks. Onlookers cowered as they drove past them, not meeting their gaze. A pair of long legs came running up the sidewalk and knelt next to her. "Marie," Brian's voice broke, "oh my god. Oh my god. Where are you hurt?"

He helped her sit, and she saw Ife. Rocking her father's body, she made an indescribably haunting sound. "Daddy, no," she sobbed, "Daddy please."

Once the trucks drove away, neighbors came running up to the Wilsons. Someone tried to untangle Ife from her dad, and she screamed, swinging wildly for them to get away. "Leave me alone!" she shrieked, cupping her dad's face.

Marie got a leg under herself. "Easy, Marie," Brian braced her, "you don't know how injured you are."

Marie held up a hand to him and limped to Ife. She was still throwing her arms out trying to protect the only family she had left. "Ife," Marie's voice came out hoarse, "Ife, please."

Marie knelt and crawled to her. Ife swung, connecting with Marie's cheek. Ife's eyes were wild like a feral animal. The smack she gave Marie took Ife off balance and Marie grabbed her, pulling her from Mr. Wilson. Marie held her tight, rubbing her back. "Shh," Marie said quietly, "I'm here. I'm here."

Ife whimpered in her arms. People surrounded them, speaking in low tones, moving about. Slowly, Brian lifted the two of them from the ground and started towards the Jeep. By the time they were standing, their neighbors had covered Mr. Wilson in a sheet and were taking his body inside.

Ife stared straight forward in the back seat. Blood had begun to dry and was peeling from her skin. Marie tried her best to wipe off the larger pieces of matter from Ife's body. She almost passed out when she tried to take off her shirt to use as a towel. Brian kept a watchful eye on the road in front and behind them and still managed to take off his shirt and give it to Marie. He tossed a water bottle in the back seat to help. Ife's lips trembled as Marie cleaned her face. Ife rambled quietly, completely disconnected from Marie's presence. Marie was in so much pain but kept a strong face, telling Ife about the warm shower and dinner waiting for her. When they pulled in the drive, Brian jumped out, running to the cabin, yelling for help. The front door nearly exploded off the hinges as her mother and Amy came running out.

Sara opened the door and gasped. Marie was so happy to see her. Ife slowly turned, meeting the gaze of all three. Amy dry heaved. "Get inside and get the shower going," her mother sternly ordered Amy.

Her mom gently took Ife's hand and led her out of the truck but not before eyeing Marie. She had to look awful. Her mom could hold a poker face in any situation, but at that moment her mother looked like the day she found out Freddie died. Marie tried to slide out of the Jeep herself and yelped in pain. "Stop," Brian said sliding his arms around her gently, "I've got you."

Marie was so tired. She hurt everywhere. The last moment she remembered was thinking how strong skinny Brian was to carry her so effortlessly. She leaned her head into his chest. He smelled like pine trees. The rocking movement from the Jeep to the cabin made her eyelids heavy. Marie passed out before she heard the cabin door close.

~

Sara held Marie's head over the bucket for the third time that night. Amy had been washing towels and clothes. Brian had emptied buckets and scrubbed out the bloody tiny shower. Sara shook her head with wrath. *How could anyone do this to another human being?*

Sara saw the bruises on Marie's body deepen before her eyes. Marie's fat lip grew and split from vomiting due to her concussion. By Brian's suggestion, someone needed to wake her every two hours. Which wasn't hard in that she kept throwing up. They checked her pupils, which seemed to be even, but Marie had a road ahead of her to heal. Luckily she was so out of it, Marie didn't hear Ife screaming in the shower. Amy had gone to help her bathe. "Daddy," echoed through the cabin, making Sara and Brian wince.

It was the most gut-wrenching thing Sara had ever heard. That level of grief could only be released by great trauma. Marie now laid back on the couch. Ife was finally asleep in the girls' bed. Brian had coaxed her into doing two shots of whiskey and a swig of allergy medicine. Not exactly the safest choice. But that girl needed to sleep. Her brain needed a break. Sara felt sick about the reality of what she'd face when she woke up. After the two were settled, Sara escaped to the nearby pond and fished out a dozen leeches.

Amy almost vomited again when Sara made a tiny nick in Marie's deepest bruises and placed the bloodsuckers over them. Brian led Amy to the kitchen, putting her in a tight hug. Sara was glad they had reconciled. For at least the moment. Soon Brian led Amy to Sara's room. Sara knew she wouldn't be able to sleep. She'd be up the entire night with worry. Amy and Brian slept in her bed after she insisted for the tenth time. They offered to take turns staying up, but Sara refused. Sara got up to check on Ife and plucked the fattened leeches from her baby's body. She woke Marie up every other hour and cleaned up the buckets and dishes from the melee. *I'm so tired. I'm so very tired of not being able to protect my children.*

When Brian rushed through the door all those hours

ago, Sara was pissed. She didn't like the idea of any of them in town. It was going to be a big *I told you so* until Brian filled her in. Sara couldn't believe Mr. Wilson was gone. That sweet, sweet man. Sara sipped her tea, looking out her window towards the north. Towards freedom. February couldn't come soon enough.

Marie groaned in pain as she woke the next morning. Sara could tell she was confused. The leeches had helped with the bruising, but Marie could very well have a cracked rib. "It hurts to breathe," Marie gasped when she sat up.

Sara had ibuprofen and water waiting for her. Marie took the pills and Sara began to walk her to the bathroom. After turning on the shower, Sara helped Marie get out of her clothes. Sara swallowed back her horror at the sight of Marie's battered body. Marie purposefully didn't look down.

"I'll be right here," Sara said, shutting the shower door.

Sara cringed, hearing Marie gasp and grunt, trying to clean herself. "Momma," her small voice squeaked, "I can't reach my hair."

Sara angled herself in the shower and scrubbed her hair clean. She hadn't washed her kids' hair in years. It brought back memories of night-time giggles and splashes with three kids under six in an overfilled bathtub. Sara rinsed the soap and got a towel ready for her. Wrapping herself tightly, Marie faced the half-fogged mirror. Sara saw her body begin to shake. Huge tears slid down her cheeks. "He's dead, momma," Marie sobbed, "I saw his head when it happened."

Sara hugged her. There was nothing else she could say or do. Marie wept. She cried and choked and wept more. "What is Ife going to do? Her family. They are all gone, mom. We have to help her."

Sara nodded hugging her tighter. They had to get out of this hell-hole. Somehow local MPs knew this area held refugees and dodgers. It was only a matter of time until they figured out who they were. Amy and Brian were walking out of the bedroom as Sara walked Marie out of the bathroom in clean clothes. The four of them saw Ife sitting on the couch. She was still in the T-shirt they had put her in from the night before.

Sara walked to Ife and knelt in front of her. "Ife, honey," Sara said, "are you physically hurt? Can I get you anything?"

Ife shook her head slowly. "I'm so so sorry, sweetheart," Sara continued, "You can stay with us as long as you want."

Ife finally tore her gaze from whatever she had been staring at. She took Sara's hand. "I have to get back to the store," Ife said robotically, "I have to get it cleaned up. There's a lot of work to do."

Sara blinked. She looked over Ife's shoulder at Brian and Amy. They looked as bewildered as she. Amy brought over a cup of tea and set it next to Ife. "What can we do to help?" Amy asked.

Marie stepped out of the bedroom dressed. She limped over to Ife and sat next to her, taking her hand. Sara went to get breakfast started, though she knew no one had an appetite.

~

Brian and Sara retired to different household chores. Ife and Marie sat on the couch holding each other, taking turns crying. Swallowing her guilt, Amy took the coat Brian had made her to shield her from the cold and slipped out the front door. Because finding a signal in the forest was tricky, Amy prepared for a lengthy hike, donning gloves and putting up her fur hood. She knew certain areas that were the honey spots for a signal. She needed to hear Anthony's voice. She wanted to come home. Amy cared for Brian, she truly did. But Amy pushed down what she felt for a one-way ticket out of this hell. Hearing what happened to Amare, and the insanity of Ife wanting to start the restaurant again, made her want to punch something. Didn't they realize that staying here was a death sentence? Even after all that, Marie and her mother stayed on track with their plan to walk the ice to Canada, which was weeks away. And at any moment, authorities could swoop down and shoot them where they stood. *I'm done*, she thought angrily, *with all of them*.

Brian tried to hold her after everything that had happened. It felt wrong. She was so nauseated and wanted to be left alone. The house smelled like vomit and blood. Every moment she spent with Brian felt like they were delaying the inevitable. She was going home to South Dakota to be with Anthony. Amy refused to go to Canada, and it wasn't like she and Brian could stay in Paradise. So even if she wanted to, there was no life for them anywhere. Furthermore, she didn't even want to be with him, or so she kept telling herself. So Amy snuck to the woods while everyone was busy under the guise of collecting kindling. To her dismay, there was a bit of a wind today, but being among the trees blocked most of it. When she got to the frozen stream, two bars popped up on her phone. *Yes*!

Quickly, she called Anthony. Two rings and his familiar voice said, "Hello?"

"Anthony?"

"Oh my god, Amy? It's so good to hear your voice. Where are you? Are you ok?"

"I'm still in Michigan," Amy shivered from the cold, "I'm so sorry I haven't been able to call. The signal is horrible out here."

Static and crackles made it hard to hear. "Why haven't you called?" he rightly asked.

Because I have been with another man, her conscience yelled at her.

"Well," she said, trying to think, "things have been really complicated around here. I needed to make sure my mom and sister were safe. And now I realize they never will be, and I just want to come home."

"I want you home too. I hate that you haven't been here," he said, "Listen, tell me where you are, and your dad and I will come and get you."

Amy paused. "I don't want my dad here, Anthony," Amy said, "you have no idea what he'd do to my mom."

Anthony sighed. She could almost hear him roll his eyes. "Anthony," she said, "this isn't funny. Marie is in a lot of trouble. I wouldn't put it past my dad to turn her in and do worse to my mom. You cannot tell him where I am."

A pause. Shuffling of the phone. "Anthony," Amy checked the signal.

Two bars. "Anthony," she called out again.

"I'm here. I'm here."

"Promise me," Amy said, "Promise me you won't tell my dad."

"I promise," Anthony said dryly, "but I think he'd help you, Amy. I just want you back. I hate how we left things."

"Me too," Amy said quietly.

"I, uh, even started looking at rings," he said with a chuckle, "Absence makes the heart grow fonder, right?"

Amy laughed, choking back a sob. The phone began to echo again with the tinny sound of bad reception. "Anthony," Amy called out.

"I'm here. Amy. Stop yelling. God."

They both laughed. It felt good. It felt like old times. "Paradise."

"What?" Anthony said.

"I'm in Paradise, Michigan."

A voice began to echo through the woods, calling her name. Amy knew before she saw him who was coming through the trees. "Paradise, huh? Is it as nice as it sounds?"

"I have to go," Amy tried to get him off the phone.

"Wait, Amy we need to set a date for me to come and get you," Anthony interrupted her.

"Amy!" Brian shouted from the tree line.

"Who is that?" Anthony's voice went cold.

Amy's mouth went dry. "Hey Ames," Brian said trotting up to her, "you need to stay closer to the house. Your mom is freaking out."

Brian saw the phone hidden in Amy's hood. His blue

eyes turned to ice. "Nice Amy. Real nice," Brian said loudly so Anthony would hear.

Brian stalked back the way he came. "Ames?" Anthony asked with a growl. "Who the hell else calls you Ames?"

Anthony drew out the pet name Anthony used for her that Brian had adopted on his own. "It's," she began, "his name is Brian."

"Why is he fetching you for your mom?"

The wind began to swirl the snow at her feet. "He is living with us," Amy stuttered, "he had nowhere else to go, and we had space."

"So you have a guy living with you," Anthony said quietly, "and he calls you Ames."

Amy went silent. She wasn't good at lying to protect herself like her mom or witty like Marie. Loud static filled her ears and a click. The call ended, and she knew it wasn't the signal.

~

The funeral was short and small. Only a handful of locals braved the weather to say goodbye to Amare Wilson. Marie's face was black and blue but held her head high as she walked into the church holding Ife's hand. Ife looked like her spirit had been ripped from her body. Her face was ashen and her shoulders hunched. At the alter sat a crudely-made pine box. Closed casket of course. Someone volunteered to speak as the preacher. Paradise hadn't had a formal service in years. The man who Sara had seen in town a few times nervously took the pulpit. Visions of Freddie's funeral haunted her memory. She pushed them down hard. Today was not the day she'd surrender to a mental breakdown. Ife and Marie needed her. She noticed Amy not sitting with Brian. Sara had hoped Amy would change her mind over these past months and come to Canada. The thought hadn't escaped her to hog-tie and drag her across Lake Superior on a sled.

Amy's beautiful dark hair was tied up in a bun. They didn't have nice clothes, and neither did anyone else. But everyone attempted to look put-together to honor Mr. Wilson. Sara scanned the crowd. About half of the faces she somewhat recognized, but the other half were strangers. They all looked tired and hungry. The children of these people clung to them, too afraid to cry. Paradise was a revolving door of the downtrodden, and it was now clear to her that Mr. Wilson had a very big hand in it.

Sara's heart broke as she turned to watch Marie. Ife was staring straight ahead. The faux-preacher took the pulpit. He began speaking in broken sentences. He took a sip of water and gripped the lectern, his fingers still trembling. "Amare was," he tried to start again, "The Lord says to be kind and help others. So Amare was.."

Sara felt terrible for the man. The people gathered sagged in their seats from the gravity of it all. Then a familiar friend caught her eye. In the corner of the pulpit, Michelle the spider was going about her life. Sara cocked her head. Spinning a web of perfect symmetry, she thrived. The world around her was crashing down, and here Michelle sent her the message: just keep moving.

Sara found herself rising from her seat. She walked down the aisle to the alter. The man at the podium let out a sigh of relief when she asked to say a few words. Amy sat up straight, and Marie's eyes went wide. Sara wasn't a talker. She was an avoider. Had been her entire adult life. Sara wanted to go unnoticed. Sara wanted to be small. But being no one solved nothing. And Amare deserved to be honored. "My name is Sara," she began, "and I didn't know Amare well. But I know his daughter."

Ife's reddened eyes looked up at her. "And I don't know many of you. And it has come to my attention that is all by design."

That gave way to a few hushed chuckles. Sara took a deep breath. She palmed the pulpit, her hands slick. "But anyone who could raise such an incredible human being has to be amazing himself. The one common denominator in Paradise is that Berry Patch café and the Wilsons. This is not the send-off he deserves. Amare should have been given a hero's goodbye with ceremonies and leaders coming to pay their respects for what he has done for countless people. Today we can only offer him a dozen people, a pine box, and a kind word. But that isn't all. We can all become a tiny bit of Mr. Wilson. We can help where we are needed and able. We can do the right thing when required."

Sara paused. She didn't need to elaborate. The right thing in this war was broad. And every little bit of kindness broke the back of the evil that started it all. "And we can rebuild our communities to be better than they were before. If we all do just a little collectively, we can bring his spirit back to life."

Sara took a deep breath. "Rest easy Amare. We are ready."

Ife's eyes shone with gratitude, and she mouthed the words *thank you.*

As they filed out of the church, people bundled into their outwear, clapping Sara on the shoulder in appreciation for her speech. Ife and Marie were the last to leave. Sara watched Ife choke out a loud sob as she hugged the coffin. Sara felt her cheeks wet with her tears. Amy and Brian waited by the door on opposite sides. Sara put an arm around Ife, and they walked the block up the street towards the Berry Patch. The weather had gotten nasty the past few days. The wind whipped the dusting of snow around the street like it was dancing. Sara watched the snow ballet move across the street when a military truck caught her eye. Sara stopped, and they all did the same, following her gaze. Sara heard a growl escape Marie's lips. Leaning on the truck was the murderer Marie had described. The man was a bit older than Sara, and his chiseled features sneered at them. It was a threat. And a warning. Marie surged towards him. Brian grabbed her by the back of her coat. "No," he said calmly.

Ife bent her head down and walked quickly into the front

of the restaurant. Marie was cursing before the door shut. "Why is he here?" Amy said, her voice shaking.

"To make sure we all know who is in control," Brian answered, not bothering to look at her.

"This is insane," Marie raged, pacing the booths.

Sara started a pot of coffee and pulled out some pie from the display fridge. Ife was in a booth, her head laying on the table. She looked so sad. Sara wanted to take it all away. "These guys can't just come in here and accuse people. Then kill them without a trial or any evidence."

Sara looked at Brian. Marie still didn't understand. "Where did all of those documents come from," Marie asked, "who would've put them there? They can't prove they were yours."

Sara had begun to put together that the Berry Patch was more than a local pie joint. "There must be some authorities you can call, Ife," Marie said, speaking faster and faster, "we could avenge him. Bring that Harrison fuck to justice."

"You can't come into town anymore," Ife said, staring straight ahead.

"Ok," Marie agreed, "then you can come to our house. We can come up with a plan to..."

"No."

Brian looked at Sara again. Sara winced. "How will I see you then?" Marie said confused.

"You won't."

Ife turned and looked at Marie. "You can't see me anymore," Ife said, "None of you can."

"What do you mean?" Marie's voice got higher.

She sat next to Ife and tried to hold her hand, "I can't just *not* see you."

"I won't lose another person I love," Ife said, shaking her off.

"You don't want me anymore," Marie whispered.

The Berry Patch was so quiet, Sara heard the sound of her tears hitting the table. Marie shuttered a breath. "You all need to leave," Ife said firmly, "Get out of Paradise."

"We are leaving in February," Sara said gently.

Ife turned to Sara. "So you have a plan," she said with relief.

They all nodded. "Good," Ife said.

Marie was the one now staring ahead. "No," Marie stammered, "I don't accept that."

Ife stood. "You have to."

Marie's lips trembled. "You can't avoid me forever," Marie argued, "I'll just…I'll just…"

Ife turned to her, taking her hands. "Please don't. Please don't make me go through this again. Find me when this is all over, ok? When the war is over, find me."

Marie searched her eyes, gasping for air. Ife wiped away her tears. "I love you, Marie," Ife said smiling, kissing her gently, "the moment you walked in here with your emo attitude and sharp tongue. I knew you were my kind of person. You were *my* person."

Brian looked up at Amy, but she avoided it, walking to Sara's side. Sara took Amy's hand.

"We will see each other again one day," Ife said, tucking a strand of hair behind her ear, "but right now, you and your family need to stay safe."

Sara, Amy, and Brian went to a window-side booth to watch the MP's and give Marie and Ife some privacy. The last thing they wanted was Harrison and his merry band of murderers to follow them home. Thankfully, not long after the funeral, the soldiers dispersed, going back to whatever cesspool they called home. Once all was clear, everyone said their goodbyes to Ife and piled in the car to wait for Marie. Sara watched them embrace. It was hard to see the pain in her daughter's eyes. Marie walked to the door and ran to the Jeep against the cold. She climbed into the front seat. Sara saw Ife sit down at a table and put her head in her hands, shoulders shaking. Sara sped away before Marie saw it too.

~

No one talked on the way home. Her Mother's Christmas CD filled the Jeep. The classic songs were a pleasant distraction. Because Brian kept trying to have a heart-to-heart. "Are we going to talk about this?" Brian whispered under Jingle Bells.

Amy stared straight ahead. "You can't ignore me forever," Brian whispered, crossing his arms, leaning back in his seat.

"And furthermore," he started again.

"Not now," Amy hissed.

She saw her mother's eyes flit up into the rear-view mirror. Mercifully, Brian nodded and didn't speak again until they got back to the cabin. Marie and her mother walked into the cabin, and Brian grabbed Amy's hand, pulling her around to the carport. "Does now work for you?"

Amy shook out of his grip.

"I don't get you," he said, "one minute we're a thing, and the next you're out hunting for dial tone. He isn't here, Amy. I am."

"The only reason he isn't here is to keep my mom and sister safe," Amy said, beginning to get angry.

She owed him nothing.

"So you're telling me," his voice began to rise, "you want to go back to live with your father who has been beating your mother and neglecting you your entire life. Just so you can be with a guy who you can't tell where you are because he'd tell your psychopath dad how to find you?"

Amy crossed her arms and looked down at the ground. "We're going to get married," Amy said defiantly, "I'm going to live with him. Start a family."

Brian laughed. He had the gull to laugh at her. The blood rose in her cheeks. "That's funny," he said, "I heard he would've broken it off a while ago, but there aren't many options in Watertown, South Dakota."

Amy's eyes snapped to his face. She saw the immediate regret on it after the words poured out. Amy fought back tears. "Amy," he said quietly, "I'm so sorry. I didn't mean it."

"At least I'm not a coward. I don't run away from people when times get tough," she got up into his face and yelled, "I didn't want to be here. But I stayed for my family. And once they are safe, I am going back home. To my home, to work on the relationship I have put years into."

Brian lowered his head. His face was a mixture of pain, anger, and sadness. But Amy was too pissed to care. "I matter to people. My mom, my dad despite his faults, hell even my sister," Amy said motioning at the cabin, "And he might not want to marry me right now, but Anthony loves me."

Amy shoved a frozen finger into Brian's chest. "And you," she said in a low growl, "no one feels that way about you."

She shoved past him and ran to the trail. She hated him. Absolutely hated him. And Amy knew why. It wasn't the fact Brian was trying to hurt her as she had him. It was because it was the truth. And then she spat his truth right back at him. Seeing his heart shatter before her eyes made Amy's breakfast start to come back up. Amy wandered through the forest with her phone above her head. Following the signal bars, she watched as they increased and decreased. She walked beyond the bend in the river and down the hill. The bars disappeared. "Shit."

Amy looked around. It was freezing outside. She put on her gloves, then pulled the fur collar around her face, nestling into the hood. Amy would not think about who made it for her. She told herself she would not feel bad for what she said. He knew, and Amy had warned him she loved someone else. It wasn't her burden to carry. Amy stopped again halfway down the hill; her tears were freezing on her eyelashes. It made no sense for a tower to be in a gully.

Amy scanned the trees looking for anything resembling a metal pole. And there in the distance was a too-perfect, too-green tree. It was so well hidden amongst the forest that anyone would miss it unless they were looking for it. Typical for the rural areas and their resistance to big-city technology ruining their landscape. A leaning cell phone tower disguised as a tree waved in the distance. Amy picked up the pace towards the faux pine. And sure enough, the bars increased too. Soon she was standing at the foot of a crudely painted cell phone tower trunk. Her phone buzzed with activity. Messages from her father and Anthony she'd never gotten. Emails poured in. Almost instantly there were three hundred in her inbox.

Too excited to think about what she said to Brian, she sat beneath the massive metal tree. She would tell Anthony she was coming home. Amy was done with Paradise, Michigan. Pulling her one hand from her warm glove, she unlocked her phone. Clearing her inbox was easy, for they were mostly old spam emails from years when companies actually used them. She frowned thinking about some lost server in some forgotten warehouse still sending *BIG SALE – TODAY ONLY* advertisements for stores that no longer existed. She then saw a subject-less email from Anthony. Amy tapped it and leaned forward reading his words.

Amy,
You need to call me. I'm done.

Amy's hands started to shake. Frantically, she dialed him. He picked up almost immediately. "Amy?" a sleepy voice asked.

"What do you mean we're done?"

"I can barely hear you," Anthony said.

"I'm underneath a damn cell tower in the middle of nowhere, and it's windy as hell," she yelled, "What do you mean we're done?!"

Anthony sighed loudly on the other line. "What do you expect, Amy," he said annoyed, "you up and disappear for months. You won't tell me where you are, and then I hear some dude in the background on our first phone call in weeks."

Amy wanted to scream. "He doesn't mean anything to me, Anthony."

Lie. "He's just staying with us until he can…."

"Defect?" Anthony's voice was cold.

"No," Amy stuttered, "He's…he's Canadian."

Anthony sighed again. "No, you're living in the woods with your crazy mother, sister, and a random guy. You should've come home when I told you to. I can't help what happens to you and your family now."

"I told you where I am…" Amy started.

She paused. "What do you mean what happens to me and my family?"

"Your dad has been going nuts looking for you," he said flatly, "and I was sick of seeing you work him and the system over."

"What?" She yelled into the phone, "What system?"

"If your number is called, you go," Anthony quoted her Dad perfectly, "you serve your country, so this war can end. You don't hide, hoping it will, without doing your part."

"What did you do?" Amy growled through clenched teeth.

"He knows where you are," he said quietly, "I told him yesterday."

Amy was in a full sprint before she had ended the phone call.

~

Amy burst through the door of the cabin. Everyone looked up startled. One look at her face had Sara running to close the door behind her. "What?" Sara said. "what happened?"

Amy was shaking, and her lips were blue. Brian stood taking a step towards her, his hand was outstretched. Amy took it. "Dad knows where we are," she squeaked out.

"Fuck!" Marie yelled, launching off the couch.

"How?" Sara asked calmly.

Amy's eyes filled with tears. Brian pulled her into his chest. "She told her boyfriend," he said without malice.

"How could you?" Marie yelled.

Sara began to knot her hands. "Stop it. This is not the time."

Amy sobbed into Brian's chest as he held and pet her hair. "We need to pack now," Sara said, grabbing duffle bags from the closet, "Marie, grab enough food for four days and two canteens."

Brian's eyes searched the ceiling for some hidden solution. "Sara, the straits might not be frozen in the middle yet." He said.

Sara began stuffing clothing into one pack. "It's going to have to do," Sara said breathlessly, "we have no other choice. We have one day, tops, until he finds us."

Marie was fighting back tears, stacking food on the table. "I'm so sorry," a small voice came from Brian's chest.

Marie shook her head, grumbling expletives. Brian sat Amy down on the couch and got her a cup of tea. And he began to get his pack together. Sara and Brian laid both guns out. Sara would take the handgun and Brian the rifle. After Amy composed herself, she aided in the preparation. The cabin was silent but for the shuffling of packs. By two in the morning, their packs were set by the door ready for their several-hour hike across a half-frozen Lake Superior. They ate a late dinner and cleaned up as though it were any other day. Marie watched her mother walk the walls of the cabin, taking it in one final time. Amy and Brian had excused themselves to the bedroom. Marie had already set up blankets to sleep on the couch. "I have to say goodbye," Marie said.

Sara turned and looked at her. "I know," Sara whispered, "I just don't know how to get you down there. Who knows if your father is close or not. Not to mention the MPs have probably already been alerted."

Marie nodded. "I love her," she choked on the words, "I

never thought I could love someone like I love her."

Sara sat down next to her, taking her hand. Marie leaned her head on her mom. "You can write her a letter," Sara said, "put it in the mailbox at the end of the street. Leave the flag up. Hopefully, she'll notice."

Sara walked to the kitchen and pulled out an ancient spiral note pad from her childhood. She found an old pen she made her dad for Father's Day when she was eight. It was decorated to look like a daisy. Sara patted the seat at the table. Slowly, Marie approached the table and sat down. Sara kissed her cornsilk blonde hair. "I love you," Sara whispered into it.

"Love you too, mom."

Sara walked to the bedroom to give her privacy.

~

Amy and Brian had escaped to the bedroom without question shortly after the packing wrapped up. Amy simply took his hand and led him there. She shut the door, and he sat on the bed looking up at her. "I'm sorry."

Brian shook his head. "I'm sorry."

Amy held up her hand. "Everything you said about him was true. He knew what telling my dad meant for my mom and Marie. He didn't care. Maybe he did once. But he doesn't now. And what I said to you…."

Brian reached for her hand, and she sat in his lap. Brian held her face, wiping the tears away with his thumbs. "I didn't mean any of it," Amy whispered, holding his face, "Someone *does* love you. I love you."

"I would've waited forever for you."

Amy smiled. Her heart broke for not seeing Brian for what he meant to her sooner. She leaned in and kissed him gently. His hands ran through her ebony hair, pulling her closer to him. She inhaled his breath as they found each other again. This time without guilt. This time without fear. Love. Only love passed between them. He scooped her up in his arms and laid her on the bed. The look on his face was one of awe. "Perfect."

Amy blushed. "Come here," she whispered.

They took their time. They were quiet. They made love to each other like they were the last people on earth. And when he collapsed on her after an hour of committing to one another, they were both weeping. They wept to have finally found each other. And they wept for fear of what was to come.

~

Marie finished her letter. It was three pages long. The clocked ticked behind her, four in the morning. She folded the pages neatly. Marie stood to rummage through the junk drawer to find an envelope. She looked up at Charlette's purse on the counter. Slowly, she pulled out her wallet. Behind Charlette's ID was Colin's Time Twister Magic card. Stuffing the letter and Colin's card into the envelope, she grabbed a big black marker.

Walking outside, the wind howled. The snow was so light it drifted onto everything. Her fingers stung as she began to write in large letters on the glass. *YOU'VE GOT MAIL.*

Hopefully, Ife would see it before the MPs or her father did. Part of her wanted her dad to know. She wanted him to know that despite what he had done to this family, they still found happiness and love. Wrapping her coat around herself, she trotted down the drive to the old mailbox. The snow was almost a complete white-out. It was why she barely saw the lights until they were almost on her. The wind was so loud, Marie didn't hear the engine. The sound of Marie's gasp was taken by the wind when a familiar pick-up pulled up alongside her. Ife rolled the window down. Marie's heart leaped. "Ife," she started.

"Get to the house now!" Ife ordered.

Marie's eyes went wide, and she took off in a sprint for

the cabin. She burst through the door. "Get up," she yelled.

Ife filed in shortly after. "They're here," Ife said breathlessly as Sara ran from her room, "That fuck Harrison and your dad too. Someone told them where you are."

Amy and Brian came out from the bedroom still pulling on clothes. "They have a convoy assembling right now off of Station and 123. They will be here in minutes. You have to go now!"

The cabin was sent into a fury of movement. They donned their winter clothes and began to load their packs into the Jeep. Marie grabbed Ife's hands in the chaos. "Please come," Marie begged.

Ife grabbed her face and kissed her deeply. "I can't," she said, searching her face trying to burn it into memory, "I have more to do."

Marie sobbed, hugging her. Marie handed her the letter. "You have to go now," Ife said, taking it from Marie.

They all filed out of the cabin as the sound of a helicopter beat in the distance. "I'll try to get them to follow me," Ife called as she got into her truck.

Marie watched her as her heart broke into pieces. As the truck drove away, Marie, for the first time, noticed the racing stripes. "Marie," a voice called her.

"Marie, get in the Jeep!"

Her mother's command snapped her out the moment, and she climbed into the Jeep. Brian was the last to join them, holding the rifle. Amy rolled down the window as he approached her. "What are you doing? Get in!"

"They are going to catch you if you don't go now."

Amy shook her head confused. "What do you mean? Get in!"

Marie and Sara realized what was happening as Brian cocked the gun. He looked at Sara. "Take the back trail until it hits Widewaters Road to Betsy, then stay right to Vermillion. Just like we discussed. Then run like hell."

"Brian, no!" Amy screamed understanding.

"I love you, Amy. Take care of them, Sara," Brian said,

trotting towards the front of the cabin.

Sounds of engines began roaring behind them. Amy screamed as Brian began shooting into the driveway. Sara hit the gas, praying she could see the trail amongst the snow.

~

Sara exhaled as they turned right on Widewaters Road. She realized she had been holding her breath for the twenty minutes it took to navigate the trail. The helicopter made wide sweeps of the area, but the dense forest had kept the headlights hidden. "They must think we are trying to escape on the highway," Sara said.

Amy was now sniffing and weeping silently. Marie leaned between the seats and held her hand. The sun wouldn't rise for another few hours, which meant they needed to hike across the ice on a perfect course, or they'd end up in the deeper part of the bay. Sara palmed the compass that was hooked to her coat sleeve. They rolled up on the shore of Old Wire Road. Several houses lined the beach that was now covered in snow. By some miracle, the wind had died down a bit. But the temperature was still near zero. "Bundle up girls," Sara said, getting out of the truck.

They put on their packs and looped their canteens to their belts. Sara shouldered Brian's pack laden with food, turning on her flashlight. Her back ached within minutes. But she would carry this extra load. Her girls needed their strength. The three stepped to the edge of the frozen water. The darkness of this place was unfathomable. And when they shut the truck lights off, they stood in silence. It was like peering into the open maw of the universe. Pitch black with flecks of snow flitting past their eyes. Sara looked up at the sky, marking the stars while holding the compass.

The ice wouldn't be completely frozen in the center, and Sara knew it. They would have to walk where it seemed the thickest. But with the wind whipping the fresh snow over the lake, it was difficult to see where thin spots might lie.

And in the dark, it was impossible. Each step was a complete roll of the dice. Sara cursed the wind as it screamed around them. It drowned out their heavy breathing as they started their trek over the narrow straits.

Sara knew the island was just visible from shore in the daylight and twenty miles from them but it seemed an incredible task against the cold. Twenty miles to freedom. Tears streaked down Amy's face as she followed behind Sara. Amy had tucked herself so tightly in her fur-lined hood, Sara could only see her nose. "Stay close to me!" Sara yelled over the hollowing wind.

Both girls nodded in response. They began walk-jogging over the ice, following Sara. Close to shore they were safe. And luckily, the ice seemed to be thicker than usual for this time of year. Still, she felt the ice groan under her feet in some spots, to which her heart answered by pounding harder. If any of them fell in, it would be over.

They had been walking for over two hours, and dawn was beginning to show above the eastern horizon. This would be the most dangerous place to hike. The girls were beginning to slow. Hiking her pack up higher on her aching shoulders, she kept her eyes on the ice, looking for dark spots. In the daylight, Sara could see small pockets of thinner ice, but to her relief, the straits seemed to be solid. Things seemed to be finally going their way.

Exhaling for the first time in hours, Sara motioned for the girls to take a sip of water. They may have been cold, but they were exerting a ton of energy on this hike. Sara stopped to take in her surroundings. It was like being on another planet. Ice and snow as far as the eye could see. Her eyelashes had already begun to freeze. Thankfully, her boots and gloves were keeping her most at-risk appendages warm against frostbite. Amy and Marie were panting as they took swigs from their canteens. "You ready?" Sara yelled.

Amy clutched her side, gasping for air. Her eyes stared into nowhere. She bent over and sobbed. Marie put her arm around her shoulder and said something into her furred hood. Amy shook her head and wiped her nose on her mitten. Marie grabbed her by her shoulders and wiped Amy's tears with her glove, all the while giving Amy words of inspiration. Sara watched as Amy nodded vigorously to her little sister. They hugged and then began to walk again towards Canada.

Another hour into the hike and a gust blew through the natural venturi, almost taking Sara off of her feet. The sun had just crested the horizon, and the world glowed. If it weren't for the imminent danger, it would have been a beautiful sight. Sara pulled out her father' binoculars to see how close they were getting. Sara turned to make sure the girls were still following. Amy and Marie braced themselves against the wind but quickly continued. Sara was about to turn back to the border when she saw headlights. Through her father's binoculars, she saw a snowmobile approaching from where they started on Paradise's shores. Sara saw the outline of a man. She knew without seeing who it was. The man who had held her in terror for twenty years. The man who gaslighted her, alienating her from friends and family. Dan had finally found her.

"Run!" Sara screamed.

The girls began to pump their legs, looking back in time to see the vehicle coming towards them. Sara knew the border was close. Quickly, she did the math in her head. He was ten miles away, going sixty miles per hour. They were maybe two miles from shore. They had nine minutes to get to that island before he was on them. Sara heard him coming now. The wind was loud, but the roar of his engine was louder. She dared not look back at the lightweight machine flying towards them.

Suddenly, the echo of gun-fire and the wet sound of a bullet across the ice broke her concentration. They all screamed. He was shooting at them. He was going to kill her. Then another shot and Amy yelped, covering her head as it missed her by a few yards. *Not the girls. He couldn't be trying to hurt the girls.*

Sara knew the range on those weapons, and they were closer to Dan than that. Too close. The wind was affecting his shot, but it wasn't going to for much longer. Another bullet rang out and struck several yards away from them. Sara's lungs were on fire. The girls were beginning to flank her. *Good, just keeping running. We are so close...*

But the shore of the island looked so far, and their packs were so heavy. Another shot and Marie yelled as she hit the hardened cover of Lake Superior. Blood stained the ice around Marie's arm where she lay. Amy and Sara ran crouching at her side. "You have to get up!" Amy cried out, trying to lift Marie from the ice.

The effort stole a scream from Marie's lips as she cradled her wounded arm. "Please get up!" Amy yelled.

Dan had stopped fifty yards away and was aiming at the windshield of the machine. He knew he had them. Amy got Marie standing and began running towards the island. "Mom," Amy called back, "let's go!"

Sara stood frozen. The wind whipped her ebony hair. The fire in her lungs was no longer from the run or fear. It was pure rage.

He shot her.

Like a Rolodex, images of his abuse and terror ripped through her mind: the slaps, names, fear, rape, bullying, bruises, humiliation, cuts, control. It burned through her like a wildfire.

He shot her.

The wind no longer chilled her. She was no longer afraid. Sara drew her father's pistol. The weight of it was welcoming in her hand.

He. Shot. Her. Daughter.

Sara looked over her shoulder. "I love you."

Amy's eyes widened.

"Now run!"

Sara did not look back as she heard the faint crunch of boots over the wind, knowing her girls were again headed for the island. Sara took off in the other direction. Towards the man she had cowered and run from most of her life. Sara raised her arm and began to fire in a dead sprint. Dan hit the ground, dropping his gun. The first shot hit the windshield, missing him by inches. The second took out the headlight. Everything was in slow motion. Her legs were powered by her white blinding fury. Sara felt nothing as her body carried her closer and closer to him.

He shot. My. Child.

She fired again. Dan covered his head. She saw the ice spray up next to his prone body. The rhythm of it all was like a song. Step, step, step, *shot*. Step, step, step, *shot*. She would be on him in seconds. She would take his life. And she would rejoice in it. A sudden clicking brought Sara to a stop. Looking down at her gun, smoke seeped out from the barrel. *I'm out.*

She was out of ammunition. The wind bit her face and blurred her eyes, yet the clear vision of the man who tortured her for years made her unafraid. Sara launched herself onto his prone body. Raising the gun above her head, she struck him again and again. Dan got a leg under himself and flipped Sara off his back. He was so fast. With blood running down his face, he looked like a madman. "You don't ever leave me. I am the only one who ever loved you," he said, kicking her in the face and then in the ribs.

Sara gasped for air and rolled on her back. Dan reached down for his gun and cocked it. Sara began laughing. She could taste the iron in her mouth. Sara managed to pull herself to her knees and then clambered to stand. Dan's eyes widened at the sight of his weak wife spitting out blood and chuckling with madness. "You've lost asshole. You are nothing."

Sara had bought her daughters precious time to escape, and saving them was worth every minute of her life. Sara watched him aim the rifle at her head. He smiled from behind the gun, "You are such a stupid bitch."

Sara braced for the shot. They stood there frozen in place with only the wind to let her know there wasn't a blip in time. Dan suddenly lowered the weapon and took a step back. "This doesn't concern you," Dan yelled over the wind.

The feeling of a presence on each side of her made her hair stand on end. Sara saw two horses from the corner of her eye appear, one on each side. She looked up at a man and a woman on horseback wearing uniforms and tribal decorations. The woman's black hair was braided and pinned atop her head; tattoos lined her cheeks. The man had two thick long pleats down his back, his facial tattoos as black as his hair against his copper skin. The braids rose and fell in the gusts like arms beckoning. Suddenly, the wind hushed. Sara's mouth hung open as the woman spoke, "You have fired on our nation. That is an act of war."

Dan raised his weapon again. "Canada is harboring criminals, and we have the right to apprehend them," Dan hissed.

The man raised his hand. "You did not fire on Canada."

The woman swept her hand over the now-silent ice and land behind her, "You are on the lands of the Batchawana Nation."

Dan let out a laugh. "An Indian resi? You're still fucking Canadian. Give me my prisoners. I am a sheriff, and that woman is harboring a fugitive!"

"We will take into account you haven't heard because your access to accurate news sources has been inhibited," the woman continued, "The native people and the Canadian government have negotiated a treaty reclaiming all of their original lands that border your warring nation."

"So you see," the man began, "you have fired upon our country, and *that* is an act of war."

"Canada may not offer asylum to your people," the woman stated, "but we most certainly do."

Dan still smirking cocked his gun, "I'll take my chances."

A loud beating sound broke into the end of Dan's words. Sara almost expected to see a line of Batchawana people with drums cresting the island. "I don't think that wise," the woman issued.

Three helicopters like doves in the light of the rising sun dotted the horizon. The black choppers were armed with guns and soldiers wearing the same uniform as her riding saviors. The snow on the ice whipped once more.

"This is Batchawana National Airforce," a loudspeaker announced, "you are within our borders. Please return to your country of origin."

Sara turned to see Dan now taking his turn to gape. The horse backed soldiers hadn't moved from their intense stare. They stood like statues amongst the noise and gusts. They looked like gods. "Lower your weapon and return to your country. Any attempt at reentering ours will be an official act of war. And we will, without hesitation, retaliate," the man boomed over the helicopters.

Dan lowered his rifle and stared up at the Black Hawks. A beautiful native sign was painted on all three. He slung his gun over his shoulder and walked back to his snowmobile. Once mounted, he gave Sara a look of pure malice. Sara inclined her head and mouthed, *fuck you.*

The helicopters retreated upon his exit. And Sara looked up at her two liberators. "Where are my children?" Sara said with gratitude.

~

Sara held her blanket with one hand and a warm cup of coffee with the other. Her eyes followed the buzz of activity with awe. A warehouse had been built as a staging area for defectors and asylum seekers. Ojibwas, Canadians, and Americans were busy restocking, going over paperwork, bringing food, and tending to every need of the nearly two dozen refugees, herself included. Sara watched as Amy sat across from her. Her eyes looked as though they would be permanently stained with tears. Marie sat down next to her mother on the cot. "This is incredible," Marie whispered.

Sara could only nod.

A woman walked up to Sara and Marie with a clipboard.

She had a tight blonde bun on her head and wore the Batchawana uniform. "Good evening," she glanced at her clipboard, "you must be the Weiderholts."

Sara nodded, and Amy looked up for the first time since arriving. "My name is Officer St. Amour, but you can call me Katie," she smiled warmly, "how is your arm, Marie?

"It's sore, but I'll be ok."

Sara took Marie's hand and swallowed. The bullet had grazed her arm. A few stitches, ibuprofen and Marie seemed to be her old self.

"I'm sure you have a lot of questions," Katie said.

"What is this place?" Sara finally asked, wincing at the pain in her jaw.

Katie smiled. "Welcome to Danakamigad. Or the Dana for short. It means 'happens in a certain place' in Ojibwa."

"You don't look Ojibwa," Marie asked sidelong.

Katie laughed, "No, I immigrated here, so I could help with the refugee crisis. Several years ago, Canada agreed they would not interfere in the wars between the Whites and Grays. They promised not to house refugees or asylum seekers to avoid being brought into the war."

"How could they not help us?" Marie raised her voice.

Sara placed a hand on her uninjured arm. Katie frowned.

"Oh, sweetheart. Canada never turned its back on you. But they had to be smart to protect Canadians and those who needed us in the south."

Marie's shoulders relaxed a little.

"Canada had already been in negotiations with the original people of this land to give back territory as completely separate nations," Katie continued, "so four of the tribal nations took over the lands bordering your country as newly-joined members of NATO. Because while Canada could not take on American refugees...."

Sara's eyes widened and said, "But the tribal nations could."

Amy and Marie both looked at their mother. Katie smiled, "And any NATO nation attacked by an outside force...."

"Will be supported by NATO and Canadian forces," Sara finished.

The girls sat in stunned silence. "I would have thought the Volunteers in Paradise would've keyed you into this information, at least partially."

The strangers living there, food coming in and out, people disappearing. It all made sense. It was the new underground railroad.

"I grew up there," Sara whispered, now understanding, "my dad had a cabin in the woods and we went there to hide."

Katie's brows rose, "Well that is quite the stroke of luck."

"Luck," Sara whispered.

Katie frowned and placed a hand on Sara's shoulder. "My apologies," Katie said quickly, "Paradise is one of many cities within the US border that acts as a staging area for people looking to escape."

"Is there any word from Paradise?" Marie asked too loudly. "Do you know if the MPs found out about what they do there?"

Katie took a deep breath and shook her head. "Paradise has been taken over by the Grays," her voice shook a bit, "we don't have confirmation, but most of our Volunteers are missing or confirmed dead."

Marie put her head in her hands, and Sara put an arm around her. "We have housing assigned to you about five hours north of here." Katie continued in a much more professional voice. "You will be giving Canadian green cards and will be issued citizenship within the first year of residency if that is your wish."

Katie lowered her clipboard and placed a hand on Sara's shoulder. "You are safe."

Sara held tightly to the paperwork Officer St. Amour had given her. *Safe.*

The word echoed in her mind. *Are we finally safe?*

Marie took the papers, wiping her eyes. "Looks like it's a condo complex," she read, "we will be allowed to stay for six months, and then we can go where ever we want."

"I'm pregnant," Amy interrupted.

Sara and Marie's head snapped up. Sara stood and knelt beside her daughter. "That's wonderful news, sweetie," Sara took her shaking hand.

Oh, God.

"I didn't even get to tell him."

Sara kissed Amy's forehead. "We will create such an amazing life for that little one."

~

The sun was shining sideways. Sara watched it reach through the tree branches, sending its yellow rays onto the grass. It made the dew sparkle like diamonds. She leaned down, grabbing another wet pair of jeans, tossing them over the line. Sara had always hated doing laundry. Now it was one of her favorite parts of the day: being alone, being outside. It was warmer than usual for this time of year, and Sara thanked the heavens for it. Marie was sitting on the porch of their tiny cottage, oiling her bow. She had shot a beautiful doe that morning. It would provide meat for two months. *Thank you*, she expressed to the deer silently.

They had been living at the tiny house in the middle of nowhere for the better part of a year. Amy and Marie had taken a bit longer to get used to living off the land than Sara, especially without the help of Brian. Fortunately, their stay in Paradise had at least thrown them into the lifestyle out of need. The house had three small bedrooms, a living room, and kitchen. Miniscule compared to their house in the Dakotas, but the warmth and love from inside made it feel larger than life.

Looking around, she saw the many things that needed to be done that day: weed the garden, prepare the deer, muck the chicken coop, and clean the Jeep. Sara smiled at the old

Cherokee. When they went to find a car for their travels in their new life, the old truck sat there in the used car lot. It was the biggest heap of them all. But the moment the three of them saw it, they all said together, "That one."

Sara finished hanging the clothes and started back towards the house. Amy appeared from the door, "Lunch is ready."

Sara smiled at her daughter with little Brian on her hip. Sara melted every time she saw his chubby little face. The moment Little B saw his Gama, the name Sara had chosen, he reached for her drooling and babbling. Sara took her grandson from his mother and balanced him on her hip. His brown-orange eyes matched Amy's, but his soft curls were all his daddy's. Sara bounced and talked to Little B as they made their way to the kitchen. "Can you believe this weather?" Amy sighed, taking a deep breath.

Marie stood abruptly from her seat, drawing the shotgun that never left her side. It was an immediate reflex. Amy grabbed the baby, who screamed at being removed from his Gama's arm and went for the door as Sara barricaded it with her body. "Who the hell are you?" Marie yelled to the male figure who had just exited a car and was now walking up the drive.

The male figure shouted back inaudibly. Marie cocked her gun, "You better stay where you are."

Suddenly, Sara felt Amy shove the baby back into her arms. In a trance Amy, pushed past them and walked down the steps into the drive. "Get back here," Marie hissed.

"Brian," Amy said, barely a whisper.

Sara and Marie looked at each other.

Amy took off in a run, "Brian!"

The male figure dropped his bag and began running towards the house. He caught her in mid-air, and they crumpled to the ground. Their sobs could be heard from the house.

Sara and Marie rushed to the pair. Brian was thin and in need of a shower, but he had retained all of his limbs and life. Questions of how and where rattled off as he tried answering and asking some in return. Suddenly, he looked up at Sara and Little Brian. His eyes lined with tears. "Is that?" was all he could utter.

Amy wiped her nose on her arm and stood, taking their son from Sara's arms. She turned to him, "I'd like you to meet our son."

~

The next few months flew by. Brian caught them up on what happened when they fled. After diverting the MP's away from the cabin, he used the knowledge of the woods to hide, back-track, and confuse the soldiers until nightfall. At that point, they called off the search. Sara watched Amy hanging on his every word, gripping his hand like he may disappear. The love in her eyes made her chest ache. Brian returning was a miracle and still seemed unreal. Brian balanced BJ, the name they had coined due to having Big B in the house, on his knee.

"I slept in the woods, changing my location for several days and then made my way into town at night," Brian continued, "the town was destroyed."

Marie turned away and looked out the window. Sara took her hand and squeezed. "They shot it up and threw grenades everywhere, you guys," Brian shook his head, his dark curls falling into his kind blue eyes, "I've never seen anything like it."

Marie's voice stunned the silence, "Was anyone left?"

Everyone turned back to Brian who sadly shook his head. Marie got up and went outside. Brian rubbed his free hand over his face, "I thought I was safe, and I wanted to follow you guys here. I knew your route would be heavily watched, so I thought I may try the other side of the bridge. I was raiding the general store for supplies when a few MP's left to guard Paradise found me."

BJ began drooling and getting fussy in his dad's lap, so

Amy took him and began to nurse. The utter joy on Brian's face made Sara look away, it was so intimate. Brian cleared his throat and continued, "They are taking dodgers and, so-called, traitors to camps. They are work camps where items are made for the war. I was grouped with this guy who had escaped from them once already."

Sara stared at the fire. *Maybe that is where Sam was sent.*

"If you were in good health, they suited you up and sent you off to the front line to handle the most dangerous fighting."

"Is that how you escaped," Sara asked, "you being on the front line? Did you run away?"

Brian took a deep breath and looked at Amy. "No," he sighed, "in the middle of the night, I woke up to the sounds of shouting and gunshots."

Amy took his hand again, realizing she had let it go. "When my eyes adjusted to the darkness, I realized the place we had set up camp for the night was under attack. But not by Whites, by unmarked civilians. Me and that guy from my group took down the solider guarding us, and within minutes the Gray soldiers were all dead."

"Who was it," Amy whispered over BJ's soft curls, "who freed the camp?"

"They call themselves the Volunteers," Brian said, "they are liberating Americans who don't want to fight and calling to action those who want the fighting to end."

"So more fighting to end the fighting?" Marie had entered the house silently. "Volunteers, Whites, Grays, Fuchsias, what the fuck difference does it make what they're called?"

"Marie this is different," Brian rose, "these are Americans who are backed by our old allies. And they are desperately trying to liberate the camps and aid in restoring resources. They are trying to fight for our country. Our true country. Not two sides. Not polarizing ideologies. Americans from both sides working together to unite us again."

Marie wrapped her arms around herself and turned to the fire. "Let me put BJ down," Amy stood, "and then we can play some Euchre. Open that bottle of whiskey you've been hiding, mom. Have ourselves a celebration."

Sara smiled and nodded, "I'd love that."

Brian walked with Amy to the bedroom: a family complete.

"You ok?" Sara said, watching Marie slump into a chair.

Her beautiful blonde hair shone in the firelight. She rested her chin on her fist, jaw flexing. Sara had a hard time remembering the girl she had been just over two years ago. Marie was nineteen but had the soul of a seasoned warrior twice her age. Marie's hands were calloused and strong from hunting and chopping wood. Her face was tanned and eyes sharp. Sara's heart swelled at the command and wisdom Marie displayed. "Do you think Ife's alive?" Marie whispered.

"I don't know," Sara whispered back, putting a hand on her leg.

Marie turned her big blue eyes towards her.

"But," Sara finished, "if there is a person who could survive and escape, it would be her."

Marie nodded slowly.

"Plus, Brian made it out, and he's a total buffoon," Sara jerked her head towards the bedroom.

Marie snorted and smiled at her mom. "I love you, mom."

"Love you," Sara stood as Brian and Amy entered the room.

The couple returned, and Amy already had the worn half of the deck out. Marie watched Brian fumble with the dealing, "I'm on mom's team!"

~

Several weeks had passed since Brian had returned, and the house had found a new rhythm with him in it. Marie was out chopping wood feeling the breeze cool the sweat on her back. She set the ax down and closed her eyes. The sounds of her home made her soul happy. Here she felt at peace. Yet her thoughts brought her time and again to the war waging hundreds of miles to the south. And Ife. Marie kept busy to keep her thoughts from Ife's face. Marie could hear her laugh like she'd heard it yesterday. Feel her soft skin on hers when they touched. Her deep brown eyes staring into hers. Her voice. Ife's voice shouting for them to run. Sacrificing herself so they could escape.

Marie sat down and sipped her canteen. Gravel crunching made her glace up. Her mom sat down beside her. "All done for the day?" her mom asked.

"I'm going to find her," Marie said so suddenly the words surprised herself.

Sara nodded slowly, looking out at the swaying grasses. Marie looked at her mom in the eyes. "I am going to find her, and then she and I are going to join the Volunteers and end all of this," Marie said calmly.

Sara tore her gaze from her daughter, looking out at their beautiful piece of land and nodded slowly.

"And…" Marie began again.

"There's an *And*?"

"And," Marie said, "I will find Charlette's family and give them her purse. To remember her."

There was a pause. The wind blew like fingers through the fields. She would walk away from this haven and safety for Ife without question. Just like that, Marie knew what she needed to do. "When are you leaving?" Sara asked.

Marie hadn't thought that far out. It was only in those moments she had come to the conclusion she needed to find Ife no matter what she found. If Ife was dead, then she would fight in her honor. But she wouldn't believe it. She knew deep in her soul Ife was still alive. Their energies forever linked; Marie knew it without question.

"Tomorrow."

"I'm coming with you," her mom stated flatly.

Marie sat back staring at her. "You want to come with me?"

"Amy has Brian here. BJ has his parents," Sara nodded towards the house, "I'll miss them of course. But I have little place here, Marie. I belong with you. With people who want what we want. I want to help you find Ife and the Millers, honey. I..."

Marie cut her mom's sentence off by wrapping her arms around her neck in a bear hug. The woman she thought was a shell, subordinate, unable to stand on her own was the strongest most resourceful person she had ever met. And when she truly needed her mom the most, she was there.

"Then that settles it," Sara smiled.

~

After a night of tears, packing, hugs, and more tears, Sara and Marie loaded into their old Jeep. Much like the one they left on the shore so long ago in Paradise, this one carried them again into the unknown. Amy and Brian stood on the porch with little BJ in their arms. Amy hadn't stopped crying since the announcement the afternoon before. Marie teased her that dehydration was a true threat through her own tears as they embraced.

Sara smiled and waved one last time at her daughter's family before shutting the Jeep door. Marie took a deep breath, "You ready, mom?"

"Let's go get your girl."

Sara patted her leg and hit the gas.

ABOUT THE AUTHOR

RANDI HARVEY is a writer, pilot, singer, blogger, and entertainer from Milford, Michigan. She has lived throughout the country and traveled all over the world following her career. These experiences led to many of the characters and ideas for her books. Randi lives in Tampa, Florida with her husband and two sons. *The Split* is her first published novel. Look for Randi's next book *I Am Your Companion* releasing in 2020.

Follow Randi Harvey
* Instagram - @randiharvey99*
* Facebook - facebook.com/thesplitnovel*
* www.randiharvey.com/books*